The daughter of a town marshal, **Linda Lael Miller** is a *New York Times* bestselling author of more than one hundred historical and contemporary novels. Linda's books have hit #1 on the *New York Times* bestseller list seven times. Raised in Northport, Washington, she now lives in Spokane, Washington.

**Brenda Jackson** is a *New York Times* bestselling author of more than one hundred romance titles. Brenda lives in Jacksonville, Florida, and divides her time between family, writing and traveling. Email Brenda at authorbrendajackson@gmail.com or visit her on her website at brendajackson.net.

#1 *New York Times* Bestselling Author

# LINDA LAEL MILLER

# THE WAY BACK TO YOU

Previously published as *Used-to-Be Lovers*

**HARLEQUIN
BESTSELLING
AUTHOR
COLLECTION**

HARLEQUIN®
BESTSELLING
AUTHOR
COLLECTION

Recycling programs
for this product may
not exist in your area.

ISBN-13: 978-1-335-20992-4

The Way Back to You
First published as Used-to-Be Lovers in 1988.
This edition published in 2021.
Copyright © 1988 by Linda Lael Miller

Risky Pleasures
First published in 2007. This edition published in 2021.
Copyright © 2007 by Brenda Streater Jackson

This edition published by arrangement with Harlequin Books S.A.

For questions and comments about the quality of this book,
please contact us at CustomerService@Harlequin.com.

Harlequin Enterprises ULC
22 Adelaide St. West, 40th Floor
Toronto, Ontario M5H 4E3, Canada
www.Harlequin.com

**Printed in U.S.A.**

# CONTENTS

## Also by Linda Lael Miller

### HQN

Visit her Author Profile page
on Harlequin.com, or lindalaelmiller.com,
for more titles!

# THE WAY BACK TO YOU

## Linda Lael Miller

For Jean and Ron Barrington,
living proof that romance is alive and well

# Chapter 1

Trying hard to concentrate on her work, Sharon Morelli squinted as she placed a wispy chiffon peignoir exactly one inch from the next garment on the rack. This was a standard antiboredom procedure reserved for days when almost no customers wandered into her lingerie shop, Teddy Bares. She was so absorbed in the task that she jumped when two dark brown eyes looked at her over the bar and a deep voice said, "Business must be slow."

Sharon put one hand to her pounding heart, drawing in a deep breath and letting it out again. Clearly, Tony hadn't lost his gift for catching her at a disadvantage, despite the fact that their divorce had been final for months. "Business is just fine," she snapped, hurrying behind the counter and trying to look busy with a stack of old receipts that had already been checked, rechecked and entered into the ledgers.

Without looking up she was aware that Tony had followed her, that he was standing very close. She also knew he was wearing battered jeans and a blue cambric work shirt open halfway down his chest, though she would never have admitted noticing such details.

"Sharon," he said, with the same quiet authority that made him so effective as the head of a thriving construction company and as a father to their two children.

She made herself meet his gaze, her hazel eyes linking with his brown ones, and jutted out her chin a little way. "What?" she snapped, feeling defensive. It was her turn to live in the house with Briana and Matt, and she would fight for that right if Tony had any ideas to the contrary.

He rolled his expressive eyes and folded his arms. "Relax," he said, and suddenly the shop seemed too small to contain his blatant masculinity. "We've got a project a couple of miles from here, so I stopped by to tell you that Matt is grounded for the week and Briana's with Mama—the orthodontist tightened her braces yesterday and her teeth are sore."

Sharon sighed and closed her eyes for a moment. She'd worked hard at overcoming her resentment toward Tony's mother, but there were times when it snuck up on her. Like now. Damn, even after all this time it hurt that Briana was Carmen's child and not her own.

Beautiful, perfect Carmen, much mourned by the senior Mrs. Morelli. Eleven years after her tragic death in an automobile accident, Carmen was still a regular topic of lament in Tony's extended family.

To Sharon's surprise, a strong, sun-browned hand reached out to cup her chin. "Hey," Tony said in a gentle undertone, "what did I say?"

It was a reasonable question, but Sharon couldn't answer. Not without looking and feeling like a complete fool. She turned from his touch and tried to compose herself to face him again. If there was one thing she didn't want to deal with, it was Maria Morelli's polite disapproval. "I'd appreciate it if you'd pick Bri up and bring her by the house after you're through work for the day," she said in a small voice.

Tony's hesitation was eloquent. He didn't understand Sharon's reluctance to spend any more time than absolutely necessary with his mother, and he never had. "All right," he finally conceded with a raspy sigh, and when Sharon looked around he was gone.

She missed him sorely.

It was with relief that Sharon closed the shop four hours later. After putting down the top on her yellow roadster, she drove out of the mall parking lot. There were precious few days of summer left; it was time to take the kids on the annual shopping safari in search of school clothes.

Sharon drew in a deep breath of fresh air and felt better. She passed by shops with quaint facades, a couple of restaurants, a combination drugstore and post office. Port Webster, nestled on Washington's Puget Sound, was a small, picturesque place, and it was growing steadily.

On the way to the house she and Tony had designed and planned to share forever, she went by a harborful of boats with colorful sails bobbing on the blue water, but she didn't notice the view.

Her mind was on the craziness of their situation. She really hated moving back and forth between her apartment and that splendid Tudor structure on Tamarack

Drive, but the divorce mediators had suggested the plan as a way of giving the children a measure of emotional security. Therefore, she lived in the house three days out of each week for one month, four days the next, alternating with Tony.

Sharon suspected that the arrangement made everyone else feel just as disjointed and confused as she did, though no one had confessed to that. It was hard to remember who was supposed to be where and when, but she knew she was going to have to learn to live with the assorted hassles. The only alternative would be a long, bitter custody battle, and she had no legal rights where Briana was concerned. Tony could simply refuse to allow her to see the child, and that would be like having a part of her soul torn from her.

Of course he hadn't mentioned any such thing, but when it came to divorces, anything could happen.

When she reached the house, which stood alone at the end of a long road and was flanked on three sides by towering pine trees, Matt was on his skateboard in the driveway. With his dark hair and eyes, he was, at seven, a miniature version of Tony.

At the sight of Sharon, his face lighted up and he flipped the skateboard expertly into one hand.

"I hear you're grounded," she said, after she'd gotten out of the car and an energetic hug had been exchanged.

Matt nodded, his expression glum at the reminder. "Yeah," he admitted. "It isn't fair, neither."

Sharon ruffled his hair as they walked up the stone steps to the massive front doors. "I'll be the judge of that," she teased. "Exactly what did you do?"

They were in the entryway, and Sharon tossed her purse onto a gleaming wooden table brought to America by some ancestor of Tony's. She would carry her overnight bag in from the trunk of the roadster later.

"Well?" she prompted, when Matt hesitated.

"I put Briana's goldfish in the pool," he confessed dismally. He gave Sharon a look of grudging chagrin. "How was I supposed to know the chlorine would hurt them?"

Sharon sighed. "Your dad was right to ground you." She went on to do her admittedly bad imitation of an old-time gangster, talking out of one side of her mouth. "You know the rules, kid—we don't mess with other people's stuff around here."

Before Matt could respond to that, Mrs. Harry, the housekeeper, pushed the vacuum across the living room carpet and then switched off the machine to greet Sharon with a big smile. "Welcome home, Mrs. Morelli," she said.

Sharon's throat felt thick, but she returned the older woman's hello before excusing herself to go upstairs.

Walking into the bedroom she had once shared with Tony was no easier than it had been the first night of their separation. There were so many memories.

Resolutely, Sharon shed the pearls, panty hose and silk dress she'd worn to Teddy Bares and put them neatly away. Then she pulled jeans, a Seahawks T-shirt and crew socks from her bureau and shimmied into them.

As she dressed, she took a mental inventory of herself. Her golden-brown hair, slender figure and wide hazel eyes got short shrift. The person Sharon visualized in her mind was short—five foot one—and sported a pair of thighs that might have been a shade thinner. With a sigh, Sharon knelt to search the floor of the closet for her favorite pair of sneakers. Her mind was focused wholly on the job.

A masculine chuckle made her draw back and swing her head around. Tony was standing just inside the bedroom doorway, beaming.

Sharon was instantly self-conscious. "Do you get some kind of sick kick out of startling me, Morelli?" she demanded.

Her ex-husband sat down on the end of the bed and assumed an expression of pained innocence. He even laid one hand to his heart. "Here I was," he began dramatically, "congratulating myself on overcoming my entire heritage as an Italian male by not pinching you, and you wound me with a question like that."

Sharon went back to looking for her sneakers, and when she found them, she sat down on the floor to wrench them onto her feet. "Where are the kids?" she asked to change the subject.

"Why do you ask?" he countered immediately.

Tony had showered and exchanged his work clothes for shorts and a T-shirt, and he looked good. So good that memories flooded Sharon's mind and, blushing, she had to look away.

He laughed, reading her thoughts as easily as he had in the early days of their marriage when things had been less complex.

Sharon shrugged and went to stand in front of the vanity table, busily brushing her hair. Heat coursed through her as she recalled some of the times she and Tony had made love in that room at the end of the workday....

And then he was standing behind her, his strong hands light on her shoulders, turning her into his embrace. Her head tilted back as his mouth descended toward hers, and a familiar jolt sparked her senses when he kissed her. At the same time, Tony molded her close. Dear God, it would be all too easy to shut and lock the door and surrender to him. He was so very skillful at arousing her.

After a fierce battle with her own desires, Sharon withdrew, wide-eyed and breathless. This was wrong; she and Tony were divorced, and she was never going to be able to get on with her life if she allowed him to make love to her. "We can't," she said, and even though the words had been meant to sound light, they throbbed with despair.

Tony was still standing entirely too close, making Sharon aware of every muscle in his powerful body. His voice was low and practically hypnotic, and his hands rested on the bare skin of her upper arms. "Why not?" he asked.

For the life of her, Sharon couldn't answer. She was saved by Briana's appearance in the doorway.

At twelve, Briana was already beautiful. Her thick mahogany hair trailed down her back in a rich, tumbling cascade, and her brown eyes were flecked with tiny sparks of gold. Only the petulant expression on her face and the wires on her teeth kept her from looking like an angel in a Renaissance painting.

Sharon loved the child as if she were her own. "Hi, sweetie," she said sympathetically, able now to step out of Tony's embrace. She laid a motherly hand to the girl's forehead. "How do you feel?"

"Lousy," the girl responded. "Every tooth in my head hurts, and did Dad tell you what Matt did to my goldfish?" Before Sharon could answer, she complained, "You should have seen it, Mom. It was mass murder."

"We'll get you more fish," Sharon said, putting one arm around Bri's shoulders.

"*Matt* will get her more fish," Tony corrected, and there was an impatient set to his jaw as he passed Briana and Sharon to leave the room. "See you at the next changing of the guard," he added in a clipped tone, and then he was gone.

A familiar bereft feeling came over Sharon, but she battled it by throwing herself into motherhood.

"Is anybody hungry?" she asked minutes later in the enormous kitchen. As a general rule, Tony was more at home in this room than she was, but for the next three days—or was it four?—the kids' meals would be her responsibility.

"Let's go out for pizza!" Matt suggested exuberantly. He was standing on the raised hearth of the double fireplace that served both the kitchen and dining room, and Sharon suspected that he'd been going back and forth through the opening—a forbidden pursuit.

"What a rotten idea," Bri whined, turning imploring eyes to Sharon. "Mom, I'm a person in pain!"

Matt opened his mouth to comment, and Sharon held up both hands in a demand for silence. "Enough, both of you," she said. "We're not going anywhere—not tonight, anyway. We're eating right here."

With that, Sharon went to the cupboard and ferreted out the supply of canned pasta she'd stashed at the back. There was spaghetti, ravioli and lasagna to choose from.

"Gramma would have a heart attack if she knew you were feeding us that stuff," Bri remarked, gravitating toward another cupboard for plates.

Sharon sniffed as she took silverware from the proper drawer and set three places at the table. "What she doesn't know won't hurt her," she said.

There were assorted vegetables in the refrigerator, and she assuaged her conscience a little by chopping enough of them to constitute a salad.

After supper, when the plates and silverware had been rinsed and put into the dishwasher and all evidence of canned pasta destroyed in the trash compactor, the subject of school came up. Summer was nearly over; D day was fast approaching.

Matt would be in the third grade, Briana in the seventh.

"What do you say we go shopping for school clothes tomorrow?" Sharon said. Helen, the one and only employee Teddy Bares boasted, would be looking after the shop.

"We already did that with Gramma," Matt said, even as Bri glared at him.

Obviously, a secret had been divulged.

Sharon was wounded. She'd been looking forward to the expedition for weeks; she and the kids always made an event of it, driving to one of the big malls in Seattle, having lunch in a special restaurant and seeing a movie in the evening. She sat down at the trestle table in the middle of the kitchen and demanded, "When was this?"

Matt looked bewildered. He didn't understand a lot of what had been going on since the divorce.

"It was last weekend," Briana confessed. Her expression was apologetic and entirely too adult. "Gramma said you'd been under a lot of strain lately—"

"A lot of strain?" Sharon echoed, rising from the bench like a rocket in a slow-motion scene from a movie.

"With the shop and everything," Briana hastened to say.

"Quarterly taxes," Matt supplied.

"And credit card billings," added Briana.

Sharon sagged back to the bench. "I don't need you two to list everything I've done in the past two months," she said. Her disappointment was out of proportion to the situation; she realized that. Still, she felt like crying.

When Matt and Bri went off to watch television, she debated calling Tony for a few moments and then marched over to the wall phone and punched out his home number. He answered on the third ring.

Relief dulled Sharon's anger. Tony wasn't out on a date; that knowledge offered some comfort. Of course, it was early....

"This is Sharon," she said firmly. "And before you panic, let me say that this is not an emergency call."

"That's good. What kind of call is it?" Tony sounded distracted; Sharon could visualize his actions so vividly—he was cooking—that she might as well have been standing in the small, efficient kitchen of his condo, watching him. Assuming, that is, that the kitchen was small and efficient. She'd never been there.

Sharon bit down on her lower lip and tears welled in her eyes. It was a moment before she could speak. "You're going to think it's silly," she said, after drawing a few deep and shaky breaths, "but I don't care. Tony, I was planning to take the kids shopping for their school clothes myself, like I always do. It was important to me."

There was a pause, and then Tony replied evenly, "Mama thought she was doing you a favor."

Dear Mama, with a forest of photographs growing on top of her mantel. Photographs of Tony and Carmen.

Sharon dragged a stool over from the breakfast bar with a practiced motion of one foot and slumped onto it. "I am not incompetent," she said, shoving the fingers of one hand through her hair.

"Nobody said you were," Tony immediately replied, and even though there was nothing in either his words or his tone to feed Sharon's anger, it flared like a fire doused with lighter fluid.

She was so angry, in fact, that she didn't trust herself to speak.

"Talk to me, Sharon," Tony said gently.

If she didn't do as he asked, Tony would get worried and come to the house, and Sharon wasn't sure she could face him just now. "Maybe I don't do everything perfectly," she managed to say, "but I can look after Briana and Matt. Nobody has to step in and take over for me as though I were some kind of idiot."

Tony gave a ragged sigh. "Sharon—"

"Damn you, Tony, don't patronize me!" Sharon interrupted in a fierce whisper, that might have been a shout if two children hadn't been in the next room watching television.

He was the soul of patience. Sharon knew he was being understanding just to make her look bad. "Sweetheart, will you listen to me?"

Sharon wiped away tears with the heel of her palm. Until then she hadn't even realized that she was crying. "Don't call me that," she protested lamely. "We're divorced."

"God, if you aren't the stubbornest woman I've ever known—"

Sharon hung up with a polite click and wasn't at all surprised when the telephone immediately rang.

"Don't you ever do that again!" Tony raged.

He wasn't so perfect, after all. Sharon smiled. "I'm sorry," she lied in dulcet tones.

It was after she'd extracted herself from the conversation and hung up that Sharon decided to take the kids to the island house in the morning. Maybe a few days spent combing the beaches on Vashon would restore her perspective.

She called Helen, her employee, to explain the change in plans, and then made the announcement.

The kids loved visiting the A-frame, and they were so pleased at the prospect that they went to bed on time without any arguments.

Sharon read until she was sleepy, then went upstairs and took a shower in the master bathroom. When she came out, wrapped in a towel, the kiss she and Tony had indulged in earlier replayed itself in her mind. She felt all the attendant sensations and longings and knew that it was going to be one of those nights.

Glumly, she put on blue silk pajamas, gathered a lightweight comforter and a pillow into her arms and went downstairs. It certainly wasn't the first night she'd been driven out of the bedroom by memories, and it probably wouldn't be the last.

In the den Sharon made up the sofa bed, tossed the comforter over the yellow top sheet and plumped her pillow. Then she crawled under the covers, reaching out for the remote control for the TV.

A channel specializing in old movies filled the screen. There were Joseph Cotten and Ginger Rogers, gazing into each other's eyes as they danced. "Does Fred Astaire know about this?" Sharon muttered.

If there was one thing she wasn't in the mood for, it was romance. She flipped to the shopping network and watched without interest as a glamorous woman in a safari suit offered a complete set of cutlery at a bargain price.

Sharon turned off the television, then the lamp on the end table beside her, and shimmied down under the covers. She yawned repeatedly, tossed and turned and punched her pillow, but sleep eluded her.

A deep breath told her why. The sheets were tinged with the faintest trace of Tony's after-shave. There was no escaping thoughts of that man.

In the morning Sharon was grumpy and distracted. She made sure the kids had packed adequate clothes for the visit to the island and was dishing up dry cereal when Tony rapped at the back door and then entered.

"Well," Sharon said dryly, "come on in."

He had the good grace to look sheepish. "I was in the neighborhood," he said, as Briana and Matt flung themselves at him with shouts of joy. A person would have thought they hadn't seen him in months.

"We're going to the island!" Matt crowed.

"For three whole days!" added Briana.

Tony gave Sharon a questioning look over their heads. "Great," he said with a rigid smile. When the kids rushed off to put their duffel bags in the van, the car reserved for excursions involving kids or groceries, Sharon poured coffee into his favorite mug and shoved it at him.

"I was going to tell you," she said.

He took a leisurely sip of the coffee before replying, "When? After you'd gotten back?"

Sharon hadn't had a good night, and now she wasn't having a good morning. Her eyes were puffy and her hair was pinned up into a haphazard knot at the back of her head. She hadn't taken the time to put on makeup, and she was wearing the oldest pair of jeans she owned, along with a T-shirt she thought she remembered using to wash the roadster. She picked up her own cup and gulped with the enthusiastic desperation of a drunk taking the hair of the dog. "You're making an awfully big deal out of this, aren't you?" she hedged.

Tony shrugged. "If you're taking the kids out of town," he said, "I'd like to know about it."

"Okay," Sharon replied, enunciating clearly. "Tony, I am taking the kids out of town."

His eyes were snapping. "Thanks," he said, and then he headed right for the den. The man had an absolute genius for finding out things Sharon didn't want him to know.

He came out with a rolled-up blueprint under one arm, looking puzzled. "You slept downstairs?"

Sharon took a moment to regret not making up the hide-a-bed, and then answered, "I was watching a movie. Joseph Cotten and Ginger Rogers."

Tony leaned back against the counter. "The TV in our room doesn't work?"

Sharon put her hands on her hips. "What is this, an audit? I felt like sleeping downstairs, all right?"

His grin was gentle and a little sad, and for a moment he looked as though he was about to confide something. In the end he finished his coffee, set the mug in the sink and went out to talk to the kids without saying another word to Sharon.

She hurried upstairs and hastily packed a bag of her own. A glance in the vanity mirror made her regret not putting on her makeup.

When she came downstairs again, the kids had finished their cereal and Tony was gone. Sharon felt both relief and disappointment. She'd gotten off to a bad start, but she was determined to salvage the rest of the day.

The Fates didn't seem to be on Sharon's side. The cash machine at the bank nearly ate her card, the grocery store was crowded and, on the way to the ferry dock, she had a flat tire.

It was midafternoon and clouds were gathering in the sky by the time she drove the van aboard the ferry connecting Port Webster with Vashon Island and points beyond. Briana and Matt bought cinnamon rolls at the snack bar and went outside onto the upper deck to feed the gulls. Sharon watched them through the window, thinking what beautiful children they were, and smiled.

Briana had been a baby when her bewildered, young father had married Sharon. Sharon had changed Bri's diapers, walked the floor with her when she had colic, kissed skinned knees and elbows to make them better. She had made angel costumes for Christmas pageants, trudged from house to house while Briana sold cookies for her Brownie troop and ridden shotgun on trick-or-treat expeditions.

She had earned her stripes as a mother.

The ferry whistle droned, and Sharon started in surprise. The short ride was over, and the future was waiting to happen.

She herded the kids below decks to the car, and they drove down the noisy metal ramp just as the heavy gray skies gave way to a thunderous rain.

# Chapter 2

Holding a bag of groceries in one arm, Sharon struggled with the sticky lock on the A-frame's back door.

"Mom, I'm getting wet!" Briana complained from behind her.

Sharon sunk her teeth into her lower lip and gave the key a furious jiggle just as a lightning bolt sliced through the sky and then danced, crackling, on the choppy waters of the sound.

"Whatever you do, wire-mouth," Matt told his sister, gesturing toward the gray clouds overhead, "don't smile. You're a human lightning rod."

"Shut up, Matthew," Sharon and Briana responded in chorus, just as the lock finally gave way.

Sharon's ears were immediately met by an ominous hissing roar. She set the groceries down on the kitchen counter and flipped on the lights as Bri and Matt both rushed inside in search of the noise.

"Oh, ick!" Bri wailed, when they'd gone down the three steps leading from the kitchen to the dining and living room area. "The carpet's all wet!"

Matt's response was a whoop of delight. His feet made a loud squishing sound as he stomped around the table.

"Don't touch any of the light switches," Sharon warned, dashing past them and following the river of water upstream to the bathroom. The source of the torrent proved to be a broken pipe under the sink; she knelt to turn the valve and shut off the flow. "Now what do I do?" she whispered, resting her forehead against the sink cabinet. Instantly, her sneakers and the lower part of her jeans were sodden.

The telephone rang just as she was getting back to her feet, and Matt's voice carried through the shadowy interior of the summer place she and Tony had bought after his family's company had landed a particularly lucrative contract three years before. "Yeah, we got here okay, if you don't count the flat tire. It's real neat, Dad—a pipe must have broke or something because there's water everywhere and the floor's like mush—"

Sharon drew in a deep breath, let it out again and marched into the living room, where she summarily snatched the receiver from her son's hand. "'Neat' is not the word I would choose," she told her ex-husband sourly, giving Matt a look.

Tony asked a few pertinent questions and Sharon answered them. Yes, she'd found the source of the leak, yes, she'd turned off the valve, yes, the place was practically submerged.

"So who do I call?" she wanted to know.

"Nobody," Tony answered flatly. "I'll be there on the next ferry."

Sharon needed a little distance; that was one of the reasons she'd decided to visit the island in the first place. "I don't think that would be a good idea..." she began, only to hear a click. "Tony?"

A steady hum sounded in her ear.

Hastily, she dialed his number; she got his message. Sharon told it, in no uncertain terms, what she thought of its high-handed owner and hung up with a crash.

Both Bri and Matt were looking at her with wide eyes, their hair and jackets soaking from the rain. Maternal guilt swept over Sharon; she started to explain why she was frustrated with Tony and gave up in midstream, spreading her hands out wide and then slapping her thighs in defeat. "What can I say?" she muttered. "Take off your shoes and coats and get up on the sofa."

Rain was thrumming against the windows, and the room was cold. Sharon went resolutely to the fireplace and laid crumpled newspaper and kindling in the grate, then struck a match. A cheery blaze caught as she adjusted the damper, took one of the paper-wrapped supermarket logs from the old copper caldron nearby and tossed it into the fire.

When she turned from that, Bri and Matt were both settled on the couch.

"Is Daddy coming?" Briana asked in a small voice.

Sharon sighed, feeling patently inadequate, and then nodded. "Yes."

"How come you got so mad at him?" Matt wanted to know. "He just wants to help, doesn't he?"

Sharon pretended she hadn't heard the question and

trudged back toward the kitchen, a golden oasis in the gloom. "Who wants hot chocolate?" she called, trying to sound lighthearted.

Both Bri and Matt allowed that cocoa would taste good right about then, but their voices sounded a little thin.

Sharon put water on to heat for instant coffee and took cocoa from the cupboard and milk and sugar from the bag of groceries she'd left on the counter. Outside the wind howled, and huge droplets of rain flung themselves at the windows and the roof. "I kind of like a good storm once in a while," Sharon remarked cheerfully.

"What happens when we run out of logs?" Briana wanted to know. "We'll freeze to death!"

Matt gave a gleeful howl at this. "Nobody freezes to death in August, blitz-brain."

Sharon closed her eyes and counted to ten before saying, "Let's just cease and desist, okay? We're all going to have to take a positive approach here." The moment the words were out of her mouth, the power went off.

Resigned to heeding her own advice, Sharon carried cups of lukewarm cocoa to the kids, then poured herself a mugful of equally unappealing coffee. Back in the living room, she threw another log on the fire, then peeled off her wet sneakers and socks and curled up in an easy chair.

"Isn't this nice?" she asked.

Briana rolled her eyes. "Yeah, Mom. This is great."

"Terrific," agreed Matt, glaring into the fire.

"Maybe we could play a game," Sharon suggested, determined.

"What?" scoffed Bri, stretching out both hands in a groping gesture. "Blindman's bluff?"

It *was* a little dark. With a sigh, Sharon tilted her head back and closed her eyes. Memories greeted her within an instant.

She and Tony had escaped to the island often that first summer after they bought the A-frame, bringing wine, romantic music and very little else. They'd walked on the rocky beaches for hours, hand in hand, having so much to say to each other that the words just tumbled out, never needing to be weighed and measured first.

And later, when the sun had gone and a fire had been snapping on the hearth, they'd listened to music in the dark and made love with that tender violence peculiar to those who find each other fascinating.

Sharon opened her eyes, grateful for the shadows that hid the tears glimmering on her lashes. *When did it change, Tony?* she asked in silent despair. *When did we stop making love on the floor, in the dark, with music swelling around us?*

It was several moments before Sharon could compose herself. She shifted in her chair and peered toward Bri and Matthew.

They'd fallen asleep at separate ends of the long couch and, smiling, Sharon got up and tiptoed across the wet carpet to the stairs. At the top was an enormous loft divided into three bedrooms and a bath, and she entered the largest chamber, pausing for a moment at the floor-to-ceiling windows overlooking the sound.

In the distance Sharon saw the lights of an approaching ferry and, in spite of her earlier annoyance, her spirits were lifted by the sight. Being careful not to look at the large brass bed she and Tony had once shared—Lord

knew, the living room memories were painful enough—
she took two woolen blankets from the cedar chest at
its foot and carried them back downstairs.

After covering the children, Sharon put the last store-
bought log on the fire and then made her way back to
the chair where she rested her head on one arm and
sighed, her mind sliding back into the past again, her
gaze fixed on the flames.

There had been problems from the first, but the trouble between Tony and herself had started gaining real
momentum two years before, when Matt had entered
kindergarten. Bored, wanting to accomplish something
on her own, Sharon had immediately opened Teddy
Bares, and things had gone downhill from that day forward. The cracks in the marriage had become chasms.

She closed her eyes with a yawn and sighed again.
The next thing she knew, there was a thumping noise
and a bright light flared beyond her lids.

Sharon awakened to see Tony crouched on the hearth,
putting dry wood on the fire. His dark hair was wet and
curling slightly at the nape of his neck, and she had a
compulsion to kiss him there. At one time, she would
have done it without thinking.

"Hello, handsome," she said.

He looked back at her over one broad, leather-jack-
eted shoulder and favored her with the same soul-
wrenching grin that had won her heart more than ten
years before, when he'd walked into the bookstore
where she was working and promptly asked her out.
"Hi," he replied in a low, rumbling whisper.

"Have you been here long?"

Tony shook his head, and the fire highlighted his
ebony hair with shades of crimson. "Ten minutes,

maybe." She wondered if those shadows in his brown eyes were memories of other, happier visits to the island house.

She felt a need to make conversation. Mundane conversation unrelated to flickering firelight, thunderstorms, music and love. "Is the power out on the mainland, too?"

Again, Tony shook his head. There was a solemn set to his face, and although Sharon couldn't read his expression now, she sensed that his thoughts were similar to hers. When he extended his hand, she automatically offered her own.

"I'm hungry," complained a sleepy voice.

Tony grinned and let go of Sharon's hand to ruffle his son's hair. "So what else is new?"

"Dad, is that you?" The relief in the little boy's voice made Sharon wonder if she'd handled things so badly that only Tony could make them better.

Tony's chuckle was warm and reassuring, even to Sharon, who hadn't thought she needed reassuring. "One and the same. You were right about the floor—it is like mush."

Bri stirred at this, yawning, and then flung her arms around Tony's neck with a cry of joy. "Can we go home?" she pleaded. "Right now?"

Tony set her gently away. "We can't leave until we've done something about the flood problem—which means we're going to have to rough it." Two small faces fell, and he laughed. "Of course, by that I mean eating supper at the Sea Gull Café."

"They've got lights?" Bri asked enthusiastically.

"And heat?" Matt added. "I'm freezing."

"Nobody freezes in August," Bri immediately quoted back to him. "Blitz-brain."

"I see things are pretty much normal around here," Tony observed in wry tones, his head turned toward Sharon.

She nodded and sat up, reaching for her wet socks and sneakers. "An element of desperation has been added, however," she pointed out. "As Exhibit A, I give you these two, who have agreed to darken the doorway of the Sea Gull Café."

"It doesn't have that name for nothing, you know," Bri said sagely, getting into her shoes. "Don't anybody order the fried chicken."

Tony laughed again and the sound, as rich and warm as it was, made Sharon feel hollow inside, and raw. She ached for things to be as they had been, but it was too late for too many reasons. Hoping was a fool's crusade.

Rain was beating at the ground as the four of them ran toward Tony's car. Plans encased in cardboard tubes filled the back seat, and the kids, used to their workaholic father, simply pushed them out of the way. Sharon, however, felt an old misery swelling in her throat and avoided Tony's eyes when she got into the car beside him and fastened her seat belt.

She felt, and probably looked, like the proverbial drowned rat, and she started with surprise when the back of Tony's hand gently brushed her cheek.

"Smile," he said.

Sharon tried, but the effort faltered. To cover that she quipped, "How can I, when I'm condemned to a meal of sea gull, Southern-style?"

Tony didn't laugh. Didn't even grin. The motion of his hand was too swift and too forceful for the task of shifting the car into reverse.

Overlooking the angry water, the restaurant was filled with light and warmth and laughter. Much of the island's population seemed to have gathered inside to compare this storm to the ones in '56 or '32 or '77, to play the jukebox nonstop, and to keep the kitchen staff and the beaming waitresses hopping.

After a surprisingly short wait, a booth became available and the Morellis were seated.

*Anybody would think we were still a family,* Sharon thought, looking from one beloved, familiar face to another, and then at her own, reflected in the dark window looming above the table. Her hair was stringy and her makeup was gone. She winced.

When she turned her head, Tony was watching her. There was a sort of sad amusement in his eyes. "You look beautiful," he said quietly.

Matt groaned, embarrassed that such a sloppy sentiment should be displayed in public.

"Kissy, kissy," added Briana, not to be outdone.

"How does Swiss boarding school sound to you two?" Tony asked his children, without cracking a smile. "I see a place high in the Alps, with five nuns to every kid…."

Bri and Matt subsided, giggling, and Sharon felt a stab of envy at the easy way he dealt with them. She was too tired, too hungry, too vulnerable. She purposely thought about the rolled blueprints in the back seat of Tony's car and let the vision fuel her annoyance.

The man never went anywhere or did anything without dragging some aspect of Morelli Construction along

with him, and yet he couldn't seem to understand why
Teddy Bares meant so much to her.

By the time the cheeseburgers, fries and milk shakes
arrived, Sharon was on edge. Tony gave her a curious
look, but made no comment.

When they returned to the A-frame, the power was
back on. Sharon sent the kids upstairs to bed, and Tony
brought a set of tools in from the trunk of his car, along
with a special vacuum cleaner and fans.

While Sharon operated the vacuum, drawing gallon after gallon of water out of the rugs, Tony fixed
the broken pipe in the bathroom. When that was done,
he raised some of the carpet and positioned the fans so
that they would dry the floor beneath.

Sharon brewed a fresh pot of coffee and poured a cup
for Tony, determined to do better than she had in the
restaurant as the modern ex-wife. Whatever that was.

"I appreciate everything you've done," she said with
a stiff smile, extending the mug of coffee.

Tony, who was sitting at the dining table by then, a
set of the infernal blueprints unrolled before him, gave
her an ironic look. "The hell you do," he said. Then, taking the coffee she offered, he added a crisp, "Thanks."

Sharon wrenched back a chair and plopped into it.
"Wait one second here," she said when Tony would have
let the blueprints absorb his attention again. "Wait one
damn second. I *do* appreciate your coming out here."

Tony just looked at her, his eyes conveying his disbelief…and his anger.

"Okay," Sharon said on a long breath. "You heard
the message I left on your answering machine, right?"

"Right," he replied, and the word rumbled with a
hint of thunder.

"I didn't really mean that part where I called you an officious, overbearing—" Her voice faltered.

"Chauvinistic jerk," Tony supplied graciously.

Sharon bit her lower lip, then confessed, "Maybe I shouldn't have put it in exactly those terms. It was just that—well, I'm never going to know whether or not I can handle a crisis if you rush to the rescue every time I have a little problem—"

"Why are you so damn scared of needing me?" Tony broke in angrily.

Sharon pushed back her chair and went to the kitchen to pour a cup of coffee for herself. When she returned, she felt a bit more composed than she had a few moments before.

She changed the subject. "I was thinking," she said evenly, "about how it used to be with us before your construction company became so big—before Teddy Bares…"

Tony gave a ragged sigh. "Those things are only excuses, Sharon, and you know it."

She glanced toward the fire, thinking of nights filled with love and music. Inside, her heart ached. "I don't understand what you mean," she said woodenly.

"You're a liar," Tony responded with cruel directness, and then he was studying the blueprints again.

"Where are you sleeping tonight?" Sharon asked after a few minutes, trying to sound disinterested, unconcerned, too sophisticated to worry about little things like beds and divorces.

Tony didn't look up. His only reply was a shrug.

Sharon yawned. "Well, I think I'll turn in," she said. "Good night."

"Good night," Tony responded in a bland tone, still immersed in the plans for the next project.

Sharon fought an utterly childish urge to spill her coffee all over his blueprints and left the table. Halfway up the stairs, she looked back and saw that Tony was watching her.

For a moment she froze in the grip of some unnamed emotion passing between them, but her paralysis was broken when Tony dropped his gaze to his work.

Upstairs, Sharon took a quick shower, brushed her teeth, pulled on a cotton nightgown and crawled into the big, lonely bed. Gazing up at the slanted ceilings and blinking back tears of frustration, she wriggled down under the covers and ordered herself to sleep.

But instead of dreaming, Sharon reviewed the events of the evening and wondered why she couldn't talk to Tony anymore. Each time she tried, she ended up baiting him, or sliding some invisible door closed between them, or simply running away.

She was painfully conscious of his nearness and of her need for him, which had not been assuaged by months of telling herself that the relationship was over. She put one hand over her mouth to keep from calling his name.

From downstairs she heard the low but swelling strains of familiar music. Once, the notes had rippled over her like the rays of the sun on a pond, filling her with light. They had flung her high on soaring crescendos, even as she clung to Tony and cried out in passion....

Sharon burrowed beneath the covers and squeezed her eyes shut and, an eternity later, she slept. When she awakened the room was filled with sunlight and the scent of fresh coffee.

After a long, leisurely stretch, Sharon opened her eyes. A dark head rested on the pillow beside hers, and she felt a muscular leg beneath the softness of her thigh.

"Oh, God," she whispered, "we made love and I missed it!"

A hoarse laugh sounded from the pillow. "No such luck," Tony said. "Our making love, I mean. We didn't."

Sharon sat up, dragging the sheets up to cover her bosom even though she was wearing a modest cotton nightgown. She distinctly remembered putting it on, and with a quick motion of her hands, she lifted the sheet just far enough away from her body that she could check. The nightgown was still in evidence.

"What the devil do you think you're doing, Tony Morelli?" she demanded furiously.

He rolled onto his back, not even bothering to open his eyes, and simultaneously pulled the covers up over his face, muttering insensibly all the while.

"You guys made up, huh?" Briana asked from the doorway. She was all smiles and carrying two cups of coffee, hence the delicious aroma.

"No, we didn't," Sharon said primly.

"Not a very diplomatic answer," Tony observed from beneath the covers. "Now, she's going to ask—"

"Then how come you're in bed together?" the child demanded.

"See?" said Tony.

Sharon elbowed him hard, and crimson color flooded her face. "I don't know," she said with staunch conviction.

Briana brought the coffee to the end table on Sharon's side of the bed, and some of it slopped over when she set the cups down. There were tears brimming in her eyes.

"Damn you, Tony," Sharon whispered, as though there were no chance of Bri's not hearing what she said. "Explain this to her—right now!"

With a groan, Tony dramatically fought his way out from under the blankets and sat up. "There's only one bed," he said reasonably, running a hand through his rumpled hair and then yawning again. "The couch is too short for me, so I just crawled in with your mom."

"Oh," Bri said grudgingly, and left the room, shutting the door behind her.

"She didn't understand," Sharon lamented.

Tony reached past her to collect one of the cups of coffee. "Kids don't need to understand everything," he said.

If the man hadn't been holding a steaming hot cup of coffee, Sharon would have slapped him. As it was, she glared at him and stretched out a hand for her own cup.

After a while Tony got up and wandered into the adjoining bathroom, and Sharon didn't look to see whether or not he was dressed. When he returned, he crawled back into bed with her, rolling over so that one of his legs rested across both of hers.

His mouth descended toward hers, smelling of toothpaste, and he was definitely not dressed.

"Tony, don't—"

The kiss was warm, gentle and insistent. Sharon trembled as all the familiar sensations were awakened, but she also braced both hands against Tony's chest and pushed.

The motion didn't eliminate all intimate contact— Tony had shifted his weight so that he was resting lightly on top of her—but it did make it possible to speak.

"No," Sharon said clearly.

Tony slid downward, kissing her jawline, the length of her neck, her collarbone.

"No," she repeated with less spirit.

His lips trailed across her collarbone and then downward. He nibbled at her breast through the thin fabric of her nightgown.

Her voice was a whimper. "No," she said for the third time.

Tony's mouth came to hers; his tongue traced the outline of her lips. "You don't mean that," he told her.

Sharon was about to admit he was right when there was a knock at the door and Bri called out in sunny tones, "Breakfast is served!"

Tony was sitting up, both hands buried in his hair, when Briana and Matt entered the room carrying trays.

# Chapter 3

The downstairs carpets were far from dry. "Leave the fans on for another day or so," Tony said distantly. Standing beside the dining room table, he rolled up a set of plans and slid it back inside its cardboard cylinder.

A sensation of utter bereftness swept over Sharon, even though she knew it was best that he leave. The divorce was final; it was time for both of them to let go. She managed a smile and an awkward, "Okay— and thanks."

The expression in Tony's eyes was at once angry and forlorn. He started to say something and then stopped himself, turning away to stare out the window at Bri and Matt, who were chasing each other up and down the stony beach. Their laughter rang through the morning sunshine, reminding Sharon that some people still felt joy.

She looked down at the floor for a moment, swallowed hard and then asked, "Tony, are you happy?"

The powerful shoulders tensed beneath the blue cambric of his shirt, then relaxed again. "Are you?" he countered, keeping his back to her.

"No fair," Sharon protested quietly. "I asked first."

Tony turned with a heavy sigh, the cardboard cylinder under his arm. "I used to be," he said. "Now I'm not sure I even know what it means to be happy."

Sharon's heart twisted within her; she was sorry she'd raised the question. She wanted to say something wise and good and comforting, but no words came to her.

Tony rounded the table, caught her chin gently in his hand and asked, "What happened, Sharon? What the hell happened?"

She bit her lip and shook her head.

A few seconds of silent misery passed, and then Tony sighed again, gave Sharon a kiss on the forehead and walked out. Moving to the window, she blinked back tears as she watched him saying goodbye to the kids. His words echoed in her mind and in her heart. *What the hell happened?*

Hugging herself, as though to hold body and soul together, Sharon sniffled and proceeded to the kitchen, where she refilled her coffee cup. She heard Tony's car start and gripped the edge of the counter with one hand, resisting an urge to run outside, to call his name, to beg him to stay.

She only let go of the counter when his tires bit into the gravel of the road.

"Are you all right, Mom?" Bri's voice made Sharon stiffen.

She faced this child of her spirit, if not her body, with a forced smile. "I'm fine," she lied, thinking that Bri looked more like Carmen's photographs with every passing day. She wondered if the resemblance ever grieved Tony and wished that she had the courage to ask him.

"You don't look fine," Briana argued, stepping inside the kitchen and closing the door.

Sharon had to turn away. She pretended to be busy at the sink, dumping out the coffee she'd just poured, rinsing her cup. "What's Matt doing?"

"Turning over rocks and watching the sand crabs scatter," Bri answered. "Are we going fishing?"

The last thing Sharon wanted to do was sit at the end of the dock with her feet dangling, baiting hooks and reeling in rock cod and dogfish, when right now her inclinations ran more toward pounding her pillow and crying. Such indulgences, however, are denied to mothers on active duty. "Absolutely," she said, lifting her chin and straightening her shoulders before turning to offer Bri a smile.

The child looked relieved. "I'll even bait your hooks for you," she offered.

Sharon laughed and hugged her. "You're one kid in a thousand, pumpkin," she said. "How did I get so lucky?"

Carmen's flawless image, smiling her beauty-queen smile, loomed in her mind, and it was as though Tony's first wife answered, "I died, that's how. Where would you be if it weren't for that drunk driver?"

Sharon shuddered, but she was determined to shake off her gray mood. In just two days she would have to give Briana and Matt back to Tony and return to her lonely apartment; she couldn't afford to sit around feeling sorry for herself. The time allowed her was too fleeting, too precious.

She found fishing poles and tackle in a closet, and Bri rummaged through the freezer for a package of herring, bought months before in a bait shop.

When they joined Matt outside, and the three of them had settled themselves at the end of the dock, Bri was as good as her word. With a deftness she'd learned from Tony, she baited Sharon's hook.

In truth, Sharon wasn't as squeamish about the task as Bri seemed to think, but she didn't want to destroy the child's pleasure in being helpful. "Thanks," she said. "I'm sure glad I didn't have to do that."

"Women," muttered Matt, speaking from a seven-year pinnacle of life experience.

Sharon bit back a smile. "Shall I give my standard lecture on chauvinism?" she asked.

"No," Matt answered succinctly. It was the mark of a modern kid, his mother guessed, knowing what a word like *chauvinism* meant.

Bri looked pensive. "Great-gramma still eats in the kitchen," she remarked. "Like a servant."

Sharon chose her words carefully. Tony's grandmother had grown up in Italy and still spoke almost no English. Maybe she followed the old traditions, but the woman had raised six children to productive adulthood, among other accomplishments, and she deserved respect. "Did you know that she was only sixteen years old when she first came to America? She didn't speak or understand English, and her marriage to your great-grandfather had been arranged for her. Personally, I consider her a very brave woman."

Bri bit her lower lip. "Do you think my mother was brave?"

Questions like that, although they came up periodically, never failed to catch Sharon off guard. She drew in a deep breath and let it out again. "I never met her, sweetheart—you know that. Wouldn't it be better to ask your dad?"

"Do you think he loved her?"

Sharon didn't flinch. She concentrated on keeping her fishing pole steady. "I know he did. Very much."

"Carl says they only got married because my mom was pregnant with me. His mother remembers."

Carl was one of the cast of thousands that made up the Morelli family—specifically, a second or third cousin. And a pain in the backside.

"He doesn't know everything," Sharon said, wondering why these subjects never reared their heads when Tony was around to field them. "And neither does his mother."

Sharon sighed. God knew, Tony was better at things like this—a born diplomat. He and Carmen would have made quite a pair. There probably would have been at least a half dozen more children added to the clan, and it seemed certain that no divorce would have goofed up the entries in the family Bible. Maria Morelli had shown her all those names, reaching far back into the past.

Sharon was getting depressed again. Before Bri could bring up another disquieting question, however, the fish started biting. Bri caught two, Matt reeled in a couple more, and then it was time for lunch.

The telephone rang as Sharon was preparing sandwiches and heating canned soup.

"It's Gramma!" Matt shouted from the front room.

"Tell her your dad isn't here," Sharon replied pleasantly.

"She wants to talk to you."

Sharon pushed the soup to a different burner, wiped her hands on a dish towel and went staunchly to the telephone. "Hello," she said in sunny tones.

"Hello, Sharon," Maria responded, and there was nothing in her voice that should have made her difficult to talk to.

All the same, for Sharon, she was. "Is there something I can help you with?"

"Michael's birthday is next week," Maria said. She was referring to her youngest son; Tony was close to him and so were the kids.

Sharon had forgotten the occasion. "Yes," she agreed heartily.

"We're having a party, as usual," Maria went on. "Of course, Vincent and I would like the children to be there."

Sharon's smile was rigid; her face felt like part of a totem pole. She wondered why she felt called upon to smile when Maria obviously couldn't see her.

A few hasty calculations indicated that Bri and Matt would have been with Tony on Michael's birthday anyway. "No problem," Sharon said generously.

There was a pause, and then Maria asked, "How are you, dear? Vincent and I were just saying that we never see you anymore."

Sharon rubbed her eyes with a thumb and a forefinger, suppressing an urge to sigh. She regarded Vincent as a friend—he was a gentle, easygoing man—but with Maria it seemed so important to say and do the right things. Always. "I-I'm fine, thanks. I've been busy with the shop," she responded at last. "How are you?"

Maria's voice had acquired a cool edge. "Very well, actually. I'll just let you get back to whatever it was that you were doing, Sharon. Might I say hello to Bri, though?"

"Certainly," Sharon replied, relieved to hold the receiver out to the girl, who had been cleaning fish on the back porch. "Your grandmother would like to speak with you, Briana."

Bri hastened to the sink and washed her hands, then reached eagerly for the receiver. The depth of affection this family bore for its members never failed to amaze Sharon, or to remind her that she was an outsider. Even during the happiest years she and Tony had shared, she'd always felt like a Johnny-come-lately.

"Hi, Gramma!" Bri cried, beaming. "I caught two fish and the floors got all flooded and this morning I thought things were okay between Dad and Mom because they slept together...."

Mortified, Sharon turned away to hide her flaming face. *Oh, Bri,* she groaned inwardly, *of all the people you could have said that to, why did it have to be Maria?*

"Right," Briana went on, as her words became clear again. "We're having—" she craned her neck to peer into the pan on the stove "—chicken noodle soup. Yeah, from a can."

Sharon shook her head.

"Listen, Gramma, there's something I need to know."

An awful premonition came over Sharon; she whirled to give Bri a warning look, but it was too late.

"Was my mother pregnant when she married my dad?"

"Oh, God," Sharon moaned, shoving one hand into her hair.

Bri was listening carefully. "Okay, I will," she said at last in perfectly ordinary tones. "I love you, too. Bye."

Sharon searched the beautiful, earnest young face for signs of trauma and found none. "Well," she finally said, as Bri brought in the fish but left the mess on the porch, "what did she say?"

"The same thing you did," Briana responded with a shrug. "I'm supposed to ask Dad."

Sharon allowed her face to reveal nothing, though Tony had long since told her about his tempestuous affair with Carmen and the hasty marriage that had followed. She had always imagined that relationship as a grand passion, romantic and beautiful and, of course, tragic. It was one of those stories that would have been wonderful if it hadn't involved real people with real feelings. She turned back to the soup, ladling it into bowls.

"I guess I could call him."

Sharon closed her eyes for a moment. "Bri, I think this is something that would be better discussed in person, don't you?"

"You *know* something!" the girl accused, coming inside and shutting the door.

"Wash your hands again, please," Sharon hedged.

"Dad told you, didn't he?" Briana asked, though she obediently went to the sink to lather her hands with soap.

Sharon felt cornered, and for a second or two she truly resented Bri, as well as Carmen and Tony. "Will you tell me one thing?" she demanded a little sharply, as Matt crept into the kitchen, his eyes wide. "Why didn't this burning desire to know strike you a few hours ago, when your father was still here?"

Briana was silent, looking down at the floor.

"That's what I thought." Sharon sighed. "Listen, if it's too hard for you to bring this up with your dad, and you feel like you need a little moral support, I'll help. Okay?"

Bri nodded.

That afternoon the clouds rolled back in and the rain started again. Once more, the power went out. Sharon and the kids played Parcheesi as long as the light held up, then roasted hot dogs in the fireplace. The evening lacked the note of festivity that had marked the one preceding it, despite Sharon's efforts, and she was almost relieved when bedtime came.

Almost, but not quite. The master bedroom, and the bed itself, bore the intangible but distinct impression Tony seemed to leave behind him wherever he went. When Sharon retired after brushing her teeth and washing her face in cold water, she huddled on her side of the bed, miserable.

Sleep was a long time coming, and when it arrived, it was fraught with dreams. Sharon was back at her wedding, wearing the flowing white dress she had bought with her entire savings, her arm linked with Tony's.

"Do you take this man to be your lawful wedded husband?" the minister asked.

Before Sharon could answer, Carmen appeared, also wearing a wedding gown, at Tony's other side. "I do," Carmen responded, and Sharon felt herself fading away like one of TV's high-tech ghosts.

She awakened with a cruel start, the covers bunched in her hands, and sank back to her pillows only after spending several moments groping for reality. It didn't help that the lamp wouldn't work, that rain was beating at the roof and the windows, that she was so very alone.

The following day was better; the storm blew over and the electricity stayed on. Sharon made sure she had a book on hand that night in case her dreams grew uninhabitable.

As it happened, Carmen didn't haunt her sleep again, but neither did Tony. Sharon awakened feeling restless and confused, and it was almost a relief to lock up the A-frame and drive away early that afternoon.

The big Tudor house was empty when they reached it; Mrs. Harry had done her work and gone home, and there was no sign of Tony. The little red light on the answering machine was blinking rapidly.

Sharon was tempted to ignore it, but in the end she pushed the Play button. Tony's voice filled the room. "Hi, babe. I'm glad you're home. According to Mama mia, I need to have a talk with Bri— I'll take care of that after dinner tonight, so don't worry about it. See you later." The message finished, and then another call was playing, this one from her mother. "Sharon, this is Bea. Since you don't answer over at the other place, I figured I'd try and get you here. Call me as soon as you can. Bye."

The other messages were all for Tony, so Sharon dialed her mother's number in Hayesville, a very small town out on the peninsula.

Bea answered right away, and Sharon sank into the chair behind Tony's desk. "Bea, it's me. Is anything wrong?"

"Where are you?" Bea immediately countered.

"At the house," Sharon replied in even tones.

"Crazy arrangement," Bea muttered. She had never approved of Sharon's marriage, Sharon's house or, for that matter, Sharon herself. "In, out, back, forth. I don't know how you stand it. Furthermore, it isn't good for those kids."

"Bea!"

"All right, all right. I just wanted to know if you were still coming over this weekend."

Sharon shoved a hand through her hair. She hated avoiding her own mother, but an encounter with Bea was more than she could face in her present state of mind. "I don't remember telling you that I'd be visiting," she said carefully, feeling her way along.

It turned out that Bea was suffering from a similar lack of enthusiasm. "It isn't like I don't want you to come or anything," she announced in her blunt way, "but Saturday's the big all-day bingo game, and one of the prizes is a car."

Sharon smiled to herself. "I see. Well, I have inventory at the shop, anyway. Call me if you win, okay?"

"Okay," Bea replied, but it was clear from her tone that her attention was already wandering. She was a beautician by trade, with a shop of her own, and an avid bingo player by choice, but motherhood had descended on her by accident. Bea Stanton had never really gotten the knack of it. "Part of the mill burned down," she added as an afterthought.

Sharon's father, who had never troubled to marry Bea, and probably would have been refused if he had proposed, was a member of the Harrison family, which owned the mill in question. Hence Bea's assumption that Sharon would be interested.

"That's too bad," she said. "Was anybody hurt?"

"No," Bea answered distractedly. "There's one of those big televisions, too. At bingo, I mean."

"Good," Sharon answered, as a headache began under her left temple and steadily gained momentum. "If there's nothing else, Bea, I think I'd better hang up. I have to get the kids squared away before I go back to the apartment."

Bea started muttering again. Sharon said a hasty goodbye and hung up, and when she turned in the swivel chair, Tony was standing in the doorway.

She gasped and laid one hand to her heart. "I really wish you wouldn't do that!"

"Do what?" Tony asked innocently, but his eyes were dancing. He left the doorway to stride over and sit on the edge of the desk.

He was wearing dirty work clothes, but Sharon still found him damnably attractive.

"That was my mother," she said, in an effort to distract herself.

Tony's smile was slow, and he was watching Sharon's lips as though their every motion fascinated him. "I hope you gave her my fondest regards."

"You don't hope any such thing," Sharon scoffed, scooting the chair back a few more inches.

Tony stopped its progress by bending over and grasping the arms in his hands. "I've missed you," he said, and his mouth was so close to hers that Sharon could feel his breath whispering against her skin.

"The kids are here," she reminded him.

He touched her lips with his and a sweet jolt went through her. One of his index fingers moved lightly down the buttoned front of her flannel shirt.

"Stop it," she said in anguish.

Tony drew her onto her feet and into his kiss, holding her so close that she ached with the awareness of his masculinity and his strength. She was dazed when, after a long interlude, the contact was broken.

In another minute she was not only going to be unable to resist this man, she could end up taking him by the hand and leading him upstairs to bed. Resolutely, Sharon stepped back out of his embrace. "Why, Tony?" she asked reasonably. "Why, after all these months, has it suddenly become so important to you to seduce me?"

He folded his arms across his chest. "Believe me," he said, "it isn't sudden. Has it ever occurred to you, Sharon, that our divorce might have been a mistake?"

"No," Sharon lied.

Tony's expression said he saw through her. "Not even once?" When she shook her head, Tony laughed. The sound was sad, rueful. "I've always said you were stubborn, my love."

Sharon was easing toward the door. "You'll talk to Bri?"

"I said I would," Tony replied quietly, his arms still folded, that broken look lingering in his eyes.

She cleared her throat. "Did your mother tell you what the problem is?"

Tony nodded. He looked baffled now, and watchful, as though he was curious about something. "I'm surprised it didn't come up before this, given the gossip factor. Sharon—"

She felt behind her for the doorknob and held on to it as though it could anchor her somehow. "What?"

"It bothers you, doesn't it? That Carmen was pregnant when I married her."

It would be stupid, and very unmodern, to be bothered by something like that, Sharon reasoned to herself. "Of course it doesn't," she said brightly, throwing in an airy shrug for good measure.

A look of fury clouded Tony's face, and in the next second he brought his fist down hard on the surface of the desk and rasped a swear word.

Sharon's eyes were wide. She opened her mouth and then closed it again as Tony shook his finger at her.

"Don't lie to me," he warned in a low, even voice.

Sharon stepped inside the den and closed the door so that the kids wouldn't hear. "Okay," she whispered angrily, "you win. Yes, it bothers me that Carmen was pregnant! It bothers me that she ever existed! Are you satisfied?"

He was staring at her. "You were jealous of Carmen?" he asked, sounding amazed.

Sharon turned away to hide the tears she wasn't sure she'd be able to hold back, and let her forehead rest against the door. For several seconds she just stood there, breathing deeply and trying to compose herself. When she felt Tony's hands on her shoulders, strong and gentle, she stiffened.

His chin rested against the back of her head; she was aware of the hard, masculine lines of his body in every fiber of her being.

"I didn't understand, babe," he said in a hoarse whisper. "I'm sorry."

Sharon couldn't speak, and when Tony turned her and drew her into his arms, she hid her face in the warm strength of his shoulder. He buried his fingers in her hair.

"I made a lot of mistakes," he told her after a long time.

Sharon nodded, lifting her head but unable to meet Tony's eyes. "So did I," she confessed. "I—I think I'd better go."

His embrace tightened for an instant, as though he didn't want to release her, and then relaxed. Sharon collected her purse, hurried out to the garage and slid behind the wheel of her roadster.

The door rolled open and Sharon backed slowly out into the driveway.

Saying goodbye to Briana and Matt didn't even occur to her.

# Chapter 4

Sharon's small garden apartment seemed to have all the ambience of a jail cell when she walked into it late that afternoon, carrying a bag of take-out food in one hand. The walls were nicotine yellow, unadorned by pictures or any other decoration, and the cheap furniture had served a number of previous tenants.

Feeling overwhelmingly lonely, as she always did when she left the house and the kids to return to this place, Sharon flipped on the television set and sank onto the couch to eat fish-and-chips and watch the shopping channel.

She was teetering on the brink of ordering a set of marble-handled screwdrivers when there was a knock at the door. Sharon turned down the volume, crumpled the evidence of her fast-food dinner into a ball and tossed it into the trash as she called, "Who's there?"

"It's me," a feminine voice replied. "Helen."

Sharon crossed the short distance between the kitchenette and the front door and admitted her employee with a smile. In her early thirties, like Sharon, Helen was a beautiful woman with sleek black hair and a trim, petite figure. Her almond-shaped eyes accented her Oriental heritage.

Helen's glance fell on Sharon's overnight bag, which was still sitting on the floor in front of the coat closet. "How were the kids?" she asked.

Sharon looked away. "Fine," she answered, as her friend perched gracefully on the arm of an easy chair.

Helen sighed. "You're awfully quiet. What went wrong?"

Sharon pretended not to hear the question. She went into the kitchenette, took two mugs from the cupboard and asked brightly, "Coffee?"

"Sure," Helen replied, and Sharon jumped because she hadn't heard her friend's approach. It seemed that people were always sneaking up on her.

She filled the mugs with water, thrust them into her small microwave oven and set the time, still avoiding Helen's gaze.

"My, but we're uncommunicative tonight," the younger woman observed. "Did you have some kind of run-in with Tony?"

Sharon swallowed, and her eyes burned for a moment. "Listen," she said in a voice that was too bright and too quick, "I've been thinking that I should do something about this place—you know, paint and get some decent furniture...."

Helen put a hand on Sharon's shoulder. "What happened?" she pressed gently.

Sharon bit into her lower lip and shook her head. "Nothing dramatic," she answered, after a few seconds had passed.

The timer on the microwave chimed, and Sharon was grateful for the distraction. She took the cups of steaming water out and transferred them to the counter, where she spooned instant coffee into each one.

Helen sighed and followed Sharon into the living room. "I stopped by to borrow your burgundy shoes," she said. "The ones with the snakeskin toes."

Sharon was looking at the television set. The sound was still off, so the man selling crystal cake plates seemed to be miming his routine. "Help yourself," she replied.

Helen went into Sharon's tiny bedroom and came out a short time later with the shoes in one hand and a firm conviction in her eyes. "Why don't you give it up and go home, Sharon?" she asked quietly. "You know you're not happy without Tony."

"It isn't as simple as that," Sharon confessed.

"Is he involved with someone else?"

Sharon shook her head. "I don't think so. The kids would have mentioned it."

"Well?"

"It's too late, Helen. Too much has happened."

Helen sat on the arm of the chair again, lifted her cup from the end table and took a thoughtful sip of coffee. "I see," she said, looking inscrutable.

Sharon assessed the dingy walls of her living room and said with forced good cheer, "It's time I got on with my life. I'm going to start by turning this place into a home."

"Terrific," agreed Helen, her expression still bland.

"If you're going to start embroidering samplers, I'm out of here."

Sharon laughed. "You know, that's not a bad idea. I could do some profound motto in cross-stitch—Anybody Who Says Money Doesn't Buy Happiness Has Never Been to Neiman-Marcus."

At last, Helen smiled. "Words to live by," she said, setting aside her coffee and standing up. "Well, I've got a hot date with my husband, so I'd better fly. See you tomorrow at the shop." She held up the burgundy pumps as she opened the door. "Thanks for the loan of the shoes," she finished, and then she was gone.

Sharon was even lonelier than before. Knowing that the only cure for that was action, she put on a jacket, gave her hair a quick brushing and fled the apartment for a nearby discount store.

When she returned, she had several gallons of paint and all the attending equipment, except for a ladder. It seemed silly to buy something like that when there were several in the garage at home; she would stop by the house when she left Teddy Bares the next day and pick one up.

Sharon had never painted before, and it took all her forbearance to keep from plunging into the task that very night before any of the preparations had been made.

She rested her hands on her hips as she considered the changes ahead. She'd chosen a pretty shade of ivory for the living room, the palest blue for the kitchenette and a pastel pink for the bedroom and bath. If it killed her, she was going to give this apartment some pizzazz and personality.

While she was at it, she might as well do the same for the rest of her life. It was time to start meeting new men.

Sharon caught one fingernail between her teeth and grimaced. "Exactly how does a person go about doing that?" she asked the empty room.

There was no answer, of course.

Sharon took a shower, washed and blow-dried her hair and got into pajamas. She was settled in bed, reading, when the doorbell rang.

She padded out into the dark living room. "Yes?"

"Mom," Bri wailed from the hallway, "I'm a bastard!"

Sharon wrenched open the door, appalled to find the child standing there, alone, at that late hour. "You aren't, either," she argued practically, as she pulled Briana into the apartment.

"Yes, I am," Bri cried, with all the woe and passion a wounded twelve-year-old is capable of feeling. Her face was dirty and tear streaked, and she hadn't bothered to zip her jacket. "My whole life is ruined! I want to join the Foreign Region!"

"That's 'legion,' darling," Sharon said softly, leading her toward a chair, "and I think you have to be older."

"Stupid rules." Bri sniffled, dashing at her tears with the back of one hand.

"The world is full of them," Sharon commiserated, bending to kiss the top of the girl's head. "Does your dad know where you are?"

"No," Bri replied without hesitation, "and I don't care if he worries, either!"

"Well, I do," Sharon answered, reaching for the living room extension and punching out the familiar number. "I take it you had that talk about your conception," she ventured in tones she hoped were diplomatic, as the ringing began at the other end of the line.

Bri was fairly tearing off her jacket, every motion designed to let Sharon know that she was here to stay. The child nodded and sniffled loudly.

Sharon turned away to hide her smile when Tony answered, "Hello?"

"It's ten o'clock," Sharon said warmly. "Do you know where your daughter is?"

"In bed," Tony replied, sounding puzzled.

"Wrong," Sharon retorted. "I'm sorry, Mr. Morelli, but you don't win the week's supply of motor oil and the free trip to Bremerton. Bri is here, and she's very upset."

"How the hell did she manage that?"

Sharon shrugged, even though Tony couldn't see the gesture. "Maybe she called a cab or took a bus—I don't know. The point is—"

"The point is that I hate my father!" Bri shouted, loudly enough for Tony to hear.

He sighed.

"I see everything went very well between the two of you," Sharon chimed sweetly. Her hackles were rising now; she was thinking of the danger Bri had been in and of the pain she was feeling. "Tony, what the devil did you say to this child?"

"He said," Bri began dramatically, "that he and my mother were such animals that they couldn't even wait to be married!"

Sharon turned, one hand over the receiver. "I'd keep quiet, if I were you," she said in warm, dulcet tones. Tony, meanwhile, was quietly swearing on the other end of the line.

"I'll be right over to get her," he announced when he'd finished.

"And leave Matt alone?" Sharon countered. "I don't think so."

"Then you can bring her home."

Sharon was angered by his presumption. "Maybe," she began stiffly, "it would be better if Bri spent the night. She's very upset, and—"

"Briana is my daughter, Sharon," Tony interrupted coldly, "and I'll decide how this is going to be handled."

Sharon felt as though he'd slapped her. *Briana is my daughter.* Tony had never hurled those words in Sharon's face before, never pointed out the fact that, in reality, Bri was exclusively his child.

"I'm sorry," he said into the stricken silence.

She couldn't speak.

"Damn it, Sharon, are you there or not?"

She swallowed. "I-I'll bring Briana home in a few minutes," she said.

"I don't want to go back there ever again!" Bri put in.

Tony's sigh was ragged. Again, he swore. "And I thought I was tactful."

Sharon's eyes were full of tears, and her sinuses had closed. "Apparently not," she said brokenly.

"She can stay," Tony conceded.

Sharon shoved a hand through her hair. "That's magnanimous of you," she replied. "Good night, Tony." Then, not trusting herself to say more, she hung up.

During the next few minutes, while Bri was in the bathroom washing her face and putting on a pair of Sharon's pajamas, her stepmother made the sofa out into a bed. Tony's words were still falling on her soul like drops of acid. *Briana is my daughter... I'll decide how this is going to be handled....*

Bri came out of the bathroom, looking sheepish and very childlike. The emotional storm had evidently blown over. "Is Daddy mad at me?"

Sharon shook her head. "I don't think so, sweetie. But you were plenty mad at him, weren't you?"

Bri nodded, biting her lower lip, and sat down on the end of the sofa bed.

Sharon joined her, putting an arm around the child's shoulders. "Want to talk?"

Bri's chin quivered. "I'm a mistake!" she whispered, and tears were brimming in her eyes again.

Sharon hugged her. "Never."

The little girl sniffled. "I was probably conceived in the backseat of a Chevy or something," she despaired.

Sharon couldn't help laughing. "Oh, Bri," she said, pressing her forehead to her stepdaughter's. "I love you so much."

Briana flung her arms around Sharon's neck. "I love you, too, Mom," she answered with weary exuberance. "I wish you could come home and stay there."

Sharon didn't comment on that. Instead, she smoothed Bri's wildly tangled hair with one hand and said, "It's time for you to go to sleep, but first I want to know something. How did you get here?"

Bri drew herself up. "I called a cab. Dad was doing laundry, so he didn't hear me go out."

Sharon sighed. "Sweetheart, what you did was really dangerous. Do I have your word that you won't try this ever again?"

Bri hesitated. "What if I need to talk to you?"

Sharon cupped the lovely face, a replica of Carmen's, in her hands. "Then you just call, and we'll make plans to get together right away," she answered softly. "Do you promise, Briana?"

The child swallowed hard and nodded, and then Sharon tucked her into bed and kissed her good-night just as she had so many times in the past. She'd reached the privacy of her room before her heart cracked into two pieces and the grieving began in earnest.

Tony arrived early the next morning while Sharon was still in the shower, and collected Briana. He left a terse note on the kitchen table, thanking her for "everything."

Sharon crumpled the note and flung it at the wall. "Thank you for everything, too, Morelli," she muttered. "Thanks one hell of a lot!"

She was in a terrible mood by the time she reached the shop. Helen had already arrived, and Teddy Bares was open for business.

Since there were several customers browsing, Sharon made herself smile as she stormed behind the counter and into the small office at the back.

Helen appeared in the doorway after a few minutes had passed. "Are you okay?" she ventured carefully.

"No," Sharon replied.

"Is there anything I can do?"

Sharon shook her head. She was going to have to pull herself together and get on with the day. It was a sure bet that Tony wasn't standing around agonizing over the fact that his family was in pieces. He knew how to set aside his personal life when it was time to concentrate on work.

Sharon drew a deep breath and went out to greet her customers. The morning was a busy one, fortunately, and there wasn't time to think about anything but taking care of business.

It was noon, and Helen had gone to the pizza place at the other end of the mall to get take-out salads, when

Tony wandered in. Instead of his usual jeans, work shirt and boots, he was wearing a three-piece suit, beautifully tailored to his build. He approached the counter and inclined his head slightly to one side, his dark eyes seeming to caress Sharon for a moment before he spoke.

"I'm sorry we didn't get a chance to talk this morning," he said.

"I'll bet you are," Sharon scoffed, remembering the brisk note tucked between the salt-and-pepper shakers in the middle of her table. "What's with the fancy clothes?"

"I had a meeting," Tony answered. Then he arched one ebony eyebrow and sighed. "I don't suppose you're free for lunch."

Sharon opened her mouth to say that he was dead right, but Helen arrived before she could get the words out. "Know what?" she chimed. "They were all out of salad. I guess you have no choice but to accept Tony's invitation."

Sharon wasn't buying the no-salad routine—the pizza place made the stuff up by the bushel—and she frowned at Helen, wondering where she'd hidden all that lettuce. "I've got an idea," she told her friend tartly. "Why don't you go to lunch with Tony?"

Like a spectator at a tennis match, Tony turned his head toward Helen, waiting for her to return the ball.

"I have plans," Helen said loftily, and marched around behind the counter, elbowing Sharon aside. "It just so happens that I'm out to build an underwear empire of my own, Ms. Morelli, so watch your back."

Tony laughed and took Sharon's arm and, rather than make a scene, she allowed him to lead her out of the shop and along the mall's crowded concourse. The place was jammed with mothers and children shopping for school clothes.

Sharon jutted out her chin and walked a little faster, ignoring Tony as best she could.

"Where do you want to eat?" he finally asked.

"I don't care," Sharon responded firmly.

"I like a decisive woman," came the taut reply. Tony's grasp on her elbow tightened, and he propelled her toward a sandwich place.

When they were seated at a table in a corner by a window, Sharon's rigid control began to falter a little. "How could you say that?" she demanded in a miserable whisper, avoiding Tony's eyes.

"What?" he asked, in a baffled tone that made Sharon want to clout him over the head with the menu that had just been shoved into her hands.

"What you said last night," Sharon whispered furiously. "About Bri being your daughter!"

"Isn't she?" Tony asked, having the audacity to read the menu while he awaited her answer.

Sharon suppressed an urge to kick him in the shin. She pushed back her chair and would have left the table if he hadn't reached out and caught hold of one of her wrists. "You know that isn't what I mean!" she said.

Tony looked as though he had a headache. *Men,* Sharon thought to herself, *are such babies when it comes to pain.* "We do not seem to be communicating, here," he observed a few moments later.

"That's because one of us is stupid," Sharon said. "And it isn't me, buddy."

Tony sighed. "Maybe I was a little insensitive—"

"A little?" Sharon drew a deep breath and let it out.

"My God, Tony, you've got insensitivity down to an art. You don't even know why I'm angry!"

His jaw tightened. "I'm sure after you've tortured me for a few hours," he responded, "you'll tell me!"

A teenage waitress stepped into the breach. "The special today is baked chicken."

"We'll take it," said Tony, his dark, furious gaze never shifting from Sharon's face.

"Right," said the waitress with a shrug, swinging her hips as she walked away.

Tony didn't wait for Sharon to speak. "So help me God," he told her in an ominously low voice, "if you say you don't want the baked chicken, I'll strangle you."

Sharon sniffed. "I had no idea you felt so strongly about poultry," she said.

Tony glared at her. "Sharon," he warned.

She sat back. "Bri is not just your daughter, regardless whose Chevy she was conceived in," she said with dignity. "I raised that child. I love her as much as I love Matthew."

Tony looked bewildered. "Regardless of whose..." His words fell away as an expression of furious revelation dawned in his face. "Last night. You're still mad because of what I said last night on the phone about Bri being my daughter."

Sharon said nothing; she didn't need to, because she knew the look on her face said it all.

"Good Lord," Tony muttered. "I apologized for that."

Sharon was dangerously near tears; she willed herself not to cry. She had a store in this mall; people knew her. She couldn't afford to make a public spectacle of herself. "And you thought that made everything all right, didn't you? You could just say 'I'm sorry' and it would be as though it had never happened."

The baked chicken arrived. When the waitress had gone, Tony demanded, "What else could I have said, Sharon?"

She swallowed and looked down at her food in real despair. Never in a million years was she going to be able to get so much as a bite down her throat. "Bri is mine, too, and I love her," she insisted miserably, and then she got up and walked out of the restaurant with her head held high.

The shop was full of customers when Sharon got back, and she threw herself into waiting on them. All the same, it was a relief when the day ended. Unlike many other shops in the mall, Teddy Bares closed at five-thirty.

"You really ought to think about getting someone in to work until nine," Helen ventured quietly as the two women went through the familiar routine of emptying the cash register, totaling receipts and locking up.

Sharon just shrugged. She felt raw inside and had ever since her encounter with Tony at noon. Going through the motions was the best she could hope to accomplish, for the moment, anyway.

Helen's gaze was sympathetic. "What happened, Sharon?" she asked. At her friend's look, she went on. "I know, it's none of my business, but I've never seen two people more in love than you and Tony. And yet here you are, divorced—unable to have a civilized lunch together."

Sharon remained stubbornly silent, hoping that Helen would let the subject drop.

She wasn't about to be so accommodating. "He loves you, Sharon," she said insistently. "The rest of us see that so clearly—why can't you?"

The numbers on the receipts blurred together. Sharon chose to ignore Helen's remark about Tony's feelings. "You know, my mother warned me that the marriage wouldn't work. Tony was already successful then, and Bea said he was way out of my league—that he'd get tired of me and start running around."

Helen was seething; Sharon didn't even have to look at her friend to know that smoke was practically blowing out of her ears. "Excuse my bluntness, but what the devil does your mother know? Who is she, Dr. Ruth?" Helen paused. "Tony didn't cheat on you, did he?"

Sharon shook her head. "No, but he got tired of me. I'm sure it would only have been a matter of time until there were other women."

Helen made a sound that resembled a suppressed scream. "How do you know he got tired of you? Did he say so?"

"No," Sharon answered in a sad, reflective tone. "He didn't have to. He worked more and more, harder and harder, and when we were together, we fought—like today."

"What did you fight about?" Helen persisted.

Sharon looked around her at the teddies and peignoirs and robes, all made from shimmering silks and satins of the highest quality. "Teddy Bares, mostly," she answered. And then she took up her purse and started toward the door.

The subject, like the shop, was closed.

# Chapter 5

Tony slammed his fist on the hood of a pickup truck marked with the company name, and swore. He'd just fired one of the best foremen in the construction business, and now he was going to have to swallow his pride, go after the man and apologize.

"Tony."

He stiffened at the sound of his father's voice, then turned, reluctantly, to face him. "You heard," he said.

Vincent Morelli was a man of medium height and build, and of quiet dignity. He'd begun his working life as an apprentice carpenter at fifteen and had passed a thriving company on to his sons fifty years later. "Everybody heard," he replied. "What happened, Tonio?"

Tony shoved one hand through his hair. "I'm not sure, Papa," he confessed, shifting his gaze to the line of condominiums under construction a hundred yards away. "I know one thing—I was wrong. I've been wrong a lot lately."

Vincent came to stand beside him, bracing one booted foot against the front bumper of the truck. "I'm listening," he said.

Tony had heard those words often from both his parents since earliest childhood, and he knew Vincent meant them. He was grateful for the solid, sensible upbringing he'd had, and he wanted desperately to give the same gift to his own children. "It's Sharon," he said. "And the kids—it's everything."

Vincent waited, saying nothing.

"I didn't want the divorce," Tony went on after a few moments, aware that he wasn't telling his father anything he didn't already know. Vincent had seen the grief and pain Tony had hidden so carefully from Sharon. "Ever since it happened, I've been trying to find a way to make things right again. Papa, I can't even talk to the woman without making her mad as hell."

His father smiled sadly. He'd always liked Sharon, even defended her desire to strike out on her own. Vincent had insisted that she was only trying to prove herself by starting the shop, while Tony had dismissed the project as silly. And worse.

"In some ways, Tonio," Vincent said, his voice quiet and calm, "you're too much like me."

Tony was taken aback; there was no one he admired more than his father. It was impossible to be too much like him.

"I worked hard building this company for many, many years. But I was also something of a failure as a man and as a father. I didn't know my own sons until they were men, working beside me, and I may never truly know my daughters."

Tony started to protest, but Vincent stopped him with one upraised hand, still callused from years of labor, and went on. "You all grew up to be successful men, you and Michael and Richard, and your sisters are fine women, but you give me too much of the credit. Most of it should go to your mother, Tony, because she taught you all the things that make you strong—confidence in yourself, clear thinking, personal responsibility, integrity."

Tony looked down at his boots.

"I was sixty years old," Vincent continued, "before I had the good sense to appreciate Maria for the woman she is. If you're wise, Tonio, you won't wait that long before you start treating Sharon with the respect she deserves."

"I do respect her," Tony said, his eyes still downcast. "She came into my life at a time when I thought I wanted to die, Papa, and she gave me back my soul. And even though she'd had a rotten childhood herself, she knew how to be a mother to Bri."

Vincent laid a hand on his son's shoulder. "These are pretty words, Tony. Perhaps if you would say them to Sharon, instead of assuming that she knows how you feel, things might get better."

"She won't listen. There are always too many demands—too many distractions—"

"That is simple to fix," Vincent broke in reasonably. "You bring the children to your mother and me and you persuade Sharon to go to the island house for a couple of days. There, you hold her hand and you speak softly, always. You make sure that there is wine and music, and you tell her that you love her. Often."

Tony grinned, feeling a certain tentative hope. "You're quite the ladies' man, Papa," he teased.

Vincent chuckled and slapped his son's shoulder again. "I did not father three sons and three daughters by accident," he replied.

Just then, the recently fired foreman drove up in a swirl of dust. Scrambling out of his car, the man stormed toward Tony, shaking his finger. "I've got a few more things to say to you, Morelli!" he bellowed.

Tony sighed, gave his father a sheepish look and went to meet his angry ex-employee. "I've got something to say to you, too," he responded evenly. "I was wrong, Charlie, and I'm sorry."

Charlie Petersen stared at him in astonishment. "Say what?" he finally drawled.

"You heard me," Tony said. "There's a foreman's job open if you want it."

Charlie grinned. "I want it," he admitted.

The two men shook hands, and then Charlie strode back toward the framework rising against the sky. "Hey, Merkins," he called out to a member of his crew. "If I see you walking around without your hard hat again, you're out of here, union steward or not!"

Tony laughed and went back to his own work.

Sharon had left the shop early in hopes of getting the stepladder from the garage without encountering Tony. Conversely, she was almost disappointed that she'd succeeded.

"I wish we could come and help you," Matt said, as they gathered in the kitchen to say goodbye, biting forlornly into a cookie, "but we're both grounded."

Bri, perched on one of the stools at the breakfast bar, nodded disconsolately.

Sharon pretended to ponder their offenses, a finger to her chin. "Let's see," she said to Matt, "you're being punished for the wholesale slaughter of goldfish, am I right?"

Matt gave Bri an accusing look, but admitted his guilt with a nod.

"And I'm on the list," Briana supplied glumly, "because Dad says running away isn't cool."

"He's right," Sharon said. "Did the two of you manage to work things out?"

Bri shook her head. "Not yet. We're supposed to talk tonight."

Sharon sighed and laid gentle hands on her stepdaughter's shoulders. "Sometimes your dad isn't the most tactful man on earth. You might try looking past what he says to what he means."

"You could try that, too, Mom," Bri remarked, with the kind of out-of-left-field astuteness children sometimes use to put their elders in their places.

"Touché," Sharon replied, kissing Bri's forehead and then Matt's.

Matt groaned, but spared her his usual, heartfelt "yuck!"

"How are we supposed to get Uncle Michael a birthday present if we're both grounded?" he demanded, when Sharon would have made her exit.

"Gramma already told us the party will have to be postponed because Uncle Michael is going to be out of town and because Daddy has other plans for the weekend," Bri told him in a tone reserved for little brothers and other lower forms of life. "Boy, are you stupid."

Sharon closed her eyes. She didn't want to give a damn that Tony had a special date lined up for the weekend, but she did. Oh, hell, did she ever.

Matt wasn't about to stand for any nonsense from his sister. "Saturday is still Uncle Michael's birthday and we still have to get him a present and you're *still* a royal pain in the rear end, Briana Morelli!"

Reminding herself that the job of worrying about these two little darlings was rightfully Tony's—bless his heart—Sharon backed out of the door, waving. "Bye," she chimed, as the argument escalated into a confrontation that might well require peacekeeping forces.

Mrs. Harry, the housekeeper, would keep them from killing each other before Tony got home.

The stepladder was leaning against the wall of the garage, where Sharon had left it. She put it into the trunk of the roadster along with her oldest pair of jeans from the dresser upstairs and two ancient work shirts that she'd stolen from Tony's side of the closet.

The refurbishing of Sharon Morelli and her surroundings was about to begin.

Two and a half hours later, when Sharon had moved and covered all her furniture and masked off every inch of baseboard, every electrical outlet and every window in her apartment, she was starting to wish she'd been more resistant to change, more of a stick-in-the-mud.

There was a resolute knock at the door—her dinner was about to be delivered, no doubt—and Sharon unwrapped the knob and turned it. Tony was standing in the hallway, paying the kid from the Chinese restaurant. He'd already appropriated her pork-fried rice and sweet-and-sour chicken.

Sharon snatched the white cartons from her ex-husband's possession and went into the kitchen to un-tape one of the drawers and get out a spoon and fork.

"Oh, are you still here?" she asked pleasantly, when she turned to find Tony standing behind her with his arms folded and his damnably handsome head cocked to one side.

"No," he answered dryly, his eyes smiling at her in a way that melted her pelvic bones. "I'm only an illusion. It's all done with mirrors."

"I wish," Sharon muttered, edging around him to march back into the living room, her feet making a crackling sound on the newspaper covering the carpet. She knew she looked something less than glamorous, wearing a bandana over her hair, those disreputable jeans, dirty sneakers and a shirt that reached to her knees, but one couldn't paint walls and ceilings in a flowing ballgown.

Tony followed her. He was too big for her apartment; he didn't fit.

Sharon wished that he'd leave and at the very same moment was glad he hadn't. "Sit down," she said with a generous gesture. Then, realizing that both chairs were covered, along with the couch, she plunked down on the floor, cross-legged, and Tony joined her.

Sharon opened her food and began to eat. "I'd offer you some," she said through a mouthful of fried rice, "but I'm incredibly greedy."

Tony's eyes left Sharon warm wherever they touched her, which was everywhere, and he let her remark hang unanswered in the air.

She squirmed and speared a chunk of sauce-covered chicken from the carton on the floor in front of her. "Are you here for some specific reason or what?" she asked.

He looked around at all the masking and newspapering she'd done. "I came to help you paint," he said.

Sharon sighed. "Tony—"

He was watching her mouth. Sharon found it very distracting when he did that. "Yes?" The word had a low rumble, like a faraway earthquake.

"I can manage this on my own."

His smile was a little forced, but it was a smile. He was trying; Sharon had to give him credit for that. "I'm sure you can," he answered reasonably. "But I'd like to help." He spread his hands. "Call it a personal quirk."

"I call it a crock," Sharon responded, but she was grinning. She couldn't help herself.

"I love you," Tony said quietly.

Sharon's forkful of fried rice hung suspended between the carton and her mouth. She remembered what the kids had said about the plans he'd made and stiffened her spine. "Are you practicing for your hot date this weekend?" she asked.

"Jealous?" he wanted to know.

"Not in the least," lied Sharon, jamming the fork into her rice as if it were a climber's flag she was planting on a mountain peak.

Tony reached out, took the carton from her hand and set it aside. Then he caught her wrists gently in his hands and pulled until she was straddling his lap. "Just this once," he suggested, breathing the words rather than saying them, his lips brushing against Sharon's, "let's skip the preliminary rounds, okay?"

Sharon's arms were trembling as she draped them around his neck. "Okay," she whispered. She knew that what was about to happen was a mistake, but she couldn't stop it. Tony was a man any woman would want, and Sharon had the added handicap of loving him.

The kiss was long and thorough and so intimate that it left Sharon disoriented. She was surprised to find herself lying on the floor, because she didn't remember moving. And she was frightened by the scope of her feelings.

Tony's hand was unfastening the buttons on her shirt when she stopped him by closing her fingers over his. "This woman you're seeing this weekend—who is she?" she dared to ask.

He kissed her again, briefly this time, and playfully. "She's you," he answered. "If you don't turn me down, that is."

Sharon withdrew her hand, and the unbuttoning continued, unimpeded. She closed her eyes as he opened the shirt and then removed it. She made a soft sound in her throat when she felt the front catch on her bra give way. "Oh, Tony—"

"Is that a yes or a no?" he asked in a husky voice, and Sharon could feel his breath fanning over her nipple.

"What's the…question?" she countered, gasping and arching her back slightly when she felt the tip of Tony's tongue touch her.

He chuckled and took several moments to enjoy the territory he'd just marked as his own before answering, "We'll talk about it later."

Sharon's fingers had buried themselves, at no conscious order from her, in his hair. She felt an inexplicable happiness founded on nothing of substance. Her eyes were burning, and there was an achy thickness in her throat.

His hand was warm as it cupped her breast, his thumb shaping a nipple still moist and taut from the caresses of his lips and tongue. "Oh, God, I've missed you," he said, and then he kissed her again, hungrily, as though to consume her.

And she wanted to be consumed.

Tony's mouth strayed downward, along the line of her arched neck, over her bare shoulder, midway down her upper arm. When he reclaimed her nipple, Sharon moaned an anguished welcome.

The snap on her jeans gave way to his fingers, closely followed by the zipper, and still he availed himself of her breasts, first one and then the other. Sharon was like a woman in the throes of an uncontrollable fever; she flung her head from side to side, blinded by the sensations Tony was creating with his hand and mouth, her breath too shallow and too quick. She grasped his T-shirt in her hands and pulled at it; if she'd had the strength, she would have torn it from him.

He finally cooperated, however, allowing Sharon to undress him, to pleasure him in some of the same ways that he had pleasured her.

Their joining, when it happened, was graceful at first, like a ballet. With each flexing of their bodies it became more frenzied, though, culminating in a kind of sweet desperation, a tangling of triumph and surrender that left both Tony and Sharon exhausted.

Tony recovered first and, after giving Sharon a leisurely kiss, sat up and began putting his clothes back on. The newspaper crackled as he moved, and Sharon began to laugh.

"What's funny?" he asked, turning and bracing himself with his hands so that he was poised over her. His eyes were full of love and mischief.

"I probably have newsprint on my backside," Sharon replied.

"Turn over and I'll look," Tony offered generously.

"Thanks, but no thanks," she answered, sliding out from beneath him and reaching for her own clothes.

"'Housing Market Bottoms Out,'" he pretended to read in a ponderous tone when Sharon reached for her panties and jeans.

She laughed and swung at him with the jeans, and that started a bout of wrestling, which ended in Sharon's bed a long time later.

"What were you going to ask me—about the weekend?" Sharon ventured, her cheek resting against Tony's shoulder. It felt good to lie close to him like that again.

Tony rested his chin on top of her head. He seemed to be bracing himself for a rebuff of some sort. "I'd like to go to the island house for a couple of days—just you and me."

Sharon absorbed that in silence. She had planned to take inventory at the shop that weekend, but a woman in business has to be flexible. She sighed contentedly and kissed the bare skin of his shoulder. "Sounds like an indecent proposal to me."

He laughed and his arm tightened around her waist. "Believe me, lady, it is."

Sharon raised her head to squint at the clock on the bedside table. "Oh, Lord. Tony, who's with the kids?"

"Mrs. Harry stayed late. Why? What time is it?"

"Boy, did Mrs. Harry stay late," Sharon agreed. "Tony, it's after midnight."

He swore and threw back the covers, crunching around on the newspaper looking for his clothes, and Sharon laughed.

"Do you realize what that woman gets for overtime?" Tony demanded, bringing his jeans and T-shirt from the living room to put them on.

Sharon was still giggling. "No, but I know how much she hates working late. I'm glad you're the one who has to face Scary Harry, and not me."

"Thanks a lot," Tony replied, snatching his watch from the bedside table. "We're leaving for the island Friday night," he warned, bending over to kiss her once more, "so make sure you have all the bases covered."

Sharon opened her mouth to protest this arbitrary treatment, then closed it again. She really didn't want to argue, and they could discuss such issues on the island.

"Good night, babe," Tony said from the doorway of her room.

Sharon felt a sudden and infinite sadness because he was leaving. "Bye," she replied, glad that he couldn't see her face.

After she'd heard the door close behind him, she went out to put the chain lock in place. This, she thought, was what it was like to have a lover instead of a husband.

She tried to decide which she preferred while picking up her clothes. Lovers had a way of disappearing, like smoke, but husbands were surely more demanding. Sharon guessed that this was a case of six in one hand and half a dozen in the other.

She also deduced pretty quickly that she wasn't going to be able to crawl back into that bed where she'd just spent hours making love with Tony and fall placidly to sleep. She took a shower, put on her clothes and mixed the first batch of paint.

The new coat of soft ivory revitalized the living room and, coupled with the after effects of Tony's lovemaking, it brightened Sharon's spirits, as well. For the first time in months—the first time since she'd filed for divorce—she felt real hope for the future.

It was 3:00 a.m. when she finished. After cleaning up the mess, Sharon stumbled off to her room and collapsed facedown on the rumpled covers of the bed. She had absolutely no problem sleeping.

She entered Teddy Bares, bright eyed and humming, at precisely nine o'clock the next morning to find Helen reading a romance novel behind the counter.

The cover showed a dashing pirate holding a lushly buxom beauty in his arms. There were eager lights in Helen's eyes as she told Sharon breathlessly, "The woman in this book was given the choice of sleeping in the hold with a lot of soiled doves on their way to Morocco or sharing the captain's bed!"

Sharon took the book and studied the hero on the cover. He was an appealing rake with a terrific body. "Share his bed or languish in the hold, huh? Decisions, decisions."

Helen reclaimed the paperback and put it under the counter with her purse. Her expression was watchful now, and curious. "You look happy," she said suspiciously.

Sharon took her own purse to the back room and dropped it into a drawer of her desk. After settling herself in her chair, she reached for a pad of legal paper and a pencil and began making notes for an ad in the help wanteds. "Thank you," she replied in belated response to Helen's remark. "We won't be taking inventory this weekend, but I'll need you to work on Saturday if you will."

Helen was reading over her shoulder. "You're hiring another clerk? Excuse me, but is there something I should know?"

Sharon stopped writing and smiled up at her friend. "Good heavens, are you asking me if I mean to fire you?"

Helen nodded. "I guess I am," she said, looking worried.

Sharon shook her head. "Absolutely not. But I've decided that you're right—it's time we got someone to work evenings, and I'd like to be able to take more time off. That means we need two people, really. Both part-time."

Out front, the counter bell rang. Helen was forced to go and wait on a customer, but she returned as soon as she could. Sharon was on the computer by that time, placing her ad.

"With any luck, we'll have applicants by Monday," she said.

Helen's eyes were wide. "I know what's going on here!" she cried in triumph. "It's like that Jimmy Stewart movie where he wishes he'd never been born and *whammie*, this angel fixes him right up. His friends don't recognize him—his own mother doesn't recognize him. His whole life is changed because he realizes how important he really is, and he's so happy—"

Sharon was shaking her head and smiling indulgently. "You can't seriously think that anything like that really happened," she said. "Can you?"

Helen sighed and shook her head. "No, but sometimes I get carried away."

With a nod, Sharon got out the books and began tallying debits and credits.

## Chapter 6

"The pictures have to go, Mama," Tony said gently, gesturing toward the photographs of Carmen and himself on top of his parents' mantel.

Maria Morelli looked down at her hands, which were folded in her lap. She was a beautiful woman who always wore her dark hair done up in an impeccable coronet, and her skin was as smooth as Italian porcelain. Although she was the finest cook in all the family, her figure was trim, like those of her daughters. "Carmen's mother was my dearest friend," she finally replied, her voice small and soft. "We might as well have been sisters."

Tony nodded. "I know that, Mama. I'm just trying to make things a little easier for Sharon, that's all."

The flawless, ageless face hardened for the merest fraction of a second. "Sharon divorced you," she reminded him. "She is not your wife."

Tony let out the sigh he had been restraining. "Do you dislike her that much, Mama?" he asked quietly, after a few moments had passed.

"I don't dislike Sharon at all," Maria replied, her dark eyes snapping as she met her eldest son's gaze. "She is my grandson's mother." She paused, probably to allow Tony time to absorb the significance of such a bond.

"The pictures bother her," Tony reasoned. "You can understand that, can't you?"

"Carmen was practically family. You were raised together from the time you were babies—"

"Yes," Tony interjected softly. "And I loved Carmen very much. But she's dead now—"

"All the more reason she should be remembered properly," Maria said, and although her voice was low, it was also passionate. "Have you forgotten that she was Briana's mother, Tonio?"

Tony shook his head. "No, Mama. But Sharon isn't asking any of us to forget."

Maria drew in a long breath, let it out slowly and nodded. Her glance strayed to the assortment of pictures she'd kept for twelve years, lingering fondly on each one in turn. "She was so beautiful, Tonio."

Tony looked at Carmen, smiling happily and holding his arm in their wedding picture, and some of the old feelings came back, if only for a moment. "Yes," he said hoarsely.

"You take the pictures," Maria said, with an abrupt sweep of her hand that didn't fool Tony in the least. "Save them for Briana—someday, she'll want them."

Tony nodded and rose to stack the framed photographs one on top of the other. Maria had left her chair to stand with her back to him. "You still love Sharon, then?" she asked.

"Yes," Tony replied. "Maybe more than before, Mama."

"There were so many problems."

He thought of the hours he'd spent with Sharon during the night just past. Although the sex had been better than ever—and it had always been good, even at the end of their marriage—it was the laughter and the quiet talk that Tony loved to remember. He cherished the images that lingered in his mind. "There isn't anything I want more in all this world than a second chance with Sharon," he told his mother, and then he left the huge house, where every item in every room was familiar.

Tony went to his condo, rather than the house, partly because he needed some time alone and partly because he wanted to give the photographs to Briana at a time when things were better between them. At the moment, his relationship with his daughter was rocky, to say the least.

When he reached the one-bedroom place where he'd been living since the final separation from Sharon, Tony set the photographs of Carmen down and immediately forgot about them. His grandmother, Lucia, made one of her surprise entrances, coming out of the kitchen with her arms extended.

Lucia went wherever she wanted, that being a privilege of age and rank in the Morelli family, and Tony kissed her forehead and greeted her in gentle Italian.

She responded by explaining that his sister, Rosa, had brought her—she knew, as did everyone in the family, where he kept a spare key hidden—and that she wanted to cook for him. Tony adored the old woman, but he wasn't in the mood to eat or to chat amiably.

"Another time," he told Lucia, in her own language. "I can't stay."

Lucia smiled, touched his face with one of her small, veined hands and replied that she would put the food in plastic containers and tuck it into the refrigerator for him to have later.

Tony laughed and shook his head, then bent to kiss her cheek. "Enjoy, Grandmama," he told her, and then he left the condo, got back into his car and drove until he reached the secret place overlooking the sound.

This bit of ground with a view of trees and water was a place to think, a place to hope and hurt and plan. Twice, it had been a place to cry.

Sharon returned from her lunch break with her book tucked away in her purse so that Helen wouldn't see it. What was happening between her and Tony was still too fragile and tentative to discuss, even with her closest friend, and she knew that an Italian cookbook would raise questions.

While Helen was out having her customary salad, Sharon called Tony's sister, Rosa, and enlisted her help. Married two years and pregnant with her first child, Rose was a willing collaborator. She promised to pick up the kids and take them home with her for the evening.

When it came time to close the shop, Sharon rushed through her part of the routine and dashed to the grocery store at the opposite end of the mall. Holding the book two inches from the end of her nose, she studied the list of ingredients needed to make clam spaghetti as she wheeled her cart up and down the aisles. If this dish didn't impress Tony, nothing would.

After leaving the supermarket, Sharon drove to the house on Tamarack Drive and let herself in. In the kitchen, on the big blackboard near the telephone, Bri had written carefully, "Dear Daddy, we're at Aunt Rose's. I told her we were grounded and she said our sentence had been suspended and you're supposed to go to the condo. Love, Bri."

Beneath this Rose had added a scrawled, "Don't worry about Grandmama—I'm on my way to collect her right now. Ciao, handsome. R."

Smiling, Sharon went to the rack where assorted keys were kept and ran her finger along it until she came to the one that would admit her to Tony's place. She dropped it into the pocket of her skirt and left the house again.

Tony's building stood on a road well out of town; Sharon remembered exactly where it was because he'd been working there overseeing the construction of the place when she'd had him served with divorce papers. The address was burned into her mind, as was the image of Tony storming into Teddy Bares with the papers in his hand, demanding answers Sharon hadn't been able to give.

He lived at the far end of the first row of condos; Bri and Matt had told her that weeks before, after a visit. Sharon pulled into the empty driveway and then sat for several minutes, trying to work up the courage to go in.

Finally, she did, her hand trembling a little as she unlocked the door and stepped inside, her bag of groceries in one arm.

The place was dim and sparsely furnished in the

way that homes of divorced men often are, and it was neat to a fault.

A lighted aquarium bubbled on one end of the raised hearth of the fireplace, boasting several brightly colored fish. On the mantel was a framed picture of the kids taken at Disneyland during happier times. Tony's mother, sisters and aunts had supplied him with hand-crocheted pillow covers and afghans, which were discreetly displayed. Sharon knew Tony kept them not because he loved the handiwork, but because he loved the family.

She felt a bittersweet mixture of hope and grief as she switched on a lamp and found her way into the kitchen. Just as she'd expected, it was small and efficient, organized down to the last olive pick. A delicious aroma of tomato sauce and mingling spices filled the air.

Humming, Sharon took the new cookbook from her purse and the groceries from their paper bag. She knew a few moments of chagrin when the telephone rang and Tony's answering machine picked up the call; maybe she shouldn't have let herself in this way without his knowing.

The caller was Tony's youngest brother, Michael. "Get back to me when you can, Tonio," he said with quiet affection. "We landed the contract on that new supermarket, so it's partytime at my place tonight. Bring the blonde."

Sharon's hands froze as Michael's closing words echoed through the condo like something shouted into a cave. She considered gathering up her cookbook and food and leaving, then drew a deep breath and reminded herself that she and Tony were divorced. Certainly, he had a right to date.

On the other hand, it hurt so very much to think of him with someone else....

In the end, Sharon decided to stay. Since she'd come this far, she might as well see this idea through to the last chopped clam and strand of spaghetti.

Sharon soon discovered that she'd forgotten to buy olive oil, and Tony's supply, if he'd ever had one, was gone. "What blonde?" his ex-wife muttered, still a little nettled, as she got down the butter-flavored shortening and plopped some into a skillet.

When she had the meal well underway—she had to admit that it didn't smell like anything Maria Morelli had ever cooked—she decided to switch on some music, touch up her lipstick and make sure that her hair was combed.

The bathroom had to be at the end of the hall next to the front door. Sharon headed that way, but was halted by an eerie glow coming from the single bedroom.

Puzzled, she paused and looked inside, and what she saw made her mouth drop open. The shock wounded her so deeply that she had to grasp the doorjamb in one hand for a moment to steady herself, and just as she found the strength to turn away, she heard Tony coming in.

Still, she stared at the familiar photographs, the ones that had once graced Maria's living room. They were neatly aligned on Tony's dresser, a votive candle flickering in front of them.

Sharon turned away with one hand to her mouth, her eyes scalded with tears, and came up hard against Tony's chest.

He took her upper arms in his hands to steady her, and even though the light was dim in the hallway, Sharon could see the baffled look in his eyes. She broke free of him and stumbled back to the living room, where she grabbed for her purse.

"Sharon, wait a minute," Tony pleaded reasonably. "Don't go—"

She dashed at her tears with the back of one hand and marched into the kitchen to turn off the burner under her clam sauce. "I guess I deserved this," she called, knowing that she probably sounded distracted and hysterical but unable to help herself. When she reached the living room again, Tony was beside the front door, as if to stand guard. "It was presumptuous of me to just walk in, thinking we could pick up where we left off—"

"You're welcome here anytime," Tony hold her. "Day or night."

"The woman Michael refers to as 'the blonde' would probably take issue with that," Sharon said, and the words, intended to be sophisticated and flippant, came out sounding like a pathetic joke. She reached for the doorknob and turned it. "Goodbye, Tony. And I'm sorry for intruding—I really am."

When she opened the door, he caught hold of her arm and pulled her back inside. The stereo was playing a particularly romantic tune, one she and Tony had once liked to listen to together.

"Damn it, Sharon, I'm not going to let you walk out. Not again."

She wrenched her arm free of his grasp. "You can't stop me," she spat, and this time there was no attempt at sounding anything but angry and hurt. She stood with her back to him, trembling, gazing out at the street and seeing nothing.

"You're too upset to drive," Tony reasoned, making no attempt to renew his hold on her arm. "Come in and talk to me. Please."

Sharon lifted one hand to her forehead for a moment. "There's no point in our talking—we should have learned that by now."

He sighed. "Sharon, if it's about the woman, we're divorced—"

"It isn't that," she said in wooden tones. "It's that spooky little shrine in your room." She paused on the doorstep, turning to look up at him. "My attorney will be contacting yours about the joint custody arrangement—our sharing the house and all that. We're going to have to work out some other way."

"Sharon." Tony's voice had taken on a note of hoarse desperation. He reached out cautiously to take her hand, and then he pulled her behind him along the hallway toward his room.

In the doorway, he paused. Sharon saw the muscles in his broad shoulders go rigid beneath the fabric of his shirt. "Oh, my God," he muttered, and didn't even turn around to face her. After giving a raspy sigh, he said, "You'll never believe me, so I'm not even going to try to explain. Not right now." His hand released Sharon's, and hers fell back to her side. "I'll call you later."

"There isn't going to be a 'later,'" Sharon said mildly. "Not for us."

With that, she turned and walked away, and Tony made no move to stop her.

Back at the apartment, she changed into work clothes and began painting with a vengeance. Tears streamed down her face as she worked, but she dared not stand still. She painted the kitchen, the bedroom and the bathroom, and gave the living room a second coat.

When that was done it was so late that there was no sense in going to bed at all. Sharon disposed of all the newspaper, leftover paint, brushes and cans, and then took a shower. As she turned around under the spray of water, she scoured her breasts and hips, all the places where Tony had touched her, hoping to wash away the sensations that still lingered.

"My God," Helen breathed, when she walked into the shop an hour later, "you look terrible!"

Sharon said nothing. She simply marched into the back room like a marionette on strings that were too tautly drawn, and sat down at her desk. She scanned the morning's mail, taking special note of a fashion show coming up in Paris in a couple of weeks. Maybe it was time to go on a real buying trip instead of ordering everything from wholesalers. She wondered numbly whether or not her passport had expired.

She felt almost ready to go out into the main part of the shop and face the customers by that time, but as Sharon slid back her chair, she got a surprise.

Michael, Tony's brother, came striding into the little room, looking very earnest, very young and very angry. Sharon had always liked him tremendously, and she was injured by the heat she saw burning in his dark Morelli eyes.

"What did you do to him?" he whispered tightly.

"Shall I call the police?" Helen put in from the doorway.

Sharon shook her head and gestured for Helen to leave her alone with Michael. "Sit down," she told her former brother-in-law.

He took the chair beside her desk, still fuming. "I had a party last night," he said, glaring at her.

Sharon sat down and folded her hands in her lap. "I know," she replied evenly.

"Tony was there."

By this time, there was a wall of ice around Sharon. "Good," she answered.

Michael was obviously furious. To his credit, however, he drew a deep breath and tried to speak reasonably. "Sharon, my brother looks like he's been in a train wreck. He showed up at my place late last night, stinking drunk and carrying on about shrines and blondes and clam sauce. The only halfway reasonable statement I could get out of him was that your lawyer was going to call his lawyer." Michael was a little calmer now. "Which brings us back to my original question. What did you do to Tony?"

Sharon was too tired and too broken inside to feel resentment, but she knew that she should. "I didn't do anything to Tony," she replied coolly. "And the problem is between your brother and me, Michael. Forgive me, but none of this is any of your business."

Michael leaned toward her, his eyes shooting fire. "Do you think I give a damn whether or not you consider this my business? Tony is my brother and I love him!"

Sharon closed her eyes for a moment. She had a headache, probably resulting from the combination of this confrontation and the paint fumes at home. She wanted the whole world to go away and leave her alone—yesterday, if not sooner.

"I salute you, Michael." She sighed, rubbing her temple with three fingers. "Tony is a hard man to love— I've given up trying."

Michael shoved a strong, sun-browned hand through his curly hair. "Okay," he said in frustration. "I gave it a shot, I blew it. Tony is going to kill me if he ever finds out I came here and told you about last night."

"He won't hear it from me," Sharon assured the young man. "Congratulations on the new contract, by the way. The one for the supermarket."

Michael looked at her curiously for a moment, then got out of his chair. He ran his palms down his thighs in a nervous gesture. "Thanks. Sharon, I just want to say one more thing, and then I'll get out of here. Tony loves you as much as any man has ever loved a woman, and if the two of you don't find a way to reach each other, it's going to be too late."

"It already is," Sharon said with sad conviction. "We shouldn't even have tried."

At that, Michael shook his head and went out. Helen appeared the moment the shop door had closed behind him.

"Are you all right?" she asked.

Sharon shook her head. "No," she answered, "I'm not. Listen, Helen, I have this wretched headache…" *And this broken heart.* "I'd like to leave for the rest of the day. If you don't want to stay, you don't have to— you can just lock up and go home."

Helen was looking at her as though she'd just suggested launching herself from the roof of the mall in a hang glider. "I'll close the shop at the regular time," she said.

Sharon nodded. "Okay, good. Umm—I'll see you tomorrow…."

"Sure," she said with a determined smile. "No hurry, though. I can handle things alone if I have to."

Sharon put on sunglasses, even though it wasn't a particularly bright day, and walked across the parking lot to the roadster. Because she wanted to feel the wind in her face, she put the canvas top down before pulling out of her customary parking space. With no special destination in mind, she drove onto the highway and headed out of town.

She'd been traveling along the freeway for almost an hour before she became aware that she was, after all, definitely going somewhere. She was on her way to Hayesville, the little town on the peninsula where she'd grown up and where her mother still lived.

As huge drops of rain began to fall, Sharon pulled over to the side of the road and, smiling grimly to herself, put the car's top back up. After another hour, she stopped at a restaurant along the roadside to have coffee and call Briana and Matt.

"Where are you, Mom?" Briana wailed. "You're supposed to be with us—it's your turn."

Matt was on one of the other phones. "School starts tomorrow, too," he added.

Sharon closed her eyes for a moment, trying hard to collect herself. It wouldn't do to fall apart in a truck stop and have to be carried back to Port Webster in a basket. "You guys aren't alone, are you? Isn't Mrs. Harry there?"

"No," Bri answered. "Dad is. But he's got a headache, so we're supposed to stay out of the den."

Responsible to the end, Sharon made herself say, "One of you go and tell him to pick up the telephone, please. I have to explain why I can't be there."

While Bri rattled on about her favorite rock group, her prospects of surviving seventh grade and what the orthodontist had said about her friend Mary Kate's broken tooth, Matt went off to the den.

After an eternity of adolescent prattle, Tony came on the line. "Hang up, Briana," he said tersely.

Bri started to protest, then obeyed.

Sharon took the plunge. "Tony, listen to me—"

"No, lady," he broke in brusquely, "you listen to me. I don't know where you are or what you're doing, but it's your turn to hold down the fort, so get your shapely little backside over here and look after these kids!"

Sharon sighed, counted mentally and went on. "I can't. I-I'm out of town."

Tony sounded so cold, like a stranger. "Wonderful. Was your lawyer planning on mentioning that to my lawyer?"

"Don't, Tony," Sharon whispered. "Please, don't be cruel."

"I'm not trying to be. I thought that was the way we were going to be communicating from now on— through our attorneys. God knows, we can't seem to manage a one-to-one conversation."

"That's true, isn't it?" Sharon reflected. "We're like two incompatible chemicals—we just don't mix."

"Where are you?" Tony asked evenly, after a long and volatile silence.

"I'm going to visit my mother." The words came out sounding stiff, even a little challenging, though Sharon hadn't meant them that way.

"Great," Tony replied. "If you catch her between bingo games, you can pour out your soul."

"That was a rotten thing to say, Tony. Did I make remarks about your mother?"

"Often," he answered.

It was just no damned use. Sharon was glad Tony couldn't see the tears brimming in her eyes. "Give my love to the kids, please, and let them know that I'll be home tomorrow. Tell them we'll have supper out to celebrate their first day of school."

Tony was quiet for so long that Sharon began to think he'd laid the receiver down and walked away. Finally, however, he said, "I'll tell them."

"Thanks," Sharon replied, and then she gently hung up the telephone and went back out to her car.

It was raining hard, and Sharon was glad. The weather was a perfect match for her mood.

# Chapter 7

It was getting dark when Sharon arrived in Hayesville. She turned down Center Street, passing the bank and the feed-and-grain and the filling station, and took a left on Bedford Road.

Her mother lived in a tiny, rented house at the end. The picket fence needed painting, the top of the mailbox was rusted out and the grass was overgrown. Sharon parked in the empty driveway and got out of her car, bringing her purse with her.

She entered through the tattered screen door on the back porch. As always, the key was hanging on its little hook behind the clothes drier; Sharon retrieved it and let herself into her mother's kitchen.

"Bea?" she called once, tentatively, even though she knew she was alone. No doubt, Tony had been right; Bea was playing bingo at the Grange Hall. She only worked part-time as a beautician these days, having acquired some mysterious source of income, which she refused to discuss.

Predictably, there was no answer. Sharon ran a hand through her hair and wondered why she'd driven all this way when she'd known her mother wouldn't be there for her, even if she happened to be physically present.

She looked at the wall phone, wishing that she could call Tony just to hear his voice, and she was startled when it rang. She blinked and then reached out for the receiver. "Hello?"

"Sharon?" Bea's voice sounded cautious, as though she wanted to make sure she was talking to her daughter and not a burglar.

Sharon smiled in spite of everything. "Yes, it's me," she answered quietly. "I just got here."

"Melba Peterson told me she saw you drive by in that fancy yellow car of yours, but I wasn't sure whether to believe her or not. She said they were going to have a thousand-dollar jackpot at bingo tonight, too, and all they've got is a few cases of motor oil and a free lube job at Roy's Texaco."

Sharon twisted one finger in the phone cord. "Does that mean you're coming home?"

Bea was clearly surprised. "Of course I am. Did you think I was just going to let you sit there all by yourself?"

After a moment, Sharon managed to answer, "Yes—I mean, no—"

"I'll be right there, darlin'," Bea announced cheerfully. "Have you had anything to eat?"

"Well—"

"I didn't think so. I'll stop at the burger place on my way home."

Sharon tried again. "I don't really feel—"

"See you in a few minutes," Bea chimed, as though she and her daughter had always been close.

By the time her mother had arrived, roaring up in her exhaust-belching dragon of a car, Sharon had splashed her face with cold water, brushed her hair and mustered a smile.

Bea dashed up the front walk, a grease-dappled white bag in one hand, her purse in the other. "What did he do to you, that big hoodlum?" she demanded, dashing all Sharon's hopes that she'd managed to look normal.

She sighed, holding the screen door open wide as Bea trotted into the living room. "Tony isn't a hoodlum, and he didn't do anything to me—"

"Sure, he didn't. That's why you're up here in the middle of the week looking like you just lost out on a three-card blackout by one number." She gestured with the paper bag, and Sharon followed her into the kitchen.

Bea was a small woman with artfully coiffed hair dyed an improbable shade of champagne blond, and she wore her standard uniform—double-knit slacks, a colorful floral smock and canvas espadrilles. She slapped the burger bag down in the middle of the table and shook one acrylic fingernail under Sharon's nose.

"It's time you let go of that man and found somebody else," she lectured.

Sharon was annoyed. "You never looked for anybody else," she pointed out, lingering in the doorway as she'd done so often in her teens, her hands gripping the woodwork.

Bea drew back a chair and sat down, plunging eagerly into the burgers and fries, leaving Sharon the choice between joining her or going hungry. "What makes you think I needed to look?" she asked after a few moments.

Sharon sat and reached for a cheeseburger. "You mean you had a romance in your life and I didn't even know it?"

Bea smiled and tapped the tabletop with one of her formidable pink nails. "There was a lot you didn't know, sweetheart," she said smugly. Then she laughed at her daughter's wide-eyed expression.

The two of them sat in companionable silence for several minutes, consuming their suppers. Finally, Sharon blurted out, "I'm still in love with Tony."

"Tell me something I didn't already know," Bea answered with a sigh.

Sharon's throat had closed; she laid down what remained of her cheeseburger and sat staring at it. "I guess you were right when you said it would never work," she said, when she could get the words out.

Bea's hand, glittering with cheap rings, rose hesitantly to cover hers. "I didn't want you to be hurt," she answered gently. "Tony was young, he'd just lost his wife, he had a little baby to raise. I was afraid he was going to use you."

"But you said—"

"I know what I said. I told you that he was out of your league. That he'd get tired of you."

Sharon was watching her mother, unable to speak. This understanding, sympathetic Bea wasn't the woman she remembered; she didn't know how to respond.

"I was hoping to discourage you," Bea confessed, a

faraway expression in her eyes. "It was never easy for you and me to talk, was it?"

"No," Sharon said with a shake of her head. "It wasn't."

Bea smiled sadly. "I didn't know how," she said. "We didn't have Dr. Phil and to tell us things like that when you were a girl."

Sharon turned her hand so that she could grip her mother's. "How's this for talking?" she asked hoarsely. "I can't think anymore, Bea—all I seem to be able to do is feel. And everything hurts."

"That's love, all right," Bea remarked. "Do you have any idea how Tony feels?"

Sharon shook her head. "No. Sometimes I think he loves me, but then something happens and everything goes to hell in the proverbial hand basket."

"What do you mean, 'something happens'?"

Dropping her eyes, Sharon said, "Yesterday I got this bright idea that I was going to surprise Tony with a real Italian dinner. Only I was the one who got the surprise."

Bea squeezed her hand. "Go on."

She related how she'd stumbled upon the pictures of Carmen with the votive candle burning reverently in front of them.

"There was probably an explanation for that," Bea observed. "It doesn't sound like the kind of thing Tony would do, especially after all this time."

Sharon bit into her lower lip for a moment. "I know that now," she whispered miserably.

"You couldn't just go back and apologize? Or call him?"

"Tony has a way of distancing himself from me," Sharon mused with a distracted shake of her head. "It hurts too much."

"It would probably be safe to assume that you've hurt him a time or two," Bea reasoned. "Didn't you tell me once that Tony went into a rage when you divorced him?"

Sharon closed her eyes at the memory, nodding. She'd never once been afraid of Tony, not until that day when he'd come into Teddy Bares with the divorce papers in his hand, looking as though he could kill without hesitation. She'd stood proudly behind the counter, trembling inside, afraid to tell him why she couldn't remain married to him—and not sure she knew the answer herself.

Bea spoke softly. "You say you love Tony, but it would be my guess that you still don't understand what's going on between the two of you. Well, you were right before, Sharon—you don't dare go back to him until you know what went wrong in the first place."

"What can I do?" Sharon whispered, feeling broken inside. She ached to be held in Tony's arms again, to lie beside him in bed at night, to laugh with him and fight with him.

"Wait," Bea counseled. "Try to give yourself some space so that you'll be able to think a little more clearly. If you love a man, it's next to impossible to be objective when you're too close."

"How did you get so smart?" Sharon asked with a tearful smile.

Bea shrugged, but she looked pleased at the compliment. "By making mistakes, I suppose." She got up to start brewing coffee in her shiny electric percolator.

Sharon gathered up the debris from their casual dinner and tossed it into the trash, then wiped the tabletop clean with a damp sponge.

"Tony's not such a bad man," Bea said in a quiet voice. "I guess I just have a tendency to dislike him because he has so much power to hurt you."

Sharon looked at her mother in silence. Their relationship was a long way from normal, but at least they were both making an effort to open up and be honest about what they thought and felt.

That night she slept in her own familiar room. When she awakened the next morning, she felt a little better, a little stronger.

Sharon found Bea in the kitchen, making breakfast. As Bea fried bacon, she told her daughter all about the new car she intended to win at that day's bingo session. And then the telephone rang.

Pouring two cups of fresh coffee, as well as keeping an eye on the bacon, Sharon listened while her mother answered with a bright hello. "Yes, she's here," she said after a moment of silence. "Just a moment."

Sharon turned, smoothing her skirt with nervous hands, and gave her mother a questioning look.

"It's Mr. Morelli—Vincent," Bea whispered, holding the receiver against her bosom.

Some premonition made Sharon pull back a chair and sit down before speaking to her former father-in-law. "Vincent?" she asked, and her voice shook.

The gentle voice thrummed with sadness and fear. "I have bad news for you, sweetheart," Vincent began, and Sharon groped for Bea's hand. It was there for her to grip, strong and certain. "There was an accident early this morning, and Tony's been hurt. The doctors still don't know how bad it is."

The familiar kitchen seemed to sway and shift. Sharon squeezed her eyes shut for a second in an effort to ground herself. "What happened?" she managed to get out.

Vincent sighed, and the sound conveyed grief, frustration, anger. "Tonio was climbing the framework on one of the sites, and he fell. He wasn't wearing a safety belt."

Sharon swallowed, envisioning the accident all too clearly in her mind. "Are Briana and Matt all right?"

"They're at school," Vincent answered. "They haven't been told. The rest of the family is here at City Hospital."

"I'll be there as soon as I possibly can," Sharon said. "And Vincent? Thank you for calling me."

"Thank heaven the housekeeper knew where you were. Drive carefully, little one—we don't need another accident."

Sharon promised to be cautious, but even as she hung up she was looking around wildly for her purse. She was confused and frantic, and tears were slipping down her cheeks.

Bea forced her to stand still by gripping both of Sharon's hands in her own. "Tell me. One of the children has been hurt?"

Sharon shook her head. "No—it's Tony. He fell— the doctors don't know…" She pulled one hand free of her mother's and raised it to her forehead. "Oh, God, it will take me hours to get there—my purse! Where is my purse?"

Bea took the purse from the top of the dishwasher and opened it without hesitation, taking out Sharon's car keys. "I'm driving—you're too upset," she announced.

Minutes later Bea was at the wheel of the expensive yellow roadster, speeding out of town, her daughter sitting numbly in the passenger seat.

* * *

Sharon nearly collided with Michael when she came through the entrance of the hospital; in fact, she would have if her brother-in-law hadn't reached out with both hands to prevent it.

"Tony...?" she choked out, because that was all she could manage. She knew that her eyes were taking up her whole face and that she was pale.

Michael's expression was tender. "He's going to be all right," he said quickly, eager to reassure her, still supporting her with his hands.

Relief swept over Sharon in a wave that weakened her knees and brought a strangled little cry to her throat. "Thank God," she whispered. And then, in a fever of joy, she threw her arms around Michael's neck.

He held her until she stepped back, sniffling, to ask, "Where is he? I want to see him."

Michael's dark eyes were full of pain. "I don't think that would be a good idea, princess," he said, his voice sounding husky. "Not right now."

"Where is he?" Sharon repeated, this time in a fierce whisper. Her entire body was stiff with determination.

Michael sighed. "Room 229. But, Sharon—"

Sharon was already moving toward the elevator. Bea, still parking the car, would have to find her own way through the maze that was City Hospital.

Room 229 was in a corner, and members of the Morelli family were overflowing into the hallway. Sharon was glad she'd encountered Michael before coming upstairs, or she might have thought that the worst had happened.

News of her arrival buzzed through the group of well-wishers, and they stepped aside to admit her.

Tony was sitting up in bed with a bandage wrapped

around his head. His face was bruised and scraped, and his left arm was in a cast. But it was the look in his eyes that stopped Sharon in the middle of the room.

His expression was cold, as though he hated her.

Vincent and Maria, who had been standing on the other side of the room, silently withdrew. Sharon knew without looking around that the other visitors had left, also.

And she was still stuck in the middle of the floor with her heart jammed in her throat. She had to swallow twice before she could speak. "I got here as quickly as I could," she said huskily. "Are—are you all right?"

Tony only nodded, the intensity of his anger plainly visible in his eyes.

A cold wind blew over Sharon's soul. "Tony—"

"Stay away," he said, shifting his gaze, at last, to the window. In the distance the waters of the sound shimmered and sparkled in the afternoon sun. "Please— just stay away."

Sharon couldn't move. She wanted to run to him; at the same time, she needed to escape. "I'm not going anywhere until you tell me what's the matter," she told him. The moment the words were out of her mouth, she wondered if she'd really said them herself, since they sounded so reasonable and poised.

Tony was still looking out the window. "We cause each other too much pain," he said after a long time.

She dared to take a step closer to the bed. Her hands ached to touch Tony, to soothe and lend comfort, but she kept them stiffly at her sides. His words, true though they were, struck her with the aching sting of small pelted stones.

Sharon waited in silence, knowing there was nothing to do but wait and endure until he'd said everything.

"We have to stop living in the past and go on with our lives. Today taught me that, if nothing else."

There were tears burning in Sharon's eyes; she lowered her head to hide them and bit into her lower lip.

"You can have the house," he went on mercilessly. At last Tony looked at Sharon; she could feel his gaze touching her. His voice was a harsh, grinding rasp. "I've never been able to sleep in our room. Did you know that?"

Sharon shook her head; pride forced her to lift it. "I've slept in the den a lot of times myself," she confessed.

The ensuing silence was awful. Unable to bear it, Sharon went boldly to the side of the bed even though she knew she wouldn't be welcome.

"I was so scared," she whispered. Her hand trembled as she reached out to touch the bandage encircling his head. It hid most of his hair and dipped down on one side over his eye, giving him a rakish look.

"No doubt," Tony said with cruel dryness, "you were afraid that Carmen and I had found a way to be together at last."

The gibe was a direct hit. Sharon allowed the pain to rock her, her eyes never shifting from Tony's. Speech, for the moment, was more than she could manage.

"The 'shrine,' as you called it, was my grandmother's doing," Tony went on, with a terrible humor twisting one side of his mouth and flickering in his eyes. "I'd talked Mama into giving up the pictures, since they bothered you so much. I planned on turning them over to Bri later on, when she and I were getting along a little better. In the meantime, Grandmama found them. Evidently, she decided to while away the time by honoring the dead."

Sharon lifted her index finger to his lips in a plea for silence, because she could bear no more. He was right—so right. They were causing each other too much pain.

She grasped at a slightly less volatile subject with the desperation of a drowning woman. "What about Bri? Will I still be able to see her?"

Tony looked at her as though she'd struck him. "You're the only mother she's ever known. I wouldn't hurt her—or you—by keeping the two of you apart."

"Thank you," Sharon said in a shattered whisper. She touched his lips very gently with her own. "Rest now," she told him, just before she turned to walk away.

He grasped her arm to stop her, and when she looked back over one shoulder, she saw that his eyes were bright with tears. "Goodbye," he said.

Sharon put a hand to her mouth in an effort to control her own emotions and ran out of the room. The hallway was empty except for her father-in-law.

Vincent took one look at Sharon and drew her into his arms. "There, there," he said softly. "Everything will be all right now. Tonio will be well and strong."

The sobs Sharon had been holding back came pouring out. She let her forehead rest against Vincent's shoulder and gave way to all her grief and confusion and pain.

"Tell me, little one," he urged gently when the worst was over. "Tell me what hurts you so much."

Sharon looked up at him and tried to smile. Ignoring his request, she said instead, "Tony is so lucky to have a father like you." She stood on tiptoe and kissed

Vincent's weathered, sun-browned cheek, and that was her farewell.

Bea, who had been in the waiting room with Maria, came toward Sharon as she pushed the button to summon the elevator. Neither woman spoke until they'd found the roadster in the parking lot and Sharon had slid behind the wheel, holding out her hand to Bea for the keys.

With a shake of her head, Bea got into the car on the passenger side and surrendered them. "Where are we going now?"

Sharon started the car and then dried her cheeks with the heels of her palms. Before backing out of the parking space, she snapped her seat belt in place. "Home," she replied. "We're going home. Tony just gave me the house."

"He just what?" Bea demanded. "The man is giving away his possessions? Tony's own mother told me, not fifteen minutes ago, that he's going to be fine. They're letting him leave the hospital tomorrow."

Sharon was concentrating on the traffic flow moving past the hospital. If she didn't, she was sure she would fall apart. "The house isn't his 'possession,' Mother. It belonged to both of us."

Sharon had addressed Bea by a term other than her given name for the first time in fifteen years; she knew that had to have some significance, but she was too overwrought to figure out what it was.

"If it's all the same to you," Bea said, when they were moving toward Tamarack Drive, "I'd like to go home tomorrow. I could take the bus."

Sharon only nodded; she would have agreed to almost anything at that point.

The moment the car pulled into the driveway, Bri and Matt came bursting out the front door, still wearing their first-day-of-school clothes. They were closely followed by Rose, who was resting both hands on her protruding stomach.

Sharon addressed her former sister-in-law first. "He's all right—you knew that, didn't you?"

Rose nodded. "Papa called. It's you we're worried about."

Bri and Matt were both hugging Sharon, and she laughed hoarsely as she tried to hold each one at the same time.

"Mom, is Daddy really okay?" Briana demanded, when they were all in the kitchen moments later.

Sharon was careful not to meet the child's eyes. "Yes, babe. He's fine."

"Then why isn't he here?" Matt wanted to know. He was staying closer to her than usual; Sharon understood his need for reassurance because she felt it, too.

"They want to keep him in the hospital overnight, probably just to be on the safe side," Sharon told her son. "He's got a broken arm, a few cuts and scrapes and a bandage on his head. Other than that, he seems to be fine."

"Honest?" Bri pressed.

"Honest," Sharon confirmed. "Now, I want to hear all about your first day of school."

Both children began to talk at once, and Sharon had to intercede with a patient, "One at a time. Who wants to be first?"

Bri generously allowed her brother that consideration, and Matt launched into a moment-by-moment account of his day.

Much later, when dinner was over and both Bri and Matt had gone upstairs to their rooms, Sharon made out the sofa bed in the den for her mother. She was like an automaton, doing everything by rote.

Bea retired immediately.

Wanting a cup of herbal tea before bed, Sharon returned to the kitchen and was surprised to find that Michael had let himself in. He was leaning against a counter, his arms folded, just as Sharon had seen Tony do so many times. As a matter of fact, the resemblance was startling.

"I tried to warn you that Tony was in that kind of mood," Michael said kindly, his eyes full of sympathy and caring. Sharon reflected again that Tony was fortunate—not only did he have Vincent for a father, he had a whole network of people who truly loved him.

"Yes," Sharon replied in a small voice. "You did."

"Whatever he said," Michael persisted, "he didn't mean it."

Sharon longed to be alone. "You weren't there to hear," she answered. And then she turned and went upstairs, hoping that Michael would understand.

She had no more strength left.

# Chapter 8

Sharon found her passport in the bottom of a drawer of her desk at home, jammed behind some of Tony's old tax records and canceled checks, which she promptly dropped. Kneeling on the floor and muttering, she began gathering up the scattered papers.

That was when she saw the check made out to her mother. Tony had signed it with a flourish, and the date was only a few weeks in the past.

Frowning, Sharon began to sort through the other checks. She soon deduced that Tony had virtually been supporting Bea for years.

Having forgotten her passport completely by this time, Sharon got to her feet and reached for the telephone. It was early on a Saturday morning and, unless Tony had changed considerably since their divorce, he would be sleeping in.

Sharon had no compunction at all about waking him. She hadn't seen Tony, except from an upstairs window when he picked up the kids, in nearly two months. She also avoided talking to him on the telephone, although that was harder.

She supposed this was some kind of turning point.

A woman answered the phone, and Sharon closed her eyes for a moment. She hadn't expected to feel that achy hurt deep down inside herself, not after all this time. "Is Tony there, please?"

"Who's calling?" retorted the voice. Sharon wondered if she was speaking to the infamous blonde of Michael's mentioning. She also wondered if the woman had spent the night with Tony.

"I'm Sharon Morelli," she said warmly. "Who are you?"

"My name is Ingrid," came the matter-of-fact response.

*Yep,* Sharon thought miserably. *It's the blonde. People named Ingrid are always blond.* "I'd like to speak to Tony," she reminded his friend with consummate dignity.

"Right," Ingrid answered. "Hey, Tony—it's your ex-wife."

"Bimbo," Sharon muttered.

"I beg your pardon?" Ingrid responded politely.

Tony came on the line before Sharon had to reply, and he sounded worried. In fact, he didn't even bother to say hello. "Is everything all right?" he wanted to know.

Sharon looked down at the assortment of checks in her hand. "Since when do you support my mother?" she countered.

He sighed. "She told you," he said, sounding resigned.

"Hell no," Sharon swore, her temper flaring. And it wasn't just the checks; it was Ingrid, and a lot of other problems. "Nobody around here tells me anything!"

"Calm down," Tony told her in reasonable tones. "You don't begrudge Bea the money, do you?"

"Of course not," Sharon said crisply.

"Then what's the problem?"

"You didn't mention it, that's what. I mean a little thing like supporting someone usually comes up in day-to-day husband-and-wife conversation, doesn't it?"

"We aren't husband and wife," Tony pointed out.

"Damn it, we were when you started writing these checks every month. And neither you nor Bea said a word!"

"Sorry. Guess we were just trying to maintain our images, having convinced everybody that we didn't like each other."

Sharon sighed and sagged into a chair. Sometimes it was so frustrating to talk to this man, but in a way it felt good, too. "Are you still sending my mother money every month?" she asked straight-out.

"Yes," Tony answered just as succinctly.

"I want you to stop. If Bea needs financial help, I'll take care of it."

"That's very independent and liberated of you, but the thing is out of your hands. My accountants see to it every month—like the child support."

Sharon drew in a deep breath and let it out again. Then she repeated the exercise. In, out, in, out. She would not let Tony short-circuit her composure; she'd grown beyond that in the past two months. "Bea is not a child," she said.

"That," Tony immediately retorted, "is a matter of opinion. I think we need to talk about this in person."

Sharon was filled with sweet alarm. She'd stayed out of Tony's range since that day in the hospital, and she wasn't sure she was ready to be in the same room with him. On the other hand, the idea had a certain appeal. "I'm busy," she hedged.

Too late Sharon realized how thin that argument was. In truth, with all the help she'd hired at Teddy Bares, she had more time on her hands than she was used to.

"Doing what?" The question, of course, was inevitable. It was also a measure of Tony Morelli's innate gall.

Sharon's eyes fell on the blue cover of her passport. She smiled as she spoke. "I'm getting ready to go to Paris on a buying trip, actually."

"The kids didn't mention that," Tony said, and the statement had a faint air of complaint to it.

So Bri and Matt were making reports when they visited their dad, just as they did when they came home to Sharon. Well, it figured.

She smiled harder. "They don't tell you everything, I'm sure."

Tony was quiet for a few moments, absorbing that. "What should they be telling me that they aren't?" he finally asked.

Sharon wound her finger in the phone cord, hoping to sound distracted, disinterested. "Oh, this and that," she said. "Nothing important. I know you're busy, so I won't keep you." With that, she summarily hung up.

Twenty-two minutes later, Tony entered the den. Sharon noted, out of the corner of her eye, that he was wearing jeans, a T-shirt and a running jacket. Tony was especially attractive when he was about to work out.

"Hi," he said somewhat sheepishly.

Sharon smiled. She knew he'd just realized that he'd forgotten to come up with an excuse for dropping by. She looked up from the ledgers for Teddy Bares, which she always liked to check before they went to the accountant. "Hi, Tony." There was a cheerful fire crackling in the den's large brick fireplace, and the radio was tuned to an easy-listening station. "I see they took off your cast."

Tony sighed and then nodded, jamming his hands into the pockets of his navy-blue jacket. "Are the kids around?"

Briana and Matt were on the island staying in the A-frame with Tony's sister Gina and her husband. And Tony knew that.

"No," Sharon answered, refraining from pointing up the fact.

Still, he lingered. "Isn't November kind of a rotten time to go to Paris?" he finally asked.

Sharon looked down at her ledgers to hide a grin. "There is no such thing as a 'rotten time to go to Paris,'" she commented.

Tony went into the kitchen and came back with two mugs of coffee—one of which he somewhat grudgingly set down on the surface of Sharon's desk. "We went there on our honeymoon," he said, as if that had some bearing on Sharon's plans.

"I know," she replied dryly.

"The Bahamas would be warmer."

"They're not showing the spring lingerie lines in the Bahamas," was the reasonable reply. Sharon still hadn't looked up into those brown eyes; if she did that, she'd be lost.

Tony went to stand in front of the fire, his broad, powerful back turned to Sharon. "I guess we still haven't learned to talk to each other," he observed.

Sharon hadn't even realized that she'd been playing a game until he spoke. "I thought we'd given up on that," she said, in a soft voice that betrayed some of the sadness she felt.

"I've always found it difficult to do that," Tony remarked somewhat distantly. "Give up, I mean. Are you going to the company party?"

The mention of the celebration Vincent and Maria held every year just before Thanksgiving brought Ingrid to Sharon's mind. "I was invited," she said, avoiding his eyes. With the speed of Matt's hamsters fleeing their cage, her next words got out before she could stop them. "Are you taking Ingrid?"

There was an element of thunder in Tony's silence. "Yes," he answered after a very long time.

*I've done it again,* Sharon thought to herself. *I've asked a question I didn't want to have answered.* "If I have time, what with my trip to Paris," she told him, putting on a front, "I'll probably drop by."

"Good," Tony answered. His coffee mug made a solid thump sound as he set it down. "I'd better get to the gym, I guess," he added as a taut afterthought.

Sharon pretended a devout interest in the figures in her ledgers, although in reality they had about as much meaning for her as Chinese characters. "Aren't you forgetting something?"

"What?" he challenged in a vaguely belligerent tone. Sharon knew without looking that he'd thrust his hands into his jacket pockets again.

"We didn't discuss your sending money to Bea. I don't like it—it makes me feel obligated." At last she trusted herself to meet his eyes.

Quiet fury altered Tony's expression. "Why the hell should it do that? Have I asked you for anything?"

Sharon shook her head, stunned by the sheer force of his annoyance. "No, but—"

He folded his arms, and his dark eyes were still snapping. "I can afford to help Bea and I want to. That's the end of it," he said flatly.

Sharon sighed. "It isn't your responsibility to look after my mother," she told him gently. "I don't even understand why you feel it's necessary."

"You wouldn't," Tony retorted, his tone clipped, and then he walked out.

The festive feeling that autumn days often fostered in Sharon was gone. She propped both elbows on the surface of her desk and rested her forehead in her palms.

At least he hadn't made her cry this time. She figured that was some sort of progress.

"You've got to go to that party!" Helen said sternly, resting her arms on the counter and leaning toward Sharon with an earnest expression in her eyes. It had been a busy day, and they were getting ready to turn Teddy Bares over to Louise, the middle-aged saleswoman Sharon had hired to work from five-thirty until nine o'clock when the mall closed. "Furthermore, you have to take a date that will set Tony Morelli back on his heels!"

"Where am I going to get someone like that?" Sharon asked, a little annoyed that the dating game was so easy for Tony to play and so difficult for her. She'd been out with exactly four men since the divorce, and all of them were duds.

Helen was thoughtfully tapping her chin as she thought. A moment later her face was shining with revelation. "You could ask Michael to help you."

Sharon frowned, nonplussed. "Tony's brother?"

"He must know a lot of terrific guys, being pretty spectacular himself."

"Yeah," Sharon said wryly. "For instance, he knows Tony. He'd go straight to big brother and spill his guts. I can hear it now. 'Tonio, Sharon is so desperate that she's after me to fix her up with blind dates.' No way, Helen!"

Helen shrugged. "I'm only trying to help. It's too bad you don't have the kind of business where you might meet more men."

"I wouldn't want one who shopped at Teddy Bares," Sharon remarked with a grin. "He'd either be married or very weird."

Helen made a face. "You are no help at all. I'm going to ask Allen what he can dig up at the gym."

Sharon winced at the thought of Helen's husband approaching strange men and asking them what they were doing on the night of the twenty-second. It could get him punched out, for one thing. "Thanks, but no thanks. I don't like jocks."

"Tony's a jock," Helen pointed out. "Or are those washboard stomach muscles of his an illusion?"

"When," Sharon demanded loftily, holding back a smile, "did you happen to get a look at my ex-husband's stomach, pray tell?"

Helen batted her lashes and tried to look wicked. "Fourth of July picnic, two years ago, on Vashon. Remember the volleyball game?"

Sharon remembered, all right. Tony had been wearing cutoffs and no shirt, and every time he'd jumped for the ball...

She began to feel too warm.

Helen gave her an impish look and went to the back room for their coats and purses. When she came out again, Louise had arrived to take over.

"I'm going to ask Allen to check out the jocks," Helen insisted, as she and Sharon walked out of the mall together.

Sharon lifted her chin a degree. "I might not be back from Paris in time for the party anyway, so don't bother."

"Maybe you'll meet somebody on the plane," Helen speculated.

Sharon rolled her eyes and strode off toward her car. When she got home, a surprise awaited her.

Maria was sitting at the kitchen table, chatting with Bri and Matt. Mrs. Harry had evidently been so charmed that she'd not only stayed late, she was serving tea.

She said a pleasant good-night and left when Sharon came in, and the kids, after collecting their hugs, ran off to watch TV in the den.

Sharon had a suspicion that their disappearance had been prearranged. "Hello, Maria. It's good to see you." She realized with a start that she'd meant those words.

Maria returned Sharon's smile. "I hope I haven't come at a bad time."

"You're always welcome, of course," Sharon replied with quiet sincerity. Mrs. Harry had started dinner— there was a casserole in the oven—so she had nothing to do but take off her coat, hang it up and pour herself a cup of tea.

She sat down at the table with Maria, who looked uncomfortable now, and even a little shy.

"I've come to ask if you were planning to attend our party," the older woman said softly. "Vincent and I are so hoping that you will. We don't see enough of you, Sharon."

Sharon was taken aback. "I'm not sure if I can come or not," she answered. "You see, I'm traveling to Paris that week."

Maria seemed genuinely disappointed. "That's exciting," she said, and she sounded so utterly insincere that Sharon had to smile. Her former mother-in-law smiled, too. Sharon had never noticed before now how sweet it made her look.

Sharon knew her eyes were dancing as she took a sip of her tea. "It's important to you that I come to the party, but I'm not sure why."

Maria looked down at her lap. "I guess I'm trying to make amends—however belatedly. I realize now that I didn't treat you as well as I could have, and I regret it."

Sharon reached out to touch Maria's hand. "I have regrets, too," she said. "I didn't try very hard to understand how you must have loved Carmen."

Maria swallowed and nodded. "She was like my own child, but I should have made you feel more like a part of our family. Forgive me, please, for letting an old grief stand in the way of the friendship we could have had."

Sharon felt tears sting her eyes. "There's nothing to forgive," she replied. After a short interval had passed, she added, "You know, Maria, if I could be the kind of mother to Matt and Briana that you were to your children, I'd count myself a resounding success."

The compliment brought a flush of pleasure to Maria's porcelain-smooth cheeks and a gentle brightness to her eyes. She was of another generation; her life revolved around her husband, children and grandchildren. "What a wonderful thing to say," she whispered. "Thank you."

Sharon leaned forward, her hand still resting on Maria's. "They're all so self-assured and strong, from Tony right down to Michael and Rose. What's your secret?"

Maria looked surprised. "Why, I simply loved them," she answered. "The way you love Briana and Matthew." She paused and smiled mischievously. "And, of course, I had the good sense to marry Vincent Morelli in the first place. The self-assurance—as you call it—comes from him, I'm sure. And there have been times when I would have used another word for what my children have—brass. They can be obnoxious."

Before Sharon could agree that Tony, at least, had been known to suffer from that condition, there was a brief rap at the back door and he came strolling into the kitchen. He spared his ex-wife a glance, crossed the room and bent to give his mother a kiss on the cheek.

Bri and Matt, having heard his car, came racing into the room, full of joy. Tony was always greeted like a conquering hero, there to save the two of them from a death too horrible to contemplate, and that was a sore spot with Sharon.

"Hi," she said to him, when the hubbub had died down a little.

"Hello," he responded quietly.

Guilt struck Sharon full force. It was getting late, and

Mrs. Harry's casserole was probably shriveling in the oven. She left her chair and hurried over to pull it out.

"Won't you stay to dinner, Maria?" she asked. Then, hesitantly, she added, "Tony?"

Both potential guests shook their heads. "Vincent and I are meeting downtown at our favorite restaurant," Maria said. "In fact, if I don't hurry, I'll be late."

With that, she went through a round of farewells including Tony, Briana, Matt, and finally, Sharon. "Don't let him push you around," she whispered to her former daughter-in-law, squeezing her hand.

Sharon grinned and, when Maria was gone, turned her attention to Tony. "Okay, what's your excuse, Morelli? Why can't you stay for dinner?"

"Because I hate Scary Harry's tuna-bean surprise, that's why," he answered. "Last time I had it, it was worse than a surprise—it was a shock."

Naturally, the kids took up the chorus.

"Tuna-bean surprise?" wailed Bri, with all the pathos of a person asked to eat kitty litter. "Yech!"

"Can't we go out?" Matt added.

"See what you started?" Sharon said, frowning at Tony. "Thanks a lot."

Tony slid his hands into the pockets of his jeans and rocked back on the heels of his boots, looking pleased with himself. "I could always take the three of you out for dinner," he suggested innocently.

Bri and Matt were beside themselves at the prospect. "Please, Mom?" they begged in pitiful unison. "Please?"

Sharon was glaring now. "That was a dirty trick," she said to Tony. "It would serve all of you right if I said no." She paused, glancing down at the concoction Mrs. Harry had left in the oven. It did have a surprising aspect about it.

"She's weakening," Tony told the kids.

Sharon tried for a stern look. "Did you two finish your homework?"

Both Briana and Matt nodded, their eyes bright with eagerness.

She shrugged. "Then what can I possibly say," she began, spreading her hands, "except yes?"

Two minutes later they were all in Tony's car. "Put on your seat belts," he said over one shoulder, and Bri and Matt immediately obeyed.

Sharon wondered how he managed to elicit such ready cooperation. She always had to plead, reason, quote statistics and, finally, threaten in order to achieve what Tony had with a mere five words.

When they'd reached the restaurant and the kids were occupied with their all-time favorite food, spaghetti, he turned to Sharon and asked, "Are you really going to Paris?"

She looked down at the swirl of pasta on the end of her fork. Maybe it was wrong of her, given the fact that their marriage was over, but she was glad that he cared what she did. "Yes," she answered. Only superhuman effort—and the presence of her children—kept her from countering, *Are you sleeping with Ingrid?*

An awkward silence fell, and Tony was the one who finally broke it.

"Remember when we were there?" he asked quietly.

There was a lump in Sharon's throat. Vincent and Maria had given them the trip as a wedding present, and it had been like something out of a fairy tale. "How could I forget?" she asked in a voice that was barely audible. She hadn't thought, until now, how many bitter-

sweet memories would be there to meet her once she
arrived in France.

"Sharon?"

She lifted her eyes and met his gaze questioningly.

"If I said the wrong thing again," he told her, "I'm
sorry."

She swallowed and worked up a smile. "You didn't,"
she answered, marveling at herself because if he'd asked
to go along on the trip to Paris, she would have agreed
with delight.

Only Tony wasn't going to ask because he had Ingrid
now and he'd only been trying to make conversation
in the first place. He probably wasn't even interested
in Sharon's plans.

She thought of how Tony would react if she told
him that she was considering opening a second shop in
nearby Tacoma and winced at the memories that came
to mind. A fairly modern man in most respects, he'd
reverted to the Neanderthal mind-set when Sharon had
opened Teddy Bares, and things had gotten progres-
sively worse....

Tony started to reach for her hand, then hesitated.
Although he said nothing, his eyes asked her a thousand questions.

She looked at him sadly. If only he'd been proud of
her, she reflected, things might have turned out so differently.

## Chapter 9

The red-sequined dress was long and slinky with a plunging neckline and a sexy slit up one side, and it looked spectacular on Sharon.

"I can't afford it," she whispered to Helen, who was shopping with her while Louise looked after Teddy Bares. The two women were standing in the special occasions section of the best department store in the mall, gazing at Sharon's reflection in a mirror.

"Tony's going to fall into the punch bowl when he sees you," Helen responded, as though Sharon hadn't said anything.

Sharon squinted and threw her shoulders back. "Do you think it makes me look taller?"

Helen nodded solemnly. "Oh, yes," she answered.

With a sigh, Sharon calculated the purchasing power remaining on her credit card—the margin had narrowed considerably after the divorce, and if she bought this dress, it would take her to her limit. "I haven't even got a date," she reflected aloud, speaking as much to herself as to Helen.

"Have a little faith, will you? Allen's checking out the hunks up at the gym—it's a matter of time, that's all."

"A matter of time until he gets his teeth rearranged, you mean."

Helen shook her head, a half smile on her face. "Stop worrying and buy the dress. If our plans don't work out, you can always return it."

The logic of that was irrefutable. Sharon returned to the dressing room to change back into her clothes and when that was done, she bought the dress. She and Helen parted company then, and Sharon hurried home.

The kids were in the kitchen obediently doing their homework, and something good was baking in the oven. "I've got it," Sharon said, bending to kiss Briana's cheek and then Matt's. "I've been caught in a time warp or something and flung into a rerun of *The Donna Reed Show*, right?"

Bri gave her a look of affectionate disdain. "Mrs. Harry had to leave early—she lost a filling and needed to go to the dentist. She tried to call you at the shop, but you were gone, so—"

"So your dad came over to pinch-hit," Sharon guessed. The prospect of encountering Tony now made her feel a festive sort of despondency. "Where is he?"

As if in answer to that, Tony came out of the den. He was wearing jeans and a dark blue pullover, and his eyes slid over Sharon at their leisure, causing her a delightful discomfort. He strolled casually over to the wall oven and checked on whatever it was that smelled so marvelous. "Been shopping for your trip?" he asked.

Sharon realized that she was still holding the dress box from her favorite department store and self-consciously set it aside. "Not exactly," she said, with an exuberance that rang false even in her own ears. "How have you been, Tony?"

"Just terrific," he answered, with an ironic note in his voice as he closed the oven door. "Somebody named Sven called. He said Bea gave him your number."

Sven? Sharon searched her memory, but the only Sven she could come up with was a Swedish exchange student who had spent a year in Hayesville long ago when she'd still been in high school. "Did he leave a message?" she asked airily, wanting to let Tony wonder a little.

"He said he'd call back," Tony answered offhandedly. Sharon knew that he was watching her out of the corner of his eye as he took plates from a cupboard. "Your accountant wants a word with you, too."

Sharon was careful not to show the concern that fact caused her. Her accountant never called unless the news was bad.

At some unseen signal from their father, Matt and Bri had put aside their homework, and they were now setting the table. "You're supposed to call her at home," Tony added. He washed his hands at the sink, took some plastic bags of produce from the refrigerator and began tearing lettuce leaves for a salad.

Sharon was really fretting now, though she smiled brightly. She took off her coat and hung it up, then went upstairs with the box under her arm. The moment she reached the sanctity of the bedroom, she lunged for the telephone.

Moments later she was on the line with Susan Fenwick, her accountant. "What do you mean I can't afford to go to Paris?" she whispered in horror. "This is a business trip—"

"I don't care," Susan interrupted firmly. "You've got quarterly taxes coming up, Sharon, and even though you've been gaining some ground financially, you're going to put yourself in serious jeopardy if you make any major expenditures now."

Sharon sighed. She'd told everyone that she was going to Paris—Tony, the kids, Helen and Louise... just everyone. She was going to look like a real fool, backing out now.

"Okay," she said, forcing herself to smile. She'd heard once in a seminar that a businessperson should keep a pleasant expression on her face while talking on the telephone. "Thank you, Susan."

"No problem. I'm sorry about the trip. Maybe in the spring—"

"Right," Sharon said. "Goodbye."

Susan returned the sentiment and then the line was dead.

Sharon hung up and went downstairs, the smile firmly affixed to her face. The kids were already eating and Tony was in the den, gathering up the ever-present blueprints.

"Are those the plans for the new supermarket?" Sharon asked, wanting that most elusive of things—a non-volatile conversation with Tony.

He nodded, and it seemed to Sharon that he was avoiding her eyes. "The kids are having supper," he said. "Don't you want to join them?"

"I'm not hungry," Sharon answered with a slight shake of her head. In truth she was ravenous, but that fabulous, slinky dress didn't leave room for indulgences in Tony's cooking. Once he was gone, she'd have a salad.

Tony's gaze swung toward her, assessing her. "Trying to slim down to Parisian standards?" he asked dryly.

Sharon longed to tell him that the trip was off, that she couldn't afford to go, but her pride wouldn't allow her to make the admission. Her need to make a mark on the world had been a pivotal factor in their divorce, and Sharon didn't want to call attention to the fact that her standard of living had gone down since they'd parted ways. She let Tony's question pass. "Thank you for coming over and taking care of the kids," she said.

"Anytime," he responded quietly. There was a forlorn expression in Tony's eyes even as he smiled that made Sharon want to cross the room and put her arms around that lean, fit waist of his. The desire to close the space between them, both physically and emotionally, was powerful indeed.

Sharon resisted it. "Did Sven leave a number?" she asked in a soft voice, to deflect the sweet, impossible charge she felt coursing back and forth between herself and this man she loved but could not get along with.

Tony looked tired, and his sigh was on the ragged side. His grin, however, was crooked and made of mischief with a pinch of acid thrown in for spice. "It isn't tattooed on your body somewhere?" he countered.

Color throbbing in her face, Sharon ran a hand through her hair and did her best to ignore Tony as she went past him to the desk. A number was scrawled on a pad beside the telephone, along with a notation about Susan's call. Conflicting needs tore at her; she wanted to pound on Tony with her fists, and at the same time she longed to make love to him.

She was startled when he turned her into his embrace and tilted her chin upward with the curved fingers of his right hand. "I'm sorry," he said huskily.

Sharon forgave him, but not because of any nobility on her part. She couldn't help herself.

She stood on tiptoe, and her lips were just touching Tony's when the doorbell rang.

"One of the kids will get it," he assured her in a whisper, propelling her into a deep kiss when she would have drawn back.

The kiss left Sharon bedazzled and more than a little bewildered, and she was staring mutely up at Tony when Bri bounded into the room and announced, "There's a man here to see you, Mom. He says his name is Sven Svensen."

"Sven Svensen," Tony muttered with a shake of his head. His hands fell away from Sharon's waist and he retreated from her to roll up his blueprints and tuck them back into their cardboard tube.

Sven appeared in the doorway of the den only a second later, tall and blond and spectacular. He was indeed the Sven that Sharon remembered from high school, and his exuberance seemed to fill the room.

"All these years I have dreamed of you," he cried, spreading his hands. But then his eyes strayed to Tony. "This is your husband? This is the father of your children?"

"No to the first question," Sharon answered, keeping her distance, "and yes to the second. Tony and I are divorced."

Sven beamed after taking a moment to figure out the situation, and she introduced the two men to each other properly.

Tony's eyebrows rose when Sven grasped Sharon by the waist and thrust her toward the ceiling with a shout of joyous laughter. "Still you are so beautiful, just like when you were a cheerleader!"

The altitude was getting to Sharon in a hurry. She smiled down at Sven. "You haven't changed much, either," she said lamely.

He lowered her back to the floor, his happy smile lighting up the whole room. Tony's expression provided an interesting contrast; he looked as though he was ready to clout somebody over the head with his cardboard tube of blueprints.

"What brings you back to America?" Sharon asked her unexpected guest, nervously smoothing her slacks with both hands.

"I am big businessman now," Sven answered expansively. "I travel all over the world."

Sharon was aware that Tony was leaving, but she pretended not to notice. If he felt a little jealous, so be it; she'd certainly done her share of agonizing over the mysterious Ingrid.

It was then that the idea occurred to Sharon. "Will you be in the area for a while, Sven?" she asked, taking his arm. "There's this party on the night of the twenty-second—"

"You talk to him!" Michael raged, flinging his arms wide in exclamation as his father entered the small office trailer parked on the site of the new supermarket.

"The man has a head of solid marble—there's no reasoning with him!"

Tony glared at his brother, but said nothing. The argument, beginning that morning, had been escalating all day.

Vincent met Tony's gaze for a moment, then looked at Michael. "I could hear the two of you 'reasoning' with each other on the other side of the lot. Exactly what is the problem?"

Tony was glad Michael launched into an answer first, because he didn't have one prepared. All he knew was that he felt like fighting.

"I'll tell you what the problem is," Michael began furiously, waggling an index finger at his elder brother. "Tony's got trouble with Sharon and he's been taking it out on me ever since he got here this morning!"

Michael's accusation was true, but Tony couldn't bring himself to admit it. He folded his arms and clamped his jaw down tight. He was still in the mood for an all-out brawl, and his brother seemed like a good candidate for an opponent.

Vincent gazed imploringly at the ceiling. "I am retired," he told some invisible entity. "Why don't I have the good sense to go to Florida and lie in the sun like other men my age?"

Tony's mind was wandering; he thought of that Sven character hoisting Sharon up in the air the way he had, and even though his collar was already loose, he felt a need to pull at it with his finger. He wondered if she found that kind of man attractive; some women liked foreign accents and caveman tactics....

"Tonio?" Michael snapped his fingers in front of

his brother's eyes. "Do you think you can be a part of this conversation, or shall we just go on without you?"

Vincent chuckled. "Do not torment your brother, Michael," he said. "Can't you see that he's already miserable?"

Michael sighed, but his eyes were still hot with anger. "You were thinking about Sharon when you fell and damn near killed yourself, weren't you, Tony?" he challenged. After an awkward moment during which Tony remained stubbornly silent, he went on. "Now, you seem determined to alienate every craftsman within a fifty-mile radius. How the hell do you expect to bring this project in on time and within budget if we lose every worker we've got?"

Vincent cleared his throat. "Tonio," he said diplomatically, "I was supposed to be at home an hour ago. If I walk out of this trailer, what is my assurance that the two of you will be able to work through this thing without killing each other?"

Tony sighed. "Maybe I have been a little touchy lately—"

"A *little* touchy?" Michael demanded, shaking his finger again.

"Unless you want to eat it," Tony said, "you'd better stop waving that damned finger in my face!"

The sound of the phone dialing broke the furious silence that followed. "Hello, Maria?" Vincent said. "This is the man who fathered your six children calling. If I come home now, I fear you will be left with only four.... Yes, yes, I will tell them. Goodbye, my love."

Michael shoved one hand through his hair as his father hung up. "Tell us what?" he ventured to ask.

"Your mother says that her cousin Earnestine has

been very happy as the mother of four children," Vincent answered, reaching for his hat. "My orders are to leave you to work out your differences as you see fit, whether you kill each other or not. Good night, my sons."

Tony and Michael grinned at each other when the door of the trailer closed behind their father.

"Come on," Michael said gruffly. "I'll buy you a beer and we'll talk about these personality problems of yours."

Tony had nothing better to do than go out for a beer, but he wondered about Michael. "Don't you have a date or something?"

His brother looked at his watch. "Ingrid will understand if I'm a little late," he answered. "She knows you've been having a tough time."

Tony was annoyed. His hands immediately went to his hips, and he was scowling. "Is there anybody in Port Webster you haven't regaled with the grisly saga of Tony Morelli?"

"Yes," Michael answered affably. "Sharon. If you won't tell the woman you're crazy about her, maybe I ought to."

"You do and a certain old lady will be lighting lots of candles in front of your picture," Tony responded with conviction.

Michael shrugged, and the two brothers left the trailer.

Helen's eyes sparkled and she lifted one hand to her mouth to stifle a giggle when Sharon described her visit from Sven Svensen the night before.

"And Tony was there when he arrived?" she whispered in delighted scandal.

Sharon nodded. "Sven has business in Seattle, but he'll be back here on the twenty-second to take me to the company party."

Helen clapped her hands. "Thank heaven Mrs. Morelli invited Allen and me," she crowed. "I wouldn't want to miss this for anything! You'll wear that fantastic dress, of course."

Again, Sharon nodded. But she was a little distracted. "There is one thing I have to tell you about my trip to Paris," she began reluctantly.

Helen leaned forward, one perfectly shaped eyebrow arched in silent question.

"I can't go," Sharon confided with a grimace. "Susan says I absolutely can't afford it."

"Well, there's always next spring," Helen reasoned. "November isn't the greatest time—"

"That isn't the problem," Sharon broke in. "I told Tony all about the trip—I made it sound like a big deal. If I say I can't go because I don't have the money, he'll laugh at me."

"I can't imagine Tony doing that," Helen said solemnly.

"You haven't seen his financial statement," Sharon replied. "He pays more in taxes for a month than I make in six."

"He stepped right into a thriving business," Helen pointed out. "You started your own. Anyway, Morelli Construction is a partnership. Maybe Tony's had a big part in the company's success, but he can't take all the credit for it."

Sharon sighed. A woman was examining the items

in the display window, but she didn't look as though she was going to come in and buy anything. It was time for the Christmas rush to begin, if only people would start rushing. "What would you do if you were me?"

Helen drew a deep breath. On the exhalation, she said, "I'd go straight to Tony and tell him that I loved him, and then I'd not only ask him to pay for the trip to Paris, I'd invite him along. Whereupon he would accept graciously and I would kiss his knees in gratitude."

"You're no help at all," Sharon said, giving Helen a look before she walked away to put each half-slip on a rack exactly one inch from the next one.

Sharon sat in front of the lighted mirror in her too-big, too-empty bedroom, carefully applying her makeup.

"I don't understand why you want to go out with that guy, anyway," Bri said, pouting. Curled up on the foot of the bed, she had been watching her stepmother get ready for the big party. "He's not nearly as good-looking as Daddy."

Sharon privately agreed, but she wasn't about to look a gift-Swede in the mouth. Her only other options, after all, were staying home from the party or going without an escort and spending a whole evening watching Tony attend to Ingrid. She shuddered.

"I knew you'd get cold in that dress," Matt observed from the doorway. "I can practically see your belly button."

Sharon gave her son an arch look. "Did your father tell you to say that?" she asked.

"He would if he saw the dress," Bri put in.

"Are you going to marry the Terminator?" Matt demanded to know.

After a smile at the nickname Sven didn't know he had, Sharon tilted her head back and raised one hand dramatically to her brow. "No, no, a thousand times no!" she cried.

"I think she should marry Daddy," Bri commented from her perch on the end of the bed.

Sharon was finished with her makeup and had now turned her attention to her hair. She let her stepdaughter's remark pass unchallenged.

"You could take him to Paris with you," Matt suggested. "Dad, I mean. You guys might decide you like each other and want to get married again."

"Paris is a city for lovers," Briana agreed with rising enthusiasm.

"Your dad and I are not lovers." Sharon felt a twinge of guilt, which she hid by reaching for her brush and sweeping her hair up into a small knot at the back of her head. She hadn't been able to tell the kids that the Paris trip was off, mostly because she knew they would go straight to Tony with the news. It would be too humiliating to have him know that she was having a hard time financially while he was making a success of everything he did.

Her plan was to hide out on the island for a few days and let everyone think that she was in Paris. She didn't look forward to living a lie, but for now, at least, she couldn't bear for Tony to think that she was anything less than a glittering sensation.

"I don't understand why no kids are allowed at this party," Bri complained, biting her lower lip. "It would be fun to wear something shiny."

"To match your grillwork," Matt teased.

Sharon was relieved that the conversation had taken a twist in another direction, away from Paris and lovers and Tony. "Don't start fighting now, you guys. Scary Harry will want double wages for watching you."

Bri had folded her arms and was studiously ignoring her brother. The combined gesture was reminiscent of Tony. "Gramma and Grampa include us kids in everything else," she said. "Why is this party for adults only?"

"You said it yourself," Sharon answered, turning her head from side to side so that she could make sure her hair looked good before spraying it. "Your grandparents include you and your nine hundred cousins in everything else. There has to be one occasion that's just for grown-ups."

"Why?" Bri immediately retorted. "There isn't one that's just for kids."

The doorbell chimed, and Sharon was grateful. "Go and answer that, please," she said, reaching out for her favorite cologne and giving herself a generous misting.

"It's probably the Terminator," Matt grumbled, but Bri dashed out of the bedroom and down the stairs to answer the door.

Five minutes later Sharon descended the staircase in her glittering red dress to greet a tall and handsome man wearing a tuxedo. Everything would have been perfect if the man had been Tony and not Sven.

The Swede had not been exaggerating when he had described himself as a "big businessman," physical stature aside. Sven was obviously successful; he'd proved it by arriving in a chauffeured limousine.

Sharon's eyes were wide as she settled herself in the leather-upholstered backseat and looked around.

"You like this, no?" Sven asked, with the eagerness of a child displaying a favorite toy.

"I like this, yes," Sharon answered. "I'm impressed. You've done very well for yourself, Sven."

Sven beamed. "You too are doing well with your store selling underwear."

Sharon laughed and squeezed his hand. "Oh, Sven," she said. "You do have a way with words."

"This will be a very interesting evening, I think," Sven replied, his pale eyebrows moving up. "This old husband of yours, the one you do not anymore want—tell me about him."

Sharon sighed, and then related a great many ordinary things about Tony. There must have been something revealing in her tone or her manner, because Sven took her hand and sympathetically patted it with his own as the sleek limo sped toward the first event of the holiday season.

# Chapter 10

The banquet room of Port Webster's yacht club shimmered with silvery lights. Even though there were hordes of people, Sharon's gaze locked with Tony's the moment she and Sven walked through the door.

Her heart fishtailed like a car on slick pavement, then righted itself. Tony looked fabulous in his tuxedo, and the woman standing at his side was tall and lithe with blond hair that tumbled like a waterfall to her waist.

Ingrid, no doubt.

Glumly, Sharon resigned herself to being short and perky. *Cute*, God forbid. In high school those attributes had stood her in good stead; in the here and now they seemed absolutely insipid.

"Someone has died?" Sven inquired, with a teasing light in his blue eyes as he bent to look into Sharon's crestfallen face. "The stock market has crashed?"

Sharon forced herself to smile, and it was a good thing because Tony was making his way toward them, pulling Ingrid along with him.

A waiter arrived at the same moment, and Sven graciously accepted glasses of champagne for himself and his nervous date. Sharon practically did a swan dive into her drink.

Sven stepped gallantly into the conversational breach. "So, we meet again," he said to Tony, but his eyes were on Ingrid.

Tony's jawline clamped down, then relaxed. Ingrid had slipped her arm through his and clasped her hands together.

Sharon wondered why the woman didn't just execute a half nelson and be done with it, but she would have eaten one of the centerpieces before letting either Tony or Ingrid know how ill at ease she felt.

"Are you Sharon?" the blonde demanded pleasantly, extending one hand in greeting before Tony could introduce her. "I've been so eager to meet you!"

*I'll just bet you have,* Sharon thought sourly, but she kept right on looking cute and perky. "Yes," she answered, "and I presume you're Ingrid?"

The blonde nodded. She really was stunning, and her simple, black cocktail dress did a lot to show off her long, shapely legs. She seemed genuinely pleased to know Sharon, though her gaze had, by this time, strayed to Sven. "Hello," she said in her throaty voice.

Sharon took a hasty sip of her champagne and spilled a little of it when Tony took hold of her elbow, without warning, and pulled her aside. "If I stick that guy with a pin, will he deflate and fly around the room?" he asked, feigning a serious tone.

Sharon glared at her ex-husband. "If you stick Sven with a pin, I imagine he'll punch you in the mouth," she responded.

Tony looked contemptuously unterrified. He lifted his champagne glass to his mouth, taking a sip as his eyes moved over Sharon's dress. "Where did you buy that—Dolly Parton's last garage sale?"

Sharon refrained from stomping on his instep only because Sven and Ingrid were present. "You don't like it?" she countered sweetly, batting her lashes. "Good."

"We are from the same town in Sweden, Ingrid and I!" Sven exclaimed in that buoyant way of his.

"Would you mind if I borrowed your date for just one dance?" Ingrid asked Sharon. She didn't seem to care what Tony's opinion might be.

"Be my guest," Sharon said magnanimously.

"Michael is going to love this," Tony muttered, as he watched Sven and Ingrid walk away.

Sharon was desperate for a safe topic of conversation, and her former brother-in-law was it. She craned her neck, looking for him. "I'd enjoy a waltz with Michael," she said. "He's the best dancer in the family."

Tony took Sharon's glass out of her hand and set it on a table with his own. "You'll have to settle for me, because my brother isn't here," he said. His fingers closed over hers and she let him lead her toward the crowded dance floor.

To distract herself from the sensations dancing with Tony aroused in various parts of her anatomy, Sharon looked up at him and asked, "Michael, missing a party? I don't believe it."

"Believe it. He's out of town, putting in a bid on a new mall."

Sharon lifted her eyebrows. "Impressive."

"It will make ours the biggest construction operation in this part of the state," Tony replied without any particular enthusiasm.

Sharon thought of her canceled trip to Paris and sighed. "I guess some of us have it and some of us don't," she said softly.

Tony's hand caught under her chin. "What was that supposed to mean?" he asked. His voice was gentle, the look in his eyes receptive.

Sharon nearly told him the truth, but lost her courage at the last millisecond. She couldn't risk opening herself up to an I-told-you-so or, worse yet, a generous helping of indulgent sympathy. "Nothing," she said, forcing a bright smile to her face.

There was a flicker of disappointment in Tony's eyes. "Is it that hard to talk to me?" he asked quietly.

Sharon let the question go unanswered, pretending that she hadn't heard it, and turned her head to watch Sven and Ingrid for a moment. "There's something so damned cheerful about them," she muttered.

Tony chuckled, but there was scant amusement in the sound. Maybe, Sharon reflected with a pang, he was jealous of Ingrid's obvious rapport with Sven. When she looked up into those familiar brown eyes, they were solemn.

Resolved to get through this night with her dignity intact if it killed her, Sharon smiled up at him. "I'm surprised I haven't met Ingrid before this," she said brightly.

Tony shrugged. "If you'd come to any of the family gatherings lately, you would have," he observed, as though it were the most natural thing in the world for a woman to socialize with her ex-husband's girlfriend.

Sharon was inexpressibly wounded to know that Tony cared enough about Ingrid to include her in the mob scenes that were a way of life in the Morelli family. Reminding herself that she and Tony were no longer husband and wife, that she had no real part in his life anymore, did nothing to ease the pain.

The plain and simple truth was that she had been replaced with the simple ease and aplomb she'd always feared she would be. Her smile wavered.

"I've been busy lately," she said, and then, mercifully, the music stopped and Sven and Ingrid were at hand. Sharon pulled free of Tony's embrace and turned blindly into Sven's. "Dance with me," she whispered in desperate tones, as the small orchestra began another waltz.

Sven's expression was full of tenderness and concern. "So much you love this man that your heart is breaking," he said. "Poor little bird—I cannot bear to see you this way."

Sharon let her forehead rest against her friend's strong shoulder, struggling to maintain her composure. It would be disastrous to fall apart in front of all these people. "I'll be fine," she told him, but the words sounded uncertain.

"We will leave this place," Sven responded firmly. "It is not good for you, being here."

Sharon drew a deep breath and let it out again. She couldn't leave, not yet. She wouldn't let the pain of loving and losing Tony bring her to her knees that way. She lifted her chin and, with a slight shake of her head, said, "No. I'm not going to run away."

An expression of gentle respect flickered in Sven's blue eyes. "We will make the best of this situation, then," he said. He looked like the shy, awkward teenager Sharon had known in high school when he went on. "There are other men who want you, little bird," he told her. "I am one of these."

Gently, Sharon touched Sven's handsome, freshly shaven face. A sweet, achy sense of remorse filled her. He'd been so kind to her; she didn't want to hurt him. She started to speak, but Sven silenced her by laying one index finger to her lips.

"Don't speak," he said. "I know you are not ready to let a new man love you. Do you want him back, Sharon—this Tony of yours?"

"I've asked myself that question a million times," Sharon confided. "The truth is, I do, but I know it can never work."

"He betrayed you? He was with other women?"

Sharon shook her head.

"He drank?" Sven persisted, frowning. "He beat you?"

Sharon laughed. Tony liked good wine, but she'd never actually seen him drunk in all the years she'd known him, although there had been that incident Michael had mentioned weeks before. Tony had always been a lover, not a fighter. "No," she answered.

"Then why are you divorced from him?" Sven asked, looking genuinely puzzled.

"There are other reasons for divorce," Sharon replied, as the orchestra paused between numbers.

"Like what?" Sven wanted to know, as he led Sharon off the dance floor. He'd seated her at a table and secured drinks for them both before she answered.

For some reason—perhaps it was the champagne—Sharon found that she could talk to Sven, and the words came pouring out of her. "Tony was married once before when he was very young. His wife was killed in a terrible accident, and he was left with a baby girl to raise. He and I met only a few months after Carmen died."

Sven took her hand. "And?" he prompted.

"I know people say this doesn't happen to real people, but the moment I saw Tony I fell in love with him."

Sven smiled sadly, and his grasp on Sharon's fingers tightened a little. "Tell me how you met your Tony."

Sharon sighed. "I was working in a bookstore here in Port Webster and going to business college at night." She paused, gazing back into the past. "He made his selections, and I was one of them, I guess. We went out that night, and six weeks later we were married."

"You say that as though you were one of the books he bought," Sven observed. "Why is this?"

Sharon shrugged, but her expression was one of quiet sorrow. "There have been times when I felt that he'd chosen me for a purpose, the same way he chose those books. He was lonely, and he needed a mother for his daughter."

"Children can be raised successfully without a mother," Sven put in.

Sharon nodded. "That's true, of course," she conceded. "And heaven knows there are enough kids growing up without a father. But Tony is—well—he's family oriented. It's the most important thing in the world to him." She swallowed. He'd remarried quickly after Carmen, and he was going to do the same thing now. Exit wife number two, enter number three.

"You're going to cry, I think," Sven said. "We can't

have that, since he's looking our way, your buyer of books." Rising from his chair, the Swede drew Sharon out of hers, as well. "Trust me when I do this, little bird," he said huskily, and then, with no more warning than that, he swept Sharon into his arms and gave her a kiss that left her feeling as though she'd had her head held under water for five minutes.

She blushed hotly, one hand to her breast, and hissed, "Sven!"

His azure eyes twinkled as he looked down at her. "Now we can leave," he said. "We have given your used-to-be lover something to think about on this cold winter night."

It seemed unlikely that Tony would spend the night thinking—not when he'd have Ingrid lying in bed beside him—but Sharon knew that Sven was right about one thing. She could escape that ghastly party now without looking like the scorned ex-wife.

She felt Tony's gaze touching her as she waited for Sven to return with her coat, but she refused to meet it. It was time to cut her losses.

After saying a few words to Vincent and Maria, and to Helen and her husband, Allen, Sharon left the party with her hand in the crook of Sven's powerful arm and her chin held high. The luxurious interior of the limousine was warm and welcoming.

"You will come to my suite for drinks and more talk of old times, no?" Sven asked.

"No," Sharon confirmed.

Her friend frowned. "You must," he said.

Sharon squirmed a little. Maybe Sven wasn't as understanding as she'd thought. "If I have to jump for it," she warned, "I will."

Sven laughed. "I am more the gentleman than this, little bird. And since I am a man, I know how your Tony is thinking now. He will either telephone or drive past your house at the first opportunity. Do you want to be there, sipping hot cocoa and knitting by the fireside? Of course you don't!"

Sven's theory had its merits, but Sharon wasn't ready for an intimate relationship with a new man, and she had to be sure that her friend understood that. "Promise you won't get me into another lip-lock?" she asked seriously.

Sven gave a shout of amusement. "What is this 'lip-lock'?" he countered.

"I was referring to that kiss back at the party," Sharon said, her arms folded. "Nobody under seventeen should have been allowed to see that unless they were accompanied by a parent."

Sven's eyes, blue as a fjord under a clear sky, danced with mischief. "I wish you could have seen Tony's face, little bird," he said. "You would feel better if you had."

Sharon bit her lip. It seemed just as likely to her that Sven's trick would backfire and propel Tony into some R-rated adventures of his own, but she didn't want to spoil her friend's delight by saying so. "I don't want to talk about Tony anymore," she said. "Tell me about you, Sven."

Since there was no hotel in Port Webster, the limo rolled toward nearby Tacoma, where Sven's company had provided him with a suite. During the drive he told Sharon about his company, which manufactured ski equipment that would soon be sold in the United States. He also mentioned his short and disastrous marriage, which had ended two years before.

As Sven was helping Sharon out of the limo in front

of his hotel, she stepped on the hem of her slinky dress and felt the slit move a few inches higher on her thigh. "Oh, great," she muttered.

Sven chuckled. "There is a problem, no?"

"There is a problem, yes, I've torn my dress," Sharon answered. "And I'm not getting the hang of this being single, Sven. I'm not adjusting."

His hand was strong on the small of her back as he ushered her toward the warmth and light of the lobby. "It takes time," he told her. "Much time and not a little pain."

Sharon was glad she was wearing a long coat when they stepped inside that elegant hotel. There were a lot of people milling around, and she didn't want them to see that the sexy slit in her dress had been extended to the area of her tonsils.

"You are hungry?" Sven asked, as they passed a dark restaurant looking out over Commencement Bay.

Except for a few hors d'oeuvres, Sharon had had nothing to eat all evening, and all that champagne was just sloshing around in her stomach, waiting to cause trouble. "I suppose I am," she confessed, "but I don't want to take off my coat."

Sven chuckled. "Little bird, there is only candlelight in there. Who will see that your dress is torn?"

Sharon succumbed to his logic, partly because she'd missed supper and partly because she wanted to delay for as long as possible the moment when she and Sven stepped inside his suite. She loved Tony Morelli with all her heart and soul, but her desires hadn't died with their divorce. Sven's kiss, back at the party, had proved that much to her.

They enjoyed a leisurely dinner, during which they laughed and talked and drank a great deal of champagne. By the time they got to Sven's suite, Sharon's mind was foggy, and she was yawning like a sleepy child.

Sven gave her an innocuous kiss and said, "How I wish that I were the kind of man to take advantage of you, little bird. Just for tonight, I would like to be such a scoundrel."

Sharon sighed and smiled a tipsy smile. By then she was carrying her shoes in one hand and her hair was falling down from its pins. "Know what?" she asked. "I wish I could be different, too. Here I am in a fancy suite with a man who should be featured in one of those hunk-of-the-month calendars, and what do I do with such an opportunity? I waste it, that's what."

Sven grinned, cupping her face with his large, gentle hands. "Always, since I was here for high school, when I think of America, I think of you," he said with a sigh of his own. "Ah, Sharon, Sharon—the way you looked in those jeans of yours made me want to defect and ask for political asylum in this country."

Sharon stood on tiptoe to kiss his cheek. "Nobody defects from Sweden," she reasoned.

Sven put her away with a gentle purposefulness that said a lot about his sense of honor, and looked down at his slender gold watch. "It is time, I believe, to take you home," he said in a gruff voice. "It would seem that my wish to become a scoundrel is beginning to come true."

"Oh." Sharon swallowed and retreated a step. She had removed her coat in the restaurant, but she'd put it on again before they left. Now she held it a little closer around her.

"When next I come to America," Sven went on, his back to Sharon now as he looked out at the bay and the lights that adorned it like diamonds upon velvet, "you may be through loving Tony. For obvious reasons, I want you to remember me kindly if that is the case."

Sharon had had a great deal to drink that evening, but she was sober enough to appreciate Sven's gallantry. "You don't have to worry about that," she said softly. "My having kind thoughts about you, I mean. I'm no sophisticate, but I know that men like you are rare."

When Sven turned to face her, he was once again flashing that dazzling smile of his. It was as reassuring as a beam from a lighthouse on a dark and storm-tossed sea. "What you have yet to learn, little bird," he told her, "is that you also are special. You are fireworks and blue jeans and county fairs—everything that is American."

Sharon shrugged, feeling sheepish and rumpled and very safe. "I'm going to take that as a compliment since I've had too much booze to fight back if it was an insult," she said.

Sven laughed again and went to the telephone to summon the limousine and driver his company had provided for him.

It was 3:00 a.m. exactly when the limo came to a stop in front of the house on Tamarack Drive, and Tony's car was parked in the driveway.

Sven smiled mysteriously, as though some private theory of his had been proven correct. "You would like me to come in with you?" he inquired.

He didn't look surprised when Sharon shook her head. She knew she had nothing to fear from Tony, even if he was in a raving fury, but she wasn't so sure that the same was true of Sven. With her luck the two men would get into a brawl, half kill each other and scar the kids' psyches for life.

"Thanks for everything," she said, reaching for the knob. As she'd expected, the door was unlocked. "And good night."

Sven gave her a brotherly kiss on the forehead and then walked away.

The light was on in the entryway, and there was a lamp burning in the living room. Barefoot, her strappy silver shoes dangling from one hand, Sharon followed the trail Tony had left for her.

He was in the den, lying on the sofa bed and watching the shopping channel. He was wearing battered jeans and a T-shirt, and his feet were bare. He didn't look away when Sharon came to stand beside the bed.

She glanced at the TV screen. A hideously ornate clock with matching candelabras was being offered for an exorbitant price. "Thinking of redecorating?"

Tony sighed, still staring at the screen. "Who do I look like?" he countered. "Herman Munster?"

Sharon tossed her shoes aside and sat down on the edge of the mattress. "What are you doing here?" she asked.

He rubbed his chin with one hand. "I seem to have some kind of homing device implanted in my brain. Every once in a while I forget that I don't live here anymore."

Sharon felt sad and broken. The slit in the dress she hadn't been able to afford went higher with an audible rip when she curled her legs beneath her. She plucked at the blanket with two fingers and kept her eyes down. "Oh," she said.

Tony's voice was like gravel. "Do you know what time it is?" he demanded.

Sharon's sadness was displaced by quiet outrage. "Yes," she answered. "It's 3:05, the party's over and a good time was had by all. You can leave anytime now, Tony."

He reached out with such quick ferocity that Sharon's eyes went wide, and he caught her wrist in one hand. Even though Tony wasn't hurting her, Sharon felt her heart trip into a faster, harder beat, and her breath was trapped in her lungs.

Before she knew what was happening, she was lying on her back, looking up into his face. A muscle flexed along his jawline. He was resting part of his weight on her, and even though she was angry, Sharon welcomed it.

"If you're in love with that Swede," Tony said evenly, "I want to know it. Right now."

Sharon swallowed. "I'm not really sober enough to handle this," she said.

Tony looked as though he might be torn between kissing Sharon and killing her. "Fine. If I have to pour coffee down your throat all night long, I'll do it."

She squeezed her eyes shut. "I really think you should let me go," she said.

"Give me one good reason," Tony replied.

"I'm going to throw up."

He rolled aside. "That's a good reason if I've ever heard one," he conceded, as Sharon leaped off the bed, a hand clasped to her mouth, and ran for the adjoining bathroom.

When she came out some minutes later, Tony was waiting with her favorite chenille bathrobe draped over one arm, and a glass of bicarbonate in his hand.

Sharon drank the seltzer down in a series of gulps and then let Tony divest her of the coat. He did raise an eyebrow when he saw that the slit had advanced to well past her hip, but to his credit he made no comment. He turned her so that he could unzip the dress, and Sharon didn't protest.

Her hair was a mess, her mascara was running and her gown—which she would still be paying for in six months—was totally ruined. She couldn't afford her trip to Paris, and she loved a man she couldn't live with.

It was getting harder and harder to take a positive outlook on things.

## Chapter 11

The hangover was there to meet Sharon when she woke up in the morning. Head throbbing, stomach threatening revolt, she groaned and buried her face deep in her pillow when she heard Tony telling the kids to keep the noise down.

Sharon lifted her head slightly and opened one eye. She was in the den.

There was a cheerful blaze snapping and crackling in the fireplace, and Matt was perched on the foot of the hide-a-bed, watching Saturday morning cartoons. Tony was working at the desk, while Briana strutted back and forth with Sharon's ruined dress draped against her front.

"That must have been some party," the child observed, inspecting the ripped seam.

"Coffee," Sharon moaned. "If anyone in this room has a shred of decency in their soul, they'll bring me some right now."

Tony chuckled and got out of his chair. Moments later he was back with a mug of steaming coffee, and the kids had mysteriously vanished. "Here you go, you party animal," he said, as Sharon scrambled to an upright position and reached out for the cup with two trembling hands.

"Thanks," she grumbled.

Tony sat on the edge of the bed. "Want some breakfast?"

"There is no need to be vicious," Sharon muttered. The coffee tasted good, but two sips told her the stuff wasn't welcome in her stomach.

He laughed and kissed her forehead. "You'll feel better later," he said gently. "I promise."

She set the coffee aside and shoved a hand through her rumpled hair. "You're being awfully nice to me," she said suspiciously, squinting at the clock on the mantelpiece. "What time is it, anyway?"

Tony sighed. "It's time you were up and getting ready for your trip to Paris. Your flight leaves Seattle this afternoon, doesn't it?"

Sharon settled herself against the back of the sofa and groaned. She wanted so much to confess that she was really planning to spend the next four days on the island, but she couldn't. She had an image to maintain. "Yes," she said.

"I'd like to drive you to the airport," Tony told her.

Sharon stared at him. Although she wanted to accept, she couldn't because then, of course, Tony would find out that she wasn't really going anywhere. "That won't be necessary," she replied, dropping her eyes.

Never a man to let well enough alone, Tony persisted. "Why not?"

Sharon was trapped. She could either lie or admit that she was a failure and a fraud. She gnawed at her lower lip for a moment and then blurted out, "Because Sven is seeing me off."

There was a short, deadly silence, then Tony stood. "Great," he said, moving toward the desk, gathering whatever he'd been working on earlier.

Sharon steeled herself against an impulse to offer him frantic assurances that she and Sven weren't involved. After all, Tony wasn't letting any grass grow under his feet, romantically speaking. He had Ingrid. "I knew you'd understand," she hedged, reaching for her chenille bathrobe and hopping out of bed. She was tying the belt when Tony finally turned around to face her again.

"I don't have the right to ask you this," he said, his voice gruff and barely audible over the sounds of muted cartoons and the fire on the hearth. "But I've got to know. Is he—Sven—going to Paris with you?"

Sharon's throat ached with suppressed emotion; she knew what it had cost Tony, in terms of his dignity, to ask that question. She could only shake her head.

Tony nodded, his eyes revealing a misery Sharon didn't know how to assuage, and said, "I'll just take the kids out for a while, if that's okay. Have a good trip."

The guilt Sharon felt was monumental. She loved these people, Tony and Briana and Matt, and she was lying to them, acting out an elaborate charade for the sake of her pride.

"I will," she said. "Thanks."

He gave her a look of wry anguish. "Sure," he answered, and within five minutes Briana and Matt had said goodbye to Sharon and left with Tony.

Woodenly, Sharon trudged upstairs, got out of her robe and the nightgown she had no memory of putting on, and stepped into a hot shower. When she came out, she felt better physically, but her emotions were as tangled as yarn mauled by a kitten.

She put on jeans and a burgundy cable-knit sweater, along with heavy socks and hiking boots. "Just the outfit for jetting off to Paris," she muttered, slumping down on the side of the bed and reaching for the telephone.

Helen answered on the second ring. "Teddy Bares. May I help you?"

Sharon sighed. "I wish someone could. How's business this morning?"

"We're doing pretty well," Helen replied. "Everything is under control. That was some kiss old Sven laid on you at the party last night, my dear."

"I was hoping no one noticed," Sharon said lamely.

"You must know that Tony did. He left five minutes after you and Sven went out the door, and your former in-laws had to take the blonde home because he forgot her."

Sharon's spirits rose a little at the thought of Ingrid slipping Tony's mind like that. She said nothing, sensing that Helen would carry the conversational ball.

"If I ever had any doubt that Tony Morelli is nuts about you, and only you, it's gone now." She paused to draw a deep, philosophical breath. "You're not still going through with this trip-to-Paris thing, are you?"

"I have to," Sharon said, rubbing her temple with three fingers.

"Nonsense."

Sharon didn't have the energy to argue. The shop had been a big part of the reason she and Tony had gotten divorced; he was very old-fashioned in a lot of ways, and she doubted that he understood even now why she wanted the hassles of owning a business. If she didn't succeed, all his misgivings would be justified. "I'll be back the day before Thanksgiving," she said firmly. "If there are any emergencies in the meantime, you know where to call."

Helen sighed. "This is never going to work, you know. The truth will come out."

"Maybe so," Sharon replied, "but it had better not come out of you, my friend. I'll explain this to Tony myself—someday."

"Right," Helen said crisply. "Tell me this—what number are you going to give him to call if one of the kids gets sick or something? He'll expect you to be registered in a hotel...."

"I told Tony several days ago that I'd be checking in with you regularly, so if anything goes wrong, you'll hear from him. All you would have to do then is call me at the A-frame."

"This is stupid, Sharon."

"I don't recall asking for your opinion," Sharon retorted.

"What about postcards?" Helen shot back. "What about souvenirs for the kids? Don't you see that you're not going to be able to pull this off?"

Sharon bit her lip. The deception was indeed a tangled web, and it was getting stickier by the moment, but she was already trapped. "I'll check out that import shop in Seattle or something," she said.

"You're crazy," commented Helen.

"It's nice to know that my friends are solidly behind me," Sharon snapped.

There was a pause, and then Helen said quietly, "I want you to be happy. You do know that, don't you?"

"Yes," Sharon replied distractedly. "Goodbye, Helen. I'll see you when I get back from—Paris."

"Right." Helen sighed, and the conversation was over.

Sharon packed jeans, warm sweaters and flannel nightgowns for the trip, leaving behind the trim suits and dresses she would have taken to Europe. Such things would, of course, be of no use on the island.

She loaded her suitcase into the trunk of her roadster and set out for Seattle and the import shop she had in mind. First things first, she reflected dismally, as she sped along the freeway.

Halfway there, she asked herself, "What am I doing?" right out loud and took the next exit. Within minutes, she was headed back toward Port Webster.

Enough was enough. Surely going through all this was more demeaning than admitting the truth to Tony could ever be.

Sharon drove by his condominium first, but no one answered the door. With a sigh, she got back into the roadster and set out for his parents' house. Reaching that, Sharon almost lost her courage. There were cars everywhere; obviously something was going on. Something big.

Resigned, Sharon found a place for her roadster, got out and walked toward the enormous, noisy house. The very structure seemed to be permeated with love and laughter, and she smiled sadly as she reached out to ring the doorbell. She didn't belong here anymore; maybe she never had.

Vincent opened the door, and his look of delight enveloped Sharon like a warm blanket and drew her in out of the biting November cold. "Come in, come in," he said, taking her hand in his strong grasp. "We're having a celebration."

Sharon lingered in the entryway when Vincent would have led her into the living room. "A celebration?" she echoed.

Vincent spread his hands and beamed in triumph. "At last, he is getting married, my stubborn son...."

Sharon's first reaction was primitive and instantaneous; her stomach did a flip, and she wanted to turn and flee like a frightened rabbit. A deep breath, however, marked the return of rational thought. Maybe things weren't very good between her and Tony, and maybe they weren't communicating like grown-up people were supposed to do, but she knew he wouldn't get married again without telling her. A man would think to mention something that important.

"Come in and have some wine with us," Vincent said gently. He'd noticed Sharon's nervous manner, but he was far too polite to comment.

She shook her head. "If I could just talk to Tony for a few minutes..."

Vincent shrugged and disappeared, leaving Sharon to stand in the colorful glow of a stained-glass skylight, her hands clasped together.

Tony appeared within seconds, slid his gaze over Sharon's casual clothes and said in a low, bewildered tone, "Hi."

Sharon drew a deep breath, let it out and took the plunge. "I have to talk to you," she said, and she was surprised to feel the sting of tears in her eyes because she hadn't planned to cry.

He took her hand and led her to the foot of the stairway, where they sat down together on the second step. Tony's thumb moved soothingly over her fingers. "I'm listening, babe," he said gently.

With the back of her free hand, Sharon tried to dry her eyes. "I lied," she confessed, the words a blurted whisper. "I'm not going to Paris because I can't afford to—Teddy Bares isn't doing that well."

Tony sighed, and enclosing her hand between both of his, lifted it to his lips. He wasn't looking at her, but at the patch of jeweled sunshine cast onto the oaken floor of the entryway beneath the skylight. "Why did you feel you had to lie?" he asked after a very long time.

Sharon sniffled. "I was ashamed, that's why. I thought you'd laugh if you found out that I couldn't spare the money for a plane ticket."

"Laugh?" The word sounded hollow and raw, and the look in Tony's eyes revealed that she'd hurt him. "You expected me to laugh because you'd been disappointed? My God, Sharon, do you think I'm that much of a bastard?"

Sharon was taken aback by the intensity of Tony's pain; he looked and sounded as though he'd been struck. "I'm sorry," she whispered.

"Hell, that makes all the difference," Tony rasped in a furious undertone, releasing her hand with a suddenness that bordered on violence. "Damn it, you don't even know me, do you? We were married for ten years, and you have no idea who I am."

Sharon needed to reach Tony, to reassure him. "That's not true," she said, stricken.

"It is," he replied, his voice cold and distant as he stood up. "And I sure as hell don't know you."

Grasping the banister beside her, Sharon pulled herself to her feet. "Tony, please listen to me—"

"If you'll excuse me," he interrupted with icy formality, "I have a brother who's celebrating his engagement." He paused and thrust one hand through his hair, and when he looked at Sharon, his eyes were hot with hurt and anger. "I hope to God Michael and Ingrid will do better than we did," he said.

*Michael and Ingrid. Michael and Ingrid.* The words were like a fist to the stomach for Sharon. She closed her eyes against the impact and hugged herself to keep from flying apart. "Can—can you keep the kids—the way we'd planned?" she managed to ask.

Tony was silent for so long that Sharon was sure he'd left her standing there in the entryway with her eyes squeezed shut and her arms wrapped around her middle, but he finally answered raggedly, "Sure. What do you want me to tell them?"

"That I love them," Sharon said, and then she turned blindly and groped for the doorknob. A larger, stronger hand closed over hers, staying her escape.

"You're in no condition to drive," Tony said flatly, and there wasn't a shred of emotion in his voice. "You're not going anywhere until you pull yourself together."

Sharon couldn't face him. She knew he was right, though; it would be irresponsible to drive in that emotional state. She let her forehead rest against the door, struggling to hold in sobs of sheer heartbreak.

Tentatively, he touched her shoulder. "Sharon," he said, and the name reverberated with hopelessness and grief.

She trembled with the effort to control her runaway feelings, and after a few more moments she had regained her composure. "I'll be on the island if the kids need me," she said.

"Okay," Tony whispered, and he stepped back, allowing her to open the door and walk out.

Sharon drove to the ferry landing and boarded the boat. She didn't get out of the car and go up to the snack bar to drink coffee and look at the view, though. She wasn't interested in scenery.

Once the ferry docked, Sharon's brain began to work again. She set her course for the nearest supermarket and wheeled a cart up and down the aisles, selecting food with all the awareness of a robot.

The A-frame was cold since no one had been there in a while, and Sharon turned up the heat before she began putting her groceries away. Her soul was as numb as her body, but for a different reason.

The warmth wafting up from the vents in the floor would eventually take the chill of a November afternoon from her bones and muscles, but there was no remedy for the wintry ache in her spirit. She went into the living room and collapsed facedown on the sofa. She needed the release weeping would provide, but it eluded her. Evidently, she'd exhausted her supply of tears in the entryway of Vincent and Maria's house.

"How did it all go so wrong?" she asked, turning onto her back and gazing up at the ceiling with dry, swollen eyes.

The telephone jangled at just that moment, a shrill mockery in the silence. Sharon didn't want to answer, but she didn't have much choice. She had two children, and if they needed her, she had to know about it.

She crossed the room, indulged in a deep sniffle and spoke into the receiver in the most normal voice she was able to manage. "Hello?"

"Are you all right?" Tony wanted to know.

Sharon wound her finger in the phone cord. "I'm terrific," she replied. "Just terrific. Is anything wrong?"

"The kids are fine." The words immediately put Sharon's mind at rest.

"Good. Then you won't mind if I hang up. Goodbye, Tony, and enjoy the party."

"Except for that night when we were supposed to paint your apartment and ended up making love instead, I haven't enjoyed anything in eight months," Tony responded. "And don't you dare hang up."

Sharon drew a chair back from the nearby dining table and sank into it. "What am I supposed to say now, Tony? You tell me. That way, maybe I won't step on your toes and you won't step on mine and we can skip the usual fifteen rounds."

When Tony answered, that frosty distance was back in his voice. "Right now I feel like putting both my fists through the nearest wall. How can I be expected to know what either of us is supposed to say?"

"I guess you can't," Sharon replied. "And neither can I. Goodbye, Tony, and give my best to Michael and Ingrid."

"I will," Tony replied sadly, and then he hung up.

Sharon felt as though her whole body and spirit were one giant exposed nerve, throbbing in the cold. She replaced the receiver and went out for a long walk on the beach.

It was nearly dark when she returned to brew herself a cup of instant coffee, slide a frozen dinner into the oven and build a fire in the living room fireplace.

The flames seemed puny, and their warmth couldn't penetrate the chill that lingered around Sharon. She was eating her supper when the telephone rang again.

Again, she was forced to answer.

"Mom?" piped a voice on the other end of the line. "This is Matt."

Sharon smiled for the first time in hours. "I know. How are you, sweetheart?"

"I'm okay." Despite those words, Matt sounded worried. "Bri and I are spending the night with Gramma and Grampa. How come you didn't go to Paris like you said you were going to?"

Sharon clasped the bridge of her nose between her thumb and index finger. "I'll explain about Paris when I get home, honey. Why aren't you and Bri sleeping at your dad's place?"

Before Matt could answer that, Bri joined the conversation on an extension. "Something's really wrong," she said despairingly. "You and Daddy are both acting very weird."

Much as Sharon would have liked to refute that remark, she couldn't. "I guess we are," she admitted softly. "But everything is going to be all right again soon. I promise you that."

She could feel Bri's confusion. "Really?" the girl asked in a small voice, and Sharon wished that she could put her arms around both her children and hold them close.

"Really," Sharon confirmed gently.

There was a quiet exchange on the other end of the line, and then Maria came on. "Sharon? Are you all right, dear?"

Sharon swallowed. "I guess so. Maria, why did Tony leave the children with you and Vincent? I understood him to say that he was going to look after them himself until I got back."

Maria hesitated before answering. "Tonio was upset when he left here," she said cautiously. "Vincent was worried and went after him. I haven't seen either of them since."

Sharon ached. Vincent Morelli was not the kind of father who interfered in his children's lives; if he'd been worried enough to follow Tony, there was real cause for concern.

"Did Tony say anything before he left?"

Sharon realized that Maria was weeping softly. "No," the older woman answered. "I'd feel better if he had. He was just—just hurting."

"I see," Sharon said, keeping her chin high even though there was no one around to know that she was being brave.

"Tonio can be unkind when he is in pain," Maria ventured to say after a few moments of silence. It was obvious that she'd used the interval to work up her courage. "But he loves you, Sharon. He loves you very much."

Sharon nodded. "I love him, too—but sometimes that grand emotion just isn't enough."

"It's the greatest force in the world," Maria countered firmly. "You and Tonio don't understand how it works, that's all."

Sharon was still mulling that over when Maria changed the subject. "You'll be back in town in time for Thanksgiving, won't you?"

"Yes," Sharon answered after a brief hesitation. She hadn't given the holiday much thought since her emotions had been in such turmoil.

"We've missed you," her ex-mother-in-law went on forthrightly. "You are still one of us, no matter what may be happening between you and that hardheaded son of mine, and—well—Vincent and I would be very pleased if you would join us all for dinner on Thursday."

Being invited to a family Thanksgiving at the Morellis' was probably a small thing, but Sharon was deeply moved all the same. Maria could have had her son and her grandchildren around her table on that special day without inviting an erstwhile wife, after all. "Thank you," Sharon said. "That would be nice."

"Of course, your mother is welcome, too," Maria added.

Bea had never made much of holidays, preferring to ignore them until they went away, but Sharon would extend the invitation anyway. "You realize that my presence might be awkward. Tony may not like it at all."

Maria sniffed. "Don't worry about Tonio. He'll behave himself."

In spite of everything that had happened, Sharon chuckled at Maria's motherly words.

"You get some rest," the older woman finished, "and don't worry about the children. I'll take very good care of them."

"Thank you," Sharon replied quietly, and after a few more words the two women said their farewells and hung up.

Sharon went upstairs to take a hot bath, and when that was done she crawled into bed and shivered under the covers. While she waited for sleep to overtake her, she laid plans for the morning.

It was time she stopped acting silly and made some sense of her life. She and Tony were divorced, but they had two children in common, and that meant they had to learn to talk to each other like civilized adults.

The task seemed formidable to Sharon.

# Chapter 12

The sound brought Sharon wide awake in an instant. She sat bolt upright in bed, her heart throbbing in her throat as she listened.

There it was again—a distinct thump. A shaky *who's there?* rose in Sharon's throat, but she couldn't get it out. Besides, she reasoned wildly, maybe it wasn't smart to let the prowler know she was there. If she kept quiet, he might steal what he wanted and leave without bothering her.

On the other hand, Sharon reflected, tossing back the covers and creeping out of bed as the noise reverberated through the A-frame again, her car was parked outside—a clear indication that someone was at home. If she just sat there with her lower lip caught between her teeth, she might end up like one of those women in the opening scenes of a horror movie.

She crept out of the bedroom and across the hall to Matt's room, where she found his baseball bat with only minimal groping. Thus armed, Sharon started cautiously down the stairs.

She'd reached the bottom when a shadow moved in the darkness. Sharon screamed and swung the bat, and something made of glass shattered.

A familiar voice rasped a swearword, and then the living room was flooded with light.

Tony was standing with his hand on the switch, looking at Sharon in weary bafflement. The mock-Tiffany lamp she'd bought at a swap meet was lying on the floor in jagged, kaleidoscope pieces.

Slowly, Sharon lowered the bat to her side. "You could have knocked," she observed lamely. Her heart was still hammering against her rib cage, and she laid one hand to her chest in an effort to calm it.

Tony was frowning. "Why would I do that when I have a key?" he asked, pulling off his jacket and tossing it onto the sofa. "Go put some shoes on, Babe Ruth," he said. "I'll get the broom."

Sharon went upstairs without argument, baseball bat in hand, wanting a chance to put her thoughts into some kind of order. When she came down minutes later, she was wearing jeans, sneakers and a heavy sweater. Tony was sweeping up the last of the broken glass.

"What are you doing here?" she asked, lingering on the stairs, one hand resting on the banister.

Tony sighed. "It was Papa's idea," he said.

Sharon rolled her eyes and put her hands on her hips, mildly insulted. "Now that's romantic," she observed.

Her ex-husband disappeared with the broom and the dustpan full of glass, and when he came back there was a sheepish look about him. He went to the hearth without a word, and began building a fire.

Sharon watched him for a few moments, then went into the kitchen to heat water for coffee. Hope was pounding inside her in a strange, rising rhythm, like the beat of jungle drums. Her feelings were odd, she thought, given the number of times she and Tony had tried to find common ground and failed.

She filled the teakettle at the sink, set it on the stove and turned up the flame beneath it. She'd just taken mugs and a jar of coffee down from the cupboard when she sensed Tony's presence and turned to see him standing in the doorway.

"I'm not going to leave," he announced with quiet resolve, "until you and I come to some kind of understanding."

Sharon sighed. "That might take a while," she answered.

He shrugged, but the expression in his eyes was anything but dispassionate. "Frankly, I've reached the point where I don't give a damn if supplies have to be airlifted in. I'm here for the duration."

The teakettle began to whistle, and Sharon took it from the heat, pouring steaming water into cups. "That's a pretty staunch position to take, considering that it was your father's idea for you to…drop in."

Tony sighed and took the cups from Sharon's hands, standing close. He set the coffee aside, and his quiet masculinity awakened all her sleepy senses. "Sharon," he said in a low voice, "I love you, and I'm pretty sure you feel the same way about me. Can't we hold on to that until we get our bearings?"

Sharon swallowed. "There are so many problems—"

"Everybody has them," he countered hoarsely. And then he took her hand in his and led her into the living room. They sat down together on the couch in front of the fireplace. Sharon, for her part, felt like a shy teenager.

"Why did you let me believe that you and Ingrid were involved?" she dared to ask. A sidelong look at Tony revealed that he was gazing into the fire.

His fingers tightened around Sharon's. The hint of a grin, rueful and brief, touched his mouth. "The answer to that should be obvious. I wanted you to be jealous."

Sharon bit her lower lip, then replied, "It worked."

Tony turned toward her then; with his free hand, he cupped her chin. "When that Swede kissed you at the party last night, I almost came out of my skin. So maybe we're even."

"Maybe," Sharon agreed with a tentative smile. She had a scary, excited feeling, as though she were setting out to cross deep waters hidden under a thin layer of ice. She was putting everything at risk, but with ever so much to be gained should she make it to the other side.

Cautiously, Tony kissed her. The fire crackled on the hearth and, in the distance, a ferry whistle made a mournful sound. After long moments of sweet anguish, he released her mouth to brush his lips along the length of her neck.

"Did your father tell you to do this, too?" Sharon asked, her voice trembling.

Tony chuckled and went right on driving her crazy. "He did suggest wine and music. I suppose he figured I could come up with the rest on my own."

Sharon closed her eyes, filled with achy yearnings. She was facing Tony now, her arms resting lightly around his neck. "Remember," she whispered, "how it used to be? When Bri was little?"

He had returned to her mouth, and sharp desire stabbed through her as he teased and tasted her. "Um-hmm. We made love on the living room floor with the stereo playing."

"Tony." The word sounded breathless and uncertain. "What?"

"I don't see how we're going to settle anything by doing this."

She felt his smile against her lips; its warmth seemed to reach into the very depths of her being. "Let me state my position on this issue," he whispered. "I love you. I want you. And I'm not going to be able to concentrate on anything until I've had you."

Sharon trembled. "You've got your priorities in order, Morelli—I'll say that for you."

He drew her sweater up over her head and tossed it away, then unfastened her bra. Sharon drew in a sharp breath when he took both her breasts into his hands, gently chafing the nipples with the sides of his thumbs. "I'm so glad you approve," he teased gruffly, bending his head to taste her.

Sharon muffled a groan of pure pleasure and buried her fingers in his hair as he indulged. "I think—I see where we—went wrong," she managed to say. "We should never have—gotten out of bed."

Tony's chuckle felt as good against her nipple as his tongue. "Sharon?"

"What?"

"Shut up."

She moaned, arching her neck as he pressed her down onto her back and unsnapped her jeans. He left her to turn out the lights and press a button on the stereo.

The room was filled with music and the gracious glow of the fire, and Tony knelt beside the sofa to caress her.

A tender delirium possessed Sharon as Tony reminded her that he knew her body almost as well as she did. There was an interval during which he drew ever greater, ever more primitive responses from her, and then he stood and lifted her into his arms. She worked the buttons on his shirt as he carried her up the stairs and into the bedroom.

The light of a November moon streamed over Tony's muscular chest and caught the tousled ebony of his hair as Sharon undressed him. In those moments she prayed to love Tony less because what she felt was too fierce and too beautiful to be endured.

He tensed as she touched one taut masculine nipple with the tip of her tongue, and she knew that the anticipation he felt was almost beyond his ability to bear. The words that fell from his lips as she pleasured him belonged not to earth but to a world that love had created, and while Sharon couldn't have defined a single one, she understood them in her heart.

When Tony had reached the limits of his control, he used gentle force to subdue Sharon; after lowering her to the bed, he clasped her wrists in his hands and stretched her arms above her head. His body, as lean and dynamic as a panther's, was poised over hers. In the icy, silver light of the moon, Sharon saw in his face both the tenderness of a lover and the hunger of a predator.

She lifted her head to kiss the curve of his collarbone. Tony could no longer restrain himself; his mouth fell to Sharon's as if he would consume her. A few hoarse, intimate words passed between them, and then, with a grace born of mutual desperation, they were joined.

Tony's and Sharon's bodies seemed to war with each other even as their souls struggled to fuse into one spirit. The skirmish began on earth and ended square in the center of heaven, and the lovers clung to each other as they drifted back to the plane where mortals belong.

When Tony collapsed beside her, still breathing hard, Sharon rolled over to look down into his face, one of her legs resting across his. She kissed the almost imperceptible cleft in his chin.

"I think my toes have melted," she confided with a contented sigh.

Tony put his arms around her, positioning her so that she lay on top of him. "Promise me something," he said, when his breathing had returned to normal. "The next time I make you mad, remember that I'm the same man who melts your toes, will you?"

Sharon kissed him. "I'll try," she said, snuggling down to lie beside Tony and wishing that this accord they'd reached would last forever. Unfortunately, they couldn't spend the rest of their lives in bed.

"What are you thinking?" Tony asked when a long time had passed. He'd turned onto his side to look into Sharon's face, and he brushed her hair away from her cheek with a gentle motion of one hand.

"That I love you. Tony, I want to make this relationship work, but I don't know how."

He sat up and reached out to turn on the lamp on the bedside table. "I've got a few theories about that."

Wriggling to an upright position, Sharon folded her arms and braced herself. She had a pretty good idea what he was going to say—that she was spreading herself too thin, that their marriage would have lasted if she hadn't insisted on opening Teddy Bares....

Tony laughed and caught her chin in his hand. "Wait a minute. I can tell by the storm clouds gathering in your eyes that you're expecting my old me-Tarzan-you-Jane routine—and I wasn't planning to do that."

Sharon gave him a suspicious look. "Okay, so what's your theory, Morelli?"

He sighed. "That we don't fight fair. We sort of collide like bumper cars at a carnival—and then bounce off each other. I try to hurt you and you try to hurt me, and nothing ever gets settled because we're both so busy retaliating or making up that we never talk about what's really wrong."

"That makes a scary kind of sense," Sharon admitted in a small voice. She couldn't look at Tony, so she concentrated on chipping the polish off the nail of her right index finger. "Where do we start?"

"With Carmen, I think," he said quietly.

Even after ten years as Tony's wife, after bearing one of his children and raising the other as her own, Carmen's name made Sharon feel defensive and angry. "I hate her," she confessed.

"I know," Tony replied.

Sharon made herself meet his gaze. "That's really stupid, isn't it?"

His broad, naked shoulders moved in a shrug. "I don't know if I'd go so far as to say that. It's certainly futile."

"You loved her."

"I never denied that."

Sharon drew in a deep, shaky breath. "Even after you married me," she said, "I was a replacement for Carmen at first, wasn't I?"

He shoved a hand through his hair and, for a fraction of a second, his eyes snapped and the line of his jaw went hard. At the last moment he stopped himself from bouncing off of her like one of those carnival bumper cars he'd mentioned earlier. "It's true that I didn't take the time to work through my grief like I should have," he admitted after a long time. "The loneliness—I don't know if I can explain what it was like. It tore at me. I couldn't stand being by myself, but hanging around my family was even worse because they all seemed to have some kind of handle on their lives and I didn't."

Tentatively, Sharon reached out and took Tony's hand in hers. "Go on."

"There isn't much else to say, Sharon. I did want a wife, and I wanted a mother for Briana—but I wouldn't have had to look beyond Mama's Christmas card list for a woman to fill those roles. Mama, my aunts and sisters and female cousins—they all had prospects in mind. I married you because I wanted you."

Sharon was watching Tony's face. "You wanted me? Is that all?"

Tony sighed and tilted back his head, gazing forlornly up at the ceiling. "No. I loved you, but I didn't realize it at the time. I was using you."

This honesty business hurt. "You—you wanted out, I suppose."

His arm moved around her shoulders, and he drew her close. "Never," he answered. "Do you know when I figured out that I loved you as much as I'd ever loved Carmen? It was at that Fourth of July picnic when you climbed fifteen feet up a damned pine tree to get some kid's toy plane and broke your arm taking a shortcut down."

Sharon was amazed. Her predominant memory of that first Independence Day after their marriage had been that she'd missed out on the fireworks and her share of cold watermelon because she'd spent most of the afternoon and evening in the hospital getting X rays and having a cast put on. "That made you fall in love with me? You're a hard man to please, Morelli."

He turned his head to kiss her temple. "You're not listening. I said I realized that day that what I'd felt for you all along was love."

They were silent for a few minutes, both of them lost in their own thoughts, but Sharon finally said, "I didn't grow up in a family like yours, Tony. I didn't—and don't—have your self-confidence. My insecurities have caused a lot of problems—I can see that now." She paused and sighed sadly. "And then there's Teddy Bares. How do you really feel about my business?"

"I hate it," he answered politely. "But that's my problem, not yours." Tony scooted down far enough to give Sharon a mischievous kiss. "I'll work through it."

Sharon felt a quiet happiness steal through her. "Are you saying that you want to try again?"

He cupped her breast with his hand. "Yes," he answered bluntly. "Will you give me a second chance?"

"At marriage, or our favorite nighttime activity?" Sharon teased.

Tony began to caress her. "Marriage. If I can dissolve your toes, lady, it would seem that I've got a handle on the rest."

Sharon laughed, then gave a little crooning groan as his hand moved downward to make tantalizing circles on her stomach. "It would—seem so," she agreed.

He slid beneath the covers, and his tongue encircled one of Sharon's nipples. "Marry me," he said. "Please?"

She gasped as Tony began to work his private magic. "Maybe—maybe we should live together first," she managed to say. "Until we learn to fight correctly."

"Fine," Tony agreed, preoccupied. "You explain it to Matt and Bri. And my grandmother. And—"

"I'll marry you," Sharon broke in. She pretty much knew when she was beaten. "But there will probably be a lot of fights. We'll both have to make a great many adjustments...."

"Um-hmm," Tony replied, sounding downright disinterested now. "Probably."

He was doing such delicious things to her that it was hard to speak normally. "Sometimes I'll win, and sometimes you will."

Tony flung back the covers and reached out to turn off the lamp. "I'm pretty sure you'll still be talking," he said, gathering her close to him.

He was wrong. Sharon was through talking.

When Sharon awakened the next morning, Tony wasn't in bed. She was worried for a moment until she heard him running up the stairs.

He burst into the bedroom, wearing running shorts and a tank top and dripping sweat. He gave Sharon a grin and disappeared into the bathroom to take his shower.

She waited until she heard the water come on, then went to join him.

That day was magical. They walked along the beach, hand in hand, talking, saying what they really felt, dreaming aloud and deciding how to interweave their separate hopes. They even argued at odd intervals.

It was late that night, when they were eating a complicated pasta concoction that Tony had whipped up, that the first real test of their resolve to be truthful came up.

Sharon had been talking about the opportunity she'd missed because she hadn't been able to go to Paris, and

Tony said, "If you needed money, you should have asked me."

Curled up in the easy chair in front of the hearth, Sharon lowered her fork back to her plate and said quietly, "I couldn't."

Tony qualified her statement. "Because of your damned pride."

"As if you didn't have any."

A tempest was brewing in those dark, spirited eyes, but it ebbed away as fast as it had arisen, and Tony smiled, albeit sheepishly. "Okay. Back to our corners—no kidney punches and no hitting below the belt."

With a mischievous grin, Sharon set aside her plate, got out of her chair and turned the music on and the lights off. There was a nice blaze in the fireplace, and she stretched out on the floor in front of the hearth, letting the light and warmth wash over her.

When Tony joined her, she reached up and put her arms around his neck. "I've missed you so much," she said as the music swelled around them like an invisible river. Soon, it would lift them up and carry them away, and Sharon had no intention of swimming against the current. "I love you," she whispered, pulling Tony downward into her kiss.

Soon they were spinning and whirling in a torrent of sensation, and it ended with Sharon arching her back in a powerful spasm of release and crying out for Tony as she ran her hands feverishly over his flesh. He spoke tender, soothing words to her even as he tensed in the throes of his own gratification.

The big house was full of laughter and the scent of roasting turkey when Sharon and Tony arrived, and Vincent smiled when he saw them. It was Maria who took Sharon's hands in her own and thus noticed the wide golden band on her finger.

"When?" she asked, her eyes bright with joy.

Tony kissed her forehead. Before he could answer, though, Briana and Matt made their way through the crowd of cousins and aunts and uncles, approaching from different directions but arriving at the same moment.

"Something's happened," Bri said, assessing her father and then Sharon. "What is it?"

"They're married, metal-mouth," Matt told her with affectionate disdain. "Can't you see those rings they're wearing?"

Sharon nodded in answer to the hopeful question she saw shining in Bri's eyes, and the girl flung herself into her stepmother's arms with a cry of joy.

Michael, in the meantime, was shaking Tony's hand. "Does this mean you're going to be fit to work with again?" he asked, his voice gruff, his eyes shining.

Tony laughed and lifted an excited Matt into his arms.

"We're all going to live together in the same house now, right?" the little boy wanted to know.

"Right," Tony confirmed.

"How did you two manage to get a license so fast?" Tony's sister Rose demanded from somewhere in the throng of delighted relatives.

"We were married in Nevada this morning, and I chartered a plane to fly us here," he explained. "Is everybody satisfied, or do I have to call a press conference?"

Sharon got out of her coat with some help from Tony, and went into the kitchen with Maria. Bri and Rose followed.

The place was a giant cornucopia—there were pies, candied yams, special vegetable dishes, gelatin salads, cranberry sauce—all the traditional foods. Sharon wanted to help, to be a part of the festivities, and she went to the sink and started peeling the mountain of potatoes waiting there.

Maria was preparing a relish tray nearby, and Bri and Rose were arguing good-naturedly over the football game that would be played that afternoon. They weren't concerned with who would win or lose; the bone of contention was which team had the cuter players.

Within the next hour, dinner was ready to be served and Bea had arrived in her old car, proudly presenting her three-bean casserole as a contribution.

Sitting beside Tony, her hand resting in his on the tabletop, Sharon counted the men, women and children gathered to give thanks under the Morelli roof. There were forty-three smiling faces around the card tables and the oaken one that had been a part of Lucia's dowry.

A reverent prayer was said, and then Vincent began carving the first of three turkeys with great fanfare. Sharon felt the sting of happy tears in her eyes when she turned to look at Tony, then Briana, then Matt.

She offered a silent prayer of her own, one of true thanksgiving, and laughed and cheered Vincent's expertise as a turkey carver with the rest of the family.

Her family.

\* \* \* \* \*

# RISKY PLEASURES

Brenda Jackson

To Gerald Jackson, Sr.,
the man who shows me what true love is all about.

To all my readers who participated in
the Madaris/Westmoreland/Steele
Family Reunion Cruise, 2007, this one is for you.

To my Heavenly Father,
who gave me the gift to write.


Plans fail for lack of counsel,
but with many advisers they succeed.
—*Proverbs* 15:22

# Prologue

"Take it from someone who almost found out the hard way, Van. Running away never solves anything."

Vanessa Steele shifted her gaze from the open suitcase to the woman standing in her doorway. Sienna Bradford had been her best friend since grade school, but it bothered Vanessa that at times Sienna thought she knew her better than she knew herself. Unfortunately, some times Sienna actually did.

"I am not running away." But not even Vanessa's short, gruff tone could convince anyone that she wasn't getting the hell out of Dodge because a certain man by the name of Cameron Cody was on his way to Charlotte, supposedly to spend some time visiting with her cousins.

"Then please explain what you're doing if you're not running away."

Vanessa sighed and tossed aside the blouse she was about to pack. "I'm leaving for Jamaica because Cheyenne called and asked if I would house-sit while the builders are putting in her pool. She hadn't planned on having to go to Italy for an unscheduled photo shoot," Vanessa said of her sister, an international model. "There's not a lot happening at work and a vacation in Jamaica is just what I need."

Sienna arched a brow. "And your leaving has nothing to do with Cameron coming to town?"

Vanessa nervously averted her gaze. "I wish I can say one has nothing to do with the other but that wouldn't be true and you and I both know it. Cheyenne's phone call gave me the out I need, and I'm taking it."

Sienna came farther into the room, forcing Vanessa to look at her. "What are you afraid of, Van? Why do you feel so much dislike and anger toward one man?"

"You of all people know why, Sienna. You know what Cameron tried to do to my family's business."

"Yes, but that was three years ago. And if your cousins have gotten over it and consider him a friend, why can't you?"

"I'll never consider that man a friend," Vanessa snapped.

"Then maybe you need to wonder why," Sienna replied smoothly. "There has to be a reason for your intense dislike of him."

Vanessa rolled her eyes. "There is, and I've told you what it is."

"I only know what you've convinced yourself it is."

Vanessa lifted a brow. "And what's that supposed to mean?"

"Only that I have eyes. I've been watching you and Cameron for a while now, especially at Morgan and

Lena's wedding last month. What I saw between you wasn't animosity, but a buildup of sexual chemistry of the most potent and compelling kind. And I think the reason you don't like being around him is because, if given the chance, you'd want to have your way with him." Sienna grinned. "You'd probably jump his bones in a heartbeat."

"What!" Vanessa exclaimed, folding her arms over her chest and giving her pregnant best friend an incredulous look. "How can you even think of anything so ridiculous?"

"Is it really so ridiculous, Vanessa? Think about it. He's the only man I know who has pushed your buttons since that guy you met in London."

"Well, yeah, that might be true, but he's pushing them the wrong way."

"And what if he starts pushing them the right way? What if one day you discover that Cameron isn't as bad as you think and that an affair with him is just what you need to take the edge off?"

Vanessa laughed. "I don't have an edge on."

"Yes, you do, and we both know it."

Vanessa walked over to her bedroom window and looked out. Yes, she had an edge on, all right. Not that she was counting, but it had been almost four years since that summer she'd spent in London with Harlan, a man she had fancied herself in love with. But Harlan couldn't hold a candle to Cameron Cody. As far as she was concerned, Cameron was the sexiest, most handsome man alive—which wasn't helping matters. It would be a lie to say she hadn't thought about doing him, because she had. A part of her saw it as the perfect way to get him out of her system. Right?

Wrong.

Another part of her saw it as dominance on his part, a sure victory for him. Eventually he'd take her over just as he'd enjoyed taking over corporations that suited his fancy. He had a reputation that made Genghis Khan look like a choirboy.

"Van?"

She turned back around to Sienna. "Are you suggesting that I engage in an affair with Cameron? Especially after what Harlan said?"

Sienna frowned and rubbed her stomach as she felt her baby kick. "Forget about what Harlan Shaw said. As far as I'm concerned, an affair with Cameron sounds like a good plan to me. You're twenty-six, old enough to know the score, and you and Cameron are spontaneous combustion just waiting to happen. I've never been around two more volatile individuals. And I'm not the only one who can feel the intensity, the passion, when the two of you are in the same room. Do us all a favor and finally do something about it."

Vanessa fought back the fear that ran through her at the mere thought of what would happen if she followed Sienna's suggestion. She would find herself at Cameron's mercy, become beholden to him—as she had to Harlan—and the thought of that filled her with disgust. On the other hand, the thought of sharing a bed with Cameron and finally letting go, putting aside her dislike of him to appease her overworked hormones, suddenly replaced the fear with red-hot pleasure. Wanton pleasure. It would be risky pleasure of the most intense type, the kind that would finally take the edge off. Her insides quivered at the very idea of Cameron giving her the best sex of her life. It was too much to think about. Downright scary.

She never wanted to be that vulnerable to a man. Especially not *that* man. There was so much about him she disliked. His chauvinistic, egoistical attitude was one a modern, liberated woman like herself couldn't stand or tolerate. Besides, there was her concern about just what kind of bed partner she would be. According to Harlan, she needed vast improvement in that area.

"Will it help matters if I promise to give it some thought while I'm relaxing on the beach in Jamaica?" Vanessa finally asked.

"You can't run forever. At some point you're going to have to stop running and do something about Cameron. It's obvious that he wants you, Van, and he comes across as a man who gets whatever he wants."

That was exactly what had her worried, Vanessa admitted silently. For some reason she had a feeling that Cameron's upcoming visit had a purpose, one that involved her. Maybe it was the way he had looked at her at the wedding, as if her time for avoiding him was up and that he was about to make his move. Unfortunately, it would be a wasted trip. When he arrived in Charlotte, she'd be long gone.

# Chapter 1

*This is paradise,* Vanessa thought as she stood on the shore of the white-sand beach that overlooked the deep blue waters of the Caribbean Sea. Cheyenne's two-story home was located on a secluded cove in Montero Bay, on a private street with one other house.

Other than the pool workers, who arrived at nine and left by five, Vanessa was alone, except for the two days a week that the housekeeper showed up.

Cheyenne had already left for Italy by the time Vanessa had arrived so her first days were spent unpacking and shopping.

This was day three and she had decided just to do nothing. Since weather reports had predicted it would be another scorcher of a late-July day, she stayed inside working crossword puzzles and sipping lemonade while reading a book she had picked up yesterday. Later that day, after the workers had left, she gathered up her large straw hat, her beach bag, which was stuffed with a bottle of wine and a glass, and a huge towel to head down to the beach.

When she reached what she considered a good spot, she casually glanced around. This stretch of private beach was shared only by whoever was living in the house next door and so far the place appeared empty. According to Helen, Cheyenne's housekeeper, the house had changed ownership several times, and rumor had it someone had recently purchased it.

Helen had gone on to say that a few years ago, the house had been owned by some gorgeous Italian jet-setting playboy by the name of Chardon Argentina. And if you went along with what everyone believed, a number of seductions had taken place in that house. It was even rumored that many of Hollywood's leading ladies had been overnight guests.

Vanessa shrugged as she spread the huge towel on the sand and sat down. She was glad she didn't believe everything she heard. Besides, what had happened in that house was not her business. After placing the huge straw hat on her head and situating the brim in such a way as to block what was left of the sun, she glanced toward the ocean, thinking she could definitely get used to this. She'd never had an entire beach to herself. She was glad that Cheyenne had invited her to stay.

She, Taylor and Cheyenne had always been close, but it was Vanessa who had decided to stick with the family business instead of pursuing other careers as her sisters had. She had returned home to Charlotte and the Steele Corporation after getting a grad degree from Tennessee State.

Taylor, who was twenty-four, had graduated from Georgetown with a degree in business and a grad degree in finance. After college, she'd moved to New York to work at a major bank as a wealth asset manager and was doing quite well for herself.

After obtaining a degree in communications from Boston University, Cheyenne, who was twenty-two, had taken a reporter position at a television station in Philly and in less than a year, her looks, personality and keen intelligence had gotten her a promotion to the position of anchorwoman on the morning news. That job was short-lived as she had suddenly realized she wanted to do something different and had become a model. Modeling meant a lot of traveling and living in some of the most beautiful and exotic places in the world. A year ago, Cheyenne had been doing a photo shoot in Jamaica when she'd stumbled across this particular house, fallen in love with it and purchased it.

Vanessa leaned back on her arms with her legs stretched out in front of her. She tilted her head back to enjoy the feel of the evening sun on her face, as well as the salty spray from the ocean on her cheeks and lips. She couldn't help wondering what was happening back in Charlotte. Had Cameron arrived yet? Had he discovered her gone? Was he upset about it? Why did she even care?

She was deep into her thoughts when a movement caught her eye, and she turned her head. In the distance, in front of the property next door, she could see a man standing close to shore. With the palm trees partially blocking her view, she couldn't make out his features, but she could tell he wore only a pair of swimming trunks. And he was overpoweringly male.

She sat up as her heart began pumping wildly in her chest, and she wondered what on earth was wrong with her. It wasn't as though she hadn't seen good-looking men before. So what was there about this tall, broad-shouldered, long-legged, fine-as-they-come brother whose aura was seeping out to her over stretches of sand? And what was there about him that seemed so oddly familiar?

Biting down on her lip, she fought against one particular ultrasexy male image that tried forcing its way into her mind. She simply refused to go there. She would not let Cameron creep into her thoughts. Tilting her head, she refocused her attention as she continued to gaze at the man, not seeing as much as she would like due to the shade cast by the palm trees, the fading evening sun and the emergence of dusk.

Since this was a private beach she quickly assumed he was the owner of the house next door and wondered who he was. A celebrity perhaps? Was he married, single or in between lovers like she was?

A lump caught in her throat when the man eased down his swimming trunks. It suddenly occurred to her that he was about to go swimming in the nude. Although their properties were separated only by a few palm trees, she wondered if he hadn't noticed her sitting here—if he had, evidently he didn't care.

She knew the decent thing to do was to ignore him, but she couldn't pull her gaze away. When he had completely removed the trunks, she held her breath and wished like hell that she had a pair of binoculars.

Reaching into her beach bag, she pulled out the bottle of wine and wineglass she had packed. By the time the man had dived into the ocean water she had not only poured a glassful but had quickly tossed back the contents, liking how the soothing liquid had flowed down her throat.

She decided to pour another glass, taking her eyes off the man for just a second. When she looked back, pausing with the wineglass halfway to her lips, he was gone. She sighed, wondering if she'd really seen him or if he'd been a mirage, a cruel trick of her imagination.

As she took a sip of her wine to calm her racing heart, a part of her knew that what she'd seen earlier had been the real thing.


Cameron Cody stood at the window and watched as the woman he intended to marry gathered up her belongings to walk back to the house where she would be staying for two weeks.

He didn't want to think what her reaction would be once she discovered he was her neighbor and that her flight from Charlotte had been for nothing. As soon as he had gotten word—thanks to her cousin and his loyal friend Morgan Steele—that she intended to leave the country for a few weeks to house-sit her sister's home in Jamaica, he had changed his plans. No big deal. Where she went, he intended to follow. Her time for avoiding him had run out. At thirty-five, he was no longer interested in playing games. He was ready to make his move.

When he was sure Vanessa was safely inside the house, he moved away from the window toward the wet bar to pour himself a drink. He glanced around the home he had recently purchased, wanting to believe that luck was still on his side. It had been easy enough to buy this house within a matter of hours, his first move to gain what he considered the most valuable asset of his life.

As he sipped his brandy, he recalled the exact moment a little over three years ago when he had first laid eyes on Vanessa Steele. He had arrived at a very important Steele Corporation board meeting, one he'd assumed would give him total control of the Charlotte-based manufacturing company.

He had walked into the conference room, confident in his abilities and pretty damn positive that one of the Steeles would defect and throw their voting shares his way. After all, past experience had shown him that if offered the right price, family members had a tendency to prove that blood might be thicker than water but not thicker than the mighty dollar.

The Steeles had proved him wrong that day.

In less than an hour he had walked away after encountering the first defeat of his career as a corporate raider. But that afternoon hadn't been a complete waste, since he had sat across the table from the most beautiful woman he'd ever seen. He could admit now that he had focused his attention more on Vanessa Steele than on taking over her family's company.

The memory of that day would forever be etched in his mind. Something about Vanessa had immediately captured his attention. The moment he had gazed into her eyes he had suffered an instant jolt in his gut. He'd been mesmerized, awestruck and captivated all at the same time. The other two Steele women had been just as good-looking, but it had been Vanessa who had caused his body and mind to react in all sorts of ways. Everything about her had turned him on, even when she had glared at him, which she'd spent most of her time doing.

During the years that followed, he and members of the Steele family had put the takeover attempt behind them. He was close friends with Vanessa's four older male cousins, especially Morgan, whom he considered one of his best friends. He even got along with her two sisters whenever their paths crossed. But Vanessa hung back, refusing to accept friendship or anything else from him.

She was different from the women he usually dated, since his taste ran to the tall, willowy, talk-only-if-you're-asked-to-speak kind. At five foot eight, she came up to his nose. He'd discovered that fact the one and only time he'd caught her unawares and had gotten up close. And instead of a willowy figure she had a feminine one, with a small waist and seductive curves to her hips. Whenever she passed, every male took notice. And then there was her face. It seemed the hairstyle she wore, short and flippy, was created just for her; it emphasized her ethereal facial features. Dark eyes, a voluptuously formed mouth, a chin imbued with intense stubbornness, and high cheekbones, compliments of her Cheyenne ancestry from her mother's side.

That day in the conference room he knew she had felt the intensity of his attention and hadn't liked it. That hadn't diminished his feelings for her, even though he'd known he should walk away and leave her alone. Ten years ago, at the age of twenty-five, he had learned one hard lesson when it came to matters of the heart. Stay clear of them. A woman who got too deep under a man's skin could ultimately become his downfall. Besides, he needed to use his time working deals and not pursuing resistant women.

But he had ignored the warning bells and now after three years of playing a no-win game, he was ready to pursue a relationship and come out a winner. Some would even go so far as to say that he'd taken drastic measures. All he said was that there came a time when a man had to do what a man had to do. Now he was finally going to do something about this chronic tug of desire that claimed his body each and every time he saw her or thought about her—which was all the time.

Today on the beach she had been wearing a wrap over her bathing suit, but she'd still looked good. He remembered the way the straps of the wrap had hung off her shoulders and how those graceful legs of hers moved when she walked. And when she had sat down and leaned back on her arms and stretched out her legs, he had gotten a nice view of her thigh, and even from a distance he had become so aroused that he'd had to jump into the ocean waters to cool off.

Cameron couldn't retract the smile that touched his lips. Experience had taught him a valuable lesson—if there was something you wanted, then you put all your efforts into getting it. You didn't wait for it to come to you or you'd never have it. And he was a man with a reputation for going after whatever it was he wanted. Hence, here he was, on this beautiful tropical island, going after Vanessa.

By this time tomorrow she would know that he was her neighbor. She would also know that for the remainder of her time on the island, he intended to seduce the hell out of her.

The last time he'd come up against the Steeles, he had failed. This time he would only be dealing with one.

Vanessa. He wanted her and no matter what it took, he wouldn't fail at having her.

The ringing of his cell phone crashed its way into his thoughts. Annoyed at the interruption, he picked it up and flipped it open. "Yes, what is it?" he said gruffly.

"McMurray is trying to fight back."

Cameron recognized the caller's voice immediately. Xavier Kane was not only his right-hand man but also a good friend. The two had met at Harvard when Cameron was in business school and Xavier in law school. Though both had been loners, somehow they'd forged a bond that was still intact today. For years Cameron had tried to convince Xavier to come work for him, knowing it would only be a matter of time before his friend got tired of defending men who were guilty of white-collar crimes. Cameron had needed someone to have his back, someone he trusted implicitly, and X was that man. Now Xavier handled all the legal aspects of Cody Enterprises.

A faint smile touched Cameron's lips. "He can fight back, although it's rather late since Global Petroleum is now legally mine."

"Well, I just thought you should know that he held a press conference today, and I don't have to tell you that he painted you as someone who won't have any sympathy or loyalty with the present workers when you clean house."

Cameron shook his head. "I bet while he was in front of the camera he didn't happen to mention how he messed up his employees' pension plan or how they were about to lose their jobs anyway at the rate he was going."

"Of course he didn't. His intent was to make you look bad. And when I called him to let him know we wouldn't hesitate to take him to court for slander, he made a threat."

Cameron raised a dark brow. "What kind of threat?"

"That you're going to regret the day you were ever born for taking his company away."

Cameron shook his head. "He brought that on himself."

"You and I both know he doesn't see things that way. And there's no telling what will happen when he finds out your connection to his company. After all this time he's evidently put behind him his bad deeds of yesteryear."

Cameron's face hardened. "He might have, but I haven't."

"Just be prepared, Cam. All hell's going to break loose when he discovers why you took his company away."

"How he handles things doesn't matter to me, X, and as far as I'm concerned, John McMurray is serving no purpose by causing problems now."

"Yes, but I've always told you that there's something about him that bothers me. It's like he's not working with a full deck most of the time. As a safety precaution I'm going to let Kurt know what's going on. I want to make sure his men know that McMurray is not allowed back on the premises. If he hasn't cleaned out his desk by now, we'll ship his things to him."

"I agree we should tell Kurt." Kurt Grainger, another college friend, headed up security for Cody Enterprises.

A few moments later, after hanging up the phone, Cameron banished John McMurray from his mind. The only thing he wanted occupying his mind were thoughts of a woman by the name of Vanessa Steele.

# Chapter 2

"What neighbor?"

Vanessa tapped her foot impatiently on the ceramic tile floor. "I'm talking about the man who lives next door, Cheyenne," she said trying to hide her frustration. She had a harder time squashing the irritation she felt with herself for being so curious about the man's identity.

It was morning and the pol workers were ten minutes late already. She couldn't wait to gather her stuff and go back down to the beach in hopes that she would see the stranger again. For some reason he had played on her thoughts all night.

"I truly don't know anything about a man living next door," Cheyenne said convincingly. "That house has been up for sale for a while, but I hadn't heard anything of a new owner. It must have been rather recent."

After a brief pause, Cheyenne then asked, "Why are you interested in my new neighbor, Van?"

Vanessa frowned and searched her mind for a reason her sister would believe and decided to be honest. "I saw him yesterday. At least I caught a glimpse of him," she said, deciding not to tell Cheyenne about the man swimming in the nude. "And I liked what I saw."

"Umm, your hormones acting up, are they?" her sister asked in a teasing voice.

"You sound like Sienna, and no, my hormones are not acting up. It was the usual reaction a woman would have to a good-looking man."

"Then do something about it. Be neighborly and go over there, introduce yourself and welcome him to the neighborhood."

Vanessa's mouth quirked. Of the three of them Cheyenne had always been the most daring. "I can't do that."

"Sure you can. You're a liberated woman. You don't have to wait for the man to make the first move. What are you afraid of?"

That was the same question Sienna had asked her about Cameron. "I'm not afraid of anything," she came back to say. She was wrong, though. She was afraid of something. Rejection. Thanks to Harlan Shaw.

"Well, my advice is, if you're interested, act on it."

"Goodbye, Cheyenne."

"Why do you always do that, Van? When someone tells you something you don't want to hear, you bow out in a hurry."

"You just answered your own question, Cheyenne," she said with a weak smile in her voice. "You're telling me something I really don't want to hear. Love you. Goodbye."

Vanessa hung up the phone.

* * *

A couple of hours later, Vanessa stood in her sister's kitchen with her back against the counter looking at the picnic basket she had placed on the table. It was her idea of a welcome-to-the-neighborhood gift and contained a bottle of spring water, a block of cheese she had picked up from the market two days ago, as well as a pack of crackers. Then there was the fruit she had added, and for dessert, oatmeal raisin cookies she had baked.

Vanessa knew if either Taylor or Cheyenne was putting the basket together they would probably include a tablecloth, the proper eating utensils and enough food for two with the intent of joining him in a picnic instead of giving him everything he needed to enjoy on his own. To say both of her sisters were bold when it came to dating was an understatement. But then neither had encountered the likes of Harlan, the man responsible for rattling her self-confidence.

In fact, neither of her sisters nor her cousins had ever heard of him. The only person who'd known about him was Sienna. Vanessa had immediately been taken with Harlan's handsome features and smooth talk while vacationing for two weeks in London four years ago. He'd been a college professor from Los Angeles on a year's sabbatical doing research for a book he was writing.

She'd thought he was special, an intellectual genius. She'd also assumed that he had fallen in love with her, as she had with him, and that he would want to continue what they'd started once she returned to the States. Instead, on the last night they spent together, the one and only time they'd been intimate, he'd told her they were through. She hadn't been everything that he fully desired from a woman in bed. After the pain of his cruel words, she had made a decision not to let any man close enough to break her heart again. That was the main reason she kept a comfortable distance between herself and Cameron Cody. She would admit—but only to herself and only when she was in a good mood—that she was attracted to him, but her mother hadn't raised her to be a fool twice over.

So instead of being as bold as she wanted to be and inviting the man next door to picnic with her on the beach, she would do the neighborly thing and present him with a welcome basket and leave. She wouldn't even enter his home if he invited her inside. He was a stranger and she knew nothing about him. He could be married or some woman's fiancé. She had enough to keep her mind occupied over the next two weeks. She certainly didn't need a man around causing problems. All she had to do when she felt weak was to remember Harlan, although she had to admit Harlan's memory had a tendency to fade to black when Cameron was around.

She walked over to the basket, opened the lid and did a quick check to make sure she hadn't forgotten anything. She wondered what Mr. Neighbor would think when she appeared on his doorstep. She intended to meet the man then put him out of her thoughts once and for all.

Little Red Riding Hood.

That was the first thought that came to Cameron's mind when he glanced out his library window and saw the feminine figure coming up his walkway dressed in a red shorts set, a red straw hat and carrying a picnic basket. He pasted a smile on his lips. It seemed that

Vanessa would be finding out his identity sooner than he had anticipated, but that was just as well.

He stood and pressed the intercom button on his desk and within minutes an elderly lady appeared. It seemed that Martha Pritchett came with the house, having been housekeeper to the previous four owners, over a period of fifteen years. She had been born and raised on the island and arrived early on Monday, Wednesday and Friday mornings. He really didn't need her that often and with little to do, she usually left by noon. But during the time she was there, he'd found her to be very efficient.

"Yes, Mr. Cody?"

"I'm about to get a visitor."

"And you want me to send them away," she said quickly, assuming what would be his position on unwelcome guests.

In most circumstances she wasn't far off the mark, but in this case, the last thing he wanted was Vanessa sent away. "No. I want you to do whatever it takes to encourage her to stay. I'm going upstairs to change and will be back down in a minute."

"Yes, sir."

"And in case it comes up in conversation, I prefer that you not give her my name."

If Martha found his request strange, her expression didn't show it. "All right."

With adrenaline of the strongest kind rushing through his veins, Cameron turned and left the room.

Vanessa stood, stretched and for the third time dismissed the idea of leaving before officially meeting her neighbor. She'd only rung his bell once when the door had been opened by an elderly lady with a huge smile who'd introduced herself as Martha.

Vanessa had given her the spiel of wanting to welcome her sister's new neighbor, and then, without batting an eye, the older woman had ushered her inside. That had been a little over five minutes ago. Explaining that the master of the house would be down shortly, she led Vanessa to the massive living room. A few moments later she had returned with a tray of hot tea and the most delicious tea cakes Vanessa had ever eaten. Then she had excused herself.

Vanessa glanced around the room, admiring everything she saw and wondering if the decorating was the taste of the present owner or if, as in the case of Cheyenne's home, the furnishings had come with the house. Whichever the case, Vanessa was in awe of the furniture's rich design, as well as the cost of the paintings that hung on the walls. Being best friend to Sienna, who was an interior designer, had acquainted her with the different designs and style of furniture and it was plain to see everything in the house spoke of wealth.

And then there was this breathtaking view of the ocean through the large floor-to-ceiling window. She could stand there looking out at that view for hours, but she didn't have that much time to spare, she thought, glancing at her watch. The five-minute wait time had stretched to seven, and a part of her refused to be kept waiting any longer. Besides, each and every time she was reminded of what she had seen of her neighbor yesterday made goose bumps form on her arms. What if he walked into the room wearing something as skimpy as the swimming trunks he'd had on yesterday? Or, worse yet, what if he was bold enough to walk into the room wearing nothing at all?

Vanessa felt her face flush at the thought and immediately decided maybe coming here hadn't been a good idea after all. She should have waited until their paths crossed on the beach or something. Sighing, she was about to turn around when she heard a deep husky voice behind her.

"Sorry to keep you waiting."

Vanessa went still. She knew that voice. She knew that sensual texture, that smooth timbre, that silky reverberation. Her throat immediately tightened around the gasp that formed in it. She felt heat flow up her arms as a tingling sensation swept through her at the same time that realization streamed all through her. It was highly unlikely that two men could produce that same sexy sound. It was a voice she'd always thought was meant to seduce, and it could only belong to one man.

She quickly turned around and her gaze clashed with dark eyes, the same dark eyes she often fantasized about at night in the privacy of her bedroom. Before she could utter his name in shock and disbelief, she watched as a small smile touched the corners of his lips right before he spoke.

"Hello, Vanessa. Welcome to my home."

"Your home?" Vanessa snapped the words as she fought the intense anger that was coursing through her, consuming every part of her body. If this was somebody's idea of a joke, she wasn't at all amused. She closed her eyes, hoping this was a bad dream. There was no way Cameron Cody could be here when he was supposed to be in Charlotte. But seconds later, when she reopened her eyes, he still stood across the room, staring at her. She could feel her blood pressure rise.

Her gaze swept over him. His head was clean-shaven, his eyes deep and dark. An angular jaw with a cleft in the chin completed an outrageously handsome face. This was the first time she'd seen him wearing anything other than a business suit or tux, but the jeans and pull-over shirt looked good on him. He appeared tall, solid, rugged and impenetrable. And just as yesterday, when she had seen him from a distance, his mere presence denoted some sort of masculine power.

"Yes, my home," he said, breaking into her thoughts and stepping into the room.

She narrowed her eyes and placed her hands on her hips. "And just when did you buy it?"

"A few days ago," he replied in a low, controlled voice, a sharp contrast to hers. She was livid and her voice reflected her emotion.

"Please don't tell me that you bought this house when you found out I was coming here."

He shoved his hands into the pockets of his jeans and met her narrowed gaze. Instead of showing any sign of wilting under her angry stare, he simply said, "Okay, then I won't tell you."

Vanessa heard her own teeth gnashing and wondered if he heard it, as well. Angrily, she strode to the center of the room to stand in front of him. "Just who the hell do you think you are?"

"I prefer to know *your* thoughts instead, Vanessa. You tell me who *you* think I am."

She tried not to notice the sexy drawl in his voice when he'd said her name, or the intense look in his eyes. She threw her head back and tilted it at an angle.

"I think you are the most ruthless, uncaring, callous, hard-nosed and unfeeling man that I know."

He nodded slowly and then said, "If you believe that, then it means you really don't know me very well, because I'm considerate, compassionate, loyal and passionate. I can prove it."

Of the four qualities he'd named the only one she could believe he had in his favor was passion. "I don't want you to prove anything. You being here and buying this house only show how far you'll go to get something you want, something you intend to possess. What is it about me that has become an obsession to you, Cameron? Is it because the Steele Corporation was the one company you couldn't get your cold, callous hands on and now you've decided to go after me for revenge?"

"My wanting you has nothing to do with revenge, Vanessa. It has everything to do with the intensity of my desire for you."

A part of Vanessa wished he hadn't said that one word, a word she'd been battling since meeting him. *Desire.* Cameron Cody wasn't a man a woman could ignore—at least not a woman with any degree of passion in her bones. There was something about him that grabbed you, snatched your attention the moment he walked into a room. It was something that went beyond just a handsome face and a well-built body. There was something perilous about him, something downright lethal. She was convinced that beneath his civilized side there was a part of him that could be downright ruthless, unrefined and plain old raw. Some women were drawn to such men, but she wasn't.

"I care nothing about the intensity of your desire for me," she finally said. "I just want to be left alone."

"I've left you alone long enough."

"Excuse me?"

"I said I've left you alone long enough," he drawled smoothly and in a way that had those same goose bumps reappearing on her arms. "I've given you more time than I've given anything I've ever wanted."

Fire flared in Vanessa's eyes. She couldn't believe the audacity of the man. "And should I feel grateful about that?"

Cameron moved a step closer. "It's not gratitude I want you to feel. Right now I want you to feel something else altogether."

Before she could blink, he stepped closer and pulled her into his arms. His mouth descended upon hers, snatching her next breath. For some reason that she didn't understand, instinctively her lips parted at the same time she felt strong hands wrap around her. Before she could register anything else, before she could regain total control of what was happening and stop it from going further, Cameron inserted his tongue into her mouth.

The moment she sampled his taste, just as bold and daring as the rest of him, she gasped. Then she moaned deep in her throat when her pulse rate escalated. Suddenly, she felt a spine-tingling sensation race through her body, along with an intense need to put all she had into this kiss.

The kiss was everything she'd hoped it would not be, the kind of kiss that drew her to him like a magnet. It was the kind of kiss that did more than give her a sampling of his taste. It was feeding her in a way she had never been fed before. His invasive tongue was doing things a male tongue had never done in her mouth before, making it an art. With other men, she had considered kissing a chore, something that was expected of you.

But Cameron was taking the art of French-kissing to a whole other level. It was downright scandalous, all the things he was doing. But a part of her didn't want him to stop. And he was getting her to join in the erotic byplay, something she had never done before.

She felt herself drowning in his sensuality, getting smothered in the passion. And she knew if she didn't put a stop to this madness now, he would claim a victory; the same way he did with anything else he went after. And she refused to become another one of his claimed possessions.

With more strength than she'd thought she had, she pushed herself out of his arms and inhaled deeply to regain control of her senses. She felt flustered and knew she probably looked it, as well. But to her way of thinking, he maintained a calm demeanor, looking totally in control, programmed and completely at ease. His coolness made her even angrier. It also proved what she'd said earlier. The man had no feelings.

"That should not have happened," she snapped.

"But it did, and it will again," he said with strong conviction in his voice. "We are two passionate individuals, Vanessa. The reason you didn't fight me off just now is because you've been aching to taste me just as long as I've been aching to taste you. And things won't stop there, sweetheart. They can only go further."

"No!"

"Yes. You can't fight me on this. Becoming mine is inevitable."

"Like hell!"

A small smile curved his wide mouth. "Actually it'll be more like heaven. That I promise you."

She took another step back. "Don't promise me anything, Cameron. Just stay away from me."

"Sorry, I can't do that."

Her mind registered his words but she refused to accept them. "I will fight you with every breath in my body."

"You do that. And at the same time I plan on claiming you with every breath in mine."

"You know nothing about me!"

"But I will. I intend to get to know everything about you, Vanessa. Count on it."

Knowing that continuing to exchange words with him was a complete waste of her time, she angrily moved around him to leave his home, pausing only to snatch her red straw hat off the table.

# Chapter 3

"Mr. Cody, what do you want me to do with the basket that Ms. Steele brought?"

Cameron forced his gaze from the window where he watched an angry Vanessa make her way down his palm-tree-lined driveway toward the path that would lead her back to her place. To say she was highly upset with him would be an understatement.

He turned slowly, took a deep breath and let it out before asking, "Where is it?"

"I placed it on the kitchen table."

"Leave it there. I'll take care of it."

"Yes, sir." She turned to leave.

"And, Martha?"

She turned back to him. "Yes, sir?"

"If Vanessa Steele ever returns, whether I'm here or not, she is welcome."

He was certain that after overhearing his and Vanessa's conversation, his housekeeper probably thought that this would be the last place Vanessa would show her face again. However, if those were her thoughts, Martha was keeping them to herself. "Yes, sir," she said instead. "I'll make a point of remembering that." Then she left the room.

Moments later, curiosity drew Cameron to the kitchen to see exactly what Vanessa had put in his gift basket. Like a kid in a candy store he started pulling things out, smiling when he saw the oatmeal raisin cookies she was famous for, the ones he'd heard Morgan rave about so many times.

As he began putting everything back in the basket he saw that her intent was for him to have a picnic without her, since there was just enough of everything for one person to enjoy. That was thoughtful of her. But then, from what he'd learned of Vanessa, she was a rather thoughtful person, which was why she was involved in so many community projects. But, as he'd told her, there was a lot about her he didn't know, and since he intended to marry her relatively soon, he needed to continue his quest to get to know her.

Ten years ago he had vowed never to become involved in a relationship with even the remotest chance of becoming serious. He had made it a point to be totally honest with women he dated, to let them know up front that there were zero odds that the affair would go anywhere. He was very selective, preferring those women within his social circle. And there were certain things he just didn't do. He didn't invite them to functions that included his closest friends. And he never gave one free rein in his home. His home—and he had several—was his sanctuary, his private and personal domain. No woman had permission to invade his place. Until now. As he'd told Martha, Vanessa was welcome to his home at any time. If he was busy, he was to be interrupted; if he was asleep, he wanted to be awakened. It was important that he got his point across to Vanessa that she had become the most important thing in his life.

He leaned back against the counter, thinking about how she'd looked standing in the middle of his living room, as angry as any woman had a right to be. While she was standing there giving him what she saw as a much-deserved dressing-down, he was giving her a dressing-down of another type. He'd been wondering just what she had on beneath that cute pair of red linen shorts with the matching top. Some of the thoughts that had run through his mind had been outright scandalous. She hadn't been wearing a bra, he could tell that. But then her breasts were just the right size and shape not to need one. And when he had pulled her into his arms and kissed her, he had known the exact moment her nipples had hardened because he'd felt them press firmly against his chest.

After their kiss, when he'd finally released her lips, he couldn't help but recall how he'd left them moist and thoroughly kissed. And then there had been that deep, dark, desire-filled look in her eyes, just seconds before they turned fiery red and she began spouting off about him staying away from her. But, as he'd told her, that wouldn't happen.

He would admit her finding out he had bought this house just to be close to her threw a monkey wrench in things for a while, but he was determined not to give up. Eventually, she would get over it, especially when she saw he wasn't going away. He intended to use whatever means he found necessary to break down her defenses.

With that in mind he walked out of the kitchen and went to the nearest intercom to summon Martha.

"Yes, Mr. Cody?"

"I want a dozen red roses sent to Ms. Steele. And I want a bottle of wine delivered with the flowers. Have the card say, 'Thanks for the basket. I'd love to share its contents, as well as this wine, with you later today on the beach.'"

"Yes, sir."

Confident the older woman was capable of carrying out his wishes, he headed toward the study.

"Calm down, Vanessa, and stop yelling. I don't understand a word you're saying."

Vanessa inhaled deeply. Sienna was right. She *had* been yelling. Pausing, she rubbed her cell phone against her cheek to calm nerves that were already shot to hell. She couldn't believe it. She just couldn't believe it.

"Now do you want to start over and tell me what has you so upset?"

Sienna's voice—calm as you please—reminded her why she was so upset. "Cameron is here, Sienna."

"Here, where?"

Vanessa rolled her eyes. "Here in Jamaica. On this island. Living right next door. He had the audacity, the gall, to purchase the house next door. I am as pissed as any woman can get."

"I can tell. You're raising your voice again. Calm down. So, you're saying he found out you were skipping town and decided to follow you?"

"Yes, that's exactly what I'm saying. Just what am I supposed to do about that?"

"Make the most of it."

"Sienna!"

"Okay, considering how you feel about the man, I guess that wasn't a good answer."

"No, it wasn't," Vanessa said, walking over to the refrigerator and grabbing one of Cheyenne's beers. "So come up with something else."

It was only after popping the top off the bottle that she remembered she didn't like beer. But what the hell, her day was a total waste now anyway. She took a swallow, straight from the bottle, and decided this particular brand wasn't so bad.

"Okay, but first I want to know how you found out he was there."

For the next fifteen minutes Vanessa filled Sienna in. It would have taken less time had Sienna not asked so many questions, especially when Vanessa told her about seeing Cameron go skinny-dipping.

"Well," Sienna said, sighing deeply, "you've warned him to stay away from you and if he doesn't adhere to your request you can have him arrested as a stalker."

"Sienna!"

"Hey, I'm serious."

Vanessa rolled her eyes upward. "Cameron doesn't pose that kind of threat and you know it. He's merely being a pain in the ass."

"All right, then, let's cover one more time why he is such a pain in your rear end. The man is simply gorgeous, any woman can see that. Even I can and you know that I only have eyes for Dane. Cameron has money, plenty of it. And he has manners. He's refined, sophisticated, intelligent—"

"He's also in the business of taking people's companies away from them."

"Come on, Van. Are you going to hold what he tried doing to the Steele Corporation over his head forever? Business is business. You can't hate all the corporate raiders out there. Look at Ted Turner, another self-made millionaire who created more jobs than he took away. Corporate takeovers have become a way of life. Besides, look at the number of people who are benefiting from all those foundations Cameron has set up. He's on the cover of *Ebony* this month, by the way. You should pick up a copy and read the article. I did. I was impressed."

"Stay impressed. There's nothing that man can do that will impress me."

"It'll be your loss, and unfortunately another sister's gain. I bet there are a number of women out there who would love getting a piece of Cameron Cody right now."

"They're welcome to him!"

"At some point I believe I'm going to have to remind you that you said that."

Vanessa rubbed the bridge of her nose, wondering why she'd bothered calling Sienna anyway. For some reason her best friend could actually envision her and Cameron as a couple. How that was possible she didn't know. Vanessa couldn't blame Sienna's pregnancy for destroying her brain cells since Sienna had reached that conclusion long before she'd gotten pregnant.

She took another swallow of beer before saying. "Look, Sienna, talking to you is getting me nowhere. I called you for advice, not for you to take sides with the enemy."

"I'm not taking sides with the enemy. You are my very best friend and I love you. But I also think you're so full of dislike for Cameron that you aren't thinking straight. If you would put your dislike aside and sit down and analyze the situation, I think you would reach the conclusion that what he's doing is rather cute, as well as bold. I visited Cheyenne's place with you last summer so I know what that house next door looks like. Just think about it, Van. He went through all that trouble to buy that place just to be close to you. Why do you think he did that?"

"I already know why he did it. He told me. He wants me."

"And is that so bad?"

"Yes, it's bad because I refuse to become just another possession to him, one that he goes about obtaining just like his corporations. I refuse to let any man take me over that way."

"And what way would you want a man to take you over?"

Vanessa tipped the beer bottle up to her mouth and drank a large swallow again. It was only when her eyes started feeling heavy that she recalled another reason she had never liked beer. It had a tendency to make her feel sleepy. "I don't want to be taken over, Sienna."

"Okay, then, how about changing the strategy. You take over Cameron."

"What?"

"Think about it. Evidently he has this well-thought-out plan to win you over. What if you put yourself in position to be the one in charge?"

"In what way?"

"Any way you want. I have an idea what Cameron

wants out of this pursuit. I see it in his eyes every time he looks at you. He definitely has the hots for you. And don't bother denying that you have the hots for him, as well. So, my question to you is this—what's wrong with an island fling? However, you'll be in charge, and you'll make the rules. Men like Cameron don't like following rules, especially if they're someone else's. But with you calling the shots, you'll be the one to decide what you want to do with him in the end, instead of the other way around."

Sienna's words reminded Vanessa of Harlan, and she was aware that her best friend knew they would. "Harlan Shaw screwed up your mind, Vanessa, but it's going to take a man like Cameron to screw it back on right. You can't see it so I won't waste my time saying it again. But I'm your best friend and I know what's going on in that head of yours. I also know what's going on in that body of yours. It's been almost four years since you've been with anyone. Cameron is available, he turns you on, so why not make the most of it?"

Vanessa glanced at the bottle and thought it must be the beer, because for one brief moment she was actually considering what Sienna had said. She shook her head, refusing to consider the suggestion.

"Look, Sienna, I'm feeling sleepy. I need to go lie down."

"Sleepy? Isn't it the middle of the day there?"

"Yes, but I just overindulged in a bottle of beer," she said, placing the empty bottle on the counter beside her.

"Okay, go to bed. But just think of how much more fun it would be if Cameron could join you there. Aren't you tired of sleeping alone? Aren't your inner muscles aching for a little hanky-panky?"

"Goodbye, Sienna," Vanessa said, not bothering to answer the questions.

"Goodbye, Van. Love you."

"Love you, too. But there are days I wished you weren't my best friend."

Even after Vanessa clicked off the line, she could still hear Sienna laughing.

# Chapter 4

Hours later when Vanessa opened her eyes she glanced around her bedroom. The first thing she noticed was that the sun had gone down. Then as she pulled herself up in bed she felt those inner muscles Sienna had teased her about earlier. They were actually aching.

She quickly blamed it on the beer she'd drunk, which would also be the reason she'd conjured up that hot and heavy dream she'd had. In her dream she and Cameron had made love on the beach, under a beautiful blue sky. She had felt the soft sand beneath her back while he loomed over her, touching and tasting her everywhere before finally taking his place between her legs.

She quickly sucked in a deep breath, forcing the memory of the dream to the back of her mind. Getting out of bed, she walked over to the window and looked out toward the beach, watching how the waves hit the shore, how the seagulls flew overhead and how—

Her breath caught when she saw a lone figure jog by, invading her line of vision. Her achy inner muscles clenched when she recognized Cameron, wearing the skimpiest pair of jogging shorts she'd ever seen on a man. Her gaze followed him. Although she was still upset over what he'd pulled, she couldn't discount the fact that Cameron Cody had a great body to go along with his handsome face. She might be mad but she definitely wasn't blind. She could appreciate a nice piece of male flesh no matter what her anger level was.

Keeping her gaze focused on him as he ran at an even pace, she couldn't help but admire his muscular shoulders, broad chest, firm stomach, healthy thighs and strong legs. Those were the same legs that in her dream had wrapped around her thighs to hold her down when he entered her body over and over again.

And, as if her dream wasn't bad enough, there was the memory of the kiss they had shared earlier, so intense and more passionate than any kiss she'd ever experienced. He was a master kisser to whom every nerve and cell in her body had greedily responded.

Even now she could feel heat seeping through all parts of her body just thinking about it. His tongue had known just what it was supposed to do and had done it well. He had tumbled her resistance the same way the Berlin Wall had met its downfall. Whenever she thought of his mouth locked to hers, and the wicked and sensuous things he could do with that tongue, all those achy parts of her body acted up.

Vanessa forced herself to take a deep breath and then let it out. She felt so hot, her brow damp, that she wondered if the air conditioner was working. When the view of Cameron was lost among the thicket of palm trees, she moved away from the window, deciding to take a shower before going downstairs to meet with Helen before she left. Today was market day and there were a couple of items she wanted Helen to pick up. Beer being one of them.

As long as Cameron was her neighbor, Vanessa refused to share the private beach with him. If she had to remain inside for the rest of her stay in Jamaica, that would suit her just fine, because she would not give him the time of day…although certain parts of her body relentlessly pushed for her to do that and more.

Vanessa picked up the scent of the flowers the moment she walked down the stairs. She glanced across the room to see the huge vase of red roses on the living-room table.

"Where did those come from?" she asked Helen upon reaching the last stair.

Busy dusting, the housekeeper didn't pause or look up when she said, "They arrived a few hours ago. Aren't they pretty?"

Vanessa had to agree, although she really didn't want to, especially when she had an idea who sent them.

"They came with a bottle of wine."

Vanessa lifted a brow. "Wine?"

"Yes. I placed it on the kitchen table."

Vanessa walked over to the roses. They were simply gorgeous. The blooms were full, and the petals looked healthy and silky. Seeing the flowers reminded her of her father. His garden was full of flowers of all types, but especially roses.

She knew his death as a result of lung cancer was the reason she had been so gullible that summer she'd met Harlan. She had needed affection and unfortunately had looked for love in the wrong places and with the wrong man. She would not be making that same mistake again.

She pulled off the card and read it, confirming her suspicions. After everything she'd said, Cameron still had the nerve to invite her to a rendezvous on the beach later.

"I'm leaving in a few minutes, Ms. Steele. Is there anything you want me to pick up for you from the market?"

Vanessa glanced up at Helen. "Yes, there are a few things I need."

A few minutes later she had given Helen her list. Before the older woman could walk out the door she called out to her. "And, Helen?"

She turned. "Yes?"

"If you happen to see a copy of *Ebony* magazine on the rack, grab one for me, please."

"Yes, ma'am, I'll do that."

Once Helen had left, closing the door behind her, Vanessa shrugged her shoulders. Okay, so she was curious about the article on Cameron. But curiosity meant nothing. It would be a cold day in hell before another man got the best of her again.

Especially him.


"So, how are things going, Cameron?"

Cameron glanced around at what were fast becoming familiar surroundings as he talked on the phone to his friend Morgan Steele. "Vanessa knows I'm here," he said slowly after taking a sip of his wine.

"Umm, and how did she take it?"

"Like we both knew she would. Let's just say I'm not her favorite person right now."

Morgan's chuckle vibrated over the mobile phone. "I hate to tell you but you've never been her favorite person. You've always been her least-liked person."

Cameron couldn't help but smile. "Thanks, Morgan, for being so brutally honest."

"That's what friends are for."

After a brief pause and another sip of wine, Cameron said, "I want you to help me understand something, Morgan."

"Okay, I'll try."

"Why does Vanessa take my actions three years ago as a personal affront? You and your brothers, as well as her sisters, were able to get over it. What's holding her back from doing the same? Is there something I'm missing here? Something you can share with me?"

"No, there's nothing I know about. The only reason I can come up with is the fact that the Steele Corporation was founded by my father and my uncle, Vanessa's father. And, as you know, her father died a few years ago. They were very close."

"You think she feels I was trying to take away his legacy?"

For a moment Morgan didn't respond and then he said, "At one time that thought did occur to me, but now I'm inclined to think there might be another reason altogether."

"And what reason is that?"

"Vanessa hasn't had a man she's ever gotten serious about, although I do recall her having a couple of boyfriends while she was in college. But there's never been anyone special, no one she's brought home for the family to meet. Now that I think of it, I believe her coldness toward you and men in general might be linked to what might have happened to her one summer."

Cameron paused with his wineglass halfway to his lips. He felt the hairs on the back of his neck stand up. "What happened?"

"I don't really know. None of us do, although I'd bet my money that her best friend, Sienna Bradford, knows. Right after my uncle died, Vanessa took some time off from her job and went to Europe for a few weeks to get away. We were worried about her and thought the trip would be a good idea. Vanessa, Taylor and Cheyenne were close to their father and took his death hard, but I think Vanessa took it the hardest. Like her mom, she felt there was something they could have done to make him stop smoking years ago."

"A smoker will only quit when he's ready."

"I know that, but still, it was hard on her. The couple of times she called home from London she seemed to be doing okay, and I'd heard through the grapevine that she'd met someone, some guy who was also vacationing over there. I'd even heard from Cheyenne— or should I say overheard when she and Taylor were deep in conversation one day—that Vanessa fancied herself in love with him. But we all figured she only assumed it was love because she was going through a vulnerable period in her life, and she would come to her senses before doing anything stupid like bringing home a husband. Anyway, the next thing we know, she returns home and to this day she hasn't mentioned him. None of us even knows his name. The only thing I can figure is that she discovered the guy was playing her, and she cared more for him than he did for her. Most likely that's why she's keeping you at arm's length, to protect her heart. She's not sure she can trust you and probably feels that you're trying to take over her life."

In a way he was, Cameron silently agreed. That was definitely his intent. He wanted her life to become ingrained in his, but he didn't see that as a negative. He could only see positives, so why couldn't she?

"I suggest you use another approach," Morgan continued. "All of us discovered real early that strong-arm tactics don't work well for Vanessa. I've told you that before."

Morgan *had* told him that before, but Cameron was used to doing things his way. Now it seemed that his way wasn't working. "So what do you suggest?" he asked.

"You're going to have to revamp and do a sneak attack."

That comment had Cameron laughing. "Like the one you used with Lena?"

"Yeah, like the one I used with Lena. Laugh all you want but I got my woman, didn't I?"

"Need I remind you that it wasn't exactly smooth sailing for you, Morgan?"

"No, you don't have to remind me, but I was still able to make it work."

Cameron had to agree, since Morgan and Lena had been married a little over a month now. Morgan had also kicked off his campaign for a seat on the city council in Charlotte. "A sneak attack, huh?" he asked.

"Yes. A sneak attack. Let her think that whatever will happen between you two is only for the moment, nothing permanent. If you go into it promising tomorrows, she won't believe you. Women expect us to have commitment-phobia, so let her think what you're proposing isn't for the long haul, although you know it really is. Vanessa won't consider a long-term relationship with a man, but she might be interested in a short-term affair if she was in control and calling the shots."

Cameron shook his head. Most of the women he knew would jump at the chance of having a permanent relationship with him, given the size of his bank account. "So you think if I use that approach it will work?"

"Yes. Try it and see. Let her assume it's nothing more than a fling and when it's over, you'll go your way and she'll go hers. Your job is to pull out the Cody charm and get her so taken with you that she won't want to go anywhere."

Cameron rubbed his chin as he pondered Morgan's advice. Then he said, "You do know this is your cousin's fate you're plotting, don't you?"

Morgan chuckled. "Yes, but my brothers and I trust you to do the right thing by her."

Cameron grinned. "Thanks for the vote of confidence."

"You're welcome. But if I'm wrong, Cameron, you'll have us to deal with. Understood?"

"Yes, Morgan. I understand completely."

Sitting down at the kitchen table, Vanessa resigned herself to the inevitable, taking the time to read the article on Cameron. Helen had put away the items she'd picked up at the market and had placed *Ebony* on the table in full view.

It didn't help matters that Cameron's picture—in living, vibrant color—was on the cover. Nor that the photographer's close-up sent a fluttery feeling all through her insides and had blood rushing through her veins. Cameron had been caught in a rare moment with a smile curving the corners of his lips. She would rather not admit that he looked so sexy that she had stared at the cover for too long before turning it facedown.

Vanessa sighed as she turned it faceup, and once again his picture sent tingly sensations all over her skin. One thing she'd discovered since that day three years ago was that Cameron was what fantasies were made of. She of all people should know, since he was a nightly invader into her dreams.

Deciding to get it over with, she opened the magazine and immediately flipped to page thirty-nine. Ignoring another picture of him—this one showing him entering the doors of one of the many corporations he'd taken away from someone—she began reading.

A short while later Vanessa pushed away from the table as she closed the magazine. Okay, she would be the first to admit it was a well-written article. As head of the public relations department at the Steele Corporation, she understood the importance of projecting a positive image, as well as a beneficial relationship with the public, and the article had definitely done that.

It showed a side of Cameron few probably got to see—his compassionate side. His philanthropic actions included establishing numerous foundations to help those less fortunate. Most of them Vanessa hadn't known about, but some, such as the Katrina Relief Fund, she was aware of; he had solicited her cousins' involvement in that particular project. Under Cameron's leadership and direction, several construction companies had rebuilt homes in New Orleans so the evacuees could return and reestablish their lives. According to the article, Cameron, acting as pilot, had gotten his private jet into the stricken city of New Orleans to provide aid and relief long before the federal government had arrived.

One thing the article hadn't focused on was how many companies Cody Enterprises had taken over in the past years, and how many people had lost their jobs because of those takeovers. There was no doubt in her mind that he was a man who liked being in total control, and he would handle any of his personal relationships the same way he handled his business.

Even when kissing her earlier today, he hadn't taken anything slowly. He had seen an opportunity and seized it. He had seen what he wanted and gone after it. With him there would be no compromise. It would be all or nothing, and only on his terms.

She walked around the house, pulling down the blinds. When she walked into the living room she couldn't help but stare at the roses. No doubt there was a purpose behind Cameron sending them. He probably assumed that this was the first step in breaking down her defenses, and that the next time he saw her she would be easier to bend his way. If that's what she thought, he definitely had another think coming.

She glanced out the window, realizing how much she'd missed spending any time on the beach today. Suddenly, the stubborn streak within her decided not to let Cameron's presence keep her from enjoying her time here. Tomorrow she would get up, pack a lunch and spend the day on the beach. She'd meant what she'd said when she'd told Cameron she wanted to be left alone.

Now she would see how good he was at following orders.

# Chapter 5

The man wasn't good at following orders, Vanessa concluded the very next morning when she opened the front door to find Cameron standing there. Evidently he hadn't taken her seriously.

"What do you want, Cameron? I thought I told you to stay away from me," she said, glaring at him.

"You did and I recall telling you that I wouldn't."

He leaned against the bamboo post, seemingly completely at ease. She watched him slip his hands into the pockets of his shorts and wished he hadn't done that. It drew her attention to what he was wearing—a muscle shirt and a pair of denim shorts that emphasized his masculine physique. She touched her stomach when her inner muscles became achy, and released a moan.

"Are you okay?"

Her glare deepened. "No, I'm not okay. I don't like being harassed."

"And you think that's what I'm doing? Harassing you?"

"Yes."

"Then I need to use another approach."

"What you need to do is turn around, go back to your place and leave me alone."

He shook his head. "I can't do that. We need to talk."

Vanessa rolled her eyes. "We have nothing to talk about since I have nothing to say to you."

"But I have something to say to you. I'd like to offer you a business proposition."

Her eyes widened slightly before returning to angry slits. "A business proposition?"

"Yes. One where you'll be in full control and calling all the shots."

Before Vanessa's mind could take in what he had said and dissect what he meant, he added, "I think I need to clear something up right now, Vanessa, something you might have assumed. I'm not interested in a committed relationship...with anyone."

Now, that really threw her. Not that she was surprised he wasn't interested in a committed relationship, since most single men weren't. But it did leave her curious as to why he had been hot on her tail for the past three years. Or was it just as she'd thought? To him it had been a challenge, nothing more than a game he'd had every intention of winning.

Evidently he read the question in her eyes because he responded by saying, "The reason I've been pursuing you with such single-minded determination is that I think you're a very desirable woman and I want you. It's as simple as that."

She crossed her arms over her chest. Nothing with

Cameron was ever simple. "So you bought a house just to be near me for a couple of weeks because you *want* me?"

"Yeah, and in a bad way. Three years' worth of wanting to be exact. I've dreamed of having you in my bed every night, and I figured it was time to turn my dreams into reality."

Although she wished it was otherwise, his words were having a naughty effect on her. Sensations, warm and tingly, began flowing all through her veins, and the salty air from the nearby ocean was getting replaced with his scent, a pungent fragrance that was all man.

"It won't happen," she said with conviction.

"What won't happen?"

"Me, you, together that way."

"I think it will, because you're a very passionate woman, although it appears you keep all that passion hidden. I would love to tap into it."

Hidden passion that he wanted to tap into? She wondered what kind of alcohol he'd been drinking this morning. "Look, I have no idea what you're talking about." She decided not to tell him that she'd been told by one man just how passionless she was.

"Then let me break everything down for you. Let me make my offer. One that you can accept or reject."

"And if I reject it?"

"Then I promise to leave you alone for the remainder of your stay here as you've requested. In fact, I'll make arrangements to fly back to the States. But I'm hoping that you will accept it."

"And if I do?"

"If you do, I will take you on the sexual adventure of your life. Entertain old fantasies and create new ones.

I plan to take us both over the edge, and when it's over, you'll go your way and I'll go mine, and I promise not to bother you again."

"Just like that?"

"Yes, just like that. My offer is that for the remainder of your days here, I will become your sex mate while we indulge in all sorts of wild and wicked playtime."

Vanessa felt her stomach fluttering again. Now she wished she'd had a taste of whatever alcohol he had consumed that morning. She needed it. What he was proposing—although similar in nature to what Sienna had suggested—was crazy, absolutely ludicrous, outright insane. Still, his words refused to stop swimming around in her mind, and, as he stood there on her front porch in the sunlight, looking more handsome than any man had a right to look, she was tempted. Boy, was she tempted.

Pulling on her last bit of control, she said, "And what makes you think I want a sex mate?"

He took a step closer. "Your kiss. A man can tell a lot from a woman's kiss. Hunger, wariness, pain. I tasted all three. You want me as much as I want you. Being honest with yourself and admitting it is the first step. I can see it even now in your eyes, the heat, the yearning, the need."

He reached out and took her hand in his. Before she could pull it back, he rubbed his thumb across the underside of her wrist. "Feel it here," he said of her pulse. "Your passion points. They're beating like crazy and drumming out a message you've ignored too long."

She pulled her hand back. "It's all in your mind," she said, then moistened her lips when they suddenly felt dry.

"I don't think so and I'm willing to prove you wrong."

Her eyes narrowed. "I don't want you proving anything."

"Don't you? Let's move on to your wariness. I tasted that, too. You want me, but you don't fully trust me. You're confused about where I'm coming from and, more importantly, where I'm going when it's over. I think I've made it clear what I want out of a relationship with you. And it's not wedding bells. But then I'm sure you feel the same way."

Before she could respond he continued, "And last but not least, I tasted pain, which is why you probably find it hard to trust me or any other man. But that's okay. I plan to take the pain away and replace it with pleasure of the most intense kind. After me you won't even remember your last fling."

Vanessa studied Cameron carefully. She gazed back into the intense eyes staring at her and felt another tug of her inner muscles. They were getting achier by the minute. Four years was a long time and her body was letting her know it. What Cameron had said wasn't helping matters. He wanted her for a sex mate. He wanted to tap into what he claimed was her hidden passion.

"Think about my proposition, Vanessa, and if you're interested in what I'm proposing, meet me on the beach at noon. Like I said, I'll let you set the parameters and call the shots. Turning over total control to anyone isn't easy for me, but I'll do it because I want you that bad. I'll take you on any terms."

She swallowed the tightness in her throat. "And what happens after you've had me? What if you get tired of me after the first time?" She couldn't forget that Harlan had done exactly that.

Cameron's soft chuckle caressed her skin. "Trust me, that's not possible. I doubt I'll be tired of you after the first thousand years. But how long the affair lasts will be up to you, and I promise to adhere to your time frame."

He took a step back. "Think about everything I've said and if you're interested, I'll see you on the beach at noon."

As Vanessa watched him walk away she knew she had to get a grip. Over the past three years the man had tilted her world, and now he was proposing to rock it in a way it had never been rocked before. She inhaled deeply, then let the breath out slowly. No, she told herself, the thought of a meaningless fling with Cameron was too much. She wouldn't even think about it.

She thought about it all morning. Pacing the confines of her sister's living room, she went through the pros and cons of Cameron's proposal, and it seemed the pros were tilting the scale.

If he had suggested such a thing five years ago, she would have told him just where he could go. But that would have been her pre-Harlan days, a time when she wanted to believe in romance and a forever kind of love.

She had grown up believing that two people could meet, fall in love and stay together for the rest of their lives, until death did them part. Her parents had done it, and so had her aunt and uncle. And when she had been looking at things through rose-colored glasses, she had wanted that same special love for herself.

But Harlan had taught her one vital lesson in life, something she wouldn't ever forget: All that glittered wasn't gold. She was older and smarter now and didn't look through those rose-colored glasses anymore. After she'd thoroughly analyzed that summer in Europe, the one thing that stood out was how each day Harlan wanted to change her, mold her into the person he wanted by suggesting certain outfits for her to wear, foods that he preferred she eat and activities he'd rather they did. It was always what he wanted, without any consideration for what she wanted. It had always been about Harlan. He had controlled everything.

Even their lovemaking.

That night he hadn't asked for any suggestions or ideas. He'd done things his way, mainly for his own satisfaction. And if he thought she had failed in pleasing him, well, if the truth were known, he hadn't pleased her, either. But at the time she had fancied herself too much in love to care.

Now she did care.

After not having been intimate with a man since Harlan, the thought of a relationship with one just for sex should be a turnoff. But knowing the man involved was Cameron was quite the opposite. He turned her on. Besides, the dynamics of a man-woman relationship weren't what they used to be. Men, she told herself, no longer courted you. They seduced you.

So what was wrong with seducing them back?

There would be no misunderstandings in their relationship. There would be a beginning and an end. And most importantly, it would be a way finally to get Cameron to leave her alone and a way finally to get the one thing her body needed. A man.

But not just any man.

It needed the man who'd so ruthlessly invaded her dreams, the man who could stare at her from across a room and make heat swell within her. The man who could start her pulse—her pleasure points—to beating in a way that sent blood racing through her veins.

And she would be the one in control.

*That* was the one thing that appealed to her. How would Cameron react once stripped of control? Once unable to call the shots? He would have a hard time of it, no doubt, but she would enjoy every single minute.

Every single inch of him.

She sighed deeply. Was she crazy to consider such a thing? Or was she crazy not to? She would be going into the affair with both eyes open, with no unrealistic expectations. There would be no future in the brief relationship they shared but at least her celibate days would come to an end. For the rest of her stay on this island, she would put out of her mind that Cameron Cody had to be the most insufferably irritating man she'd ever met and instead concentrate on how he was also the handsomest and sexiest. Being around him, looking into the darkness of his eyes, studying those intriguing lips and knowing what it would feel like being touched by those big, strong hands, being made love to with an intensity that took her breath away, was worth the risk.

For a short while she wouldn't feel guilty about being so incredibly attracted to him. She would take Sienna's advice and finally take her "edge off." And what better person to do it with than a man who was so utterly male? She and Cameron were spontaneous combustion just waiting to explode, just as Sienna claimed.

Besides, it was about time someone taught Cameron a lesson in humility. Not everything in life got played by his terms, his wants and his desires. People weren't like corporations; he couldn't just come in and take over their lives because they caught his eye for the moment.

A smile touched the corners of her lips. For the second time in his life Cameron Cody was about to get outdone by a Steele. The first time her family had effectively shown him that family devotion was worth a lot more than his money. Now, with single-minded determination, she intended to show him that there were some things you just couldn't control. He was about to discover that all his management theories couldn't be applied to a personal relationship, not even a short-term one.

Whether Cameron realized it, he had met his match.

# Chapter 6

It was high noon.

For Vanessa, the path leading from Cheyenne's home down to the beach had never seemed so long. She had changed from the sundress she'd been wearing earlier to a pair of shorts and matching top that were meant to capture Cameron's full attention, not that she didn't think she'd had it earlier when he had been standing on her doorstep.

She had seen the way his eyes had roamed over her. She had felt the heat in the gaze that had touched different parts of her body. At the time she'd been so taken aback by his proposal she had dismissed the intensity of his look.

In the future, when it came to him she wouldn't dismiss anything. She would keep her eyes and ears open, and, more than anything, she would keep her heart intact. She would not make the same mistake with him that she had with Harlan.

As soon as her bare feet touched the heated sand, another kind of heat quickly spread through her. Cameron had laid out a towel on the beach a safe distance from the water, and he had brought the basket she'd given him yesterday. But what caught her eye was the man himself.

He was shirtless, wearing only a pair of khaki shorts. Probably he had on his swimming trunks under the shorts, just like she was wearing her two-piece bathing suit under her outfit.

Regardless of the smell of the ocean water, she discovered the closer she got to him that his scent enveloped her. He was standing, looking out over the ocean with his back to her, but not for one minute did she think he wasn't aware of her approach. Her gaze traveled over him, appreciating the corded muscles of his back.

When she got within five feet of him, he slowly turned and her gaze automatically latched on to the bare, muscular contours of his chest and the sparse dark hairs covering it. Bringing her gaze back to his face, she watched the corners of his lips tilt in a slow, devastatingly handsome smile, the impact of which she could feel all the way to her womb. It was an intense tug that made her inner muscles clench.

"Thanks for coming," he said in a low, sexy voice that made her heart begin thumping and made goose bumps rise on her arm. "I'm going to make sure you don't regret your decision."

She came to a stop beside him. "We'll see, Cameron, but first we need to talk, to get a few things straight up-front. I want to make sure we understand each other completely."

He nodded. "All right. And after we talk I suggest we eat since it's lunchtime. Do you want to sit here to talk or do you want to walk along the beach?"

The thought of the two of them strolling along the beach together set up a romantic picture in her mind, and she didn't want to think romance. "We can sit and talk right here."

He nodded before taking her hand to assist her down on the huge towel. The moment their hands touched, she felt an electric current charge through her body and knew he felt it, as well. He sat down beside her. When one of his bare legs brushed against hers, her heartbeat quickened. The sexual chemistry between them was overpowering. Even if she had had on layers and layers of clothing, she still would have felt his touch. Every fiber of her body was attuned to him, but she was determined to dispel some of that high-voltage sexual tension that gripped them, made her forget about talking and want only to lie on this towel with him, naked, instead.

"So what are your rules?"

His words interrupted her thoughts and she glanced over at him. Even sitting there as casual as he wanted to be, he still looked dominating, far more powerful and commanding than she liked.

The sooner she told him just how things would be between them, the better. Then he could take her proposal or leave it. She was inclined to think he would leave it, because a part of her refused to believe he could put total control in her hands.

The next few minutes would tell.

"I want to share an affair with you, Cameron, for the remainder of the time I have left on the island. Twelve days to be exact. During that time I will forget my dislike of you, and I want you to forget your dislike of me."

"I don't dislike you. In fact I like you. A lot."

His words gave her pause, and it took a few moments to regroup her thoughts. "Okay, maybe your feelings for me are not as intense as my feelings for you, but even you would admit we really don't get along."

"That was your choice. You turned me down each and every time I asked you out. You refused to get within ten feet of me."

Glancing down, Vanessa rubbed the bridge of her nose, wondering how they had strayed off the subject. She decided to use the opportunity to make him see that, unlike in the past, she wouldn't be putting distance between them now...not as long as she was in control.

"Forget about the past, Cameron, because I'm within ten feet of you now, aren't I? I'm sitting so close to you, I'm practically in your lap."

A naughty smile touched his lips when he said in a low voice, "If you want to ease over into my lap, I won't have a problem with it."

She rolled her eyes. "I'm sure you won't, but I need us to finish our discussion."

"All right."

"Like I said, we will put the past and our feelings behind us and start on that adventure you alluded to. But at the end of the twelve days, whatever we've shared will come to an end. No future. No promises. You will go your way and I will go mine, and if our paths cross again, which I'm sure they eventually will, given your close relationship with other members of my family, we will act as though nothing ever happened between us. There won't be any repeat or any suggestion of such a thing. When this affair ends, it's over. Totally and completely. Understood?"

He stared at her for a long moment but she refused to back down or wither under his gaze. She remained quiet and still while he considered her proposal.

Finally he spoke. "Yes, I understand but what happens if—"

When he stopped in midsentence she arched a brow and asked, "If what?"

"If we become addicted to each other. What if the intimacy is so good and we get so embodied into each other's systems that we don't want things to end? What if—"

Not wanting to hear any more, Vanessa reached out and pressed her fingers to his lips to silence his next words. She wished she hadn't when the tip of his tongue lightly flicked across her fingers.

The action made her gasp, nearly took her breath away. But for some reason she couldn't pull her hand back. She stared at him, felt those same inner muscles clench again at the heated lust forming in his eyes. Then she wondered if such a thing was possible. Could she possibly become sexually addicted to him? Or was he thinking too much of himself? There was no doubt in her mind that he probably could whip up some delicious sexual fantasies, but…an addiction? She shook her head. That couldn't and wouldn't happen.

She moistened her lips as she pulled her fingers away from his mouth, but not before his tongue flicked out for one more quick taste. She watched as he took that same tongue and licked his lips as if he had enjoyed the taste of her.

"It won't happen," she finally said, barely getting the words out. "I've never gotten addicted to anything in my life."

"Maybe the reason you've never gotten addicted is because you've never overindulged. For the next twelve days, with me, you will."

She saw something flicker in his eyes and for some reason she suddenly felt on her guard. "It doesn't matter. I won't get addicted."

She watched as his gaze dropped to her mouth and he said, "But if when our affair is over you find you still want me, just let me know and I will make myself available. Anytime, anyplace and any position."

A wave of heated desire, larger than one of the waves forming out in the ocean, shot through her. Any position? Just what kind of fantasies had he conjured up for the next twelve days?

Vanessa had to struggle against the excitement that tried grabbing her in its clutches. He had painted one hell of a picture; the imagery was too sensual even for a graphic artist to try his hand at it. Someday, when this affair was over, she would wonder just how she got through it with all her senses intact.

Had she perhaps bitten off more than she could chew? But then she remembered that she would be the one in control. He couldn't do any more than she let him. She had the last word.

Struggling to regain power of her senses, she said, "Thanks for the offer but I don't intend to use it."

"That will be your choice, Vanessa, but it's out there if you change your mind."

"I won't."

He gave her a look that said, "we'll see." "And another thing, Vanessa, just so you don't accuse me of having an ulterior motive later, I might as well tell you that I've decided to make Charlotte my primary home."

His words shocked the hell out of her and she was grateful she was sitting down. It had been bad enough to endure his occasional trips to the city, but the thought of him setting up permanent residence in her hometown was too much.

"Why?" she snapped. "Why are you moving to Charlotte?"

"I happen to like the town. I own several homes, most of them in the areas where I have extensive business interests—Atlanta, Austin and Los Angeles—and of course, now this place here. But the home I recently purchased in Charlotte is where I intend to stay most of the time."

"Exactly where in Charlotte? What side of town?" she asked, clearly annoyed.

"The same subdivision where Morgan lives. I like the area and the homes there."

She nodded. So did she. It was a very beautiful area and the homes, all in the million-dollar range, were simply breathtaking. At least he would be living on the opposite side of town, quite a distance from her, so the chances of their paths crossing too many times were low enough not to worry about now.

"Well, I'm trusting you to stay on your side of town and I'll stay on mine," she said.

He smiled. "Don't worry. Charlotte is big enough for both of us," he said, standing.

She gazed up at him, hoping that it was.

"Now that we've come to an understanding about a number of things, do you want to go for a walk before we have lunch? Of course, the decision is yours," he said smoothly.

*Walk?* Vanessa thought, smiling humorlessly. *He wants to go for a walk?* She would have thought that a man like Cameron would immediately initiate his role as her sex mate by suggesting that they go to one of the houses and get it on. Was he trying to throw her off by using a different strategy?

She regarded him for a moment and was about to pull herself to her feet when he reached out his hand to her. His fingertips grazed her knuckles before his hand tightened around hers, effortlessly tugging her up. Trying to downplay the stirrings she felt between her thighs, she said in a tight voice, "A walk sounds like a good idea. It's a nice day out."

"Yes, it is."

He surprised her even more when he kept her hand tucked in his as they began strolling along the shoreline. She glanced up at him, and he looked at her and slanted a crooked smile before asking, "Is anything wrong?"

*Nothing other than that I can actually feel my heart leaping in my chest,* she thought. But instead she said, "No, nothing's wrong. But I would like to know something."

"What?"

"Who told you that I was coming here? Although I have an idea."

"Do you?"

"Yes."

"Umm, how would you like to go to dinner?"

She shook her head, knowing what he was trying to do. "You're trying to avoid my question."

"Am I?"

"Yes."

He glanced sideways at her and gave her an easy grin. She had seen more smiles from him in the past few hours than she'd thought possible. "You're right. I am avoiding your question. But I won't reveal my sources."

"I think I know who it was."

He chuckled. "But you're not sure so leave it alone."

"I can't. I want to know who told you I was coming here."

"Why?"

"So I can deal with him."

Cameron chuckled. "Are you sure it's a he?"

She glanced over at him. "Pretty much."

"You're only guessing, Vanessa, and I'm not telling you. Now, back to my earlier question of how you want to spend dinner?"

She wondered why he was asking. Did he have an idea? She decided to play her hunch. "I don't know. Any suggestions?"

"Yes. There's a concert tonight on the beach of the Half Moon Royal Villas. I think you might like it since I understand you enjoy reggae music."

Irritation stiffened her spine. Someone had again given him information about her. He evidently felt her displeasure and glanced down at her. "Why does it bother you that someone mentioned that to me?"

She stopped walking and turned to him. "Because that meant I was the topic of your conversation, and I'm not sure I like that."

Cameron stared at Vanessa, resisting the urge to pull her into his arms and kiss her. He wanted to indulge in the taste he'd sampled. Instead he said, "I think we need to clear the air about something. I've wanted you from the first moment I saw you, but I'm sure you know that already. And because I wanted you, I became fixated on knowing all there was about you, so I asked questions. Trust me, if my sources thought I was asking for the wrong reasons, they would not have told me anything."

"And you think wanting to know everything about me for the mere reason of sleeping with me is the right reason?"

Cameron smiled blandly. He had decided after talking to Morgan on the phone yesterday that he would modify his sneak-attack plan. When possible, he intended to be as honest as he could with her. Because of that, it would only be fair that she knew how much he'd wanted her initially.

"Yes, I think so. I'm a private person. I don't bring a lot of people into my life and I have established a certain standard for the women I date."

He saw the frown that appeared on Vanessa's face. Evidently she didn't like the thought of being grouped with the other women he dated. In the past he had always enjoyed a pretty healthy sex life, making sure no woman got close. But with Vanessa he had wanted more than a toss between the sheets. He had wanted a whole hell of a lot more and he still did.

"I saw my relationship with you as different," he said honestly. "With someone else it might not have mattered what was her favorite food, her taste in music or her favorite sports, but when it came to you, it mattered."

"Why?"

"Because, like I said earlier, and I've been saying now, I wanted you, and the depth of that want went beyond anything I've ever known. I've never been attracted to a woman this much before."

Vanessa shrugged. "It was probably the challenge. You didn't get the Steele Corporation so you decided to go after a Steele."

Cameron shook his head. "First you accuse me of seeking revenge. Now it's the thrill of a challenge. It's neither of the two. You're a very desirable woman, Vanessa. Why is it so hard for you to believe that?"

Morgan had mentioned something about the possibility of a man screwing up her life one summer a few years ago and since that time she hadn't dated much. Had the man done or said something to make her question her appeal, her femininity? If that was the case, he would make sure in the coming days that he did the opposite. The last thing Vanessa Steele needed to worry about was whether a man actually found her desirable.

"It's hard for me to believe because I know how men are. I have four older male cousins, remember."

"Yes, but three of them are happily married, so what's your point?"

She evidently took offense at his question. Her frown deepened. "My point is that while they're happy now, there was a time they dated frequently with no thought of settling down."

"And are you saying that women don't date frequently? I know some women who are just as bad as men when it comes to getting what they want, using whatever means possible."

She glared at him. "We aren't talking about women. We're talking about men."

Cameron raised a brow. "Are we? And why is that?"

Vanessa inclined her head to get a better look into Cameron's face and to keep the glare of the sun out of her eyes. "I don't know why that is and I would appreciate it if you didn't confuse me."

In that instant Cameron knew only one thing for sure: he had to kiss her. The way she had tilted her head back made her lips too accessible and he had a deep, compelling need to ravish them, kiss her crazy. Every nerve in his body was pushing him to do just that, so he leaned closer.

Evidently she picked up on his intent but didn't take a step back. Instead their gazes held, locked. She tried clearing her throat lightly and said, "You never finished telling me about the plans for dinner."

"Dinner?"

"Yes. I think that's what we should be concentrating on."

His gaze moved from her eyes back onto her mouth. If she thought she could get him thinking about anything other than kissing her, she was wrong. Leaning closer, he said huskily, "The only thing I want to concentrate on, Vanessa, is your mouth."

"Cameron…" When his lips touched hers, his name became a shuddering breath from her mouth.

The last time they kissed he had tried zapping her of her senses, but this time he wanted to take things slow and tender. She parted her mouth beneath his and the moment she did so, he drank of her greedily but in a leisurely and unhurried way. He wanted every dip, swipe and lick of his tongue to solicit a reaction from her, a sensuous response. And if for one minute she thought she wouldn't get addicted to this, then he intended to prove otherwise. He had gotten addicted to her even before their first kiss. Her scent had been his downfall, but he could admit that her taste was doing a close second.

The kiss was incredible. It was heated and it made a tortured groan escape his throat when she began returning it, tangling her tongue with his, making an already heated situation even hotter.

He wrapped his arms around her, pulling her closer to fit into him. He felt her bare legs rub against his, felt the hardened tips of her breasts press against his bare chest, and he felt the hardness of his erection settle between her thighs. And when he heard her moan, blood rushed through his veins.

Cameron knew that if they didn't stop soon he would be tempted to lay her down on the beach, right here, and make love to her, to claim her as he wanted. He wanted to say to hell with a sneak attack. He wanted to operate on the got-to-have-you-now strategy but knew that he couldn't. Contrary to what she thought, he was fighting for long-term here and he intended to get it.

With that thought in mind, he drew back and heard her soft, breathless protest when he did so. He gazed down at her swollen lips, and the eyes that met his looked drugged in the most passionate way.

He knew he should say something, anything, or else he would be devouring her mouth once again. "I think the Tapas restaurant would be nice."

It took a second for her to comprehend that he had spoken. "For what?" she asked softly.

He smiled and wondered if she realized her arms were still wrapped around his neck and she was inching her lips closer to his.

"For dinner," he said throatily, deciding to inch his lips closer to hers, as well. "We can do dinner there and then do the concert. What do you think?"

Instead of answering him, she released a whimper the moment her lips touched his, reconnecting with his mouth again. As far as he was concerned, if they kept this up they could forgo dinner and just feast on each other; especially when he felt her taking the lead by wrapping her tongue around his.

He might work hard at making her addicted to this, but for him, things were even worse. For the past three years, Vanessa had been a fascination to him. Now she was fast becoming an obsession.

## Chapter 7

It was a beautiful evening, Vanessa thought, as she leaned back against the headrest, feeling the wind off the ocean gently caress her face. She was in Cameron's convertible sports car as they made their way down the narrow beach road toward the restaurant where they would be having dinner.

She had to admit that her noontime meeting on the beach with him had gone well. After their walk they had returned to the towel and shared lunch. Their conversation had mostly been about the new addition to the Steele family, a beautiful little boy named Alden who had been born to Chance and Kylie, who had joined his teenage son and her teenage daughter together into an amazing blended family. They also talked about Morgan's bid for political office and how Cameron intended to be a part of Morgan's campaign staff. After they had finished eating, Cameron had walked her back to her place and, with nothing more than a peck on the cheek, he'd left.

"I never did thank you for the roses. They're beautiful," she said, finally breaking the silence surrounding them in the two-seater vehicle. "And the wine was a nice touch."

He gave a quick glance over at her. "You're more than welcome for both."

When silence settled between them again she decided to ask, "Is this car yours or is it a rental?"

"It's mine. I purchased it the first day I arrived, and I plan to keep it here on the island to use whenever I'm here. Do you like it?"

She smiled. "Yes, actually I do. Morgan bought a sports car for Lena as a wedding gift, but I'm sure you know that."

He chuckled. "Yes, I know. It's a nice set of wheels."

Vanessa nodded in agreement. "Lena said she'd always wanted one, but had always stuck to purchasing something practical. Morgan decided to indulge her and she loves it."

"And he loves her."

Vanessa glanced over at Cameron. He sounded so sure of that, but then everyone was aware of how Morgan felt about his wife. He wasn't ashamed to wear his heart on his sleeve. Neither were Chance and Sebastian. They had been fortunate enough to meet women who were worth every ounce of their love, and since getting to know them and seeing what beautiful people Kylie, Lena and Jocelyn were, both inside and out, Vanessa understood why.

Deciding to keep the focus of the conversation on anyone but them, she said, "At what point do you think he fell in love with her?"

She had heard the story of how Morgan had been swept off his feet the moment Lena had walked into the ballroom at some charity function, but since Cameron and Morgan were close friends she wanted to hear his thoughts.

"According to Morgan, he fell for her the first time he saw her. Instant love. I understand it can happen that way sometimes."

"Do you really believe that?"

They had arrived at the restaurant and Cameron noticed he was behind a few other cars waiting for valet parking. He turned to Vanessa, thinking that she had asked a good question and he wanted her to see the similarities between their situation and Morgan and Lena's.

"Yes. I believe a man can meet a woman and fall in love the moment he sets eyes on her." He could tell by the gentle lift of her brow that she was surprised by his response.

"That's interesting to hear you say that. Please elaborate."

He smiled. He'd figured she would want him to. "There's really nothing to elaborate on, Vanessa. Contrary to what some women think, all men aren't horrid."

"Women don't think *all* men are horrid."

"Maybe not all of you, but enough of you do to give some of us a bad rap. All it takes is for one man to mess up, and the masses of your gender assume the next one will do the same."

She straightened in her seat, her body going on the defensive as she frowned at him. "Are you saying if the roles were reversed that a man wouldn't be just as cautious? That a man wouldn't protect his heart from further pain?"

Cameron smiled weakly, remembering that he was currently at that stage in his own life. Stacy McCann had definitely done a job on him when she'd claimed that although she loved him, she had to obey her father and marry a man who'd been born into wealth instead of considering marriage to Cameron—a man her father referred to as a "young punk with pipe dreams."

"No," he said. "All I'm saying is that at some point you have to move on and take another chance, risk all." At least to a certain degree.

He didn't utter those last words but he definitely believed them. He was certain he could not totally and completely give his heart to another woman ever again. But what he could do for Vanessa was to pledge her his undying devotion. While he hadn't felt love the moment he'd seen her, he'd felt an instant attraction, the kind he'd never before experienced. Vanessa might not have his love but she would have the next best thing.

"Dinner was wonderful, Cameron," Vanessa said as they sat in what she thought had to be one of the most exquisite restaurants on the island. In addition to the exceptional food and service, they'd been seated at a table with a breathtaking view of the ocean.

"I'm glad you enjoyed it," Cameron said, taking a sip of his wine. "It came highly recommended."

She didn't have to ask by whom since Chance and Kylie had come here on their honeymoon, and had raved about what a fantastic time they'd had. They had stayed at the Half Moon Royal Villas, where she and Cameron would be going later for the concert on the beach.

Feeling Cameron's eyes on her, she glanced across the table. The moment their gazes connected, a shimmering heat flowed all through her, pooling in the lower part of her body. Earlier, while they were eating and exchanging polite conversation, she had allowed herself to relax a little and let her guard down. Now, seeing the intense look in his eyes, she quickly pulled her guard back up.

His look was more than just intense, it was purposeful. The lighting of the restaurant played along his features, highlighting his angular jaw, cleft chin and sexy lower lip. Then there was something about the slickness of his bald head that gave him such a manly appeal. He looked so good in the tailored trousers and a white shirt that when she'd opened the door to him earlier, he had momentarily taken her breath away.

She continued to study his lower lip while she gently traced the stem of her wineglass, thinking just what she would like to do with those lips. She'd never been a woman who felt comfortable making the first move, but she felt like doing so now. Besides, he was her sex mate and she was in full control and calling the shots. The big question was whether she was going to use that control. Could she ask him to make love to her as if it was nothing more than asking him to pass the butter?

She swallowed tightly, feeling the intense heat and awareness of the unbroken eye contact they were sharing. Why was she just now noticing things about him, things she hadn't taken time to notice before? Like the long lashes that covered his dark eyes, the pearly white teeth that seemed so perfect and straight, or the way he could never keep his fingers still for long. They were either holding something or drumming restlessly on the table.

"Ready to go?" he asked, his voice seemingly gentle.

"To the concert?"

"Yes. But if you prefer to call it an early night—"

"No," she said quickly, calling herself a coward. "I'm looking forward to the concert."

"All right."

She took another sip of her wine. Why couldn't she have told the truth? *Yes, I prefer calling it an early night, so we can go back to my place or yours and tumble between the sheets.* But she hadn't, and it wasn't a good idea for her to even think it.

Moments later, while they waited for their check, she decided to ask, "Have you moved into your place in Charlotte yet?"

The corners of his lips tipped into a smile. "No. That's the reason I was coming to Charlotte, to spend a few days getting settled."

"And you changed your plans to follow me here?"

"Yes."

Vanessa shook her head, still not sure what to make of that. "You'll have a lot to do when you get back."

"I'll manage."

Probably with hired help, she thought. Before she could think of another topic to keep the conversation going, the waiter returned with their check. She watched as Cameron signed off on the bill while thinking just how little she knew about him other than what she'd read in the newspaper or, more recently, in that magazine.

He was a high-school dropout who had gotten himself together to end up graduating cum laude from Harvard Business School. A self-made millionaire, he was one of the most successful men in the country.

She hadn't noticed that the waiter had gone, and she was still sitting there staring at Cameron. When she did realize it, she saw that he was staring back at her. For a moment she couldn't breathe and it felt as if her heart was pounding in her chest.

"Are you ready to leave now, Vanessa?"

Her gaze dropped to his mouth, and she saw it move, but for the life of her she had no idea what he'd said. Her mind, her thoughts, her entire body were centered on him and on how, just by looking at her, he could make a compelling need thicken inside of her.

"Vanessa?"

"Yes?"

A smile touched those full, irresistible lips. "I asked if you were ready to leave for the concert."

Sighing deeply, she nodded. She would go to the concert, but all she'd do was think about what would happen between them later.

Some women, Cameron thought, were meant to be made love to, day and night, twenty-four hours a day, seven days a week. Vanessa Steele was that kind of woman.

He was standing in line at the bar to get a refill on their drinks and couldn't help but stare at her. She was standing, leaning against a palm tree, listening to the music, her body swaying to the reggae beat.

He had been on edge all night, ever since picking her up. She had come to the door wearing a peasant blouse that hung off her shoulders and a matching skirt whose hem came to her ankles. And she had the cutest-looking sandals on her feet. He had been tempted to kiss her then and there and suggest they forgo dinner and the concert and go somewhere and make love.

But he hadn't made such a suggestion. Instead he had taken her hand and led her to his car, all the while knowing this would be one hot night for him in more ways than one.

The need for her was sharp and compelling. He wanted to touch her all over, kiss her all over, make love to her inside and out. Each thought intensified his need, his desire. Raw, primitive passion clawed at him. He could no longer hold it beneath the surface. It was there, forcing its way free, gripping him, slicing through him.

As if she felt the heat of his eyes on her, she glanced in his direction and their gazes connected and then locked—something they'd done a lot tonight. At that moment a deep, intense sensation sent flames flaring through him and he knew he had to leave with her. Now.

"What would you like to have, sir?"

He blinked when he realized the bartender had asked him a question. He broke eye contact with Vanessa to glance at the man long enough to say, "Nothing."

The only thing he wanted to have was Vanessa. He turned to stride back to her, hoping that she would take his suggestion that they leave now.

Vanessa watched as Cameron began walking toward her, his eyes locked with hers. Even across the distance she felt his heat and read the intense look in his gaze. His shoulders looked massive and he appeared larger than life with every step he took. There was a profound sexiness about him. The way his pants fit his body had her mesmerized because she could tell when she glanced below his waist that he was aroused. From what? Just looking at her? Hidden fantasies in his mind?

She was glad that everyone else around them was caught up in the concert and didn't notice that she and Cameron were caught up only in each other. The closer he got the more she could feel her heart thundering, beating wildly in her chest. She no longer wondered how their night would end. He was painting a very clear picture.

"Our drinks?" she asked, when he finally reached her empty-handed.

"I think we need more than alcohol to cool off," he said huskily, reaching out and gently drawing her to him.

She met his heated gaze. "Do we?"

"Yes."

She then surprised Cameron by placing her arms around his neck, bringing her body up close to his. He knew there was no way she couldn't feel his erection, the intensity of his desire for her. Hell, she probably had noticed it when he was walking back toward her.

"And what do you think we need, Cameron Cody?" she asked, breaking into his thoughts.

The corners of his lips turned up slightly as he stared down at her. Then he leaned close to her ear and whispered, "I think we need to go someplace where we can be alone."

She gazed into his eyes for several long moments before saying softly, "I think you're right."

# Chapter 8

"Would you like to see the progress that's been made on Cheyenne's pool, Cameron?"

*No. Not really,* Cameron thought as he leaned against the closed door. He dug his hands into the pockets of his trousers and watched as Vanessa crossed the room, her skirt twirling in fluid motion around her legs when she walked.

The ride from the concert had been the hardest drive he'd ever made. More than once he'd been tempted to pull to the side of the road, tug her into his arms and start something that he could handle a lot better in a bedroom. Right now the last thing he was interested in seeing was a swimming pool under construction.

"Cameron?"

When he hadn't answered, she turned and was looking at him with one beautifully arched eyebrow raised.

He could tell she was nervous and that it would be to his advantage to do whatever it took to make her comfortable. And if that meant seeing her sister's pool then so be it.

Pulling his hands out of his pockets, he stepped a little farther into the room. "Yes, I'd like to see it." He then tilted his head in the general direction where he figured the pool to be and said, "Isn't it dark out back?"

"With the flip of a switch the area will become well lit."

*Great.* "All right, then, show me."

He followed as she led him through the living room where she opened a set of French doors. The scent of the ocean immediately filled their nostrils, but it was her scent that was driving him wild, and it had done so all evening.

When he followed her onto the patio, she flipped a switch and, true to her word, the area lit up and he saw it—a huge cemented hole in the ground. "When I first arrived they were just digging it out," she was saying. "Now it's begun to take shape. Already I can tell it's going to be beautiful."

He shook his head and his mouth curled into a smile. "Pools aren't beautiful, Vanessa. People are beautiful."

Thinking they had wasted enough time already, he crossed the patio to where she was standing staring out at the pool. When he reached her he took her hand in his and turned her to him. His gaze took in the features of her face, moving from her dark eyes, her high cheekbones, her delicious-looking mouth and back to her eyes again. "*You* are beautiful," he said in a deep, husky voice.

She shook her head. "You're either seeing things or have bad eyesight."

"It's neither," he said, reaching out and gently looping his arms around her shoulders and taking a step closer, bringing their bodies right smack against each other. "I know beauty when I see it, Vanessa, and *you* are beautiful."

She sighed, and he knew she'd figured it would be a waste of time to argue with him, so she said, "Thank you."

"You're welcome."

At that moment a million scenarios began filling Cameron's mind, all of them fantasies or dreams in which she was a willing participant. His dreams were what had kept him going even when it seemed Vanessa's icy attitude toward him would never melt. Now he was ready to turn one of those dreams—didn't matter which one since there were many—into reality.

He decided to take things slow and dipped his head to brush a kiss across her lips. "I like tasting you," he said, watching her eyes darken.

"Do you?"

"Yes." He then dipped his head to kiss her again, this time gliding the tip of his tongue across the fullness of her mouth. "I do. You taste good. You smell good. And…you can do this to me," he said, slowly sliding his hands from her shoulders to her backside and pressing her against him so she would know exactly what he was talking about.

She arched into his erection, and his breath caught at such a bold move. "Are you sure *I* did this?" she asked in a whisper close to his ear.

A chuckle rumbled deep within his throat. "Baby,

I'm positive you did it. I haven't thought of anything but making love to you all evening," he said, trailing kisses down her throat.

"Is that a fact?"

"Yes, definitely nonfiction." While one hand remained on her backside, the other gently caressed her back while he continued to taste her slowly, letting the tip of his tongue move to the underside of her ear.

"Cameron." Her voice was barely a whisper, but he could hear the deep desire in it.

"Yes?"

"Stop torturing me." She arched into him some more.

"You're the one in control, Vanessa. Just say the word."

"Take me."

She didn't have to say a single thing more. As far as he was concerned those two words said it all. He swept her into his arms and headed back into the house, pausing only long enough to adjust his hold on her so she could reach out and pull shut the French doors.

"Where to?" he asked, glancing down at her when he stood in the middle of the living room. Adrenaline was pouring through his veins at an alarming speed. He wanted her. Now. But he refused to allow their first time to be anywhere other than a bed. Later, all the others could be anytime, anyplace, any position, just as he'd said.

"The guest room is upstairs. First door on your right."

Before she had finished what she was saying, he was already moving in that direction. When he reached the room he gave the furnishings nothing more than a quick glance. His attention, however, was definitely drawn to the huge sleigh bed. It looked sturdy and that was good. He crossed the room and leaned down to place her on it and was surprised when she pulled him down on the bed with her, hungrily latching on to his mouth. He groaned deep in his chest when she slipped her tongue between his parted lips and knew her degree of need was just as high as his.

"Now, Cameron. I couldn't stand it if you waited." Her voice was filled with tension and desire and her words reflected a desperation that hit him below the gut.

In a tangle of ardent open-mouthed kisses and eager, frantic hands, he began removing her clothes, pulling the blouse over her head and sliding the skirt down her hips. He tossed her sandals aside and then she lay there, in full view, wearing nothing more than a white lace bra and a matching thong that barely covered her feminine mound.

Although the lingerie was fairly revealing, he wanted to see the real thing and reached out and unclasped her bra. Her breasts, in all their fine glory, were exposed to his eyes. He reached out and touched them, caressed them, then leaned over and took a hardened tip into his mouth, sucking relentlessly.

"Cameron…"

He pulled back to lower the thong down her thighs. She lifted her hips as he slowly slid the flimsy material down her legs. Tossing her thong aside, he reached out and touched her center. Finding it wet, he began stroking it, stirring up the scent of her in the room.

"Cameron…" She murmured his name again in a tortured groan. "Don't play with me. Just do it."

"If you're absolutely, positively sure that's what you want."

"I'm absolutely, positively sure," she moaned.

He stood back as his gaze moved all over her naked body, over her breasts, down to the core of her femininity then down the length of her gorgeous long legs, before inching back toward her center, the part of her that drew him. That's where he would get the ultimate, succulent taste he craved.

Unable to resist any longer, he quickly began removing his clothes while she watched him, feeling the heat of her eyes over him as he bared all. Her sexy scent now permeated the room, driving him crazy with the need to make love to her after three years of wanting her. He took the time to ease the condom he had taken from his wallet over his shaft before moving back toward the bed.

"I told you earlier that I liked your taste. Remember?"

She gazed at him through heavy-lidded eyes filled with desire. "Yes."

"Now I intend to show you just how much."

Vanessa gasped when his mouth took hers with heated possession, at the same time he moved his hand lower, past her stomach to settle right between her legs. He stroked her there again, ardently fondling the swollen bud of her womanhood.

"You're playing with me again," she accused in a breathless moan.

"Then let me try something else," he whispered in her ear.

Before she realized what he was about to do, he eased her back onto the fluffy bed coverings and began kissing a trail down her stomach. Every place his mouth touched made her skin feel sensitized. When he reached the spot between her inner thighs, he began placing heated kisses there.

Vanessa lifted her hips, barely able to tolerate the intense sensations overtaking her. Her need for modesty vanished, and she instinctively opened her legs when his mouth moved to the center of her.

She screamed his name at the first stroke of his tongue on her and her body quivered from the inside out when he began feasting on her hungrily, as if he'd been waiting a long time to do what he was doing. A strangled moan got caught in her throat and her hips rose off the bed when he stopped nibbling on her and began a tormenting lick.

"Cameron!"

She screamed his name again when her body exploded in one mind-bending, earth-shattering climax. By the time the sound echoed off the walls, he had leaned up to position his body over hers. The moment her trembling subsided, she looked up and gazed into his eyes.

"I've wanted you for so long," he whispered, his erection homing in on the heat of her like iron toward a magnet.

Still recovering from the effects of one hell of an orgasm, Vanessa somehow found the strength to lift her hips, and the moment his hardened tip grazed her womanly core, he threw his head back and slid into her body. She wrapped her legs around him when he began moving back and forth inside her. With each thrust, her body was being navigated to a place it had never been before.

She might be the one in control, but he was the one plotting a course that was pushing her toward another skyrocketing experience. She had never known pleasure this intense, this extreme and forceful. It was as if his body knew just what position, what angle to take to hit that precise spot—her ultimate erogenous zone.

Each mind-blowing plunge was made to send her over the edge, and she felt her thighs quaking and her muscles spasming. When he bucked his body with an intensity that tested the endurance of the mattress springs, she felt her body explode at the same time his did.

"Vanessa!"

He hollered out her name, giving one last long, hard thrust into her body. She seemed to break into a million tiny pieces upon impact, never realizing something like this could be so powerful and earth-shattering. And then he was back at her mouth, kissing her with a hunger that was sending her body into an erotic spin all over again.

At that moment, the only thing she was totally aware of was that whether she wanted him to or not, Cameron Cody was rocking her world.

Neither wanted to move so they lay there, wrapped in each other's arms, their bodies connected, their limbs entwined for the longest time while their breathing returned to normal and their pounding heartbeats abated.

Sometime later, Cameron eased off Vanessa to look down at her. He was mesmerized, slightly shaken at what had taken place. He'd wanted her for so long, he wasn't surprised at the magnitude of his need, his craving, his desire. But what he hadn't counted on or expected was the intense degree of satisfaction and fulfillment he'd received.

Never before had any woman made him feel what he'd felt with her. If he had to describe it, he couldn't.

No words could. Sensations he'd never before encountered had rammed through his body, overtaking his mind, as well. It was totally bizarre, impossible to comprehend and even a tad bit alarming that one single woman could make him feel that way.

But she had.

Somehow, Vanessa Steele had tunneled her way under his hardest covering, his most tightly sealed wrap, and was embedded under his skin. No woman had ever done this.

His gaze studied her face. Her eyes were closed and she was breathing evenly, but he knew she wasn't asleep. Like him, she was probably trying to get her mind and body in sync, which wasn't easy after what they had shared.

"You're one amazing woman," he said softly, truthfully, breaking into the quiet silence surrounding them.

He watched a smile touch her lips as she slowly opened her eyes to him. "Thank you. That was a wonderful thing to say."

He considered the look in her eyes. It was as if she was both surprised and relieved by his words. Why? Had someone once told her differently? An old lover perhaps? He pushed the thought aside, thinking if that was the case, the person evidently hadn't recognized true passion when he saw it. Besides, he didn't want to think of anyone else having shared something so special with her. That was all in the past. Whether she knew it or would accept it, she belonged to him now and that was all that mattered. He would always tell her how remarkable she was.

"It's true," he said, staring down into her face. From that first day he'd known she was a beautiful woman, but he hadn't known just how beautiful until now. She had that afterglow look, that aroused look in her eyes that said she could and would take him on again. Even now, after what they'd just shared, he still wanted to devour her, and he was certain she knew it because his erection had grown hard against her belly.

He leaned down, deciding that he wanted to play with her lips again, and began licking them from corner to corner. He liked the purr of pleasure that eased from her throat. He liked it even more when he felt her hand travel down his stomach to close over his shaft. He sucked in a deep breath and groaned when she began stroking him.

"Two can play your game, Mr. Cody," she whispered. Her hands were steady, her fingers confident, and he felt a rush of blood surge through his veins, especially the ones located where she had touched.

"You're playing with dynamite," he whispered, barely getting the words out when pleasure as raw as it could get shot all through him.

"Umm, I can believe that," she said softly, in a sultry voice. "I'm still recovering from the aftershocks of the last explosion."

"Vanessa…"

Cameron said her name, whispered it from deep within his gut. He leaned down and kissed her, at the same time positioning his body over hers again. He slid into her, slowly, easily, and felt as if he was getting a piece of heaven. He groaned in pleasure as he continued to kiss her hungrily while slowly moving in and out of her body.

He felt on fire, scorched, and when her body began quivering beneath his, he literally went up in smoke.

She called out his name, clenched his shaft with her inner muscles, pulling him deeper inside her, and he threw his head back and growled as he experienced yet another mind-blowing, body-ramming orgasm.

He had only one conscious thought: Just who was getting sexually addicted to whom?

# Chapter 9

With her eyes still closed, barely released from sleep, Vanessa reached for the ringing telephone next to her bed. "Hello."

"So, who's my neighbor? Have you checked him out yet?"

Cheyenne's question jerked Vanessa out of her slumberous state and she immediately opened her eyes. Sunlight was pouring into the room and she could hear the shower running. Memories of last night came flooding back and a quick glance at the spot beside her in bed indicated tumbled sheets and an indentation where a man's body had been.

Cameron's body.

"Vanessa, hey, are you awake? I asked about my neighbor and if you'd had a chance to check him out yet."

Vanessa sighed, knowing there was no way she was

going to tell her sister that not only had she checked him out, but she'd gone a step further and had slept with him, as well. "Yes, I'm awake, Cheyenne, and yes, I've checked him out."

"And?"

Vanessa rubbed a hand across her face. "And it's Cameron."

There was a pause. Then Cheyenne said, "Cameron? As in Cameron Cody?"

"Yes, as in Cameron Cody."

She could hear Cheyenne's soft chuckle and frowned. It always annoyed Vanessa that her two sisters had found Cameron's hot pursuit of her rather amusing. "So, I assume buying the house next door was a calculated move on his part after finding out you would be house-sitting for me for two weeks."

Vanessa sighed. If only her sister knew the whole story. "Yes, it was."

"Wow, that's really something for a man to want you that bad to go to those extremes. Why don't you put him out of his misery and go ahead and have an affair with him, Van?"

Vanessa couldn't help the smile that touched her lips. She doubted Cameron was in much misery this morning since they *were* having an affair. But it even went deeper than that. They were officially sex mates for the next eleven days. "I'll think about it."

"He's not going away. Determined men are like pimples. They keep reappearing."

"I'll keep that in mind."

"I don't understand why you don't like the guy. He's good-looking, sexy, wealthy and—"

"Goodbye, Cheyenne."

"Hey, don't you want my opinion?"

"Not really. Call Taylor and harass her." She then hung up the phone.

"It's not good to hang up on people."

Vanessa flicked her gaze in the direction of the deep male voice. Cameron was leaning against the bathroom door wearing only a towel wrapped around his waist. His body was glistening, still wet from his shower, and just as Cheyenne had said, he was good-looking, sexy…

She wondered how much he'd heard. "Cheyenne is used to me hanging up on her. We have that kind of relationship."

He took a few steps into the room and she had to struggle with the breath that was forcing its way through her lungs. The only thing worse than a good-looking Cameron was a half-naked good-looking Cameron. Although there was the towel, it didn't take much for her to visualize him wearing nothing at all, as he'd done most of last night. She had seen enough of him in the buff. Or had she? She then decided it hadn't been enough and that she would love seeing even more.

"And what kind of relationship is that?" he asked, coming to sit on the edge of the bed beside her. He had a just-showered scent. His smell was fresh, manly.

"It's the kind where she expects me to hang up on her when she starts getting bossy, which she has a tendency to do. I'm the oldest and she's the youngest but sometimes I think she believes it's vice versa."

His sexy chuckle seemed to rumble off the walls in the room. "And what about your other sister? Taylor. The one living in New York."

Vanessa sat up in bed and braced her back against the headboard. "Taylor likes keeping everyone out of her business, so she makes sure she doesn't get into anyone else's. She's the one we call the Quiet Storm."

He lifted a brow. "And why is that?"

"Because she doesn't have a lot to say. She's usually mild-mannered and easygoing. But if you piss her off, there's plenty of hell to pay."

"Oh, I see."

Cameron stared at her for a long moment and Vanessa began getting uncomfortable under his fixed gaze. "What?" she asked.

He smiled. "It just occurred to me that I hadn't kissed you good morning."

"Oh, were you supposed to?"

"Definitely."

And then he was inching his face closer to hers for a kiss. It was soft and gentle, but it didn't take long for it to turn into something desperate and hungry. When he finally lifted his mouth from hers, she kept her eyes on his lips and asked, "So what would you like to do today?"

The look and smile he gave her told her she hadn't needed to ask. "I'll let you think of something," he said.

A part of her felt that maybe she should send him away, put distance between them to lessen the impact his mere presence was having on her. An idea formed in her mind; perhaps they should each do their own thing during the day and just come together at night. But she immediately squashed it. The thought of planning only their nights together seemed too calculated, nonspontaneous and such a waste of valuable time. There was that part of her that wanted him around both day and night, and they only had eleven days left. "Would you like to go shopping?" she asked.

He lifted a dark brow. "Shopping?"

"Yes. There're some wonderful shops in town."

He nodded. "All right, shopping it is. I need to go home and change but I'll be back within the hour. Unless you want to go back to sleep for a while to get some rest. We were up pretty late."

That was an understatement, she thought. They had been awake practically all night. She had used muscles she hadn't used in years, if ever. Those same achy muscles from yesterday were now aching for another reason.

"No, I'm fine. I don't need any more sleep."

"Okay," he said, standing slowly. "I'll see you in an hour."

Vanessa watched as he dropped the towel and began dressing. Although seemingly unbothered by his nakedness, she was *getting* bothered by it. Her skin was beginning to feel tingly, and the memories of last night were beckoning for a repeat performance.

He was about to slip into his pants when she got up enough courage to act. "Cameron?"

He glanced over at her. "Yes."

"I don't need any more sleep, but there is something else I can use right now." She was certain the look in her eyes and the low pitch of her voice were a dead giveaway.

"And what's that?" he asked.

She sighed. He was deliberately making her spell things out for him. No problem. She could do that. "Come here and I'll show you," she said.

He slowly walked back over to the bed, and she leaned over toward him and kissed his bare stomach before reaching out and gliding her hands over his thick erection. "This," she said looking up at him, "is what I can use right now."

The smile that touched the corners of his lips sent all kinds of sensations throbbing through her, and when he stepped back and removed his shirt she knew that being a sex mate to this man was better than she had ever imagined. And the thought that he'd found her amazing in bed had boosted her confidence level sky-high.

The moment his knee touched the mattress she was reaching out to him, rubbing her naked body against his. And when he wrapped his arms around her and eased her down into the thickness of the bed coverings, she knew it would be late when they got to town to do any shopping. But then, some things just couldn't be hurried.

"So what do you think of this one?"

A surge of desire raced through Cameron as he sat in the chair at the dress shop surveying yet another outfit on Vanessa. It was hard to believe women did this sort of thing every time they purchased clothes. First, it took them forever to find exactly what they wanted on the rack, then they had to go into the dressing room to try it on and then come out wearing it to get someone's opinion. So far this was her sixth outfit. He had liked them all except for the one that had barely covered her thighs, definitely showing too much leg. He'd told her he hadn't liked the little black skirt, but she had smiled and placed it in her "to buy" stack anyway.

He smiled when he thought of those legs of hers, the same ones that had wrapped around him tightly, locking him inside her body, clenching her muscles to draw everything out of him while they had—

"Cameron, I asked what you thought."

Her words reclaimed his attention. He tapped his fingers on his knee. This would be another one he didn't like. It showed too much breast. Hell, her twin globes were pouring out of it and the swath of light overhead was making it nearly impossible not to notice the hardened tips of her nipples pressing against the fabric. This dress would make a lot of women jealous. But it was the men he was worried about. Men would see her in this dress and immediately want to take her out of it.

"I don't like it," he finally said.

"Why?"

Last time, with the skirt, he hadn't given her a reason and she'd decided to purchase it anyway. Maybe if he told her why he didn't particularly care for this dress, she wouldn't buy it. "It shows too much cleavage. Your breasts are all but pouring out of it."

He then dragged his gaze over the rest of her and said, "The outfit leaves very little to the imagination. It's clinging to you like a second layer of skin. A man will look at you in that dress and immediately think of sex."

She glanced down at herself in the outfit. "You think so?"

"Hell, yeah."

She glanced back up, met his gaze and smiled. "In that case I think I'll take it."

Cameron immediately saw red and wondered if steam was coming out of his ears. Before he had a chance to say anything, she had darted back into the dressing room. She was lucky they were in a public place or he would be striding into that dressing room to teach her a lesson about tempting him.

He was about to settle back in his chair to wait for her to come out wearing yet another outfit when his cell phone rang. The caller ID indicated it was Xavier. "Yes, X, what's going on?"

"The main office at Global Petroleum was broken into last night. Security has been tight there for the past few days so we figure it might have been an inside job. A McMurray loyalist. We're discovering he had quite a few."

Cameron tightened his grip on the cell phone. "Was anything taken?"

"No, just a mess made with papers scattered all about. But a message was left for you, smeared on the wall."

Cameron rubbed the bridge of his nose. "What did it say?"

"Told you to give the company back to McMurray or you'll be sorry. Kurt told me to let you know that he's determined to find the person responsible."

Cameron nodded. There was no doubt in his mind that Kurt *would* find the person or die trying. "Okay, keep me posted."

"Do you want me to advise Kurt to let the local police know what's going on?"

"No, not yet. If we go to the authorities it will eventually get leaked to the papers. If the person is a McMurray loyalist then that's what they're counting on. Free publicity. I don't intend to oblige them."

"All right. I'll get back to you if anything else comes up."

Cameron clicked off the phone at the exact moment a rustling sound caught his attention. Glancing up, he saw the outfit Vanessa was now wearing. It had to be

made of the flimsiest material ever created. He immediately came to his feet. "No. Hell, no," he said, almost
growling. "I don't like it."

He couldn't believe someone would design such a
thing for public wear. It was so thin he could even see
she wasn't wearing any underwear. The dark area between her legs clearly showed that.

An innocent smile touched her lips. "What do you
mean you don't like it?"

He crossed his arms over his chest. "Just what I said,
Vanessa. I don't like it."

She placed her hands on her hips and he saw that
the top part of the dress was just as transparent as the
bottom. She might as well have been standing there
naked. "In that case it's a good thing you don't have
to wear it because I happen to like it," she said. "And
I'm getting it."

She turned around to leave and he called out to her,
annoyed. "I thought you wanted my opinions."

She turned back around. "I do."

Cameron frowned, puzzled. "Then please explain
why the outfits that I don't like, you're buying anyway."

She smiled sweetly. "I want your opinion, Cameron, but that doesn't necessarily mean I'll take it.
Those are all the outfits I intend to purchase today
and I'll be back in a second." She slipped back into
the dressing room.

Cameron couldn't stop the smile that curved his lips.
It seemed some women were just born to be stubborn,
and the one he intended to spend the rest of his life with
was doubly obstinate.

He shook his head in despair. How could he have
been so lucky?

* * *

Vanessa smiled at Cameron from across the table. They were sitting in one of those café-style restaurants that overlooked the bay while enjoying an early dinner. "I think we got a lot accomplished today."

He lifted a dark brow. "We?"

She dabbed her mouth with the corner of her napkin. "Yes. With your help I was able to pick out eight outfits that I think will enhance my wardrobe."

He rolled his eyes. "I didn't like half of them."

"Yes, but I liked them." *And you will, too, once you see me in them,* she thought. He had no idea she had bought the outfits with him in mind.

She placed her elbows on the table and supported her chin with her knuckles. "You're an only child, right?"

"Yes."

"It's unfortunate that you didn't have a sister, then you would understand how a woman's mind works."

"I don't need a sister to understand the workings of a woman's mind."

She gave him a quick smile. "It would have helped. Then you would have realized you were approaching the situation all wrong in going after me. You're not a forever kind of guy, Cameron. And on top of that, you have controlling tendencies. You aren't the type of man a woman would consider getting involved with for the rest of her life. But you are fling material, which is why I decided to have an affair with you."

Cameron didn't like what he was hearing but decided not to contradict anything she said. She would find out how wrong she was when he had her just where he wanted her—when he had her good and addicted. "So, what's on the agenda for tonight?" he asked, placing his napkin down and leaning back in his chair. Anticipation of what was yet to come was already flowing through his bloodstream.

"Umm, let's not plan anything. Let's go with spontaneous during our time together."

Cameron sighed. If he went with spontaneous she would be on this table, flat on her back with him on top of her, making out as though there was no tomorrow. Sitting across from her and watching her eat and drink had been torturous. Each time she had taken a sip from her glass and he had seen how her perfectly shaped mouth had fit on the rim, he'd wished it was fitting that way on a certain part of him instead. And as if that wasn't bad enough, there had been the way her throat had moved when the liquid had flowed down it, making him wonder just how deep her throat was. Just the thought had given him an erection as hard as a nail.

"So, will spontaneous be all right with you, Cameron?"

He really didn't think she knew what she was asking, and he had no intention of telling her. "Spontaneous is fine with me."

"Good. You won't be sorry."

He lifted a brow. He knew he wouldn't be sorry and hoped like hell that she wouldn't be, either. But what she'd said did give him pause. "Why would you think I'd be sorry?"

Her face broke into a smile. "Because you come across as a man who prefers structure. I take it you like to think things through thoroughly before taking action."

She had him there. Rash decisions didn't sit well with him. But spontaneous with her was a no-brainer.

He knew he wanted her and if given the opportunity to have her whenever and wherever, he would be a fool not to take it and run...to the nearest bedroom.

"Typically, I am that kind of guy, but I'm here to enjoy myself, and for the next eleven days there aren't any limitations."

Not wanting to give her too much time to ponder what he'd said, he tilted his head toward the bar. "Would you like another drink?"

She glanced at her almost-empty glass. "No, I think I've had enough. But I would like to walk on the beach later tonight. Would you?"

He regarded her for a minute, thinking of the unlimited spontaneous possibilities. Then he nodded his head slowly and said, "Yes, I'd love to do that."

A smile curved her mouth and she murmured, "Great. I'm looking forward to later."

# *Chapter 10*

Later could have come sooner, Cameron thought, as he walked barefoot along the beach. After their dinner date he had dropped Vanessa at home with the understanding they would meet on the beach after dark. When he'd asked if he needed to bring anything, she had simply smiled and said, "Just yourself."

So here he was with no specific plan in mind since spontaneous was the order of the evening. He looked past the palm trees toward her place and saw how well lit it was. Light spilled out, illuminating certain areas of the private beach.

"Cameron."

He turned toward the sound of his name and saw her standing next to a palm tree in a semilighted area. She was wearing the last outfit she had modeled for him. The one he had liked least. But seeing her in it now, the material as transparent as could be, had blood gushing through his veins.

As if mesmerized, he drifted toward her, his eyes never leaving her. With each step he took, his heart pounded out a heated rhythm and his teeth were clenched to stop the flood of sensations overtaking him.

Her outfit might have been provocative as hell, but it was her stance that was his undoing. She leaned against the tree, her legs braced apart in such a way that the flimsy material flowed all over her lush softness, her magnificent curves. Tantalizing. Sexy. Seductive.

The latter had him entranced. Standing there in that outfit she was the epitome of sensual femininity. He could clearly see everything, the puckered tips of her shapely breasts, the flat stomach and small waist and the dark triangle between her legs. His mouth watered, his erection hardened and his breathing became a forced act.

The closer he got, the longer he looked into her passion-filled eyes, the more he wanted her.

The more he wanted spontaneous.

Every muscle in his body clenched with desire the moment he came to a stop in front of her. He reached out and, with a flick of his wrist, he unclasped the hooks on both her shoulders, and the dress slithered down her body and lay in a pool at her feet.

He whisked his eyes over her naked body and when, as if in a moment of nervousness, she lowered one of her hands to cover her center, he caught her wrist and moved her hand aside. She was his. And as far as he was concerned, what she was trying to hide was his. And he intended to have it. Now.

He took a step back and whipped his shirt over his head and with trembling, hot fingers he fumbled at his belt before jerking it free and tossing it aside. Then came his shorts. Anticipating what would happen tonight, he hadn't bothered with underwear.

Vanessa just stood looking at him, letting her gaze move from his face slowly down his body, stopping at his shaft.

It actually twitched under her direct perusal and he felt it harden even more right before her eyes. When she licked her lips, he released a tortured moan.

Instantly, she sank to her knees on the sand in front of him, and before he could draw his next breath, her hands closed over his erection just seconds before she took him into her mouth.

The impact of that sensual contact made his entire body shudder. She began stroking him all over with her tongue, then raking that same tongue across the sensitized tip, nibbling gently with her teeth before sucking deeply. He tangled his fingers in her hair, trying to tug her away one minute and then trying to hold her mouth hostage on him the next.

When he felt an explosion starting right there at the tip, he jerked back, and in one quick move he eased her down and positioned his body over hers. The moment she lifted her hips to him, he entered her in one smooth thrust, driving deep into her wetness.

She screamed his name at the same exact time he screamed hers, and it seemed every cell in his body fragmented as he was thrown into mind-boggling pleasure. Too late he realized that he hadn't used a condom just as he felt his body explode, releasing everything he had deep into her womb.

He held her there, her body locked to his, and somehow, moments later, he found the strength to thrust deep into her again, and in no time felt himself succumbing, exploding once more.

This was rapture so pure, so unadulterated and perfect.

He knew it could only be this way with Vanessa.

"Would you like to watch a movie?" Cameron asked. "The previous owner left his DVD collection behind."

Vanessa glanced over at Cameron from across the kitchen and wondered if he was serious. After the rendezvous on the beach that had left them both naked and covered in sand, he had carried her to his place where they had used his outside shower. He had shampooed her hair and she had washed his back, then they had made love all over again, right there in the shower. Afterwards, he made her promise never to wear the outfit again and had given her one of his T-shirts to put on. They had decided they were hungry and now were in the kitchen.

"I'm going to have to pass on the movie, but I would like you to tell me who taught you how to cook."

He leaned back against the counter, holding a cup of coffee in his hand. He had thrown together an omelet and biscuits. "My grandfather. After my grandmother died it was just the two of us."

She nodded. "Is he still living?"

He shook his head and she could see the sadness reflected in his deep-set eyes. "No, he died when I turned eighteen. Right before I entered college."

"The two of you were close. I can tell," she said softly. She could hear the special love in his voice.

She watched a smile touch his lips. "Yes, we were very close. He was the best."

She didn't say anything for the longest time until finally she admitted, "My dad was the best, too. He never had sons but it didn't matter to him. My mom, Taylor, Cheyenne and I were the apples of his eye and he always let us know it. I only wish…"

"What?"

"That I could have convinced him to stop smoking. He died of lung cancer, and a part of me wished I could have done something, hidden his cigarettes, anything."

"That wouldn't have helped, Vanessa. The person smoking is the one who has to want to stop. Your father would have continued to smoke until it was his decision to quit."

What Cameron was telling her was no different from what her family and Sienna had told her. But when she remembered her father in his last days, how the cancer had left a robust man barely recognizable, a part of her still believed there was something she could have done.

Not wanting to discuss her father any longer, she decided to ask Cameron more about his childhood. In all the media releases she'd read on him, very little had been mentioned about it, except that he'd dropped out of school at sixteen.

"Was your grandfather your mom's father or your dad's?"

She watched him take a sip of his coffee before glancing over at her. "He was my father's father. My parents were killed in a fire at our apartment complex when I was six. My dad was able to get me out but when he went back in for my mother, the building collapsed."

Vanessa gasped and she immediately felt a tug on her heart. "Oh, how awful that must have been for you."

Cameron stared down into his coffee cup a long moment before finally lifting his head and meeting her gaze. "It was. And for the longest time, like you, I was on a guilt trip. I would often ask myself, What if Dad had gotten Mom out first? What if I had awakened and smelled the smoke first? What if I had convinced them to have a fire-escape plan like they had taught us in school? There were so many what-ifs, but I soon realized that none of them would bring my parents back."

Vanessa's heartstrings tugged tighter. She could just imagine the guilt that had consumed his young mind. "Is that when you went to live with your grandparents?" she asked.

"Yes, and they were great. It was as if they knew exactly what I needed." He chuckled. "My grandparents were pretty big on hugs. The warm and cuddly kind."

Vanessa smiled. She wondered how a man with such a warm and cuddly childhood with his grandparents could grow up to be the hard and controlled man that he was.

She opened her mouth to ask him another question when his cell phone rang. "Excuse me." He picked it up off the counter. "Yes, X."

Vanessa could tell from the expression on Cameron's face and the tenseness of his body that he didn't like whatever the person was telling him.

"Tell Kurt that I want this person found before he does any more damage." He snapped the phone shut.

"Trouble?"

Cameron jerked his head up and looked at her. "No, everything's fine."

"You're sure?"

"Positive."

She doubted he would tell her if things weren't fine and decided not to get upset by it. He really had no reason to share his business matters with her, since she certainly wouldn't be sharing any of the Steele business with him. "I've changed my mind."

The gaze holding hers was steady. "About what?"

"The movie. I'm not sleepy and I would love watching one if you still want to."

A small smile touched the corners of his lips. "Yes, I want to and I'll even let you choose something sappy."

Vanessa stood. "That's mighty generous of you, Mr. Cody."

He grinned. "Haven't you figured out by now that I'm a very generous person?"

"Need more tissue?"

Vanessa looked over at him with tear-filled eyes. "Sorry. I always cry whenever I watch this movie."

"Then why do you watch it?"

"Because it's a good movie."

"It's a tear-jerker."

She eased off the sofa to stand in front of him. "It's still a good movie. In fact, it's my favorite and has been since the first time I saw it when I was eight. I'm surprised you don't like it."

He shrugged. "It took Dorothy too long to find her way back to Kansas. As far as I'm concerned she wasn't too bright. She should have figured out a lot sooner there was no yellow brick road that would get her there."

Vanessa placed her hand on her hips, not liking his critique. "Do you have a favorite movie?"

"No."

"Not a one?"

"No, not a one. I like creating my own action," he said. With her standing right in front of him, her luscious scent was filling his lungs, and his T-shirt, which barely hit her at midthigh, was looking sexy as hell on her.

Not able to resist temptation any longer, he reached out and pulled her down into his lap. A naughty grin touched his lips. "In addition to creating my own action, I especially like taking part in my own love scenes."

And then he leaned over and kissed her.

Vanessa returned the kiss, doubting she would ever tire of kissing him. She wrapped her arms around Cameron's neck and tasted him with the same hunger with which he was tasting her. Beneath her, his erection nudged her hip and his hand began tracing a path up her inner thigh.

Suddenly Cameron pulled both his mouth and hand away. "We need to talk," he said, resting his forehead against hers. "We need to discuss something I should have brought up earlier."

She kept her arms wrapped around his neck and met his gaze. "What?"

"I didn't use any protection when we made love on the beach tonight."

His words were like ice water thrown on her. No protection. How had she not realized? She'd never had sex with a man without using some type of protection. She'd been taking the Pill since her college days but when it came to sex these days, women had more to worry about than an unwanted pregnancy. There were serious health issues to consider.

"I'm safe, Vanessa. Don't worry about that," Cameron said as if reading her thoughts. "I get a physical every year."

"So do I," she quickly said, needing to reassure him, as well. "I'm safe, too."

He smiled and tightened his arms around her waist. "I know you are."

She was tempted to ask why he was so certain, but just the thought that he was sent a warm feeling through her.

"Now that we've covered that part, we need to discuss the other."

She lifted a brow. "What other?"

"The possibility of a pregnancy."

She shook her head. "That's not possible. I'm on the Pill."

He nodded slowly. "Anything is possible. The Pill isn't 100 percent guaranteed and if a child has been created, Vanessa, the agreement is off."

"What do you mean?"

"We agreed that once this affair ended we wouldn't be in contact with each other. But if you're pregnant that changes everything since I'd want to know about my child. Understood?"

She frowned, not liking the tone of voice he'd taken, and definitely not liking the way he was trying to take control of things. "I told you I'm on the Pill, so relax, Cameron. There won't be a baby."

"If there is—"

"Then I would let you know. But you're worrying for nothing."

He met her gaze for a long moment before standing with her in his arms. "Are you ready for bed?"

After that last conversation a part of her wanted to leave, to go back to Cheyenne's place and sleep in her own bed tonight. He had made her mad. But another part of her wanted to stay, to sleep cuddled under him and wake up with him in the morning. That was the part telling her to get over it.

She quickly made a decision and tightened her arms around his neck. "Yes, I'm ready."

# Chapter 11

Four days later, Cameron leaned against the rail on his patio watching the sun rising over the ocean. Vanessa was upstairs, still asleep in his bed. He had slipped away momentarily to come downstairs to wait for a call he expected from Kurt…and also to think.

Although he had no intention of doing so, if he were to adhere to their agreement, he had only one week left to spend with Vanessa. And if he were to analyze their days together since becoming sex mates, he would be the first to admit that they had been some of the best days of his life. He smiled, thinking that a lot could be said for spontaneity.

There hadn't been too much they hadn't tried in the bedroom. But then the bedroom hadn't been the only place they'd made love. In fact, come to think of it, the only times they had actually made it to the bed was when it was time for them to retire for the night. Otherwise, spontaneous meant spontaneous.

Vanessa had seduction down to an art form, and he'd discovered the hard way—literally—that she was a woman of incredible talents. She had to be the most passionate human being on the face of the earth. Already his body was whirring with thoughts of what today would bring.

Although the sex was great, Cameron knew it wasn't the only reason he was enjoying every moment that he spent with Vanessa. Whether it was playing tennis, looking for seashells on the beach, swimming together, cooking, even shopping, everything with her was turning into an adventure.

They never talked about work but had shared their thoughts about the many charitable organizations they were both involved with. He had also discovered that she was a very compassionate person who gave her time to others generously. When he'd told her about his involvement in Angel Flight, an organization in which CEOs volunteered their private jets to transport needy patients, she promised to propose it at the next Steele board meeting, now that the company was purchasing a private jet.

The ring of his cell phone interrupted his thoughts. He answered it. "Yeah, Kurt, what do you have for me?"

"An arrest has been made, Cameron."

He nodded, relieved. At first he'd tried not to get the authorities involved, but when there had been a third incident, he'd been left with no choice. For the next ten to fifteen minutes he listened while Kurt detailed how they had discovered the identity of the person responsible for vandalizing the offices of Global Petroleum on three separate occasions.

"Of course he won't admit McMurray put him up to anything," Kurt was saying. "But that's okay since the man was caught in full color on video. I'm going to make sure he does jail time for what he did, which will give him a chance to think about it."

Cameron nodded. "Good job, Kurt. The charges being brought against him will send a clear message to others that I mean business and I won't tolerate such behavior from any employee."

After ending the call with Kurt, Cameron leaned back against the rail and stared across the ocean. For some reason he had a gut feeling that this thing with McMurray was far from over. Bitter, John McMurray would continue to make problems or would hire others to do his dirty work for him.

Not wanting to think about McMurray anymore, Cameron switched his thoughts back to Vanessa. They had gone shopping again yesterday, this time for baby items. She was excited about the new addition to the Steele family, Chance's son, Alden. Cameron was grateful she hadn't asked for his opinion on anything since he couldn't recall the last time he'd been around a baby.

*A baby.*

He remembered his conversation of a few nights ago with Vanessa when they'd discussed the possibility of her being pregnant. Yesterday, while shopping for Chance and Kylie's baby, a part of him had wished that he and Vanessa had been shopping for their own child. He had never entertained any thoughts of sharing a child with a woman until now, but the more he thought about it, the more he liked the idea…with Vanessa.

He shook his head. First he needed to secure a strong

relationship with the mother before he could even contemplate bringing a baby into the mix.

But he definitely was thinking about it.

"Okay, I'm stumped," Vanessa said, tossing aside the crossword puzzle she'd been working on for the past half hour. A few hours ago she and Cameron had made love upstairs in his bed and now they were stretched out beside each other by his pool in a double chaise longue.

"Maybe I can help," Cameron said, glancing from the book he was reading. "What's the clue?"

Vanessa picked up the book. "It's a five-letter word for 'a fruit-loving bug.' The second letter is a *P*."

Cameron turned on his side and stretched his arm around her. "Aphid." He proceeded to spell it for her.

She stared at him, amazed. "And you knew the answer…just like that," she said, snapping her fingers for emphasis.

He shrugged. "No great mystery. I love science, always have."

Vanessa shook her head. He evidently loved math, as well, if the last two shopping trips were anything to go by. By the time they'd reached the cash register, he had totaled the purchases in his head, almost to the penny. She wondered…

She flipped on her side to face him. "Cameron?"

"Yes?"

Her heart began to race. It happened every time his sexy smile was directed at her. "It's plain to see that you're a very smart and intelligent man, and I don't believe you acquired those traits since reaching adulthood. So why did you drop out of high school?"

She watched what amounted to pain form in his eyes

and he shifted on the lounger, seeming uncomfortable with her question. He lowered his arm from her shoulders. For the first time ever, Vanessa could feel him withdrawing from her. Though he seldom discussed his childhood, he had told her about his parents and how they'd died and about the grandparents who'd raised him. Why did this particular question bother him?

"I'm sorry if I asked you about something that's too personal, Cameron."

He glanced back at her and then, as if he had reached a decision about something, he pulled her back into his arms. "No, it's not too personal, at least not for you. I dropped out of school at sixteen because my grandfather lost his job. The company he had been employed with for over forty years deliberately laid him off less than a year before he was to retire so he couldn't receive any retirement benefits."

"Oh, how awful."

"Yes, it was. He was sixty-four and because of his age, there was no other place for him to go or anything else that he knew how to do. My grandfather wasn't the only person that particular company ruined that way. There were a number of others."

Vanessa sat up. She was angry. "But couldn't something be done about that company? Surely the government could have stepped in and—"

"The government did nothing," Cameron said, just as angry and very bitter. "There were no laws in place to protect workers against such tactics. And with no money coming in, I had to do something. I couldn't let my grandfather worry himself to death. His health hadn't been at its best as it was, and he was trying to make that final year."

"So you dropped out of school to help." It was a statement rather than a question.

"Yes. Gramps didn't want me to do it, neither did my teachers, but there was nothing else to do. There was still a mortgage on the house and Gramps was still paying the medical bills my grandmother had left behind."

For a moment he didn't say anything then he added, "I'm just thankful for Mrs. Turner."

Vanessa raised a brow. "Mrs. Turner?"

"Yes. She was one of my teachers who thought I had a bright future ahead of me, so she volunteered to tutor me. When I turned eighteen I passed the GED and got my high-school diploma that way."

Vanessa nodded. She was thankful for someone like Mrs. Turner in Cameron's life, as well. "And what type of work did you do for those two years?"

"I worked at Myers Feed Store for a while, driving his truck, making deliveries, and then I went to work for Handover Construction Company. With the money I made I was able to keep food on the table for me and Gramps and buy his medication each month."

Vanessa knew from what he'd told her last week that his grandfather had died right before Cameron had entered college. That must have been a lonely time for him. "Thanks for sharing that with me, Cameron."

Instead of saying anything, he pulled her into his arms and just held her close.

"I can't believe you're taking time to call me," Sienna teased. "I thought Cameron was occupying most of your time these days. Don't tell me you've had enough of each other already."

Vanessa dropped down on her bed and glanced out the window. Down below she could see Cameron driving off, going to town to pick up the items they needed for dinner. Tonight they would get into the kitchen together. "No, we haven't had enough."

She thought about what she'd said then decided she couldn't really speak for Cameron and modified her reply. "At least I haven't had enough."

Sienna was the only person to whom Vanessa had admitted that she and Cameron were having an affair. To Cheyenne, who called periodically, she hadn't said anything, deciding to let her sister keep guessing, although Vanessa was pretty sure Cheyenne knew the score.

"How many more days?" Sienna asked her.

"Seven."

"Then what happens?"

"Then Cameron returns to Charlotte. I'll be leaving a day or two afterward when Cheyenne returns."

"What's after that?"

Vanessa rolled her eyes. "Sienna, why are you asking me that? I told you that nothing happens after that. Cameron will go his way and I'll go mine. This was an island fling and nothing more."

"And what if you fall in love with him?"

Vanessa shook her head stubbornly. "Won't happen. You of all people know that I've learned—the hard way, I might add—how to keep my emotions in check."

"But why would you want to if the right person came along? You know that I wasn't ready for Dane when we first met. Talk about night and day. He was the rich kid and I was the one whose parents had more issues than *The New York Times* had newspapers. I tried to fight his interest, tried convincing him of all the reasons we were wrong for each other. Then I finally talked him into letting me be his bedmate for a night, thinking that would definitely get us out of each other's systems. You of all people know that didn't work."

"Yes, but you and Dane were meant to be together, I've always told you that. I never knew why you were fighting it and fighting him."

"The same way I don't understand why you're fighting Cameron. Okay, he can be a control freak at times, he likes being in charge, the master of his game. But even you said he's been letting you call the shots, allowing you to take control, so that means at least he's flexible. And can you honestly say that after spending a week with him, he's still the monster you always thought him to be?"

Vanessa remained quiet for a moment as she pondered Sienna's question. She thought about the time she and Cameron had spent together, all the fun they'd had. Then she said, "No, I don't think he's a monster."

Sienna must have heard the tiny catch in her voice because her friend didn't say anything for a while, until she asked, "Are you okay, Vanessa?"

"No, I'm not okay," she confirmed with a bit of gloom in her tone. "But I will be. It's just that…"

"What?"

"Nothing. I knew what I was getting into."

"Are you sure about that?"

Despite all the misgivings she was suddenly feeling, Vanessa refused to give in to the racing of her heart and summoned every ounce of her common sense. No, she told herself, what she was feeling was nothing other than good old-fashioned lust. "Yes, Sienna, I'm sure."

Vanessa held out her hand to Cameron. "The sharp knife."

He carefully placed the item she had requested into

her hand and then watched as she expertly removed the bone and skin from the four chicken breast halves before tossing the meat into the slow cooker.

"Bell pepper."

He scooped up the bell pepper strips that he'd cut and tossed them in the pot to join the chicken.

"Now the can of pepper-jack cheese soup and the chunky salsa mixture."

Before handing those items to her, he eased closer to her while she stood at the kitchen counter. "My mouth is watering already."

His closeness and the low chuckle that rumbled close to her ear actually made her shiver. Even after a week her body still reacted whenever he was near. "Then I expect you to have a clean plate later," she said, placing the lid on the cooker and setting it to cook on low for six hours. "This is what I call easy and tasty."

"I can certainly see that."

Considering her mind had been elsewhere all day, ever since talking to Sienna, Vanessa had wanted to prepare something that didn't take a lot of thought, and this was the first thing that had come to mind. It was one of the first dishes she had prepared in her home economics class in high school and she had served it to her family, or anyone else who wanted to eat it, for three nights in a row.

"So it's going to take six hours?" Cameron asked, easing still closer to her.

She smiled, already knowing where his mind was going. "Yes, just about."

"Would you like to go swimming while we wait?"

"Sure. Why not? But I didn't bring a bathing suit over here with me."

Cameron's smile nearly sizzled her insides. "Who

said anything about you needing a bathing suit? Let's be daring."

Vanessa chuckled. "If I recall, you've already been daring. I was sitting on the beach that day you decided to bare all before diving into the ocean."

He leaned over and touched her lips with his. "I saw you and even from a distance, I got turned on and needed to take a quick dip to cool off."

"You expect me to believe that?"

He took her hand in his. "Yes, because it's true. Haven't these past days we've spent together proved it?"

To Vanessa's way of thinking, these past days they'd spent together proved how quickly she had succumbed to his charm. What bothered her most was knowing that sooner or later she would have to start withdrawing. Their time together was now a clock slowly ticking away, and every second, minute or hour counted…until the end.

*The end.*

She inhaled deeply and instinctively snuggled closer to him, and he wrapped his arms completely around her. They'd had a lot of these types of moments, usually after making love when there were no words left to say and he would just hold her. Making the decision to have an island fling with him had been hard, but now what would be even harder was walking away knowing there would not be a repeat. This was all they would have.

"Yes, I'll go skinny-dipping with you, Cameron," she finally said, turning in his arms and looking up to meet his gaze. "But I won't walk out of this house down to the beach naked," she added. "I'm going to need something to wear."

A smooth grin curled the corners of Cameron's mouth. "Will one of my T-shirts do?"

She couldn't help but laugh, recalling how many times she had walked around in his T-shirts and how very little they covered. She remembered one night in particular when, in one of her seductive moods, she had seduced him while wearing his L.A. Lakers T-shirt. He had practically ripped the thing off before taking her right here on the kitchen table.

"If that's the best you can do, then yes, one of your T-shirts will do," she decided to say, trying to block the memories of that particular night from her mind.

"You know where they are."

A grin tugged at her lips. "Yes, I do, don't I?" She pulled herself out of his arms. "I'll be back in a second."

Vanessa was halfway up the stairs when she glanced back over her shoulder. Cameron was standing in the doorway separating the kitchen from the living room. His hands were braced on either side of the arch and his stance was as sexy as sexy could get. At that moment she wished she had a camera to capture that pose on film so she could take out the photo on those lonely nights after she returned to Charlotte.

She quickly turned back around and made it up the rest of the stairs. Damn, she didn't need this now, especially not when she was trying hard to keep what they were sharing in perspective. And she definitely hadn't counted on it.

Cameron Cody was truly beginning to grow on her. Even worse, he was slowly but surely getting under her skin in a way she hadn't thought possible.

*Chapter 12*

Cameron heard Vanessa return even before her bare feet touched the last step. He glanced up and tried not to stare. But he couldn't help himself. The woman did wonders for his T-shirts.

It was his opinion that her body was outright and unreservedly perfect, and as she walked toward him, putting those long gorgeous legs out in front of her, his blood raced, literally pounding through every part of him. His gaze traveled all over her. This particular shirt—the one promoting his construction company—seemed shorter than the rest. The cotton fabric clung to her full breasts and curvy hips.

When she finally reached the bottom step she slowly twirled around with her hands on her hips. "So, what do you think?" she asked as a smile twitched her lips.

He groaned inwardly. What he really thought was

that now was a good time to kiss that lush mouth of hers, or better yet, to whisk her into his arms and take her back upstairs. Everything about her, every sensuous detail, was wreaking havoc on his control, his ability to think straight, his ability to resist emotions he'd never encountered before.

"I think," he said, taking a step forward, "that you are the most beautiful woman I've ever met, whether you're wearing an outfit I personally don't like, my T-shirt or nothing at all. You are simply stunning."

A warm tingle started in Vanessa's breasts and moved lower, toward her midsection. The dark, tense eyes staring down at her seemed both serious and deeply enthralled. She bit her lower lip, trying not to let his words affect her so, and found it difficult. They *had* affected her.

She took a deep breath and glanced down at him. The only thing covering his body was a pair of outlandishly sexy swim trunks that left nothing to her imagination. They seemed like a second layer of skin and clearly emphasized the fact that he wanted her. Her heartbeat sped up at the thought of what would happen once they got down to the beach.

"I'm taking a large blanket and a bottle of body cream."

Vanessa hitched a brow. "Body cream?"

He smiled. "Yes, I want to rub it all over you after we take a swim."

A tremble ran through her body. She had a feeling that wasn't all he intended to do.

Vanessa lay on her stomach on the thick blanket with the sand as a cushion. She closed her eyes at the feel of Cameron's hands moving slowly, lightly over her shoulder, gently massaging the slope of her back and the curve of her neck. The cream he was rubbing into her skin smelled of tropical fruits, and his calloused fingers were working magic as he caressed her skin.

She released a long sigh when he rubbed more of the cream onto her back, tenderly kneading her muscles, working out her aches and pains at the same time he caused a different type of throbbing in her body.

"What are you thinking about?" he asked in an almost-whisper, leaning down close to her ear. He was on his knees straddling her butt. She could feel his nearness, his heat, and the way his hands were touching her, moving down her back, the rear of her thighs and then her behind was sending all kinds of sensations through her body.

"Umm, I'm thinking about how good your hands feel on me," she said, almost in a purr. "I've never gotten this much attention from a man before."

"And is that good or bad?"

She paused, thinking about his question, before she answered. "Before this trip, I would have thought it was bad. But now I can't help but think it's all good. I can't imagine another man touching me this way, making me feel this way, and—"

She never finished what she was about to say. Cameron had gently turned her over and rubbed some of the cream onto her chest. He began rubbing it into her skin, caressing her breasts in a circular motion around the nipples while they hardened at his touch.

After smearing more cream onto her body, his fingers moved lower to her stomach and with the tip of his finger he drew rings around her navel, sending a rush of sexual pleasure through every pore on her body. A part of her wanted to reach out and cover her feminine mound from his gaze, but she couldn't. Besides, it would be a waste of time. She might be the one in control, but Cameron had a way of using anything she did to his advantage. She was beginning to see that he was smart in more ways than one.

"I didn't tell you everything there was to know about this particular cream, Vanessa," he said, his voice a low, sensuous timbre.

She let go of a shaky breath at the mere sound. "What didn't you tell me?" She looked up into his face.

He was above her, straddling her body. Then he began lowering his head closer to hers. When he was just inches from her face he said, "The cream I've rubbed all over you is edible. Do you know what that means?"

Her gaze was locked with his and was filled with hunger, heat and a hefty dose of arousal. Of course she knew what he meant, what he was alluding to, but she decided to play dumb. "No, what does that mean?" she asked innocently.

Bracing his hands on both sides of her head, he leaned down to within inches of her lips. "It means, Vanessa Steele, that tonight, under the beauty of this Jamaican moon, you will become my treat."

"Your treat?" she asked, her voice barely audible against the waves rushing toward the shore.

"Yes, but first this…"

And then he leaned closer, captured her lips and kissed her as though she was everything he had ever wanted, everything he had ever needed, and that kissing her was his lifeline for the next minute, hour, day.

His mouth was feeding on hers with a hunger that made her whimper.

He slowly pulled his mouth away, and she immediately felt the loss of his lips on hers.

"Did I tell you that mango is my favorite fruit and this cream has plenty of mango in it?"

"Mango?"

"Yes. There's also a pinch of pineapple and avocado. Real tasty fruits. Exotic fruits. Fruits with mouthwatering flavor."

He picked up the bottle of cream and with his hands he smeared a trail of it from the tips of her breasts down to her stomach. When he came to her feminine mound with its smooth bikini wax, he stared at it for a moment before taking his hand and fully coating it with the fruity cream. It was like piling whipped cream on top of a hot fudge sundae.

"Cameron?"

"Yes?"

"What are you doing?"

"Fulfilling one of my fantasies. And I might as well confess right now that there's nothing spontaneous about this. This is something I've been thinking about for quite some time. And when we do part, Vanessa, I plan to take the taste of you with me. I want it embedded so deeply in my tongue that it becomes a permanent part of my taste buds. I want the scent of you to inflame my nostrils for all eternity."

"But we agreed—"

"I know what we agreed, Vanessa. This is an island fling and I will keep my word. But that doesn't mean I shouldn't remember what I consider to be some of the most special days I've ever had with a woman who has more passion in her little finger than some women have in their entire body. I won't do anything intentionally to look you up when we return to Charlotte, but as I told you in the beginning, I want to make love so good that you'll want to look me up."

"I won't," she said stubbornly, frowning.

"Then I really have my work cut out for me over the next six days, don't I?" he said softly, with a confidence she heard. His nostrils flared slightly when he continued. "You are in my system, and all these days of loving you only implanted you deeper. And before we separate, I'm going to make sure that I'm as entrenched within you as you are within me."

Vanessa glanced away, breaking eye contact as she looked out at the ocean. It was dark, and somewhere in the distance she could see the lights from a huge ship, probably a cruise liner. She was grateful they couldn't be seen from that far out at sea.

She breathed in deeply, wondering if she could become addicted to Cameron. Could he become an itch she would need to have scratched at some point? She shook her head, refusing to believe it. People engaged in affairs all the time and walked away. But the big question was this: Could she really and truly walk away from his loving? Endless passion, earth-shattering orgasms, an easy camaraderie with a man who made her feel desirable?

Yes, she could do it, because, although she had gotten to know Cameron a lot better than before, there were still some things about him that she wouldn't be able to tolerate. Such as his need to control and to be in control.

She turned back to look at him when she heard him removing his shorts. She watched almost spellbound as he slowly slid the garment down his legs, then she blinked, thinking that tonight his erection looked larger than usual. Was that possible?

A warm, hot tingle began in her midsection and quickly spread to the area between her legs when he slowly eased back to her, settling on his knees in the middle of her opened thighs.

"I'm going to lick you all over, starting here." He lifted her hips and placed her legs on his shoulders, bringing her feminine mound level to his. "Enjoy, sweetheart, because I certainly intend to."

Vanessa gasped at the first touch of Cameron's tongue on her sensitive flesh. Each stroke of his tongue was methodical, focused, greedy. He was giving her his undivided attention and it took everything she had not to scream out.

The intimate kiss might have started out as a late-night treat for him, but it was an entirely different thing to her. Each sensuous nibble was taking her to a place she had never been before, a place where only the two of them belonged. She didn't want to question the rightness of her thoughts, she just knew they were so.

The more he loved her in this most cherished way, the more sensations consumed her, taking over her mind and body. Her heart beat faster and her breathing became difficult. When the rumble of a scream was close to pouring forth from her throat, she bit down on her lips to hold it back. Her fingers dug into Cameron's shoulders, holding his mouth in place.

But the sensations became too much to bear. She tightened her grip on his shoulders even more and drew in a deep breath before letting it out by screaming his name when an orgasm hit.

"Cameron!"

The moment she called out his name he pulled his mouth from her and moved his body in place over hers. Then in one smooth and swift thrust, he entered her, going deep. "Wrap your legs around my waist," he whispered in her ear, and as soon as she did so, locking their bodies, he began thrusting in and out of her with the speed of a whip.

Her entire body clenched tightly, pulling everything she could out of him. She could tell he was fighting against an orgasm, trying to make it last, but she wanted more and she wanted it now.

Using her teeth she bit gently into his shoulder, then soothed the mark with her tongue. She felt him shudder, felt his body get harder inside hers and heard him moan close to her ear.

And then she felt it happen as he thrust into her hard. For the second time that night she didn't want to question the feeling of oneness with this man, the feeling that he could become her entire world, and that she was haphazardly tumbling into his.

She didn't want to think about anything, especially not the fact they had only six days left after tonight. The only thing she wanted to think about was how he was making her feel. This instant. This moment.

Vanessa knew that no matter what, after this time with Cameron, her life would never be the same.

# Chapter 13

Cameron's eyes opened slowly during the predawn hours. Something had awakened him. He reached out to pull Vanessa closer into his arms and came up empty-handed. All that was there, other than the slight indentation on the pillow where her head had lain, was her scent, an arousing fragrance that had become such an innate part of his life.

He gazed around the room and saw the open patio door. Evidently she hadn't been able to sleep. For a long while, neither had he. It was hard as hell to accept that their twelve days were over and that today at noon he would be flying out, returning to the States.

He tightened his fists at his sides, damning their agreement. There was no way she could deny that their time together had been special, especially the last six days. They had taken early-morning walks on the beach, picnics on the bay and had made love under the moonlight in a number of places. He would miss her like hell when he left, and he hoped and prayed each day that she would realize they were meant to be together.

A shiver passed through him at the thought of the separation they faced. What if, when she returned to Charlotte, she had no problem in keeping her end of the agreement and would not want to see him again? What if their time together meant more to him than it did to her? What if his entire plan backfired and he wasn't any closer to having her as a part of his life than he had been before taking Morgan's advice?

He pulled himself up in bed, suddenly thinking about all the things he'd never wanted from a woman before but now had to have from Vanessa. He'd thought he wanted possession, wanted to make her a part of his life without any deep emotional attachment or binding commitment. After all, he was a man who didn't do emotional attachments. But now he wanted it all. He wanted her.

*He loved her.*

He sucked in a deep, shaky breath with that admission. It was one he had thought he would never make again after Stacy. But Vanessa had proven him wrong. She had brought out in him something no woman had in over ten years—his desire to love unconditionally. She had broken down his defenses and made the twisted reason he'd wanted her in his life into something he hadn't counted on. Love.

He had always wanted Vanessa but hadn't realized or accepted that he also loved her.

Now he did, and what the hell was he supposed to do about it? He slowly slid back down in the bed. One thing he would not do was let her have her way and turn her back on what they could have together. His heart was at stake, and he was determined that, in the end, she would love him as much as he loved her.

He heard the sliding of the patio door and lowered his eyelids, pretending sleep. He wasn't ready to admit his feelings to Vanessa just yet. Not until he had another workable plan.

Through half-closed eyes, he watched as she dropped her robe and eased her naked body into bed beside him. She cuddled close, skin to skin, and lowered her head to his chest. Then, moments later, she glanced up, placed a kiss on his lips and whispered, "I'm going to miss you when you leave, Cameron Cody. A hell of a lot more than I should."

He didn't say anything since he knew she assumed he was asleep and her words hadn't been meant for him to hear. But those words sent every cell in his body vibrating. If she was fighting any feelings for him and was pretty close to the edge, he intended to push her over. He would try to be patient, but he wouldn't let her send him out of sight and out of mind.

When she cuddled back in his arms to reclaim sleep, a smile curved his lips. There were some risks worth taking, and no matter what it took, he intended to convince Vanessa of that.

"Are you sure you don't want to go to the airstrip with me?"

Vanessa shook her head as she watched Cameron get dressed. They had awakened that morning and made love. Then they had gone downstairs, and as they'd done on a number of other mornings, they had prepared

breakfast together. Afterward, they had come back upstairs to make love again. Now she was sitting up in bed
half-naked and he was putting on his shirt and pants.
A limo would be arriving in less than an hour to take
him to the airport where his private jet would return
him to the States.

"No, I think it's best if we say our goodbyes here,"
she said.

He glanced up and looked at her and then he slowly
walked over to the bed and pulled her into his arms.
"What we shared was special, Vanessa. I'm going to
miss it and I'm going to miss you. Why can't we—"

She quickly reached out and placed her fingers to
his lips. "Don't, Cameron. You promised. All this was
supposed to be was an island fling. We both agreed.
Flings aren't meant to last."

Taking a deep breath, Cameron fought back the
words he wanted to say. He would let her have things
her way for now, but once she set her feet back on American soil, he would intensify his plan.

"Regardless, I meant what I said. If your days or
nights become lonely and you find you still want me,
just let me know and I will make myself available to
you. Anytime, anyplace and any position."

A small tremble rippled down Vanessa's spine at
Cameron's offer. A part of her was tempted, but she
held on to her resolve. Cameron had been wonderful
these past few weeks only because he had allowed himself to put his guard down. He had been stripped of
his control. Back in the States it would be business as
usual, and he would go back to being the kind of man
she did not want in her life. The kind of person who
got what he wanted regardless of how he went about

getting it. Ruthless, powerful, demanding. Those were three things she could not accept in any man.

But still…she would miss him. She would miss everything they had shared. For a little while he had stripped away her inhibitions, robbed her of her common sense and had filled her days and nights with more pleasure than any one woman had a right to receive.

"Vanessa."

She met his gaze, saw the deep longing there and knew what he wanted. She shook her head. "You'll miss your plane."

He smiled. The smile where the corners of his lips tilted so sexily, the one that sent tingly sensations all through her. "I can't miss the plane since I own it," he said huskily. "And I can't leave here without being with you again."

He kissed her then, a hot, openmouthed kiss that was filled with more passion than Vanessa thought she could handle. She would never get tired of savoring the taste of him. It was the kind of kiss that stirred everything inside her to life once again, that activated a dull, throbbing ache right between her legs.

"Cameron."

He gently eased her down on the bed, while running his hands up her legs, her thighs and finding that very spot that ached for him. Instead of clamping her legs together to stop him, she parted them and he slipped his finger inside her. Her response to his intimate touch was immediate, and she released a moan of need from deep within her throat.

How could she still crave this when she had made love more times in two weeks than in her entire life? How could his touch alone make an insufferable long-

Risky Pleasures

ing erupt deep within her? Those questions were oblit-
erated from her mind, squashed by the sensations that
began taking over.

Intense pleasure suffused her entire body as his fingers worked their magic on her, and then shock wave
after delicious shock wave consumed her. She literally
gasped at the magnitude. Her body trembled and she
clutched him, held tightly to his shoulder as an orgasm
rammed into her.

He held her for long moments, waiting for the aftershocks to cease, to ease from her body. Then he slowly
released her and stepped back, and she watched as he
began removing his clothes. He took a condom from
his nightstand and put it on.

Vanessa could tell from the intense look in Cameron's eyes that even with the time restraints this wouldn't
be a quickie. He intended to leave her with something
she would remember for a long time. He was determined to get her addicted to him.

A rainbow of emotions arced through her. Resentment. Inflexibility. Stubbornness. But all three were
overshadowed by desire, a need that was deeply intense
within her, even after what she'd just shared with him.

When he came back to the bed, gloriously naked,
she pushed all those unwanted emotions aside. Instead
she wanted to concentrate on this one last time. Rising up, she eagerly went into his arms, kissing him
with the same hunger and intensity with which he had
kissed her earlier.

Later, after he left, she would question her sanity,
drum up all that common sense that he had blown to
pieces. She would go back to being her own person, a

confident woman who didn't want or need a man in her life.

The tiny hot flames licking her body made any more coherent thoughts impossible. And when Cameron broke their kiss and eased her down in bed, she wrapped her arms around his neck, needing to hold on to him for just a little while longer.

The look in his eyes made her breathless, and when he positioned his body over hers and continued to look at her, she could feel her body surrendering to him. To his wants and his desires.

When he entered her, she moaned at the impact and wrapped her legs around his waist. The way he made love to her, thrusting in and out, was making her delirious, and she held on, needing as much as he was giving. She felt the muscles in his back straining with each powerful thrust.

And just when she felt the earth move, he leaned toward her and dipped the tip of his tongue into the corners of her mouth, licking her as though she was a taste he had to have.

At that moment the earth didn't just move, it exploded, and she felt herself being blasted to a place Cameron had never taken her before. She screamed his name until her throat seemed raw and still the sensations kept ramming her, nonstop. She was slightly taken aback by the intensity of her passion, the force of her need, and when he followed her over, when that same explosion tore into him, she tightened her hold on him, lifted her hips and locked him in place.

And then she felt it, that affinity she had never felt before with a man, a special oneness. And no matter how much she tried fighting the feeling, it wouldn't go away.

She was forced to admit that if she hadn't gotten addicted, she was pretty close to it.

Vanessa kept running down the beach, along the shore. Cameron was probably back in the States now, back on Charlotte's soil, and she needed to run.

She kept jogging, mindless of the exhaustion that had seeped into her bones. She wanted to be tired so she could sleep tonight, so the dreams wouldn't come. It would be bad enough when she reached out and found the place beside her empty.

She had stood at his upstairs bedroom window and looked down below to watch him leave. Right before he got into the car, he glanced up, knowing she would be there. He had stared at her for a long moment before lifting his hand. She had expected a wave but instead he had blown her a kiss.

That single action had gotten under her skin, and for the rest of the day, all rational thoughts had been reduced to a mess of emotions.

So, for now, she kept running to release that wild, reckless streak that Cameron had encouraged. She was determined to be all right and to put her island fling behind her. Cheyenne had called. The photo shoot had ended and she was on her way home. That meant in a day or so Vanessa would be free to leave this island that would always hold so many special memories.

She kept running, feeling her muscles ache, feeling the heaviness of her heart, but she refused to acknowledge the pain, the anxiety, the deep, intense need Cameron had so effortlessly fulfilled. She had begun missing him the moment he had gotten into the car that had taken him away. He had left his door key with her and also his car key, both generously offered for her use.

Vanessa inhaled deeply as she continued to jog. She had taken a chance. She had trodden on dangerous grounds. She had indulged in a very special kind of risky pleasure. But she didn't have any regrets. What she and Cameron had shared was priceless and the memories would be endless.

When she returned to work on Monday, it would be business as usual. That was the way she wanted it and that was the way she intended it to be.

# *Chapter 14*

"Welcome back, Vanessa."

Vanessa glanced up to find her four cousins standing in the doorway to her office. She smiled. "Thanks, guys. It's good to be back."

"And you really want us to believe that you prefer being here over Jamaica?" Donovan, the youngest of the Steele brothers, asked.

She chuckled. "Hey, I didn't admit that, but you know what they say. There's no place like home."

Referring to that quote from *The Wizard of Oz* made her think of Cameron and the night they had watched that particular movie together.

"Vanessa?"

She was jerked from her thoughts. She glanced over at Chance. "Yes?"

"I asked if you wanted to come to dinner on Sunday. We're having a small dinner party to celebrate the baby's arrival."

She smiled. "I'd love to come." She wondered if Cameron had been invited, as well, but decided not to ask.

"And mark your calendar for Friday night, two weeks from now," Morgan said.

She raised a brow while grabbing the calendar on her desk. "What's going on that night?"

"I'm hosting a party to officially kick off my campaign. The election is in three months."

Vanessa nodded. She didn't have to wonder if Cameron would be attending that event. He was committed to Morgan's campaign. She sighed deeply, and after penciling in the date on her calendar, she smiled up at Morgan. "Consider it done. Do you need me to do anything?"

"Ask my campaign manager," he said, nodding over at Donovan. "Or I could send you to Cameron since he's the second in command."

Vanessa frowned at Morgan. "No, that's okay. I'm sure Donovan can tell me anything I need to know."

She saw the quirking of Morgan's lips and knew it was business as usual between them. He was still trying to shove Cameron down her throat. Well, little did he know, Cameron had already been there. She flushed at the memory.

"Vanessa, are you okay?"

She drew a deep breath and glanced over at Sebastian. "Yes, Bas, why do you ask?"

"You seem preoccupied about something."

*If only you knew.* "I'm not preoccupied, just a little

overwhelmed with the amount of work piled high on my desk."

"Well, bring your thoughts off Jamaica. We have a lot of work to do this week. We need to call a press conference later today."

Vanessa raised a brow. "Why?"

With irritation in his voice, Chance informed her, "An article appeared in this morning's paper that we would be laying off over two hundred employees due to outsourcing."

Vanessa shook her head. "I can't believe someone has started that rumor again."

"Well, they have, and now we need to work on damage control both with our employees and the community. Although I do find it really strange it's started up again only since Morgan is seeking public office. It wouldn't surprise me if someone is trying to play dirty politics."

Vanessa nodded. She thought the same thing. It was her job to make sure the Steele Corporation maintained a positive image, and the sooner she got back into her job, the less time she would have to think about Cameron.

"What time is the press conference?" she asked Chance.

"At noon."

"All right, how about if we meet in an hour so you can go over some things with me?"

"That's a good idea. We'll leave so you can get settled."

"Thanks."

When her cousins walked out of her office, closing the door behind them, she leaned back in her chair, grateful she had plenty to do to keep her mind occupied. The last thing she needed was to dwell on the memories of the past two weeks.

"I saw the press conference on television the other day. I think it went well, Vanessa," Sienna said as she sat across from her best friend at lunch.

"Thanks, I can't believe we're still tackling that issue but all it takes is a rumor to make people panic when it comes to their livelihood," Vanessa responded. The two women were grabbing a quick bite at the Race-track Café, a popular restaurant in town and one they frequented often.

Moments later Vanessa smiled over at her friend. "I can't get over just how pregnant you look. I've only been gone for two weeks and your stomach has grown tremendously."

Sienna chuckled. "To hear Dane tell it, I'm still not showing much, although I can't get into any of my clothes. Heck, I'm five months already, but the doctors told me the baby will probably be small. But then, Dane was a preemie when he was born."

The smile left Vanessa's face. "Are you worried the baby might come early?"

"Not really, but if it does, I'll be getting the best medical care. Dane's mother tried to insist that we use Dr. Tucker, but Dane and I told her we were perfectly satisfied with the doctor I'm using. Needless to say, she wasn't happy about it, thinks I'm to blame and hasn't said too much to me since. She doesn't know how close I finally came to telling her off."

Vanessa frowned. The rift between Sienna and her mother-in-law was an ongoing one that had started when

Sienna and Dane had first begun dating. Sienna was not the woman Mrs. Bradford had wanted for her son. Dane had been born into a rather wealthy family, while Sienna was what Mrs. Bradford considered a "nobody."

Vanessa clearly recalled how a little over three years ago, Sienna and Dane's marriage had seemed doomed, headed for divorce, until a snowstorm had left them stranded together at their cabin in the mountains. The forced togetherness had given them a chance to talk, to analyze what had gone wrong in the marriage and to decide that they still loved each other enough to stay together and make things work. Now they were doing just fine and would continue to do so as long as they kept Dane's interfering parents out of their business.

After the waiter had delivered their meals and left, Sienna glanced over at Vanessa. "Well, are you going to tell me what went down in Jamaica between you and Cameron Cody?"

Vanessa glanced at Sienna over the rim of her glass of iced tea. After taking a sip, she said, "Come on, Sienna, you know what a couple do when they're involved in an affair. Ours was no different and it was fun and enjoyable while it lasted."

"And you think it's over?"

"I know it's over. Cameron and I were very clear on the terms," Vanessa said. She hoped, for both their sakes, that he honored the agreement as he'd promised. But then, she had no reason to think he wouldn't, given that she'd been back in Charlotte for almost a week and he hadn't tried contacting her.

It would have been easy for him to do so. Her office was down the hall from Morgan's, so it would have been relatively simple for him to drop by and visit Morgan and find a reason to seek her out. She didn't want to admit it, but she was a little disappointed that he hadn't.

"I take it the sex was good."

Vanessa blinked when memories assailed her mind. The sex wasn't just good, it was amazing. She couldn't help but think of all the satisfaction she had gotten from Cameron that she hadn't gotten from Harlan. Cameron had been a thoughtful, caring and unselfish lover.

"Well?"

Vanessa was pulled out of her thoughts. She glanced across the table and saw a silly-looking grin on Sienna's face, as if she'd been privy to her thoughts. Gosh, she hoped not! She cleared her throat. "Well, what?"

"Was the sex good? I happen to think it must have been."

Vanessa raised a brow. "Why would you think that?"

"Because you seem more at ease, relaxed, less tense. I can tell you've taken the edge off. And I have a feeling I should be thanking Cameron for that."

Vanessa didn't want to admit it, but Sienna *did* have Cameron to thank for it. An affair with him had been just what she'd needed and just what she'd known it would be. Unforgettable. Since returning to Charlotte, she hadn't been able to sleep a single night without reliving those moments in her dreams.

"Don't look now, but he's here."

Vanessa's stomach suddenly clenched. "Who's here?"

"Your lover boy. Cameron Cody. He just walked in with another man, and the waiter is leading them over to a table near the wall. I don't think he's seen us."

*Thank God for that,* Vanessa immediately thought, fighting the thousands of butterflies that had been released in her stomach. Maybe they could finish eating and leave before he did notice them.

"Oops. He glanced over this way and saw us."

Sienna's words weren't what Vanessa had wanted to hear. "Then let's pretend we haven't seen him."

Sienna smiled. "Too late. I looked right in his face."

Vanessa picked up her tea glass with somewhat shaky fingers. "Fine, then I'll be the one to pretend."

"Too late again. He's coming over this way."

"Great! That's all I need."

Sienna lifted a brow. "If you keep acting this way, I'm going to think you're in need of something else. Are you getting your edge back on again?"

Vanessa hadn't thought Sienna's comment the least bit funny and was about to tell her so when she saw a shadow cross their table. She swallowed as she glanced up into the darkest, sexiest eyes that had ever been given to a man. And at that moment she remembered how those same eyes got even darker just moments before he—

"Sienna. Vanessa."

Cameron's greeting broke into Vanessa's thought, just at the right time. "Hello, Cameron," both she and Sienna said at the same time. Vanessa couldn't help but take in the sight of him. He was standing beside their table, dressed in a designer business suit, seeming completely at ease in the sexy stance she liked so well, his feet planted apart as if he was ready to take on anybody, especially her. And he would do it in such a way that would leave her totally breathless if not totally wrenched from never-ending orgasms.

"I saw the two of you and wanted to come over and say hello," he said to both while fixing his gaze directly on Vanessa.

Vanessa cleared her throat. "That was kind of you," she responded.

He nodded slightly and then said, "Well, I'll let the two of you get back to your meal. I'm dining with my attorney."

"Thanks for dropping by and saying hello," Sienna said smiling.

"It was totally my pleasure," he assured them.

Vanessa caught on to that one word. *Pleasure.* The man was the king of it. He could deliver it like nobody's business.

"It was good seeing both of you."

"Same here," Sienna said.

Vanessa, who was trying to recover from a flash of one particular memory that had taken place in Cheyenne's shower, merely nodded.

He turned and walked off. When Sienna was sure he wasn't in hearing range, she asked, "Am I to assume you no longer dislike him as much as you used to?"

Vanessa shrugged as she bit a French fry. "He's all right."

"That's not what I asked you, Van."

Vanessa frowned. Sienna wanted things spelled out for her. "Yes, you can assume that. But…"

"But what?"

"Cameron Cody is still Cameron Cody. He just happens to handle things differently in the bedroom than he does in the boardroom. I've seen him in action in both, Sienna."

"And the way he carries himself in the boardroom is the one you can't get over, isn't it?"

"Should I be able to? It showed me what I can expect after the touching, kissing and the deep thrusts. You still have a man who likes being in control. A man whose actions can actually destroy a person's livelihood when they find themselves out of a job."

"Didn't you read that article in *Ebony?* Although there tends to be some changes whenever a new management team comes on the scene, from what I gather, Cameron actually looks out for the employees of any company he acquires. In fact, the benefits package he brings is usually better than the one it replaces. He ends up being a blessing in disguise."

*A blessing in disguise.* Now, that was a different way to look at him, Vanessa thought. And although he had been exactly that to her in the bedroom by literally destroying Harlan's claim that she was not worth a damn in bed, she could not imagine him being thought of that way in the boardroom.

"Well, it no longer matters what I think of Cameron," she finally said, wiping the corner of her mouth with her napkin and fighting the urge to tilt her head, ever so slightly, and look over to where he was sitting. The tension that had invaded her stomach moments earlier was now a warm, melting feeling of longing that was seeping right to her center. It was a part of her that knew Cameron by name.

"Well, I hate to be the one to tell you this, Van, but Cameron still wants you. Evidently he didn't get enough in Jamaica."

Sienna's words sent heat pouring through her. She swallowed deeply. "What makes you think that?"

"The way he was looking at you. He was talking to both of us, but he was looking at you, with that I-want-you-in-my-bed look. I recognized it since I've seen it in Dane's eyes plenty of times."

"Well, he might as well get it out of his eyes," Vanessa said with irritation in her voice. "We made an agreement and I expect him to keep it. We reached a clear understanding before he returned to the States. What we shared in Jamaica ended in Jamaica."

"And you actually believe that?"

Vanessa couldn't fight it anymore. She gave in to the urge and took a quick glance across the room to where Cameron sat. Automatically, as if he'd been expecting her to look, their gazes caught, locked, held. She felt something. A hypnotic connection that was having a strange effect on her. From across the room she could feel his gaze. It was an intimate caress, touching her everywhere, leaving no part of her body without contact. And she could smell his scent. It was as if they were still out there on the beach and his scent, all manly, robust and sexy, mingled with the salty ocean air.

"Vanessa?"

She drew in a deep breath, forcing her gaze to return to Sienna. She found her friend studying her intently. "Yes?"

"Why are you fighting it? Why are you still fighting Cameron?"

Vanessa's hand tightened on the glass of tea she picked up. She needed a sip to cool off. Instead she took a long swallow. "I don't want to be just another thing that he controls," she managed to say moments later.

"And that's all you think you would be to him?"

"Yes."

"Well, you might not want my two cents but I happen to think you're wrong. I believe, if given the chance, Cameron could be the best thing ever to happen to you, and how he conducts business has nothing to do with you."

A part of Vanessa wished that was true, but still, she couldn't separate the parts of the man. She didn't want to know there were two parts of him: one she liked and one she didn't. She wanted to like the whole man. "Can we talk about something else now?" she quietly asked.

Sienna nodded as she leaned back in her chair. "Okay, what do you want to talk about?"

"How about names for your baby? Have you come up with any more since the last time we talked?"

Vanessa needed this, a change in subjects. It would help her ignore the sensations flowing through her. As she sat and listened to Sienna, she fought the urge to look at Cameron one more time. It wasn't easy.

"Who's the woman, Cam?"

Cameron didn't have to ask what woman X was referring to. "The one in the green pantsuit is Vanessa, Morgan's cousin, and the other woman is her best friend, Sienna Bradford."

Xavier nodded. He studied his friend over the rim of his wineglass. "And what's going on with you and Ms. Steele?"

Cameron lifted a brow. "What makes you think something is going on?"

Xavier chuckled. "Mainly that you can't seem to keep your eyes off her, and I've never known you to be that attentive to any woman."

Cameron placed his fork down by his plate and leaned back in his chair to meet X's curious gaze. "Vanessa isn't just *any* woman."

"She isn't?"

"No."

"Then who is she?"

Cameron glanced back over to where Vanessa was sitting, wishing she would look over at him again, feel everything he was feeling, want everything he was wanting. When time ticked by and she didn't look his way, he finally returned his attention to X to answer his question.

"Vanessa is the woman I intend to marry."

Cameron thought that the shocked look on Xavier's face was priceless. "Marry?"

"Yes."

Xavier shook his head, chuckling. "Does she know that?"

"She doesn't have a clue. Vanessa has no idea that she will be the most important merger of my life."

# Chapter 15

"Alden looks so much like you that he could be your son," Kylie Steele leaned over and whispered to Vanessa as she stood holding the newest member of the Steele family.

Vanessa grinned. "Only because people always said Chance and I favored each other. For a long time all my friends at school thought he was my big brother instead of my cousin."

She looked back down at the baby she held in her arms. "He's simply gorgeous, Kylie, and I can see him being a heartbreaker just like his uncle Donovan when he grows up."

"Gosh, I hope not." Kylie laughed. "There's the doorbell. Another guest has arrived. I'll be back in a minute."

"Wait! You want me to hold him until you get back? I know nothing about babies."

Kylie grinned. "You'll be fine, but if you start feeling an anxiety attack coming on, Chance is right across the room talking to Bas and his parents, and I'm sure Tiffany or Marcus will be coming in off the patio at any time. They enjoy taking care of their baby brother."

Before Vanessa could say anything else, Kylie was gone. She glanced down at Alden, almost tempted to cross the room and hand him over to his father, but then she couldn't help but be taken in by those dreamy dark eyes staring back at her. Yeah, this kid would grow up to be a heartbreaker. He was such an adorable baby.

She'd never given any thought to having a child of her own, at least not that she could recall. At some point she probably had, most likely during her childhood years when she'd played with dolls. After that, all she'd ever wanted to do was grow up and work alongside her father, uncle and cousins at the family corporation.

She would admit that after meeting Harlan and assuming she had fallen head over heels in love, the idea of having a baby might have slipped into her thoughts for one fleeting moment, but that was about it.

And then there was that time, just a few weeks ago in Jamaica, when Cameron had brought up the possibility of a baby after they had carelessly made love on the beach without any protection. She was certain she was fine, but he evidently didn't trust the potency of the Pill. As she gazed down into Alden's beautiful face, although she didn't want to she could imagine holding another baby, *her* baby. He would look just like his father with dark eyes, a deep cleft in his chin...

She sucked in deeply, wondering why she was even going there. Why was she imagining Cameron as her baby's daddy? He should be the last person that she would envision in that role.

Suddenly her pulse kicked up a notch and she quickly glanced around. Most of the people Chance and Kylie had invited to their dinner party were family members and close friends. She'd overheard Donovan mention to Bas earlier that Cameron had left Charlotte a few days ago to check on problems he was having at his company in Texas; he wasn't expected back for another week or so. Upon hearing that news, she had immediately let her guard down and relaxed, thinking she didn't have to worry about seeing him here tonight.

But now...

She recalled Kylie had gone to the door and she turned toward the foyer. Her breath caught. Cameron was standing there, leaning in the doorway, staring at her. Under his intense gaze she felt tense, exposed, taut, and she turned around, intending to leave the room. But before she could take a step, Cameron was there, standing behind her.

"Vanessa."

His voice, deep and husky, made goose bumps rise on her skin, and she could feel the heat of him standing so close. She knew it would be rude to walk off now, so she was forced to turn around to face him.

"Cameron."

The moment her gaze locked on his face, up close and personal, she felt her heartbeat kick up another notch. This was the face she had awakened to each morning in Jamaica. This was the man whose body had cuddled so close to hers at night. The man who could make her scream out at a mind-blowing orgasm—anytime, anyplace and in practically any position.

She felt her cheeks flush at all the memories that flashed through her mind. She dragged in a deep breath and forced herself to speak. "I thought you were out of town."

"I flew back for a few days, then I'll be leaving again."

She nodded. "Is everything all right? I understand you left town because you were having problems at one of your companies."

"Yes, there was the matter of a small explosion I had to deal with."

Vanessa gasped. "An explosion?"

"Yes."

"Was anyone hurt? Was there much damage?"

"Luckily no one was hurt and the damage was minimal. I gather whoever set it didn't intend to hurt anyone, they merely wanted to make a point."

Vanessa raised a brow. "A point?"

"Yes, to me."

Vanessa was about to ask what he meant by that when Kylie walked up. "I guess you thought I had deserted you, Vanessa, but I wanted to check on everything in the kitchen. Jocelyn's sister Leah is a sweetheart for volunteering to come to Charlotte and prepare such a feast for everyone. She's a fantastic cook." She then reached out to relieve Vanessa of Alden.

"Yes, I heard that she was," Vanessa said, gently placing the baby into his mother's arms.

"Dinner will be ready in a few minutes, so the two of you can continue to enjoy yourselves until then," Kylie said, smiling at the both of them before walking off to join her husband, who was talking to one of their neighbors.

Vanessa knew there was no reason she should feel nervous about being with Cameron. She certainly knew him well enough. Just thinking of all the things they had done together was downright scandalous. And she knew that although they were here together, neither one of them had actually broken their agreement. She couldn't blame him for his relationship with her family and it would be unfair to do so. Today they were victims of circumstances, and it would not be right to expect him to stay away from various functions and events just because she might be there.

"How have you been, Vanessa?"

She looked into his face but tried not to gaze directly into his eyes. "I've been fine. What about you?"

"I've been doing okay. Did your sister return to Jamaica in time to finish overseeing the construction of her pool?"

"Yes. I talked with her a few days ago and the pool's almost completed. They're putting water in it next week."

She suddenly felt tense and swallowed deeply, then she flicked her tongue out to wet her lips. When she saw Cameron's gaze latch on to the movement of her tongue, her stomach clenched and intense heat settled right smack between her thighs.

She inhaled deeply. The more they stood here talking to each other, the more they were playing a game of self-torture, wanting something neither could have again. It was time to move on. "Well, I think I'll go talk to Sienna for a while. It was good seeing you again."

And without giving him a chance to say anything, she quickly walked off.

* * *

Later that night, after her shower, Vanessa slipped between the cool, crisp sheets. She stared up at the ceiling, her mind consumed with thoughts of the time she had spent this evening at Chance and Kylie's home.

There was no way she could deny there was still a very strong attraction between her and Cameron. In fact, it was possibly even stronger than before. How else did she expect her body to react when it came within ten feet of the man who had indulged it, made love to it?

It seemed that no matter where she had gone in Chance and Kylie's home, all she had to do was turn around and Cameron was there, staring at her with those deep, dark eyes of his, though always keeping his distance. That hadn't stopped her body from desiring him, though, from wanting him and from needing to indulge in the forbidden just one more time with him.

She flipped on to her stomach and buried her face in the pillow. How could she even consider such a thing? She had risked an affair with him before and she was paying dearly, mainly because he had brought her body back to life. He had made her aware of places on her body that could stir feelings within her from a mere touch.

*His touch.*

She shook her head, determined to get under control these hot emotions she was experiencing so that when she saw him again she could handle herself in a totally professional manner. Any other reaction toward Cameron was unacceptable.

She jumped when the phone on the nightstand rang. It was her landline. Most people called her on her cell phone; few had her home number. Glancing at the caller

ID, she smiled. It was Taylor. Neither Cheyenne nor Taylor had made it to the dinner party tonight. It was unusual for either to miss a family function of any kind. Chance indicated both had called with their regrets. Cheyenne had come down with a stomach virus and Taylor was knee-deep in trying to work out a large business deal for a very influential client.

Vanessa quickly picked up the phone. "Okay, Taylor, it's not my birthday, and there's no such thing as Sister's Day, so why do I deserve the honor of a phone call?"

She could hear Taylor laughing on the other end of the line. It wasn't that Taylor never called, she just didn't call as often as Cheyenne. But lately even Cheyenne's calls didn't come as often as they used to. And there were times she couldn't be reached at all. Donovan had once teased her about leading a double life, which was something Cheyenne hadn't thought amusing at the time. She had simply explained that as a model she would often frequent countries with poor cell service.

"Don't mess with me, girl," Taylor said. "I shouldn't be calling now. I still have tons of work to do on this deal I'm trying to close for my client."

"It's that big?"

"Bigger. With the commission alone I'll be able to buy that place I've been eyeing for a while in D.C. The one that's right on the Potomac."

Vanessa smiled. Taylor had fallen in love with the nation's capital when she'd lived there while attending Georgetown University. At the time, she'd had an apartment in Virginia but had always had dreams of returning one day and buying a place right in the heart of D.C., preferably on the water.

"Hey, I'm not mad at you. Go for it," Vanessa said, knowing what a workaholic her sister could be at times.

"Speaking of going for it, I talked to Cheyenne earlier and she told me that you and Cameron finally hooked up."

Vanessa frowned. Cheyenne had a big mouth. And she didn't know the full details of what had transpired between her and Cameron those two weeks. Since Vanessa hadn't told her youngest sister anything, she'd evidently drawn her own conclusions. "Cameron and I have not 'hooked up.'"

"Sorry. I was just going by what Cheyenne said."

"And you of all people should know better than that. He bought the house next to Cheyenne's in Jamaica, so he was there at the same time I was. No big deal."

"Sure, if you say so," Taylor said chuckling. "You know I'm not one to get in anyone's business, Van."

"Please, don't start now."

"I won't, but I wasn't born yesterday. I know the man wants you. Now, whether or not he's finally gotten you is your business. But I think he's cool and handsome and everything you need."

"And just what is it that you think I need?"

"The same thing most women need. A good man in your life. A man to hold you close at night, keep the demons away, be there when the going gets tough."

"And you think Cameron would do all those things?"

"I don't know why he wouldn't. He seems like the type of guy who takes his obligations seriously. You could do a whole lot worse."

Vanessa fought the urge to tell her sister that at one time she had. And "worse" was a man by the name of Harlan Shaw. Before Harlan there had been Dr. Derek

Peterson. She'd met Derek at a party right after returning to Charlotte from college. She had liked Derek and
had quickly accepted his date, although her cousins had
warned of his reputation.

Derek had come to pick her up one Saturday night
and they hadn't been out of her driveway five seconds
before the good doctor began growing hands. They were
hands he intended to use on her at every traffic light and
stop sign. The words *No, Behave yourself* and *Keep your
hands to yourself* had fallen on deaf ears. By the time
they'd reached the restaurant, she had taken as much as
she intended. As soon as he came around to open the
door for her, she had kneed him in the groin so mercilessly that the restaurant manager had thought they
needed to call an ambulance. An embarrassed Derek
had assured everyone that he was okay before literally
crawling back into his car and leaving her stranded.
She had called her cousins to come get her, and to this
day there was still bad blood between them and Derek.

"Vanessa?"

She remembered she still had her sister on the line.
"Yes?"

"Think about what I've said about Cameron, and I
promise that will be the last time you hear anything
from me on the subject."

"I'd appreciate that."

"Touchy, touchy."

"Only when people get into my business. I can't wait
until you get a love interest so I can get into yours."

"Is Cameron a love interest, Van?"

Before Vanessa could utter the denial on her lips,
Taylor giggled and said, "That's okay. You don't have

to tell me anything. It's your business. So tell me, how is Sienna doing?"

Vanessa was glad for the change in subjects. The mere mention of Cameron had ignited a throbbing between her thighs, and that wasn't good, especially since she would be sleeping in her bed alone tonight. But later, she would have her dreams.

"Yes, X, I'm flying back to Texas tomorrow. I returned to Charlotte because there was a function I couldn't miss attending." *And a person I couldn't miss seeing.* "Arrange a private meeting between me and McMurray. What he's paying his thugs to do has to stop," Cameron said angrily, rubbing a hand down his face. "It's time for him to know who I am, why I took his company away and why I intend to keep it, no matter what he does."

Hours later, a tense Cameron couldn't sleep. His restlessness had nothing to do with his ongoing problems with McMurray but with a certain young woman by the name of Vanessa Steele.

He had needed to see her again. He had needed to know that that same potent chemistry he'd felt all during their time together in Jamaica was stronger than ever.

She was fighting him. He could feel it every time their eyes met. He knew he was gambling, but he had to believe their island affair meant more than just sex to her, just as it meant more to him. She might not be able to put it all together now, but eventually she would. Although he would keep their agreement, he intended to be at every function that she attended if he could. His flights back and forth to Texas were becoming a nuisance, costing him valuable time; time he should be using to get on the good side of a certain woman.

That was why his ongoing problems with McMurray were unacceptable and had tried his patience for the last time. For some reason the man believed that if he kept up his dirty work Cameron would eventually throw in the towel and sell the company back to him.

McMurray couldn't be more wrong.

John McMurray sat at the conference table beside his attorney with his arms crossed over his chest and fixed Cameron with a mean, level stare. "I have no idea what you're talking about, Cody, and you don't have any proof, so don't waste your time accusing me of anything."

Cameron sat at the head of the table, with Xavier Kane on one side and Kurt Grainger on the other. "But we do have proof, McMurray, which is why one of your men is behind bars now."

McMurray's attorney touched his client's elbow, cautioning him from saying anything more. He then spoke on his client's behalf. "Again, Mr. Cody, contrary to whatever proof you think you might have, my client is innocent, which means you are mistaken."

A smile split Cameron's face. "Then ask your client if the name Samuel Myers means anything to him."

The attorney didn't have to ask McMurray anything. The nervousness that darted into McMurray's eyes was a dead giveaway. However, the attorney said, "My client doesn't know a Samuel Myers."

Cameron leaned forward. "Myers says differently. Let's cut the bullshit. Frankly, I'm getting fed up with this entire ordeal. Your client lost his company."

"You took it from me!" McMurray yelled out in anger.

Cameron nodded. "Yes, I took it from you, and do you know why?"

When neither McMurray nor his attorney responded, Cameron said, "Because you don't deserve to have a company, McMurray, and how you solicit loyalty in a few of your employees is beyond me. But then, for the right price, anyone can be bought."

"Are you accusing my client of bribery?"

"Yes, for starters. Does the name Fred Cody ring a bell?"

John McMurray's face twisted with more anger. "I wish you would stop throwing out the names of people I don't know. Judging by the surname, I can only assume he's some relative of yours."

Cameron shot the man another forced smile. "Yes, he was my grandfather. He had worked for your company for over forty years, and right before he was to retire—less than a year before, in fact—you had him fired. That was almost twenty years ago."

"Twenty years ago! You're getting back at me for something I did twenty years ago? Hell, I was in my late thirties. Whatever I did then was because I was following my father's orders. What else was I to do?"

"Have a conscience. That year you released six men from your employment, men who had given Global Petroleum their blood, sweat and tears, yet you fired them without any compensation or benefits. And when they tried banding together to take your company to court, you and your father paid people to harass them and their families, scaring them to the point where they wouldn't fight the big corporation that had done them wrong. They barely had money to eat and live on, and you and your father made it impossible for them to afford to fight you any longer by deliberately dragging things out in court."

"If we fired them, then there had to be a reason for it," McMurray snapped.

"Oh, you had a reason all right. You and your old man didn't want to give them what they deserved after working for you all those years. But now I will. For the first five years, any profit I make from Global Petroleum will go to those men and their families. Of the six, four are still living, almost impoverished. So as you can see, McMurray, I'm trying to right a wrong that you and your family did."

Cameron nodded to Xavier, who slid a manila envelope over to McMurray and his attorney. "I suggest the two of you read those documents, ponder them," Cameron said. "If I'm forced to expose them, I will. I have sworn affidavits from Samuel Myers, as well as from the woman who was your father's secretary, Hannah Crosby. Ms. Crosby claims she was paid to falsify documents, and Samuel Myers has confessed to being one of your father's henchmen. He's provided us a list of all the bad deeds that your father paid him to do. If you're willing to have the press dig into history and dishonor your family's name, then go ahead, keep doing what you're doing, in other words, basically the same tricks your father pulled years ago."

Cameron leaned over the table and his smile was gone. Instead his face was a mask of pure anger. "The only difference is, your henchmen don't bother me, McMurray, and I'm not going anywhere. Do yourself and your family a favor, accept your loss and take an early retirement. Otherwise, you leave me no choice but to

send a copy of what's in that envelope to every newspaper in Texas."

McMurray jumped out of his chair, almost knocking
it over. "You won't get away with this, Cody."

"I already have. You don't own Global Petroleum
anymore. I do. Accept it. And let me give you a friendly
word of warning. If there are any more mishaps to *my*
company that I trace back to you, instead of spending
your remaining days in retirement, I'll going to see to
it that you rot in jail. Count on it."

An angry John McMurray stalked out of the conference room with his attorney—who'd taken the time
to grab the envelope off the table—following right on
his heels.

Xavier shook his head and glanced over at Cameron.
"That man is bad news."

Kurt nodded in agreement.

Cameron released a deep breath as he leaned back
in his chair. He had a feeling they hadn't seen or heard
the last of John McMurray.

## Chapter 16

Cameron walked into the kick-off party for Morgan's campaign with two purposes in mind. He wanted to show his support for his friend and he needed to see a certain woman again.

It had been two weeks since he'd last seen Vanessa at the small gathering in Chance's home and now he was in a bad way. And no matter what it took, he was going to make sure she was in a bad way, too, by the time the night was over.

"Cameron, it's good to see you."

He smiled when he was approached by Jocelyn Mason Steele. She was the woman he had chosen to run his construction company based in Charlotte. Already nearly one hundred people were on payroll, with several lucrative projects lined up to keep them busy.

He leaned over and gave her a peck on the cheek.

"You look beautiful as usual. Where's that husband of yours?"

She grinned. "Bas is around here somewhere. I think he's trying to dodge his old girlfriend," she said teasingly.

Cameron glanced around. The party was being held on the main floor of the Steele Building and decorative streamers and red, white and blue balloons were everywhere. "Cassandra Tisdale is here?" he asked.

"Yes, Cassandra and the entire Tisdale family. Time will tell if she's here to throw her support to Morgan or to be nosy. But then, we really don't care. Since throwing his hat into the ring, Morgan has received numerous financial backers even if the Tisdales decide to support Roger Chadwick."

Cameron nodded: He knew the story. The Tisdales had wanted Morgan to marry a member of their family by the name of Jamie Hollis, a senator's daughter. When Morgan had refused and told them in no uncertain terms that he would be marrying the woman he loved, namely Lena Spears, that hadn't sat too well with them…until Morgan had taken matters into his own hands and made sure Cassandra and her cousin Jamie knew that he meant business. He'd warned if they continued spreading gossip about him and Lena, he would start spreading some of his own about them.

"The buffet table is set up on the other side of the room and there's plenty to eat," Jocelyn told him.

"Thanks, but I'm going to let Morgan and Lena know I'm here before I start mingling."

A few minutes later he found them, talking to Vanessa and another man. He frowned. Was the man her date? His stomach clenched at the possibility. There was only one way to find out. Without wasting any time he approached the two couples.

Lena was the first to see him and turned and smiled radiantly. Not for the first time he thought Morgan had struck a gold mine with this woman. A Queen Latifah look-alike, she looked gorgeous in her mint-green pant-suit. Whoever thought Lena Spears would not complement Morgan was sadly mistaken.

"Cameron, I'm glad you could make it," Lena said, reaching out and giving him a hug. "I understand you've been out of town a lot."

"Yes, I have." He then shook hands with Morgan. "Seems like a nice turnout."

"It is," Morgan said. He turned to Vanessa. "Cam, you already know Vanessa."

"Yes. How are you tonight, Vanessa?"

He picked up on the unevenness of her breathing when she responded in a soft voice, "I'm fine, Cameron. And you?"

"I'm fine, as well." He glanced over at the man standing by her side. Too close, as far as he was concerned.

"And this," Morgan was saying, "is Reverend David Carrington. He recently moved to town to become the new pastor of the Redeem Baptist Church."

The man might be a minister, but there was no wedding band on his finger, Cameron noted, so anything was possible. But not with *his* woman. "Nice meeting you, Reverend. I'm going to have to visit your church one of these Sundays."

Reverend Carrington smiled. "Please do. In fact, I plan on having a blazing sermon this coming Sunday."

Cameron nodded. His mind was not on the good man's Sunday sermon. Instead he was trying to come up with a way to get Vanessa alone without breaking their agreement, even if only for a few minutes.

"Oops, I left my speech upstairs on my desk," Morgan said, looking apologetic.

"I can go get it for you," Lena quickly volunteered.

"No," Morgan said just as quickly while settling his arms around her waist. "I need you to stay down here with me and greet our guests. Vanessa can catch the elevator and get it for me."

Vanessa looked surprised. "I can?"

"Yes, you don't mind, do you?"

Vanessa sighed. What could she say? Of course she didn't mind. Besides, it would give her a chance to escape Cameron's presence. She had seen him the moment he had walked into the room. It was as if she had radar and it had homed right in on him. He was impeccably dressed in a dark suit and looked as though he had just stepped off the cover of *GQ*. Her equilibrium hadn't been the same since he'd arrived. Weeks of nonstop dreaming about the man was taking its toll. Standing so close to him, breathing in his manly scent, was definitely too much.

"Of course I don't mind. I'll be back in a second," she said, turning to walk off.

"Thanks. And take Cameron with you."

She swirled back around. "What? Why do I need to take Cameron with me?"

"Because Derek Peterson is here. Surprised the hell out of us."

At the swift elbow he received in his side from Lena, Morgan glanced over at the Reverend and said apologetically, "Sorry about that. What I meant to say is that he surprised the *heck* out of us, since he dislikes the Steeles so much."

"Who's Derek Peterson?" Cameron asked curiously.

Morgan wanted to paint the true picture of the man, but out of respect for Reverend Carrington again, he merely said, "Let's just say he's a not-so-nice person who has it in for Vanessa."

She frowned. "He doesn't have it in for me, Morgan."

Morgan chuckled. "Yes, he does. You almost crippled the man."

Vanessa rolled her eyes. "That was almost six years ago."

Morgan smiled. "Doesn't matter. There are some things a man doesn't forget and almost losing his balls—"

He cleared his throat and glanced over at the Reverend again. "I mean, almost losing his *jewels* is one of them."

Reverend Carrington tried to hide his grin. "Please point this gentleman out to me. I definitely need to invite him to church on Sunday."

"If you think it will help," Morgan said, more than happy to oblige.

"The Word always helps," was the minister's response.

"Then I say go for it," Morgan replied. "And you can kill—or save—two birds with one stone since he's standing over there by the punch bowl talking to Cassandra Tisdale. I think she's a person who will need to hear your sermon on Sunday, as well."

Reverend Carrington nodded. "My sermon will be for everyone, so I'm looking forward to seeing your face in the congregation on Sunday, too, Mr. Steele." He then walked off to where Derek and Cassandra were standing with their heads together.

"I'm going upstairs now," Vanessa said, turning to walk off.

"Now that I've heard about this Derek guy, I think I'll go with you after all." Cameron followed in step beside her. He owed Morgan for this. Chances were Morgan hadn't left his speech on his desk upstairs. Cameron had a feeling it was right in his friend's pocket.

He and Vanessa didn't say anything as they walked toward the bank of elevators. They slowed their steps when they heard loud, angry voices coming from behind a closed door, Vanessa chuckled.

Cameron glanced over at her. "What's so funny?"

"From the sound of things, Sienna has finally gotten fed up and is giving her mother-in-law hell. It's about time."

They rounded a corner to the elevators. Luckily, one opened right away. The moment they stepped in and it closed behind them, Cameron could feel the heat. He moved to the far side of one wall and she moved to the other.

"I'm sorry that Morgan put you on the spot like that, Cameron. I really didn't need an escort."

He glanced over at her. "I don't mind."

He averted his eyes from her so he wouldn't be tempted to close the distance between them, take her into his arms and kiss her. She looked so good in her red dress that showed just what a gorgeous pair of legs she had. And it didn't take much to remember how those legs could wrap around him, holding him tight inside her and—

"How's that problem going with your business in Texas?" she asked, looking everywhere but at him.

He released a deep sigh, glad for her interruption into his thoughts. "I'm hoping it's been resolved. Time will tell."

She nodded and turned to stare at the wall again. Moments later he couldn't fight it any longer and looked at her. Gosh, he loved her. And he wanted her. Here. Now. Right this second. As if she read his thoughts, she slowly turned toward him.

The moment their gazes connected, sexual tension seemed to crackle in the air between them. He saw the deep look of desire in her eyes and took a step toward her at the exact moment the elevator came to a jolting stop.

That seemed to snap her to her senses and she took a step back. "We need to get off now."

He'd had enough. He refused to torture himself any longer. "I personally think what we need to do is go somewhere and make love."

He watched her eyes darken even more, confirming she was thinking the same thing but was still fighting it.

"What about our agreement?" she asked softly when the elevator door opened and she backed up slowly, stepping off.

A smile touched his lips as he followed her. "I won't tell anyone that we broke it if you don't."

She stopped walking. He waited for her to say something, to respond. It seemed like forever before she asked quietly, "You promise?"

His mind was muddled and at the moment he didn't understand the question. "I promise what?"

"Not to tell anyone that we broke our agreement?" she whispered.

His smile deepened and took a step toward her. "I'll promise you anything."

She inhaled deeply and glanced down at her watch. "Morgan is expecting us to return with his speech."

At that moment, Cameron's cell phone rang. He pulled it out of his pocket and answered. "Yes?"

After a brief pause, he said, "No, we hadn't made it to your office yet. No problem, I'll tell her."

He clicked off the line and put the phone back in his jacket pocket. "That was Morgan. He didn't leave the speech on his desk after all. It was in his pocket."

Vanessa frowned. "Umm, now, isn't that amazing. Seems like perfect timing."

Cameron nodded. "Yes, it does, doesn't it?"

"We were set up," she said.

"Looks that way."

"And you're not upset about it?"

His low chuckle sent soft shivers all through her body. "Not in the least. Are you?"

"I should be."

He nodded. "But *are* you?"

"No." She glanced around. "While we're up here I might as well show you my office. You've never seen it before."

"No, I haven't."

"All right, it's this way, right down the hall from Morgan's."

They walked side by side and all Vanessa could think about was that he was here, and they were alone, hot and horny. Thanks to him she knew what horniness felt like; she'd been suffering from it for weeks.

When they got to her office door she pulled a key out of her small purse, but her hands were shaking so hard she couldn't fit the key in the lock.

"Let me help," he said, sliding a hand around her to the door. When he opened it, she quickly stepped inside and he followed, closing the door behind them. And relocking it.

He didn't even glance around. Instead he snaked out his hand and captured her wrist and pulled her to him.

The moment he did so, it seemed something between them broke loose, and he went for her mouth at the same moment she went for his.

Spontaneity.

He'd missed it. He wanted it. Now.

He picked her up and swirled around, placing her back against the closed door while their mouths were still locked. Hungry, they devoured each other like starved, crazed addicts. He broke the connection just long enough to flip her dress up and push her silk panties down. With one hand he unzipped his pants, pulled out his shaft, and before either could take another breath, he thrust into her.

"Cameron!"

She screamed his name and just that quickly, an explosion went off inside her, sending shivers of pleasure all through her body. But he kept going, demanding that she come again. She did and with her legs wrapped tightly around him, and the way her fingers were digging into his shoulders, he could tell that this orgasm was just as powerful as the first.

"Don't stop, Cameron. Please, don't stop," she whispered frantically, kissing his face all over.

Little did she know he couldn't stop now even if he wanted to. Not even if the building were to catch on fire. They were burning to a crisp right now anyway. He kept thrusting into her, nonstop, fast, hard, needing her, needing the connection with the woman he loved.

When he felt it, the sensation started in his toes and slowly worked its way up to his shaft. Vibrations, shock waves. It was an orgasm so powerful, it tore into him. He threw his head back to the point that his veins nearly burst in his neck. But he didn't feel any pain. He felt only ecstasy. Pleasure. Vanessa.

Breathing once again, he buried his head on her chest, between her breasts. He could die at this moment and he'd go happy, satisfied, feeling total completeness.

When the shivers stopped, he pulled back, but he did not pull out of her. He kept her pinned against the door while he was still inside her. He met her gaze and said softly, "Please don't say this shouldn't have happened."

She licked her lips before asking, barely with enough breath to speak, "Can I think it?"

He shook his head. "No."

She nodded. "You did say, anytime, anyplace and… any position."

A smile touched his lips. "Yes, I did."

"And I see that you meant it."

"Every word."

Vanessa felt him growing hard inside her again and tightened her legs around his waist to keep him locked to her. "Some people might be wondering where we've disappeared to."

"Let them wonder. I'm sure Morgan will tell them something believable."

She nodded again. "I hope so because I haven't gotten enough of you yet."

"And I haven't gotten enough of you, either."

And then he leaned forward and captured her lips at the exact moment he thrust deeper inside her. Once, twice. Again and again.

The heat was on again and he planned to take it to the limit.

# Chapter 17

"Woman, you're killing me," Cameron said through clenched teeth. They were at his house, in his bedroom, and Vanessa was on top of him, riding him like crazy. He clutched the bedspread and balled it in his fist. The woman was amazing, simply amazing. He had thought that same thing in Jamaica but now, on American soil, he was doubly sure of it.

After leaving her office they had finally gone back downstairs to join the party, barely hearing the last of Morgan's speech. Then they had quickly said their goodbyes, not caring that after having been missing from the party for over an hour, they were making a grand escape.

She had followed him home and they had barely made it inside the door before they were at it again. This time she was in control. First they had made love on the floor in his living room until their strength was depleted. And then he had carried her upstairs to his bedroom, where he had undressed her properly before making love to her again.

They had fallen asleep, but she had awakened him—less than ten minutes ago—saying she needed to ride him, and he had flipped on his back, happy to oblige. Now he was looking death in the face. The woman was going to kill him.

"I won't kill you if you stop holding back. I made it clear what I want."

Yes, she had. For some reason she enjoyed the feel of him exploding inside her, shooting his semen all the way to her womb. The moment he did so, she would clench her inner muscles and pull everything out of him, as if his release was something she had to have.

"Damn, you're really asking for it this time," he warned, barely able to get the words out.

"Good, now let go and give me what I want, Cameron. Now!"

"You better hope those pills you're on do their job tonight. If not, this is a baby in the making," he muttered just seconds before his body bucked and he exploded, giving her just what she wanted.

As if his orgasm had lit her sensuous torch, she climaxed, as well, clenching him more deeply while calling out his name. Knowing she needed this from him, he gently flipped her on her back without breaking contact, taking control and riding her. This was crazy. This was madness. This was making up for weeks of going without her in his bed—something he never wanted to do again.

After they came again, simultaneously, he lay against her, breathing hard but thinking how great life was. He was a man in love and he had the woman he wanted in his bed. Now if he could only convince her to become a forever part of his life, as well.

"Sneaking out on me, Vanessa?"

Vanessa swirled around, holding her shoes to her chest. "I thought you were asleep, Cameron. It's time for me to leave."

He glanced to the window. It was daybreak. In essence she had spent the night. He moved to get out of bed. "Let me slip on something and walk you to your car."

"No. Please don't. I'm fine."

He stayed put, seeing the look of uncertainty in her eyes. Did she regret what had happened last night? There was only one way to find out. "When will I see you again?"

He watched her nervously lick her lips, and his stomach clenched when he recalled just what she had done to him with those same lips and tongue last night. He also noticed she was backing up slowly toward the door. "I'll call you."

"When?"

She shrugged. "I don't know. I hadn't counted on this."

He figured now was not a good time to tell her that he had. A part of him had wanted to believe she still desired him and the attraction between them was just as strong and hot as it had been in Jamaica. What had happened last night had proven him right.

He knew he couldn't be completely honest with her anymore. He stood. "Can I give you something to think about?"

"Yes, what?"

"I love you."

She closed her eyes and her shoes dropped to the floor. The sound made her snatch her eyes open and she dropped to her knees to pick her shoes up. Without looking at him she gathered them in her arms and said, "This is getting complicated. I have to go."

He took a few steps toward her. "What's so complicated about me loving you?"

She looked at him as she stood up. "Because I'm not sure how I feel about you."

He reached out and pulled her to him again, making her drop her shoes for a second time. He picked her up in his arms and moved to sit on the bed with her cradled in his lap. His teeth caught her earlobe before he whispered huskily, "Don't you? I'm betting my money that you love me, too."

She pulled back and stared down at him. "Why do you think that? Because we enjoy great sex together? A lot of people enjoy great sex, Cameron."

He shook his head. "We're not talking about a lot of people. We're talking about *us*. And we share more than great sex. You're everything I want in a woman, Vanessa. You're compassionate, honest, trustworthy and—"

"But I'm having doubts about you, Cameron. You take people's companies away. What you do affects their lives. I read an article on the internet a few weeks ago about what you did to that company in Texas, Global Petroleum, and how the people resent you for taking it over and that's why you're having problems there."

Cameron moved her off his lap and stood, somewhat irritated and trying like hell to hold on to his temper. "You can't believe everything you read, especially not off the internet, Vanessa, and particularly not off that particular site. John McMurray had that site up and running for a while mainly to discredit me."

"But—"

"But you have to trust me. I know what I'm doing."

"But I don't. My family could have been in the same boat that Global is in now had you succeeded in taking over the Steele Corporation."

"No, the circumstances are different, Vanessa."

"I don't think that they are."

Cameron inhaled deeply. He loved this woman with all his heart and soul but more than anything, he wanted her to believe in him and trust him completely. "I'm leaving for Texas tomorrow and will probably be gone for a week or two. When I get back, let's have dinner and talk. There are a few things I think we need to clear up, okay?"

She slowly nodded and then stood and slipped into her shoes. "I have to go. If I don't see you or talk to you before you leave, I hope you have a safe trip."

And then she was gone, hurrying out of the bedroom and down the stairs to leave his home.

"So, Vanessa, how do you think things went at the party the other night?"

She glanced up from the document she was reading to see Morgan in the doorway of her office, a silly grin on his face. He knew better than anyone that she had missed most of the party while she was in this very office playing hanky-panky with Cameron.

Even now the memories were still vivid. She wished she had gone to church on Sunday to hear Reverend Carrington's sermon. She glared over at her cousin. "I have a bone to pick with you, Morgan."

He smiled. "What kind of bone?"

"Not a juicy rib-eye, that's for sure. I don't like being set up."

"And you think you were set up?"

"Yes."

"Umm, I don't recall you complaining about it that night when you came back downstairs. In fact, you looked rather giddy. Like the cat who'd gotten the canary."

"That's not the point."

"Then what is the point?"

She inhaled deeply and decided to use another approach. "What is it with Cameron? Other guys have tried dating me, and you, Bas, Donovan and Chance have always been overly cautious, checking them out to make sure they don't intend to run off with the family china. Yet, Cameron is a man known to take over companies and it seems like the four of you, especially you, Morgan, are all but handing me to him on a silver platter. Hell, let's forget about silver, let's even try a gold platter."

"We like Cameron. He had a rough life with the way he lost his parents, yet he made it. He's a survivor."

"But look at what he's doing to those companies," she implored.

Morgan rolled his eyes. "Name one company where the employees haven't benefited from Cameron's takeover."

"What about that one in Texas? Global Petroleum."

"That's personal for Cameron."

Vanessa arched a brow. "And how is it personal?"

"He had a score to settle with the owner."

"And for that reason he took over an entire company? What about the employees?"

"Like I said, they will end up in better shape. A lot better than Cam's grandfather did over twenty years ago."

Vanessa frowned. "What about Cam's grandfather?"

Morgan came into her office and closed the door behind him. "You know about him?"

She shrugged. "Only what Cameron shared with me. I know he was fired from his job of forty years less than a year from retirement, and he lost all his benefits."

"And did Cam tell you the name of the company responsible?"

"If he did, I don't remember. Why?"

"Because Global Petroleum is the same company that fired not only Cam's grandfather but five other men who were about to retire. None of them had a grandson like Cam who was willing to drop out of school to help make ends meet. Two of the men died within the first five years, the others still living are destitute. They're old men, in their late eighties. One is in his nineties. Cam took over Global Petroleum not only for revenge, but he's taking the company's first five years of profits to give to those remaining four men so that they can live out the rest of their lives without wanting for anything. All the profits will be split among the survivors and their families."

Vanessa leaned back in her chair, amazed. "He's actually doing that?"

"Yes. And in my book that's a pretty nice gesture for a guy you think is nothing more than a jerk."

"I never said he was a jerk. I just never understood him, until now."

Morgan shook his head. "And you still don't understand him, Vanessa. The man loves you. That's why I don't worry about what may or may not be happening between the two of you. One thing I've discovered since becoming Cam's friend is that true friendships are important to him, and because of it, he picks his friends carefully. And the reason he loves you is that he truly believes you're more than worthy of his love."

Morgan crossed his arms over his chest and met her gaze. "The big question of the hour is whether you're going to prove him right or wrong."

That night, after taking her shower, Vanessa slipped into bed with Morgan's words from earlier that day on her mind.

*"...And the reason he loves you is that he truly believes you're more than worthy of his love."*

She shook her head. If Cameron did think at one time that she was worthy of his love, chances were that after what she'd said to him their last morning together he didn't feel that way now. She had told him that she doubted him, and now he probably wouldn't want to see her.

She sighed deeply, knowing she would go stark raving crazy if she had to wait another week before he returned to Charlotte to find out. She quickly reached across the bed for the phone.

A sleepy feminine voice answered after three rings. "Hello, Lena, how are you? May I speak with Morgan for a minute?"

It took another minute for him to get on the phone. "Vanessa, it's almost midnight. What is it that can't wait until you see me at the office in the morning?"

"I hope to be on my way to Texas by then."

"What are you talking about?"

"I'm going to Austin and I need Cameron's address. Hold on, let me grab a pen."

A few minutes later, she ended her call with Morgan. She believed she was worthy of Cameron's love. Now she had to make sure he still believed it, as well.

# Chapter 18

"Cam?"

Cameron glanced up from the papers he'd been reading and saw both Xavier and Kurt standing in the doorway to his office. It was late afternoon and the three of them were working at his Austin home. So far, since his meeting with McMurray a few weeks ago, things had been running smoothly at Global Petroleum and he hoped they continued to do so.

"I thought the two of you were leaving to pick up dinner."

Kurt cleared his throat. "We were, but you got a visitor."

Cameron frowned, wondering who it could be. Very few people knew about the small ranch-style home he had inherited from his grandfather. He had to assume his visitor was one of the neighbors. Lately, more than one had come forth offering to buy his house mainly to get the land, which consisted of over ten acres. "Tell whoever it is that I'm busy."

"I don't think you want us to do that," Xavier said with a smirk on his face.

"Why not?" Cameron asked, not understanding just what was wrong with his two friends.

Kurt grinned. "Maybe you ought to see for yourself and then I think you'll understand."

"Fine," Cameron said angrily, tossing the report on his desk. He stood. "Where's this person?"

"In your living room."

Cameron left the office with Xavier and Kurt right on his heels. He'd taken a few steps and then turned around with an arched brow. "Just what the hell has gotten into you two?"

Kurt gave a sly chuckle. "Ask us that after seeing your visitor."

Cameron frowned, thinking he really didn't have time for this.

He walked into the living room and stopped dead in his tracks. The first thought that came into his mind was that he *did* have time for this. Vanessa was standing in the middle of his living room wearing that black skirt he didn't like, the one she had purchased in Jamaica. His throat went dry and his gaze traveled the full length of her, up and down her legs, her thighs... Speaking of her thighs, the skirt barely covered them.

Their gazes connected. He felt the heat. It didn't matter why she had come, all he cared about was that the woman he loved was here in his place, invading his space, affecting the very air he was breathing.

"Now you understand what we meant, Cam?"

Brenda Jackson 373

He blinked, suddenly remembering Xavier and
Kurt. He quickly turned to them. "Leave!"

Kurt, being the smart-ass, said, "Are you sure? She
could be an enemy. Maybe we ought to search her first."

"Touch her and I'll have to kill you," he said through
clenched teeth. "Leave and don't come back."

Xavier raised a curious brow. "I thought we had a
lot of work to do. You said we'd be working well into
the night."

"Out!"

He watched the two men make a beeline for the door,
and, as soon as the door shut behind them, Cameron
turned his attention back to his visitor.

He took a couple of steps forward. "I never liked
that skirt on you."

Vanessa met his heated gaze and said, "Then take
it off me. But I need to warn you it's the only thing I
have to wear."

He frowned. "You wore that all the way from Charlotte?"

She shook her head. "No, but I did wear it from
the hotel in downtown Austin. I had that full-length
raincoat over it," she said, indicating the yellow slicker
tossed across a chair. "A lot of people stared since the
sun was shining outside."

He released a deep sigh. "Thank God for that."

"For what? That the sun was shining outside?"

"No, for that full-length raincoat."

She nodded. "Aren't you going to ask why I'm here?"

He shook his head as he crossed the distance of the
room to stand in front of her. "You can tell me later.
Right now I can only concentrate on one thing."

"And what are you concentrating on?"

"Taking that damn skirt off of you."

Vanessa's body reacted instantly to Cameron's words. Blood rushed through her veins, every cell seemed sensitive. The tips of her nipples beneath her top tightened and a warm pool settled between her thighs. He was the only man who had the ability to do this to her. With just words and an intense look, he could put an achy need within her so compelling and deep that she knew of only one way to soothe it.

"Don't concentrate too hard," she heard herself saying.

He didn't.

The next instant Cameron reached out and with a flick of his wrist he undid the fastener at her waist and the skirt dropped to her feet. Just that easy. Just that quick. She was left wearing her top and a silky strap of barely nothing that was meant to cover her feminine mound. He thought it wasn't doing a very good job and he licked his lips in anticipation of tasting her. Without wasting any time, he removed her top and then got down on his knees and eased her thong down her legs.

He inhaled deeply, taking in her scent, and then he dipped his head and tasted her, right in the juncture of her thighs.

"Cameron."

He sucked in a deep breath when he rose to his feet. Every muscle in his body ached for her. God, he wanted her. He wanted to make love to her all day and all night. And he didn't intend to waste any time.

He swept her into his arms and strode quickly to the bedroom where he placed her on his bed. He drew back to remove his own clothes but she caught hold of his collar and pulled him back to her and began nipping at his bottom lip, licking it from corner to corner with the tip of her tongue.

Sensations within him intensified, making his need for her monumental, nearly insane. He was so fully aware of this woman—his woman—and he intended to leave his imprint all over her. He pulled back again and this time he swiftly removed his clothes, then rejoined her on the bed. He wanted to erase whatever doubts she had about him. He wanted to fill her with his love, so much that it would spread to her own heart. He had enough for both of them.

"Cameron."

When she opened her arms, he went into them, and when she captured his mouth, he surrendered all. Something akin to desperation swept through him, and he ran his hands everywhere on her body, needing the feel of her beneath his palms and fingers.

A distant part of his brain told him to take things slowly, but he couldn't. He needed this session to be fast and quick, deep and hard, and he needed it now. He eased his body into place over hers and entered her, and the moment she arched against him, he felt a climax coming on. But he held it back, needing the connection a little while longer.

It was a challenge when every cell in his body was electrified, every pore open to sensations he felt only when he was inside her. And when he felt her own orgasm rip through her, his heartbeat accelerated and his pulse kicked up another notch. He was too far gone to hold on any longer and when the world seemed to explode all around them, he felt it. It seemed the bed rocked, the ground shook, the lights in the ceiling began falling…

"What the hell!"

He jerked up. He was not imagining things. He pushed Vanessa out of the way before a layer of plaster fell down on her.

"Cameron, what's going on?"

Instead of answering her, he snatched her wrist and handed her his shirt as he quickly slipped into his pants. "Hurry up and put it on so we can get the hell out of here."

It didn't take long for him to figure out that someone was outside firing explosives into his home with the use of a handheld missile launcher. He dropped to the floor and pulled Vanessa down with him when all the walls seemed to start tumbling down.

When they crawled to the living room the place was in shambles, and he jerked her head down as a missile flew past her head. He cursed. The damn thing had barely missed her. He knew whoever was on the outside expected him to run out through either the front or the back entrance, thinking that they had him cornered.

"Cameron, what's going on? What are we going to do?" Vanessa whispered.

He glanced down at her. She didn't deserve to be involved in this. The person on the other side of that door had a beef with him and not her. He needed to get them to the part of the house that he knew was safe. The storm cellar his grandfather had built right after Hurricane Gilbert.

He glanced down at her. "I need you to trust me, Vanessa," he said meeting her gaze and gently rubbing her cheek. "I'm going to get us out of here."

She nodded. "I do trust you, Cameron, and I love you. That's why I came all the way to Texas. I couldn't wait to tell you."

Her words touched him and he wanted to kiss her, but time was not on their side. He needed to get them out of there. They made it to the kitchen and he pushed open the cellar door. It had been years since he'd been down there but this would be their refuge until help arrived. Someone had to have alerted the authorities by now that his ranch had become a war zone.

He led Vanessa down the stairs and except for a little dust and a few spiderwebs here and there, the place was okay. He took them as far back into the cellar as he could and then pulled her into his arms. This was a waiting game and he only hoped whoever was out there would eventually assume he had succeeded in what he came to do and haul ass.

In the meantime...

He turned Vanessa to him and leaned down and kissed her, needing the taste of her, the assurance she was all right and they were together. She wrapped her arms around him and held him tight.

Cameron wasn't sure how long they huddled down there before he heard someone call his name. He placed his fingers to Vanessa's lips, not yet certain whether the person beyond the cellar door was friend or foe.

A smile touched his lips when his name was called out again and he recognized Xavier's voice. "Stay put for a second while I let him know we're down here."

Vanessa watched as Cameron raced up the wooden stairs and responded to his friend's call through the door.

"Stand back, Cam!"

He did and then she saw the head of a huge ax slice through the door frame before it was kicked in. And then those two men stood there, the ones who had let her into Cameron's house earlier. The expressions on their faces showed they were relieved to see he was okay, but they were mad as hell.

Cameron turned, opened his arms to her and she raced across the cement floor and up the stairs to him. And when he gathered her into his arms, she knew that everything would be all right.

Later that night, back in her hotel room, Vanessa cuddled close to Cameron in bed. "I'm sorry about your home, Cameron."

When Xavier and Kurt had pulled them out of the cellar and they'd had a chance to see the damage, her heart had ached for him. But then that same heart had filled with anger that someone had wanted to do that much harm to the man she loved. He was not intended to survive the attack.

"I was thinking of rebuilding anyway. I've received a number of offers to sell but couldn't bring myself to part with it. That land is where I spent some of the happiest days with my grandfather and I needed that link."

Vanessa nodded, then frowned. "Well, at least they caught those guys."

"Yes, and they're spilling their guts. I can't believe John McMurray would go that far. The man is truly demented." McMurray's arrest had made national news. The shame that had been brought on his family had come from his hands and not Cameron's.

"And how on earth were they able to get those types of weapons? Something like that could probably shoot a plane out the sky."

"It can, which is why in most states they're outlawed. I'm just glad that Kurt brought Xavier back here to get his car and saw what was happening."

Vanessa nodded. She was, too.

Cameron glanced down at her. "Did you mean what you said earlier, just before we made it to the cellar? That part about loving me?"

She smiled. "Yes, I meant every word. You're not only my sex mate, you're my soul mate, as well. I do love you, Cameron."

"And I love you. Does this mean you'd consider marrying me?"

She grinned. "Yes, if you ask."

He turned toward her in bed, took her hand in his and gazed deep into her eyes. "Vanessa Steele, will you marry me? For better or for worse? Will you be my soul mate and my sex mate? The mother of my children? My best friend? My—"

She placed her finger to his lips. "Cameron Cody, I will be your everything."

He leaned closer, and, right before he captured her lips with his, he whispered huskily, "You already are. You were definitely one risky pleasure worth taking."

* * * * *

We hope you enjoyed reading

# *The Way Back to You*

by *New York Times* bestselling author

## LINDA LAEL MILLER

and

# *Risky Pleasures*

by *New York Times* bestselling author

## BRENDA JACKSON.

Both were originally Harlequin® series stories!

From passionate, suspenseful and dramatic
love stories to inspirational or historical,
Harlequin offers different lines to
satisfy every romance reader.

New books in each line are available every month.

Luxury, scandal, desire—welcome to the lives of
the American elite.

Harlequin.com

BACHALO0221

*Wealthy Alaskan Cash Outlaw has inherited a ranch and
needs land owned by beautiful, determined
Brianna Banks. She'll sign it over under one condition:
Cash fathering the child she desperately wants. But he
won't be an absentee father and makes his own demand...*

*Read on for a sneak peek at*
The Marriage He Demands
*by* New York Times *bestselling author Brenda Jackson.*

"Are you really going to sell the Blazing Frontier without
even taking the time to look at it? It's a beautiful place."

"I'm sure it is, but I have no need of a ranch, dude or
otherwise."

"I think you're making a mistake, Cash."

Cash lifted a brow. Normally, he didn't care what any
person, man or woman, thought about any decision he made,
but for some reason what she thought mattered.

It shouldn't.

What he should do was thank her for joining him for
lunch, and tell her not to walk back to Cavanaugh's office
with him, although he knew both their cars were parked there.
In other words, he should put as much distance between them
as possible.

*I can't.*

Maybe it was the way her luscious mouth tightened when
she was not happy about something. He'd picked up on it
twice now. Lord help him but he didn't want to see it a third
time. He'd rather see her smile, lick an ice cream cone or...
lick him.

He quickly forced the last image from his mind, but not before a hum of lust shot through his veins. There had to be a reason he was so attracted to her. Maybe he could blame it on the Biggins deal Garth had closed just months before he'd gotten engaged to Regan. That had taken working endless days and nights, and for the past year Cash's social life had been practically nonexistent.

On the other hand, even without the Biggins deal as an excuse, there was strong sexual chemistry radiating between them. He felt it but honestly wasn't sure that even at twenty-seven she recognized it for what it was.

That was intriguing, to the point that he was tempted to hang around Black Crow another day. Besides, he was a businessman, and no businessman would sell or buy anything without checking it out first. He was letting his personal emotions around Ellen cloud what was usually a very sound business mind.

"You are right, Brianna. I would be making a mistake if I didn't at least see the ranch before selling it. Is now a good time?"

The huge smile that spread across her face was priceless... and mesmerizing. When was the last time a woman, any woman, had this kind of effect on him? When he felt spellbound? He concluded that never had a woman captivated him like Brianna Banks was doing.

*Don't miss what happens next in*
The Marriage He Demands
*by Brenda Jackson, the next book in her*
*Westmoreland Legacy: The Outlaws series!*

*Available April 2021 wherever*
*Harlequin Desire books and ebooks are sold.*

Harlequin.com

# HARLEQUIN
# DESIRE

Luxury, scandal, desire—welcome to the lives of the American elite.

## Save $1.00

on the purchase of ANY Harlequin Desire book.

Available wherever books are sold, including most bookstores, supermarkets, drugstores and discount stores.

---

# Save $1.00

**on the purchase of ANY Harlequin Desire book.**

Coupon valid until April 30, 2021.
Redeemable at participating outlets in the U.S. and Canada only.
Not redeemable at Barnes & Noble stores. Limit one coupon per customer.

**52616974**

**5  65373 00076  2    (8100)0  12488**